THE FORGIVING JAR

WANDA E. BRUNSTETTER

LARGE PRINT PRESS
A part of Gale, a Cengage Company

GALE
A Cengage Company

Farmington Hills, Mich • San Francisco • New York • Waterville, Maine
Meriden, Conn • Mason, Ohio • Chicago

Copyright © 2019 by Wanda E. Brunstetter.
The Prayer Jars #2.
Large Print Press, a part of Gale, a Cengage Company.

LIBRARY OF CONGRESS CIP DATA ON FILE.
CATALOGUING IN PUBLICATION FOR THIS BOOK
IS AVAILABLE FROM THE LIBRARY OF CONGRESS

ISBN-13: 978-1-4328-6081-3 (hardcover)
ISBN-13: 978-1-4328-6082-0 (paperback)

Published in 2019 by arrangement with Barbour Publishing, Inc.

Printed in the United States of America
1 2 3 4 5 6 7 23 22 21 20 19

To my special Amish friends who live by the scriptures and know the meaning of forgiveness.

And be ye kind one to another, tenderhearted, forgiving one another, even as God for Christ's sake hath forgiven you.

EPHESIANS 4:32

PROLOGUE

Strasburg, Pennsylvania

It was a beautiful clear night, but even as the stars twinkled above, they shone in stark contrast to the mood inside Ezekiel King's truck. As they approached the home of Willis and Mary Ruth Lapp, Michelle Taylor's apprehension grew. She clutched her purse straps so tight the lack of circulation tingled her fingers. Michelle was no stranger to being cast away, but right now she felt more nervous and fearful of rejection than at any other time in her life.

Ezekiel must have sensed Michelle's anxiety, for he let go of the steering wheel with one hand and reached over to touch her arm. "It's gonna be all right. You have nothin' to worry about."

"That's easy for you to say. You're not the one who has to face the Lapps." She released her purse straps and pushed a lock of shoulder-length hair away from her face.

7

"I'd rather have a tooth pulled without anything to deaden the pain than speak to the Lapps in person. I don't know if I can forgive myself, let alone expect them to."

"Don't say that." Ezekiel's tone was reassuring. "I've known the Lapps a long time. You'll soon find out that your worries are for nothing."

As they passed more familiar places, Michelle's fretfulness intensified, even though Ezekiel tried to help her cope. "I really blew it when I didn't come clean with them before. What if they don't want to see me? They might slam the door in my face."

Taking hold of the wheel with both hands again, Ezekiel shook his head. "The Lapps aren't like that. They'll let you in and listen to whatever you have to say."

"I don't expect them to invite me to live with them again. I just want the chance to tell Mary Ruth and Willis how sorry I am for impersonating their granddaughter." Michelle blew out a puff of air. "I've never been more ashamed of myself than doing that to people who have made me feel loved like no one else ever did."

"I'm sure they will forgive you."

"I hope you're right, because if they won't speak to me, I can't return to Harrisburg. I quit my job, remember? Maybe I'll have to catch a bus and head for Ohio after all. If I beg my foster parents in Columbus, they might take me in." Michelle bit the inside of her cheek and winced. "I deserve whatever I get."

Ezekiel turned up the Lapps' driveway. "I don't think it'll come to that, but even if things don't go well, I am not letting you leave." He turned off the engine and reached for her hand. "We'll figure out something together."

Michelle nodded. She didn't know what she would do without Ezekiel. If he hadn't come to Harrisburg to get her, she wouldn't be here right now. She'd have probably spent the rest of her life moving from town to town, trying to hide from the past. Well, however things ended up, it was time for her to face the music.

CHAPTER 1

One month later

Glancing in her rearview mirror as she slowed for a stop sign, Sara Murray smiled when she noticed a horse and buggy coming up behind her car. She rolled down her window to listen to the steady rhythm of the hooves engaging the pavement. Sara breathed in the crisp, fresh air. It was good to be back in Amish country, and even better to be heading to her grandparents' house to celebrate Thanksgiving a few days from now.

She still couldn't get over the fact that her mother had been raised in an Amish home, or that she hadn't known anything about it until she'd arrived in Lancaster County earlier this fall. A letter Sara found after Mama's death had revealed her grandparents' names and stated that they lived in Strasburg. Sara had wanted to meet them right away, but due to her part-time job at a dentist's office, plus taking some business classes, she was unable to go to Strasburg until fall.

Another shock had awaited Sara: a young woman had been living with the Lapps for several months, pretending to be her. It was hard not to be bitter about that, but Michelle Taylor had left the first day Sara arrived, so it was behind her now. Sara had spent several weeks getting to know Willis and Mary Ruth Lapp and was glad for this opportunity to spend more time with them.

Last week, the dentist Sara worked for had decided to retire, so she was currently out of a job. She hoped to move out of the duplex she rented from her stepfather in Newark, New Jersey, and move to Strasburg permanently. Perhaps, if her grandparents were willing, she could live with them — at least until she found another job and could rent a place of her own.

When Sara came upon another horse and buggy, in front of her this time, she waved at the cute little girl peeking out the back of the buggy, then pulled into the oncoming lane to pass. There was something about being in these surroundings that filled her with a sense of tranquility. It almost felt as if she belonged in Strasburg.

I probably would be living here now if Mama

had remained Amish and not run off when she was a teenager. It grieved Sara to know her mother had given birth to her out of wedlock, and never explained who her biological father was. *If he knew Mama was expecting a baby, why didn't he marry her? Was my father Amish, or could Mama have gotten involved with an English man?* These questions had plagued Sara ever since she'd learned of her heritage. As much as she hated to acknowledge it, the truth was, she might never learn all the facts. In any case, it wouldn't stop her from asking questions in the hope of uncovering the truth. Deep in her heart, Sara believed she had the right to know.

When Sara pulled onto the Lapps' driveway, she felt a sense of lightness in her chest. After staying with her grandparents and enjoying their warm hospitality previously, this seemed like coming home. Of course, things had been a bit strained between them at first — especially before they'd accepted the fact that Sara was truly their granddaughter and the other woman, Michelle, had only pretended to be her.

"What a dirty trick to play on someone as kind and trustworthy as my grandpa and grandma," Sara muttered. "I don't understand how that young woman could live with herself for taking advantage of two sweet people. I hope she's miserable and is paying for her misdeed." She tapped the steering wheel with her knuckles. "I'm glad I won't have to deal with Michelle. Who knows what I might say?"

It wasn't like Sara to be vindictive or wish something bad would happen to someone, but reflecting on what her grandparents had gone through filled her with irrational thoughts.

Just relax and enjoy spending the holiday with Grandpa and Grandma, she told herself. *I will not allow anything or anyone to spoil our first Thanksgiving together.*

Sara pulled her car up near the barn, turned off the engine, and got out. After removing her suitcase from the trunk, she headed for the house.

Sara knocked on the front door and waited. When no one answered, she knocked again, a little harder this time. She'd called and left a message last night, letting them know she would arrive this afternoon. Sara expected they'd be waiting for her arrival, since Grandma had said during their phone conversation a week ago last week that she and Grandpa were looking forward to Sara's visit.

She knocked a third time. When there was still no answer, Sara stepped off the porch and walked around back. Maybe they were doing something outside, despite the chilly day. Seeing no sign of anyone in the backyard, she rapped on the back door. When that failed too, Sara glanced toward the barn. *I wonder if they could be in there.*

Sara entered the barn and was greeted by two collies — one slightly larger than the other. "Hey, Sadie. Hey, Rascal. How are you doing? Are you glad to see me?"

The dogs responded with barking and wagging tails.

Sara giggled and went down on her knees to pet them. She glanced over at the pen where the pigs were kept. Some slept next to the snoring sow, while others rooted through the straw. "My how those piglets have grown." Sara turned and gave the two excited collies her full attention. "Where are your owners?" She stroked one dog's ears, while gently patting the other dog's head. The question was silly, since the dogs couldn't talk, but the words came out before Sara thought about what she was saying.

Rascal nuzzled her hand with his nose. Then his pink tongue came out and slurped Sara's arm. "You two are quite the welcoming committee. Just wish I knew where my grandparents are."

"They went to the grocery store to get some things for our Thanksgiving meal."

Sara jumped at the sound of a woman's voice, and a sudden coldness flooded her soul when she saw who had spoken. "Wh–what are you doing here?" she asked as Michelle stepped out of the shadows. "I — I thought you were gone. Have you been hiding here in my grandparents' barn?"

Michelle shook her head. "Course not. I've been living with them for the past month."

Sara's mouth gaped open. "What?"

"I came back to apologize for making them believe I was you. And they graciously forgave me. Even invited me to stay until I found a job."

"Is that so? Well then why were you hiding in the shadows where I couldn't see you?"

"I didn't know anyone was here till I heard you talking to the dogs. At first I didn't realize who you were." Michelle's voice lowered. "These days you can't be too careful."

"Don't I know it?" Sara wanted to say more to this person who could not be trusted, but she held her tongue. Her body temperature had gone from chilly to hot. *What were Grandpa and Grandma thinking, inviting this imposter to stay with them? And why didn't they tell me Michelle was living here?* Sara felt betrayed. She was tempted to return to Newark. But she would stay put until they got home, for she needed some answers. In the meantime, she wouldn't say another word to the deceitful young woman in the barn. Sara would wait in the car until her grandparents returned.

Sara's hands shook as she sat in her vehicle, fuming. *How could Grandpa and Grandma have let that devious young woman back into their lives?*

Glancing at the barn, where Michelle had remained, Sara shifted on her seat. *How am I supposed to spend Thanksgiving with them now?* She couldn't imagine staying in the same house with Michelle for even one day. This put a damper on her asking Grandpa and Grandma if she could live with them until she found a job. *Maybe if I explain how I feel about Michelle, they'll ask her to leave. After all, she's not part of the family.*

The more Sara stewed about this, the angrier she became. If she had a job to return to and her stepfather, Dean, hadn't found a renter for the duplex, she'd turn around right now and head back to Newark. *Maybe I should go anyway. The duplex won't be rented out until next week, so I'd have a place to stay until then. But if I leave, the little conniver will have the upper hand.*

Sara didn't have long to contemplate things, because the *clip-clop* of a horse's hooves drew her attention to Grandpa and Grandma's arrival. When their horse and buggy pulled up to the hitching rail, she got out of the car.

Her grandparents stepped down from the buggy, and while Grandma headed toward Sara's car, Grandpa waved at Sara before securing the horse. Forcing a smile, Sara gave her grandmother a hug.

"It's so good to see you again," Grandma said with feeling. "We've been looking forward to your visit and hope you can stay with us a bit longer this time."

Sara bit her lip, pondering how best to say what was on her mind.

"Is everything all right, Sara? You look upset."

Sara pointed to the barn. "When I first got here, I went in there, looking for you and Grandpa. I found Michelle Taylor instead."

Grandma nodded. "Why, yes. She's been with us for almost a month now. Didn't I tell you in one of our phone calls?"

"No. I would have remembered if you

had." *And I would not be here right now.* Sara shifted from one foot to the other. "Michelle was the last person I expected to see this afternoon."

"She came back with Ezekiel, to apologize in person for what she had done," Grandma explained. "So your grandpa and I decided Michelle could stay here until she's able to find a job."

"You could forgive her, just like that?" Sara snapped her fingers.

Grandma nodded. "The Bible teaches us to forgive."

Before Sara could comment, Grandpa joined them and gave her a hug. "It's mighty nice to see you again, Granddaughter. How have you been?"

"Other than losing my job last week, I was okay until I got here and found Michelle in the barn. I had planned to ask if I could stay with you until I find a job and am able to get my own place. But since she's here, that won't work out. I should just go back to Newark." Sara figured she may as well be honest.

Grandma slipped her arm around Sara's waist. "Now don't be silly. We'd love to have you stay with us. Since we have more than one guest room, it won't be a problem to have both you and Michelle living in our home. We've been looking forward to having you, and would be very disappointed if you left."

Sara made a feeble attempt at smiling. "Oh, okay." While she didn't want to be in the same house with the imposter, at least she would be here to keep an eye on things and make sure Michelle didn't do anything else to hurt Grandpa and Grandma Lapp.

CHAPTER 2

Michelle fluffed up her pillow and rolled onto her side, trying to find a comfortable position. Lying there, she put a finger to her mouth and bit the end of a rough cuticle. *After I help out with the morning chores with Willis, I'll make some time to cut and file my nails.*

Tucking her hand back under the covers, she smiled. *I've grown to enjoy helping out here at the Lapps' place, even if the work is hard on my hands.*

When she first went to bed, Michelle had looked through a magazine she'd gotten a few days ago, reading some of the articles and smelling the sample perfumes it had inside. She still couldn't shut off the thoughts that crept in and ended up setting the publication on the floor.

She released a long sigh, one of many given since she'd been in the privacy of her room. *I'm the last person Sara wanted to see, but I can't let her negative attitude get to me.*

Normally, Michelle would have no trouble getting to sleep, but tonight was different. All thoughts were on the young woman in the room across the hall — the person she'd pretended to be.

Sara would barely even look at me during supper this evening. Guess I can't blame her. Seeing me here is a constant reminder of how I led her grandparents on. I'd probably feel the same way if the situation was reversed.

Michelle turned onto her back. *But if the Lapps can forgive me, why can't Sara? Maybe she's not the forgiving kind. Sara might not even be a Christian.*

Michelle's lips pressed together as she heaved another weighted sigh. *Of course, until I had read some scriptures and felt God's love for the first time, I wasn't a believer either. But if Sara knew the kind of life I've had, maybe she would be more understanding and realize that during the time of my deception, I needed the Lapps really bad.*

A little voice in the back of Michelle's head reminded her that Sara had lost out too, not knowing for so many years that she had grandparents as wonderful as Willis and Mary Ruth.

One thing was sure, Michelle wanted Sara to know how sorry she felt for all the wrong she had done.

I don't feel right about being in her mother's room either. Michelle punched her pillow as she made a decision. *Tomorrow I'll suggest that we switch rooms. But if things don't improve between us soon, I'll have no choice but to move out, with or without a job. Maybe Ezekiel knows someone who would take me in. It won't be his folks though; of that much I am certain.*

Sara sat on the end of the bed in the guest room across the hall from Michelle. As she brushed her long hair, she heard the "pretender" across the way, snoring. *Oh great.* Sara frowned. *Tack on one more thing to keep me awake tonight.*

It wasn't right that the imposter had been given the bedroom that used to belong to Sara's mother. She should be sleeping there, not Michelle. Didn't Grandma and Grandpa care anything about her feelings? Surely they had to realize how uncomfortable it was for her to be staying in their house with a person who had no right to be here.

Sara got up and went over to the window. It was chilly outside, but she needed fresh air, so she opened it a crack. She drew several deep breaths to clear her head.

Outside, Sara heard dried leaves rustling in the breeze as they blew across the yard below. *I wonder if I'll be able to sleep tonight, with the queen of sawing logs close by.* She grimaced. *I'd like to go over there right now, knock on her door, and holler at her to stop.*

Standing rigidly, she continued to look out at the night sky. *Hopefully this awful noise won't occur every night.*

It wasn't good to let stress control her like this, but Sara couldn't move past it. *Do Grandma and Grandpa care more about Michelle than they do their own flesh-and-blood granddaughter? Is that why they gave her Mama's room?* It was foolish to have such thoughts, but it was hard to think differently.

Rubbing her hands up and down her arms to ward off the shivers, she turned away from the window. Grandma had said during supper this evening that she hoped Sara and Michelle could get to know each other and become friends.

Fat chance! I'm not interested in getting to know the great pretender. But I'll keep my feelings to myself so I don't upset Grandpa and Grandma. If I complain, it might give them a reason to choose Michelle over me.

She flopped back onto the bed. *They can*

forgive her if they want to, but I'm not that forgiving. Sara hadn't admitted it to her grandparents or anyone else, but she still struggled with mixed feelings about her own mother's deception. It didn't make sense that Mama had kept her Amish heritage a secret. While she may have been embarrassed about having a baby out of wedlock, it didn't excuse her for not telling Sara about her grandparents. Sara had been cheated out of knowing them all those years. What fun she could have had with Grandma and Grandpa, coming to visit and staying on the farm.

As a child, Sara had envied other kids whose grandparents doted on them. Her stepfather's parents had lived in Canada and traveled a lot before they died. Sara had only met them once, when Dean and Mama first got married. Unfortunately, on one of their trips, they'd been killed when their plane crashed. So she had grown up with no grandparents at all.

Sara couldn't understand why some people weren't honest. She'd never liked being lied to or kept in the dark. Sara had always tried to be honest. "If everyone were honest, the world would be a better place," she muttered.

As her thoughts wandered, something else

came to mind. *What did I do with that letter from Brad Fuller?* In October, when Sara first visited her grandparents, a letter had come for her. Sara's muscles tensed. *It wasn't really meant for me, but for the person pretending to be me, whom he thought was Sara.*

From the things Brad said in his letter, he sounded nice. He'd mentioned being settled in at a seminary. As Sara recalled, he'd also included a Bible verse with the letter. So she assumed he was religious.

The scent of country air lingered in her room as Sara got up to close the window. *Brad mentioned his studies, and stated that he would pray for me. Was he going to school to be a preacher?* She sat back down on the bed and plopped backward, staring at the ceiling. *Oh yeah, now I remember. . . . I threw the letter out. It's a good thing too, or else I'd feel obligated to give it to Michelle. But, I can't fret about this stuff all night. I need to try and get some sleep.* Sara pulled back the covers and climbed into bed, as she breathed in the scent of clean sheets. She would deal with everything in the morning.

"You're tossing and turning quite a bit. Are you having trouble getting to sleep?" Willis asked Mary Ruth.

26

"Jah." She sat up in bed, pushing the pillow up to support her back.

He sat up too, and reached for her hand. *"Was is letz do?"*

"I'll tell you what's wrong here." Mary Ruth used her other hand to massage her pounding forehead. "The two young women we care about are not getting along well. Couldn't you feel the tension between them before, during, and after our evening meal? Why, they barely said more than two words to each other."

"True. And I have to admit it was a little awkward just you and me doin' most of the talking while we ate supper."

"Jah. We'd toss questions out to the girls, but hardly got responses from either of them."

"You're right," Willis agreed. "But maybe things will go better in a few days or so. Sara and Michelle need a little more time to get to know each other. It's only the first day."

Mary Ruth shook her head. "I don't believe a few days of getting to know each other will solve the problem. Truthfully, I think Michelle feels uncomfortable around Sara because of how she pretended to be her. And if I'm not mistaken, Sara is upset with Michelle and has not forgiven her for letting us believe all those months that she was our granddaughter."

"Bet you've hit the nail right on the head." Willis gave Mary Ruth's fingers a gentle squeeze. "I keep forgetting what a *schmaert* woman I married."

"I'm not that smart — just perceptive."

"So besides faithfully praying, what are we gonna do about the situation between Sara and Michelle?"

Mary Ruth tilted her head. "I think we should talk with them."

"Together or individually?" He shifted under the covers.

"It might be best to speak to each of them alone. Maybe you could talk to Michelle, and I'll speak with Sara. What do you think, Willis?"

"It's worth a try. Michelle likes to help me with the animals. So tomorrow morning while we're feeding the horses, I'll bring up the subject of Sara."

"Okay. While you're doing that, I'll ask Sara to help me with something in the kitchen. Then, while we are working, I'll speak with her about Michelle."

"Sounds like a plan." Willis released Mary Ruth's hand. "Ready to go to sleep now?"

"I — I hope so."

"Lie down, close your eyes, and give the

28

situation to God." Willis's gentle tone was soothing.

"I'll try." It wasn't always easy to give up control and turn things over to God, but Willis was right — that's what she needed to do.

Mary Ruth flattened her pillow. She appreciated the discussion they'd had and felt thankful for her dear, caring husband. She couldn't imagine trying to deal with this situation on her own.

Yawning, she closed her eyes and prayed, asking the heavenly Father to give her the right words when she spoke to Sara. *And please soften her heart toward Michelle so she's willing to listen,* she added before falling asleep.

CHAPTER 3

The hickory-smoked aroma of frying bacon drew Sara into the kitchen. Grandma turned from where she stood at the stove and offered a wide smile. "Good morning, Sara. Did you sleep well?"

Sara slowly nodded. She wasn't about to admit that she'd barely slept. Grandma would likely ask why, and then Sara would either have to make something up or admit that her stress over Michelle's presence was the reason she'd tossed and turned most of the night. That had been coupled with the nerve-racking snoring filtering across the hall.

"What can I do to help with breakfast?" Sara asked, hoping her grandmother hadn't noticed her unhappy mood.

Grandma gestured to the refrigerator. "You can get out some eggs and scramble them up while I finish frying the bacon."

"Okay." Sara got out the items and closed

the refrigerator door. How nice it was to have some quality time with Grandma this morning. "Is Grandpa outside doing chores?" She grabbed a bowl from the cupboard and started cracking the eggs into it.

"Yes." Grandma placed the cooked bacon aside on a paper towel. "He took a mug of freshly brewed coffee with him before heading out the door."

Sara shook some salt and pepper into the bowl. "There seem to be plenty of things to do around a farm like this." She picked up the wire whisk and mixed in the seasonings. *Why didn't my mother appreciate the simple life? I'd like some answers, but I need to be patient.*

Sara had finished mixing the eggs with a small amount of milk, when Michelle entered the room.

"Good morning. Did you get a good night's sleep?" Grandma gave Michelle the same friendly smile she'd shared with Sara.

"Sure did." Michelle glanced at Sara. "Good morning."

"Morning," Sara mumbled, barely looking at Michelle. *Sure wish I could come right out and say what's on my mind.*

Michelle moved over to stand beside Grandma and kissed her cheek. "What do you need me to do this morning?"

Sara's jaw clenched. *Michelle acts like she's the granddaughter, not me. Is she still pretending, or it is just wishful thinking?*

"Since Sara is mixing the eggs, why don't you set the table?" Grandma suggested.

"I can do that. Should I get out some milk or juice too?"

Grandma nodded. "We have orange and apple juice in the refrigerator, so you can set out both, if you like. That way, we'll have beverage choices."

"Okay."

While Michelle set the table and took out the juices, Sara put the egg mixture in a frying pan with a little vegetable oil and placed it on the propane stove. She was reminded once again that she'd been looking forward to spending time with Grandpa and Grandma, and now she had to share them with Michelle. To make matters worse, Michelle had given Grandma a kiss on the cheek. *I should have done that instead of dwelling on my negative feelings.*

"I'm going to start looking for a job today." Sara glanced over at Grandma.

"Can't it wait till after Thanksgiving?" Grandma placed the bacon on a plate and covered it with foil. "I was hoping you'd be free to help me do some baking after breakfast, and it would be nice to sit and visit with you this afternoon."

"I suppose I could wait until Monday." Sara stirred the solidifying eggs in the skillet.

Grandma smiled. "That'll be fine."

"What about me?" Michelle asked. "Won't you need my help with the baking, Grandma?"

Sara nearly had to bite her tongue to keep from saying anything. *Who does Michelle think she is, anyway? She shouldn't be calling my grandmother Grandma. Michelle had some practice when she'd lived here before, pretending to be me, but that doesn't make it right.*

"If you want to help, that's certainly fine, but I assumed you would help Willis take care of the animals after breakfast," Grandma replied.

Sara pressed her lips together to keep from blurting out her thoughts. She had a feeling Michelle only wanted to help bake so she could horn in on her time with Grandma.

The more Sara thought about it, the more upset she became. *Why does my life have to be so complicated?*

By the time Grandpa came in for breakfast, Sara had no appetite for food. Even the scrambled eggs didn't appeal to her. She forced herself to sit at the table for the prayer so she wouldn't appear impolite.

"I checked phone messages before coming into the house." Grandpa looked over at Michelle, who sat to the left of him. "There was a message for you from Ezekiel."

Michelle's blue-green eyes lit up. "What did he have to say? He's still joining us for Thanksgiving, I hope."

"Ezekiel's still coming, but he wanted you to know that he may only be here for dessert."

Michelle's brows furrowed. "How come? He said he would eat dinner with us."

Sara drank her glass of juice as she listened to Grandpa's explanation. She too was curious about why Ezekiel wouldn't be joining them until after dinner tomorrow.

"Ezekiel said in his message that his family wanted him to join them for their Thanksgiving meal." Grandpa took two slices of bacon and passed the platter to Michelle. "Guess now that he's gettin' along better with his folks, he wants to keep the peace."

From her seat next to Michelle, Grandma reached over and patted the imposter's arm. "At least he'll be joining us for pie and coffee."

Michelle nodded slowly.

Sara toyed with her fork. It was too bad Ezekiel wasn't coming for dinner, because it would keep Michelle busy with him instead of gushing over Grandma and Grandpa and hanging on their every word. This would've given Sara an opportunity to spend more time with her grandparents.

Sara had to wonder, though, how things could work out between Michelle and Ezekiel, since he was Amish and Michelle was not. Of course, if it did work out, she'd be married and out the door. *Goodbye to her, and all the troubles she's caused,* Sara mused. *But the odds are he'll see through her phony bologna and drop Michelle like a bare hand holding a hot skillet.*

Sara forced herself to eat the last bite of egg on her plate. *It's none of my business how Ezekiel and Michelle work things out. I have enough of my own problems to muddle through. And it's good I'm not involved in a relationship with a man right now. It would complicate my life even more.*

"You're kinda quiet this morning," Willis said as Michelle helped him groom his horse Bashful. "Are you still upset because Ezekiel won't be eating dinner with us tomorrow?"

She shook her head. "As long as he can

come for part of the day, I'm okay with it."

Willis set the curry comb aside and gestured to a bale of straw outside his horse's stall. "Let's have a seat over there. I'd like to talk to you about something."

"Okay." Michelle set the brush down that she'd been using on Bashful's mane, opened the stall gate, and took a seat on one end of the straw bale. She sat quietly until Willis joined her. "What did you want to talk to me about?"

"Sara."

"What about her?"

He pulled a piece of straw from the bale and stuck it between his teeth. "Mary Ruth and I have noticed the tension between you and Sara."

"Yeah, it's there, but I think it's mostly because she resents me being here." Michelle bent down to pet Rascal when he bounded up to her, wagging his tail. "I was planning to talk to her after breakfast, but she went into the bathroom before I had the chance. And since I wanted to help you with the animals, I came out here."

"It would be a good idea for the two of you to talk things out." Willis stroked the top of Sadie's head, for it appeared she wanted some attention too.

"I'm gonna ask if she'd like to trade

bedrooms with me. I figured Sara might like to have the room her mother slept in when she was a girl."

Willis nodded. "She slept there during her brief visit with us, when you were living in Harrisburg."

"I should have guessed as much and insisted on taking the other guest room when Ezekiel brought me back here."

"I think Mary Ruth suggested you sleep in there because it's the room you had during your first stay with us."

"Right. Before you knew I wasn't your granddaughter." Michelle stopped fussing with Rascal and placed her hand on Willis's am. "I still feel terrible about all the lies I told you and Mary Ruth whenever you asked questions about my past. It's hard to understand how you could both be so forgiving."

"Forgiveness doesn't come easy when a person has been wronged, but according to scripture, it's the right thing to do."

"Maybe you should tell Sara that. I'm sure she hasn't forgiven me for impersonating her."

"Give her some time and try to be patient and kind. I believe in due time, she'll come around."

■ ■ ■ ■

"What kind of pies will we be making this morning?" Sara asked after she'd finished her cup of tea.

"Pumpkin is your grandpa's favorite, so we'll need to make a few of those. Since your mother's brother and his family will be joining us, I'll make sure there are a few apple pies too because apple is Lenore's favorite. If some of the pies aren't eaten, then they can take one or two home with them." From across the table, Grandma smiled at Sara. "What kind of pie do you like best?"

Sara shrugged. "I like most pies — except for mincemeat. I've never acquired a taste for it."

"I understand, and don't worry, there won't be any mincemeat pies for our Thanksgiving dessert." Grandma rose from the table and placed her empty cup into the sink. Then she sat down again. "Before we get started, there's something I want to talk to you about."

Sara squirmed in her chair. *I bet it's about the pretender.* "What is it, Grandma?"

"I can't help noticing how cool you've been toward Michelle. Are you upset because she's staying here with us?"

Sara slid her finger around the edge of her cup as she weighed her options. *I can either pretend I have no problem with Michelle or blurt out the truth.* She went with the second choice.

"To be honest, Michelle being here does upset me. What she did to you and Grandpa was deplorable, and now she's living here — even sleeping in my mother's old room — like she's one of the family."

"I'm sure she'd be willing to switch rooms with you." Grandma lifted her glasses and rubbed a spot on the bridge of her nose. "When she returned from Harrisburg, I wasn't thinking when I offered her that room. She'd occupied it before, when we thought she was you, so —"

The back door opened, and Michelle stepped into the room, interrupting Grandma's sentence. Michelle glanced at the stove, then looked at them. "I thought you two were baking."

Grandma shook her head. "Not yet. We decided to drink some tea and talk awhile." She gestured for Michelle to take a seat at the table. "Would you like me to fix you a cup?"

"No thanks. I just came in to speak with Sara about something. Then I'm going back outside to help Grandpa — I mean, Willis, feed the hogs."

"Okay. I'll leave you two alone while I go down to the basement to get some apples." Grandma left the table, picked up a large plastic bowl, and hurried from the room.

When Michelle took a seat across from her, Sara tipped her head to one side. *I feel a bit railroaded into this talk. I wanted to spend some downtime with Grandma, not engage with the imposter this morning.* She offered Michelle full eye contact. "What did you want to talk to me about?"

"Well, for starters, I'd like to switch rooms with you. The bedroom I've been sleeping in was your mother's, and I think you should have it."

Sara slowly nodded. "Thank you. I feel the same too."

Michelle leaned forward, her elbows on the table. "I'm not asking you to be my best friend or anything, but as long as we are both living here, I hope we can be civil to each other and try to get along."

"Okay." Sara's words came out in a near whisper. Earlier, she had been ready to let Michelle have it, but now that she had the opportunity to unleash her feelings, the words wouldn't come. It wouldn't be easy to act cordially toward the imposter, but for

Grandma and Grandpa's sake, she would try.

CHAPTER 4

Clarks Summit, Pennsylvania

On a day meant for families, Brad looked at the piece of turkey on his plate and wrinkled his nose. Neither it nor the mashed potatoes and gravy held any appeal. Looking around, it seemed a few others had also ended up at this restaurant. A man trying to calm a fussy little boy looked as miserable as Brad felt. Eating by himself at a local all-you-can-eat buffet was not the way he'd hoped to spend Thanksgiving. He had planned to spend this holiday in Harrisburg with his folks, but Mom had come down with the flu last night, so Dad called and asked Brad not to come. Not only was Mom not well enough to cook, but she also didn't want to expose Brad to what she had. Brad would keep his mother in his prayers and later today check in on her and Dad to see how they were doing.

Since most of the other seminary students

Brad knew had gone home to be with their families, he was left alone to eat by himself. He'd thought about driving down to Strasburg to spend the day with the Lapps but changed his mind. It wouldn't be fair to drop in on them without an invitation, and even if he'd called yesterday and left a message, he wouldn't have felt right about inviting himself to share their Thanksgiving meal. Maybe during his Christmas break he would go down to see his old friends. He was especially eager to see how Sara was doing and find out if she'd received his letter. Brad had hoped she might write back to him, but maybe it was for the best that she hadn't. A long-distance relationship wasn't a good idea — especially with a young woman who was not a believer. It had been a difficult decision for Brad, because he enjoyed Sara's company, but his faith in God and calling to be a minister came before anything else.

He forked a piece of meat into his mouth. While it was nowhere near as tasty as the turkey his mom always made, at least he wouldn't go hungry. The families dining together around him appeared to be happy. Even the fussy little boy had calmed down and was eating the mashed potatoes on his plate.

Brad lifted his glass and sipped some ice water. When classes started up again next week, his mind would be on his studies.

Strasburg

"You outdid yourself with this meal today, *Mamm,*" Grinning at his mother, Sara's uncle Ivan made a sweeping gesture of the array of food on the table. "I bet you got up at the crack of dawn to fix all this for us. And look at the size of that turkey. It must be at least a twenty-four pounder."

Grandma gestured to Sara and Michelle sitting beside each other at the table. "I can't take credit for all the work. These two did their share and then some."

Michelle's cheeks turned pink, and Sara's face warmed too. "I was more than happy to help," she said.

Michelle bobbed her head. "Same here."

"Mary Ruth, you should have let us furnish some of the food," Ivan's wife, Yvonne, spoke up. "After all, with us being here, there are five extra people at your table. And you know how our boys like to eat." Yvonne glanced over at her two grown boys, who were eyeing the big bowl of mashed potatoes.

Sara looked at Grandma to see her response. She wasn't surprised when

Grandma smiled and said, "Not a problem. I enjoy the opportunity to cook a nice meal for my *familye.*"

Sara had heard her grandmother say that word before, and knew it meant "family." The Pennsylvania Dutch language intrigued Sara, and she hoped she would eventually learn to speak it too — or least understand more of the words so she would know what was being said when Grandma and Grandpa spoke it to one another or other family members. Even Michelle had one up on her, sometimes using Pennsylvania Dutch words Sara's grandparents had taught her.

"The food looks good, Grandma." Ivan's twenty-year-old son Benjamin spoke up. "I was invited to eat at my girlfriend's home today, but I'm glad I came here to be with our family. I'll see Marilyn tomorrow instead."

As everyone bowed their heads to say a silent prayer before partaking of the meal, Sara's thoughts went to her mother and how she'd taught Sara to pray silently when she was a girl. Back then, Sara hadn't realized praying this way was a tradition Mama had grown up with. She'd always thought it was her mother's way of praying without offending Sara's stepfather, who was not a religious man.

But now that I look back, Sara thought, instead of praying, *if Mama thought Dean would disapprove of her praying out loud, then why did she send my brother and me to Sunday school? Wasn't she worried that Dean would be upset about that too?* Some things about Mama still made no sense to Sara, although she still missed her mother and wished she could have her back.

Sara heard Grandpa's napkin rustle, so she opened her eyes and looked up. Everyone else did the same. She had to admit all the food on the table looked mighty tempting, not to mention the delicious aromas enveloping her senses.

Grandpa rose from his seat and cleared his throat. "This year something different will occur. I'd like to pass the tradition of carving the Thanksgiving bird on to Ivan."

"I'd be honored, *Daed.*" Ivan stood and waited for his father to pass him the plump turkey.

All eyes were on Grandpa as he picked up the platter and held it out to his son. Sara licked her lips, but nearly jumped out of her seat when Grandpa lost his grip. The platter tilted, and the turkey slid onto the floor. Following a huge *splat,* the stuffing shot out of the bird's cavity like a bullet, and smeared all over the floor.

It looked like Ivan had made a valiant effort to save the catastrophe from happening, but in so doing, he banged his knee against one of the table legs, knocking over the two burning candles adorning the Thanksgiving feast.

"Fire!" Ivan's oldest son, Peter, yelled as everyone jumped back from the table.

Sara gasped, watching as the beautiful white tablecloth caught fire.

All the guests scurried, trying to help. Grandma scooped up one of the fallen candles, and Michelle retrieved the other one. Yvonne grabbed the pitcher of water that was on a side table and threw it on the smoking cloth. Ivan picked up the turkey, put it back on the platter, and took it out to the kitchen, while Lenore went to get a grocery bag to spoon up the steaming filling all over the floor.

Sara couldn't do anything but stand with her mouth gaping open. *This reminds me of a movie I once saw.* She had to bite her lip to keep from giggling.

"I'm sorry, Mary Ruth." Grandpa's regret could be heard in his voice. "You worked so hard to make dinner perfect." He grabbed several napkins and dabbed up the water on the table where the tablecloth now smoldered.

"It was an accident." Grandma chuckled as if she was used to this sort of thing happening. "What would a family gathering be without a bit of chaos? And just think about the memory we can all talk about in years to come."

"What can I do to help?" Sara asked.

"How about pulling the skin off the turkey?" Grandma suggested. "There's nothing wrong with the meat under the skin, since it landed upright on the floor."

Grandpa snorted. "Guess if the turkey was gonna take off like that, it couldn't have landed any better."

By now everyone was laughing and making jokes about the flying turkey that tried to get away from the table. What was even funnier was watching Benjamin and Peter scooping mashed potatoes onto their plates, and eating as if nothing was amiss.

Sara couldn't recall having this much fun on any Thanksgiving she and her family had ever celebrated. All this laughter had taken her mind temporarily off Michelle crowding her space.

"I think we have everything under control now." Grandma hiccupped from laughing so hard. "We'll give the stuffing from the floor to the pigs. That way they'll have a Thanksgiving treat too. Peter and Benjamin, would you two mind taking it out after we eat?"

"Sure, Grandma," they said in unison.

"It's a good thing we made an extra pan of filling," Michelle said.

"That's what I usually go for first," Yvonne chimed in.

Even though there was a hole in the tablecloth, everything else was back in order. "We'll have to get a new covering for our table to use for future Thanksgivings." Grandpa pointed at the blackened material.

"Or maybe we should keep using this one." Grandma winked at him. "Think of the conversations we'll have each year when Ivan carves the turkey."

Again, Sara was amazed at how the family worked together to remedy the situation and could still laugh about it. The people at this table were not only good hearted and deeply rooted in their faith, they found humor in what most folks would be upset about.

The skinless turkey sat near Ivan, who stood over it, swiping two carving knives together. "Okay, let me get this turkey sliced so we can eat. I don't know about the rest of you, but I'm starving." He looked over at his sons. "I hope you two saved us some mashed potatoes."

"There's still plenty, Daed." Peter grinned

mischievously.

As the food got passed, conversation around the table began. Sara's cousins, Benjamin and Peter, talked fishing with Uncle Ivan and Grandpa, while the women exchanged information about quilting and baking. It was a different experience, seeing how the Amish celebrated this holiday. Growing up in Sara's home, they may have had harvest-colored decorations in several of the rooms. And Mama's scented candles burning in the kitchen always permeated the house with pumpkin pie or cinnamon-apple fragrance. But there was no joyful camaraderie, like these good people shared. Oh, there were some good times, Sara had to admit, but for the most part, holidays were quiet and dull by comparison.

Sara listened quietly as she enjoyed the succulent turkey and other tasty food. It was as if the turkey mishap had never happened. Being here with her newly found family felt right. It made her wish once again that she'd grown up knowing her grandparents, aunt, uncle, and cousins. If Sara's mother had remained Amish, then perhaps she too would be a part of the Amish community. She wondered where her mother would have sat at this same table as a young child, and later, as a young lady.

Sara could only imagine how Mama would have spent her holidays here in this house. Playing indoors after the meal, enjoying her cousins with a board game, and maybe warming up by the fire singing songs together — were these the things Mama used to do?

Sara poured gravy over her mashed potatoes and held out the bowl to Grandpa. At first he didn't seem to notice, because he sat, looking intently at Grandma. Sara could see he still felt bad, but Grandma winked again, probably to let him know everything was okay.

Glancing across the table at her cousin Lenore, Sara blotted her lips with a napkin. *Could I fit in here if I were to become Amish? Would I be able to give up my modern ways?* She didn't know why she was thinking such thoughts. Turning Amish when she'd grown up English would be a challenge — one Sara didn't feel up to — at least not right now. Maybe someday, after she'd lived here hile, she might ponder the idea. For now though, she would concentrate on getting to know her Amish relatives better and, of course, finding a job. Hopefully, some business in the area would be in need of a receptionist. If not, then she would consider some other type of work when she went job hunting next week.

Sara forked some creamy mashed potatoes into her mouth. She couldn't help smacking her lips — the potatoes were so smooth and free of lumps. *How in the world did Grandma do it without using an electric mixer? No wonder Ivan's sons made sure they got to the mashed potatoes first.* Yvonne was right — her boys sure liked to eat. Both were already on second helpings.

Sara looked forward to dessert and tasting at least one of the mouth-watering pies she had helped Grandma bake. She hoped she wouldn't put on extra weight while living here, because of her grandma's hearty cooking. While living under her grandparents' roof, Sara looked forward to learning how to fix some Pennsylvania Dutch meals. Her forehead wrinkled. *Too bad Michelle lives here too.*

Sara had to admit she felt a little better toward the pretender since she had switched rooms with her. It felt right to be back in her mother's old bedroom. It made Sara feel closer to Mama to sleep in the same bed she'd had until she left home so unexpectedly.

A knock sounded on the front door, bringing a halt to Sara's contemplations. Grandma excused herself and went to see who it was. She returned to the dining room a few minutes later with Ezekiel at her side.

"Sorry I'm late," he apologized. "My mom insisted I stay there until I'd tasted a little bit of everything on the table." Removing his straw hat, Ezekiel looked at Michelle. "When you're finished eating, and if you're not gonna eat dessert right away, would you like to go for a buggy ride?"

Her gaze went to Grandma.

"You two go ahead. I won't get the pies out till everyone's meal has settled."

"Okay, great." Michelle ate the last piece of turkey on her plate, and then she pushed away from the table. "I'll get a jacket, and then we can go." She sent a smile in Ezekiel's direction.

Sara struggled not to say anything as Michelle hurried from the room. Didn't the young woman have the good manners to stick around long enough to help clear the table and do the dishes? Apparently her desire to spend time with her boyfriend took precedence over anything else.

Sara's face tightened when Michelle returned several minutes later, wearing a jacket. "I'm ready to go, Ezekiel."

Grinning, he nodded. As they headed for the door, Ezekiel stopped and turned around. "We'll be back in plenty of time for dessert."

"Well, if you're not, there won't be any *boi* left to eat, 'cause my *fraa*'s pies are always the best. In fact, everyone just wants to gobble them up."

Grandma smiled in response to her husband's compliment. "Don't worry about that." She poked Grandpa's arm. "There's plenty to go around. Even if someone wants seconds." Grandma glanced at her grandsons, both nodding their heads.

Ezekiel snickered, as he guided Michelle out the door.

Sara's teeth clenched as she fought the temptation to call Michelle out on not clearing her dish before leaving. But she kept her thoughts to herself and let the little pretender waltz happily away.

I wonder what it'd be like to have a boyfriend who'd look at me the way Ezekiel looks at Michelle. I wonder what Ezekiel sees in Michelle. Apparently, he's forgiven her too, but I don't see how. The truth is she also lied to him when she pretended to be me.

CHAPTER 5

As a chilly breeze blew through Michelle's hair, she looked over at Ezekiel and smiled. The weather was typical for this time of year, but the crispness of the air was invigorating as it blew into the buggy where the flaps were open.

Michelle took a deep breath, enjoying the scents of the season. The fragrance of dried leaves still lingered from autumn, and the tang of wood smoke drifting out of chimneys from nearby homes permeated the air. The whiffs of smoke reminded her of campfires from cookouts her foster parents used to have in the backyard. Ezekiel's horse, Big Red, exuded a pleasant aroma too, and over it all drifted the sweetness of dried hay.

Riding in Ezekiel's buggy was more fun than riding in his truck. Hearing the steady *clip-clop* of his horse's hooves was a soothing sound. Michelle had missed seeing and hearing Amish horse and buggies during the brief time she'd lived in Harrisburg. And of course she'd missed Ezekiel. Every time she was with him, the moments seemed to go by so quickly. Michelle was thrilled to have some time to talk privately with Ezekiel. The Lapps' house was full of company this evening, so she and Ezekiel probably wouldn't even be missed.

Her thoughts transferred to Sara. The only downer wasn't the fire earlier at the table, or the turkey that flew off the platter, but the ongoing cold treatment from the Lapps' granddaughter. *Will she ever warm up to me? Is there something I could do or say to make things better between us?*

"How was your meal today?" Ezekiel asked, halting Michelle's thoughts. "From what I saw on the table, it looked like there was plenty of food to eat."

"There sure was." Michelle patted her stomach. "I ate more than my share too. But we almost didn't have any turkey."

"How come?"

She relayed the story of how the turkey had ended up on the floor. "I thought Mary Ruth would be upset, but she took it all in stride. Once the fire was out and the mess cleaned up, we all had a pretty good laugh."

"What fire?"

"Ivan tried to save the turkey, but in doing so, he hit his knee on a table leg," Michelle further explained. "That, in turn, toppled the candles over, and then the tablecloth caught fire. You almost had to be there to believe what you were seeing; it all happened so fast."

"I bet."

"Then we all jumped in to help. Well, Sara didn't at first. She looked stunned by it all. But eventually she did pitch in. And Benjamin and Peter . . . They both sat there, eating through it all." Michelle laughed. "It was kinda comical now that I think about it. Oh, and poor Ivan. You could tell he felt terrible. And so did Willis."

"I probably would have too if had happened to me." Ezekiel chuckled. "But then, things like that can happen to the best of us."

"Mary Ruth was so good about it. She even joked about keeping the tablecloth with the burned hole in it. Said it would give them something to talk about during future Thanksgivings."

"That's not somethin' they're likely to forget. It'll be some memory, all right." He leaned over and sniffed her hair. "Jah, I believe the whole story now, 'cause your hair smells like smoked turkey."

"Are you kidding?"

"Nope."

She squinted, and then laughed.

He joined in. "A good belly laugh feels good. Jah?"

"Definitely. And *danki,* because I needed that today."

"Glad I could help." He spoke softly, close to her ear, sending shivers up Michelle's spine.

"I'm glad you can take my teasing. Some folks, like my little brother, don't like it when I joke around. And if I pester Henry too much, he really gets upset." Ezekiel paused to flick the reins. "He's always been kinda sensitive."

"I can relate, on both counts, because sometimes I'm sensitive too. And when we were kids, still living with our abusive folks, my youngest brother, Jack, didn't appreciate it whenever I teased him. Ernie never seemed to mind it much though, 'cause he was a jokester himself." Swallowing against the lump that had formed unexpectedly in her throat, Michelle folded her hands tightly in her lap. She still thought about her two brothers, even though she hadn't seen them since they were all separated and put in foster care. She hoped the boys were happy and had made good lives for themselves.

But oh, how she wished she could see them again.

Michelle closed her eyes. *But I have no desire to see my biological parents. They messed up royally and don't deserve to have any contact with their children.* Her nails pressed tightly into her palms. *Probably wouldn't be glad to see us, anyhow.* Despite Michelle's unhappy childhood, she still prayed for her parents. She hoped someday they would see the error of their ways and get help for their addiction to alcohol, as well as some anger management assistance.

They rode along quietly for a while, until Ezekiel broke the silence. "I've made a decision."

Her eyes snapped open. "What about?"

"I'm gonna sell my truck and join the church."

"For sure?"

"Jah. Thought I wanted to be English, and it might be all right for some. But I've come to realize it's not for me."

"Was it getting beat up outside the restaurant where I worked in Harrisburg that led you to that decision?"

"That may have been part of it, but the biggest reason is my family. It would be hard on my folks if one of their children went English." He paused, releasing a breath so loud it sounded more like a groan. "I don't want to hurt them like that."

"I understand, but if you join the Amish church, you won't be able to see me anymore. At least not socially or . . ." Her voice trailed off.

"That's the only reason I'm holding back from joining the church."

"What do you mean?"

"I don't want to lose my relationship with you." Ezekiel let go of the reins with his left hand and reached for Michelle's right hand, sending shivers up her arm.

"So what are we going to do?" she asked.

"Would you consider joining the Amish church?"

Stunned, Michelle could only stare ahead into the darkness, as her mind reeled with his sudden question.

"Hey, did you hear what I said?" He squeezed her fingers.

"Yes, I did. I'm just not sure how to respond."

"I don't expect you to give me your answer right away, but would you at least think about it?"

"Of course. In fact, the idea of becoming Amish has crossed my mind more than once since I first came to Lancaster County."

"Really? How come you haven't mentioned it?"

"I figured it wouldn't be possible, so there was no point in saying anything." Michelle shrugged. "Besides, am I good enough?"

"That's not what you should be asking yourself. If you want it bad enough, anything is possible, Michelle. The question is — do you want to join the Amish church?"

"I–I'm not sure. I need to give it more thought. And lots of prayer," she quickly added.

"I wonder why Michelle and Ezekiel aren't back yet." Grandma looked at the grandfather clock in the living room.

"I don't know, but I'm more than ready for dessert. And if I don't move around a bit, there's a good chance I'll fall asleep in my chair." Grandpa got up from his recliner and stretched. Then he walked over in his stocking feet to the front window and gazed out toward the road. "I'm sure they'll be here soon — especially since you have those delicious pies waiting to be sliced."

Grandma stood too. "You're probably right. I suppose we could begin setting things out." She looked around the room. "Is anyone else ready for dessert?"

"I am," Benjamin and Peter said in unison. Their mother made a clicking noise with her tongue. "You two are always hungry. You could leave the table from eating a big meal and be ready to eat again within an hour."

"Yeah — especially when we are offered some dessert," Peter said, while Benjamin nodded his head.

Sara left her seat on the couch. "Why don't you stay here and relax, Grandma? I'll go to the kitchen, set the desserts out, and get a pot of coffee going."

"And I'll help her." Lenore rose from her seat. "I'll get some water heating for those who want tea."

"Thank you." Grandma smiled. "You girls are so thoughtful."

"Think while you're doin' that, I'll take a walk out to the barn." Grandpa looked at Uncle Ivan, then over at his sons. "Anyone want to join me?"

"Jah, sure." Uncle Ivan, Benjamin, and Peter got up and followed Grandpa to the door.

"Wait a minute, boys," Yvonne called. "Don't forget to take this stuffing out to feed the hogs."

Benjamin turned around and took the bag of filling his mother held.

"Thanks, Mamm." He grinned. "Sure wouldn't want Grandpa's pigs to miss out."

Grandma sat down on the couch, and Aunt Yvonne took a seat beside her. Sara, accompanied by Lenore, went to the kitchen.

"The pies you and Grandma made sure look good." Lenore pointed to the array of desserts sitting on a small table in one corner of the room. "Oh, and I see there's even a loaf of bread. Is it pumpkin?"

Sara nodded. "I made that one myself. It's from a recipe my mother used to make during the fall and winter months."

"I can't wait to try it." Lenore took a stack of dessert plates from the cupboard. "How are things going? Does Michelle living here bother you?"

Leaning against the counter, Sara sighed. "Everything about Michelle irritates me. I may seem judgmental, but I don't condone her actions and can't understand how she could have lied to Grandma and Grandpa all those months, pretending to be me." She lifted her shoulders. "Maybe she had a reason, but no one has ever told me what it was. I hope one of these days I'll find out why. For Grandpa and Grandma's sake though, I've been trying not to say anything negative about Michelle, but it's not easy."

Lenore nodded. "I felt the same way when I learned she had let our grandparents believe she was you."

"How did you get past it?"

"After talking with my folks and praying about it, we all realized we needed to forgive Michelle." Lenore filled the coffee pot with water and set it on the stove.

"I might be able to forgive her for pretending to be me and deceiving our grandparents, but I'm having a hard time with her living here."

Lenore filled the teakettle with water and set it on the burner near the coffee pot. "It would be a challenge, but Michelle doesn't really have any other place to go right now."

Sara nodded. "Neither do I."

"Really? I thought you had a duplex in New Jersey."

"It belongs to my stepfather. I was only renting from him." Sara explained how she'd been hoping to move to Strasburg and live with her grandparents until she found a job and a place of her own.

Lenore smiled. "I'm sure Grandma and Grandpa are happy to have you here, and they'd probably be pleased if you stayed with them indefinitely."

"That may be true, but if Michelle continues to live here, I'm not sure I can stay and watch her trying to win them over. It seems as if she's competing with me for their love and attention."

Lenore moved over and slipped her arm around Sara. "Please try to give it a little more time. I'm sure things will work out."

"I hope so." Sara lifted her chin. "But if they don't, I'll definitely move out. I don't want to be the cause of any more discord in this house."

Sara and Lenore had just taken the desserts into the dining room when Michelle and Ezekiel showed up.

"Sorry for being gone so long," Michelle apologized. "Is there anything I can do to help?"

Sara made an effort to smile as she thanked Michelle for her willingness to help. "I think we have everything set out."

The men came inside a few minutes later, and everyone gathered around the table. As they enjoyed dessert and drank their hot beverages, Sara received several compliments on her pumpkin bread.

She smiled. All in all, with the exception of the turkey incident, it had been a nice Thanksgiving. But the next few days might be very different — especially with Michelle involved.

CHAPTER 6

Michelle sat on the back porch, petting Rascal. It had been two days since her buggy ride with Ezekiel, and since then, she'd barely thought of much else. While he hadn't actually proposed marriage, Ezekiel had let Michelle know he wanted to pursue a relationship with her. But in order for him to do that, she'd have to become Amish.

"Could I do it?" she murmured, stroking her dog's ears. "Would it be possible for me to make all the necessary changes in order to become an Amish woman and fit into this community?"

Rascal's ears perked up, and tipping his head to one side, he looked at Michelle as if to say, "I bet you could do it."

She grinned. *If only I could read your mind. Or any other animal's, for that matter.* Her thoughts went to Willis's horse, and how she'd mistrusted him at first. Michelle had done much better when Ezekiel taught her to drive, using his docile horse and comfortable buggy.

At least that's one thing I could do well if I decided to join the Amish church. And I wouldn't mind dressing plain or doing without electricity or modern things either.

Michelle stopped petting Rascal and shifted her position on the porch step. While she had picked up a few of the Pennsylvania Dutch words, the hardest part for her would be learning to speak the Amish language fluently. She'd also have to learn German, in order to understand what was being preached during church and other Amish services, such as weddings and funerals. Although Michelle respected the way of the Plain people, and wanted Ezekiel to court her, taking classes to prepare for church membership was a big decision — one she couldn't make on a whim. She needed to be certain it was the right thing for her before she committed to anything. More prayer was needed — of that much Michelle was certain.

A smile touched Michelle's lips as she remembered how she'd felt when Ezekiel had held her hand. His grip was firm and warm, even reassuring. She could hold onto his hand forever. Michelle didn't think it was possible, but the more time she spent with Ezekiel, the more she loved him.

"Would you mind taking these down to the basement for me, Sara?" Grandma pointed to the freshly washed canning jars on the kitchen counter. They'd used the applesauce the jars had contained this morning, when Sara helped Grandma make several loaves of applesauce bread that they would take to church tomorrow. One of Grandma's good friends was hosting church at her home, so Grandma wanted to take something to help out. The bread would be served with the noon meal.

"No problem. I'll put the jars in one of the empty cardboard boxes I saw on the back porch and take it to the basement. Is there any particular place you want me to put the jars down there?"

"There's a row of shelves on one side of the room for empty jars," Grandma replied. "On the opposite wall are the shelves for glass jars I've filled with the fruits and vegetables I canned this summer and early fall."

"Okay." Sara smiled. "I'll get the box and be back here soon to pick up the jars."

When Sara stepped out the back door, she spotted Michelle sitting on the porch step with Rascal in her lap. She appeared to be deep in thought and didn't seem to notice Sara had come out to the porch. Either that or she chose to ignore her. Without saying a word, Sara picked up the cardboard container.

Back inside, Sara loaded the canning jars into the box. Turning on the battery-operated light at the top of the stairs, she walked carefully down into the nearly darkened room. Once she reached the bottom, she placed the box on a small wooden table near her grandmother's old-fashioned washing machine. Seeing a battery-operated lantern nearby, she clicked that on for additional light.

Sara spotted the wooden shelves where the empty canning jars were kept. After putting each of the jars from the box in place, she was about to head back upstairs when something caught her attention. It appeared to be a very old canning jar, partially hidden behind some other antique jars. What piqued Sara's interest the most, however, was the fact that the antique jar looked as though it had been filled up with folded pieces of paper.

Thinking perhaps the papers had been inserted to protect the old glass, she looked away. But then, Sara's curiosity got the best of her. She reached up and took it down from the shelf.

Placing it carefully on the wooden table, she removed the old lid and reached inside. Surprised, she discovered the piece of paper she'd taken out had writing on it.

Sara squinted at the words: *"We pray because we need to see God work."*

She pursed her lips. *I've prayed for many things over the years, but I've never seen God work. At least not in the way I wanted things to happen.*

Even though Sara's mother had taken her and Kenny to church a few times when they were children, Sara never understood why there was so much emphasis on prayer. She wondered sometimes if people only prayed because they thought it was the right thing to do — something to prove they were religious — and that praying might get them into heaven.

Sara's thoughts were temporarily halted when, from the exposed ceiling above, she heard water rushing through the pipes that lead to the kitchen. *Grandma must be busy at the sink still. Is she wondering what is taking me so long down here?*

It didn't seem right to go snooping through something that wasn't hers, but hopefully she wouldn't get caught.

When the water stopped running, and Sara heard footsteps above, she froze in place. She hoped Grandma wouldn't come down to check on her. Sara wanted to see if something had been written on the other papers inside the jar. She couldn't stop at one.

She reached in and took out another slip of paper. Sure enough, something had been written there too. Sara read the words silently to herself: *"And we know that all things work together for good to them that love God, to them who are the called according to his purpose" Romans 8:28.*

She stared at the jar. *Whoever wrote these notes must have been a religious person. But I wonder what their purpose was in putting the slips of paper inside this jar. Should I ask Grandma about it or keep silent? If she's the one who wrote them, she might have done it secretly. If Grandma is the author of these notes, could she be hiding them for some reason? Maybe I shouldn't mention it to her.*

She let out a long breath. If Sara chose to tell about this, it would be obvious that she'd been snooping. *I'll remain silent about those papers in the old glass jar — at least for now.*

Sara refolded the papers and put them back in the jar. She might come down here another time and see what some of the other papers said. Right now, she needed to get back upstairs and see what else Grandma needed help with today.

At least I am helping out. Sara frowned, as her muscles tensed. *That's more than I can say for Michelle today. Apparently she thinks more about herself than others.* Sara clenched her fingers around the jar. *But then, that doesn't surprise me. If the imposter could live here with my grandparents all those months, pretending to be me, she's obviously selfish and self-centered. I wish Grandma and Grandpa would see her for what she is instead of expecting me to accept Michelle and even be her friend.* Sara shook her head. *That's never going to happen.*

Ezekiel paused to look around while a customer dug through her purse for a wallet to pay for the purchases she'd placed on the counter. Here it was, the Saturday after Thanksgiving, and shopping season had jumped into full swing. The family's greenhouse buzzed with activity, and the entire King family — even Ezekiel's sister Sylvia, who'd gotten married early last spring — had been helping out today. In addition to being Saturday, when normally they were busy with customers who worked during the week, an air of excitement could be felt. Christmas was less than a month away. Holiday orders needed to be filled, and customers came and went, buying poinsettias and sprigs of holly to decorate their homes. Even a few English clergymen had stopped by to get flowers for their churches.

It was a good thing Ezekiel had prepared the bee boxes for the long winter months ahead. There would be no need to do much more than monitor the boxes from time to time until spring approached. This was a blessing, since the greenhouse needed the whole family's attention.

In November, all the honey had been collected, processed, and jarred, ready for his steady clients. Ezekiel left plenty of honey for the bees, so they would have enough food to survive the cold weather ahead. He made adjustments to the bee boxes, protecting the hives from the snowfalls and bitter air but making sure to allow good ventilation. Ezekiel even weighted down the tops of the hives to guard them against toppling over from the strong winds that often accompanied winter storms.

"Thank you and come again soon." Ezekiel smiled at the lady, who waited patiently for him to box up her poinsettias.

"I will. You have some lovely flowers and

plants here in the greenhouse." The customer left, carrying her poinsettias with care.

As another patron got ready to pay, Ezekiel heard a crash and glanced in the direction of the sound.

A child had accidentally knocked over a flower, sending dirt and a shattered clay pot into one of the aisles. The little boy wailed when his mother pointed a finger and scolded him. Ezekiel's mom got on it very quickly and had it cleaned up in no time. The child calmed down right away when she handed him a candy cane.

Ezekiel smiled. His mother had always been good with children. He was sure she and Dad looked forward to the day one of their adult children would make them grandparents.

His sister Amy kept busy helping another customer pick out flowers for a centerpiece she wanted to make. Meanwhile, Ezekiel's brother Abe and their father were busy adding freshly made Christmas wreaths to the wall, as several customers gathered around to look at those too. It was a good thing Abe and Dad had made some extra wreaths this morning, because they were selling quickly. Ezekiel didn't see his younger brother anywhere. Most likely, Henry was still in the barn, cleaning the horses' stalls. Dad had sent him there a while ago, giving him a list of chores to do.

Ezekiel's customer smiled and glanced toward the wreaths before leaving. "There is nothing like the smell of fresh pine. I may have to go look at those before I leave."

When she walked toward the wall of wreaths, Ezekiel waited on the next customer who didn't have any purchases in his hands. "Good afternoon, Mr. Duncan. Are you here to buy some flowers or one of our Christmas plants?"

"You could say that, I guess." The middle-aged man smiled and handed Ezekiel his receipt. "I'm here to pick up my order that I placed two weeks ago. Remember, I purchased fifty poinsettias to give out to my employees, plus a few extra to decorate the office too." Mr. Duncan was the manager of an insurance office in Lancaster. "I believe you waited on me when I stopped by a few weeks ago to put in my request."

"Oh, you're right. Give me a minute, and I'll go in the back and bring them out." Feeling a bit confused, Ezekiel took the customer's order form. He'd had a hard time concentrating on his work today. Unlike other times when the greenhouse was busy and he was at the point of being frazzled, today a warm and lighthearted feeling kept his mood a happy one — although distracted. All he could think about was Michelle and the good time they'd had on Thanksgiving. Especially the ride when they were alone in his buggy.

He would have liked nothing more than for Michelle to have said yes about joining the Amish faith so their courtship could happen sooner and progress at a faster pace.

Ezekiel blew a puff of air through his lips. *I can understand why she was hesitant though. After all, I didn't jump in and become English just because I thought that's what she wanted. Patience is what I need, and the willingness to give her some time.*

Ezekiel came to where the larger orders were waiting and was surprised to find Abe putting poinsettias into a box. "Do you know where Mr. Duncan's order is?"

"I'm filling it now," Abe answered. "I have a few more boxes to fill, and then it will be complete. This is a big order and should have been filled last evening."

Ezekiel pinched the bridge of his nose. "It says on the receipt he'd be picking it up today."

"I guess it was missed," Abe muttered. "Don't want to disappoint Mr. Duncan, so I'm working on it as fast as I can."

"Here, let me help you. We shouldn't keep the man waiting. He's one of our best customers."

Abe looked at Ezekiel with lowered brows. "Exactly."

They worked together quickly to complete the order, and filled five boxes of poinsettias. "I'll go get the cart so we can load these into his car," Abe volunteered.

While Ezekiel waited, his thoughts turned to Michelle once more. He couldn't wait to see her, but with the way things were going and the busy days ahead at the greenhouse, he wasn't sure when it would happen.

CHAPTER 7

Monday morning after the breakfast dishes were done, Sara slipped into a jacket, grabbed her purse, and headed for the back door.

"Where are you going?" Grandma called from the kitchen table, where she sat writing a letter.

Sara turned around. "Out to find a job. Remember, I told you I wanted to start looking today?"

"Yes, but I thought you might decide to wait a few more days." Grandma peered at Sara over the top of her reading glasses. "There's no rush in finding a job, is there?"

Without making reference to what she'd previously said about finding another place to live, Sara explained that she'd seen several job openings in this morning's newspaper and wanted to check on them. "With the way the market is these days, it's important that I do this when the opportunity strikes. The positions being advertised may not be available long."

"I suppose you are right."

"One of the jobs is working in a flower shop. I thought that seemed interesting."

"Have you ever worked in a flower shop?"

"No, but I think it might be fun to learn. I've always liked flowers, and I'm a quick learner."

Grandma tapped the end of the pen she held against her chin. "I wonder if the Kings might need someone to work in their greenhouse. They sell poinsettias this time of the year, and with Christmas only a month away, they might need some extra help."

"I'll keep that in mind." Eager to be on her way, Sara smiled and said, "Well, I'd better go." She turned and reached for the doorknob, but before she could open the door, Grandma spoke again.

"Will you be back in time for lunch?"

"I don't think so, Grandma. I might be gone until late afternoon."

"Oh, okay. I'll see you later then." She put her pen to paper again.

Sara gave a backward wave and opened the door. When she stepped outside, she was surprised to see Michelle hitching Grandma's horse to one of Grandpa's closed-in buggies. Sara was even more taken aback when Michelle got into the buggy, picked up the reins, and headed down the driveway toward the road. The pretender sure hadn't taken long to adapt to the new mode of transportation. Sara frowned. *What is that girl up to, and what's she trying to prove?*

It seemed odd that Michelle would be going anywhere with the horse and buggy by herself, not to mention wearing denim jeans and a long-sleeved sweatshirt under her teal blue puffer coat. The only people Sara had seen riding in the typical gray carriages here in the Lancaster County area were dressed plain.

I bet she's going over to her boyfriend's house. Sara had noticed the sick-cow looks exchanged between Michelle and Ezekiel when everyone sat down to enjoy their Thanksgiving desserts.

Sara got into her car and started the engine. *Whatever happens between Michelle and Ezekiel is none of my business. I need to concentrate on landing a job. Hopefully, I'll find one today.*

Michelle guided Grandma's horse to the hitching rack outside the Kings' greenhouse, got out, and secured Peanuts to the rail. Peanuts nickered to another horse already at the rail. In fact, several horse and buggies, as well as many vehicles, were parked outside the greenhouse. Due to the number of customers who were probably shopping inside, Michelle assumed most of Ezekiel's family was here working today. She wanted to speak to him about the things she'd thought about last night before going to bed, but didn't want any of his family to hear their conversation. While she wasn't sure yet about joining the Amish church, Michelle needed to know more about taking classes and what all would be expected of her. She was also eager to find out when Ezekiel planned to join the church.

When Michelle entered the greenhouse, she noticed right away that they appeared to be having a good day. A number of customers had come out, despite the cold weather. She found Ezekiel's mother, Belinda, setting some poinsettia plants on a shelf. A heater nearby blew warm air, which helped keep the plants at the correct temperature.

Walking up to Belinda, Michelle smiled. "Hi, Mrs. King. Is Ezekiel here?"

Belinda shook her head. "Not in the greenhouse, at least. I wish he was though, because we could use his help right now."

"Where is he?" Michelle glanced around.

"Out checking the beehives — although

I'm not sure why, since he already winterized them." Ezekiel's mother's tone was cool, and she barely made eye contact with Michelle.

She still doesn't like me — even though I came back to Strasburg to apologize to the Lapps for letting them believe I was Sara. Michelle fidgeted with her purse straps. *Should I talk to Belinda about what I did — maybe apologize to her too, since she probably thinks I offended the entire Amish community?*

Before Michelle had a chance to say anything, an elderly Amish couple entered the building. Belinda walked away from Michelle and went to see what they wanted.

It's just as well. I may have said the wrong thing anyway, which would have only made things worse. Truth be told, no matter what I say or do, Belinda will probably never think I'm good enough for her son. Maybe it'd be best if I don't see Ezekiel anymore. He'd be better off with some nice young woman who grew up Amish.

Michelle hurried from the greenhouse. She was almost to her buggy, when Ezekiel came around the corner of the building. "Hey, Michelle. I didn't expect to see you here today." He pulled his jacket collar tighter around his neck. "Did you come to buy something?"

"No, I came to see you."

"I'm glad you did." He stood next to her. "I just came from checking on the bee boxes. It's good to monitor them from now until spring. Anyways, I'm heading to the house for something to drink before I help in the greenhouse again. Why don't you come along and we can visit awhile?"

"I was just in the greenhouse with your mom, and it's pretty busy in there. Are you sure you don't want to go in and help them right now?"

"We won't be long." He smiled and gestured toward the house.

Michelle hesitated but finally nodded. *I may as well get this over with. It's best that I let him go now.*

After Ezekiel and Michelle entered the kitchen, he pulled out two chairs and motioned for Michelle to take a seat at the table. "Would you like something hot or cold to drink? I can heat up some hot water for tea or cocoa."

She shook her head, watching as he went to the sink to wash his hands. "No thanks."

"How about some of my mamm's banana bread? It's pretty tasty."

"I'm sure it's delicious, but I'm not hungry right now. As I said before, I came over here to talk to you about something."

"Oh? What about?"

Michelle had almost worked up the nerve to say what was on her mind when Ezekiel's sister Amy entered the room. She glanced at Michelle, looked away, then turned to face her again. "I was surprised to see you at church yesterday. I didn't realize you'd come back to Strasburg."

"I've been back a month already. And I attended church two weeks ago."

Amy's brows furrowed. "I didn't realize that. I visited a friend's church district two weeks ago, so I wasn't at the service you attended and had no way of knowing you were there."

"Oh, I see." Michelle couldn't judge by Amy's tone of voice whether she disapproved of her, but the young woman's expression said it all. Apparently, like Ezekiel's mother, his sister thought Michelle wasn't good enough for him. *The truth is, I'm not. He deserves better.*

Ezekiel cleared his throat real loud, looking right at his sister. "Did you come to the kitchen for any particular reason?"

She shrugged. "No, not really. I heard voices and came to see who was here."

"I brought Michelle into the kitchen so we could visit without interruptions."

Amy poked her brother's arm. "Okay. Okay. I can take a hint. I have to get back out to the greenhouse anyway. Business is booming, as you well know. Don't be too long, Ezekiel. Your help is also needed today." She glanced briefly at Michelle, then hurried from the room.

Ezekiel took a seat across from Michelle. "That sister of mine . . . She says things sometimes just to get under my skin." He leaned his elbows on the table. "Now what was it you wanted to talk to me about?"

She drew a deep breath. "It's about joining the Amish church. I've been thinking a lot about it these past few days."

"I hope your answer is yes."

"Not yet. I need to ask you some questions about everything that would be expected of me if I did decide to become Amish." Michelle massaged her forehead. "But now I'm having second thoughts."

"What are your second thoughts?" Ezekiel questioned.

"For one thing, it would be a big change for me to give up the only way of life I've ever known." She held up two fingers. "I'd have to learn, not one, but two languages."

Ezekiel folded the fingers she held up, and encompassed her hand in his. "Not a big problem. I can help you with that."

Michelle's gaze flitted around the room. "It's obvious that your mother and sister don't approve of me. So I think it would be best if you forgot about me joining your church and found someone else to court — someone who is honest and upright. You ought to choose a young woman who is already Amish."

Ezekiel shook his head vehemently. "It's not up to them, and I don't want anyone else."

"You may think that right now, but if the right girl came along —"

"You are the right girl, Michelle. I thought that when I believed your name was Sara, and I still think it now."

Fearing she might cave in, Michelle pushed her chair away from the table and stood. "I can't talk about this anymore. Please, give me some space. I'm confused and afraid of failing," she confessed, putting a hand to her hip. "Furthermore, please don't try to force me into this."

His cheeks puffed out. "I won't force you to do anything you don't want to do, but I hope you will think about it more. Don't say yes now, and don't say no. Just pray about whether you should join the Amish church." He stood too and placed his hand on her arm. "The first of nine instructional classes in preparation for baptism and joining the church start next Sunday." He paused and moistened his lips. "I've already agreed to take the classes that will be taught about thirty minutes before church service begins. So if you decide to take part in those classes, please let me know before then."

"When would the baptism take place?" Michelle asked.

"In the spring. And if you have some specific questions concerning what all would be expected of you, I'm more than willing to answer them and put your mind at ease." Ezekiel moved his hand from Michelle's arm to her waist. "Don't give up on us, please."

Offering no response to his statement, Michelle looked at her watch. "I've gotta go, Ezekiel. I want to buy something in your parents' greenhouse, and then I'll need to get back to the Lapps'. Willis is expecting my help with some things today." She made a beeline for the door. It had been a mistake coming here to speak with Ezekiel. Being near him made her want to say she would do whatever it took in order to join the Amish church so they could be together. But that would be the wrong motive for making such a drastic change. If Michelle were to become Amish, it had to be for the right reasons.

CHAPTER 8

"How did the job hunting go?" Grandma asked when Sara returned home at three o'clock. "Were you successful?"

Sara smiled, quickly hiding a purchase she had made around the corner so Grandma wouldn't see. Fortunately, the surprise was well hidden in a big shopping bag. "I sure was. Starting tomorrow, I'll be working at a flower shop." She hung up her jacket and purse, then took a seat at the kitchen table. "They hired me on the spot."

"Oh, at Kings' Greenhouse?"

"No, it's a florist here in Strasburg."

"That's wonderful, Sara. What will you do there?"

"I'll be doing the books, answering the phone, and waiting on customers. Since I've taken some business classes, the flower shop is a good fit for me."

"So you won't be making the flower arrangements?"

"Nope. Don't know if I'd be good at that, although it might be fun to learn. Think I'm better with beads." Sara snapped her fingers. "Speaking of which . . . I keep forgetting to give you and Grandpa something I made. Is he around? If so, I'll go up to my room and get the gifts right now."

"Yes, he's here." Grandma motioned to the living-room door. "After we ate lunch he said he wanted to catch up on his reading before doing more chores, so he's relaxing in his easy chair." She snickered. "The last time I checked though, your grandfather had dozed off. But he may be awake by now."

"Okay, I'll go up and get the gifts and meet you in the living room."

When Sara entered the living room with gifts behind her back, she found her grandparents sitting on the couch engaged in conversation. They appeared to be quite interested in what the other was saying. Sara hated to interrupt, so she waited a few minutes until they finished talking. *These two truly have a special connection. Someday I hope to have that same kind of relationship with my husband. If I ever fall in love, that is.* Sara wasn't about to settle for second best when it came to choosing a mate for life.

Although Dean had treated her mother fairly, to Sara, he and Mama didn't seem like soulmates. Sara's mother had her interests, and Dean had his. Mama had a quiet personality, and Dean was outgoing.

"Your grandma said you have something for us." Grandpa's deep voice pulled Sara's thoughts back to the present.

"Yes, I do. I was going to give them to you when I visited last month but I didn't have Grandma's gift done yet." Sara held out her right hand and handed the beaded keychain she'd made to her grandfather.

His face lit up as he pointed to the initial "L" she had etched into the leather patch. "This is a great gift. Thank you, Sara. I'll keep my house keys on it."

Pleased that he liked the gift, Sara presented Grandma with the black-and-blue coin purse. "I made this from an old scarf my mother used to wear."

"Oh my! Thank you so much." Grandma's eyes teared up as she held the item against her chest. "Knowing you used something of my daughter's makes this even more special to me."

She stood and gave Sara a hug. "And now, how about the three of us sharing a cup of hot tea?"

"And don't forget to bring in some of

those pumpkin cookies you made after lunch." Grandpa smacked his lips.

"How would you know what I baked, Husband? You came right in here after lunch and took a snooze." Grandma flapped her hand at him.

He wiggled his bushy brows. "My eyes may have been sleeping, but my sniffer was wide awake."

Sara laughed. "You are so comical, Grandpa."

"Jah, well, I don't set out to be. Funny stuff just comes out of my mouth." He winked at Sara.

"Okay, I'm going to get the goodies now." Grandma turned toward the kitchen.

"I'll help you." Sara hurried along behind her grandmother.

"Where's Michelle?" she asked when they entered the kitchen. "Will she be joining us for tea and cookies?"

Grandma shook her head. "She hasn't been back since she left this morning. Said she was going over to see Ezekiel."

"Oh, I see." Sara wouldn't admit it to Grandma, but she was glad Michelle hadn't returned yet. It was nice to have some time alone with her grandparents. If the pretender was here, she would have monopolized the conversation.

As Sara got the water heating for tea, Grandma took out several cookies and placed them on a tray.

"You know," Grandma said, "dark blue was one of your mother's favorite colors."

"Yes, she wore the scarf I used to make your coin purse a lot. Mama had a couple of blue dresses too."

"She took after me in that way." Grandma sniffed. "I still miss her so much. I am sure you do as well."

Nodding, Sara touched her chest. "The memory of Mama will always be with me." She wished she could express how she felt about her mother's deceit. Grandma didn't need to know Sara hadn't forgiven her mother for keeping her heritage a secret. Sara couldn't imagine the pain Mama had put her folks through by leaving home and never contacting them. Grandma and Grandpa Lapp were kind and loving. Surely they would have welcomed their daughter back with open arms. *How could Mama not have known how much they loved her?* Sara wondered. *Her parents did not deserve to be treated that way.*

Once the tea was ready, Sara carried the cups and teapot to the living room, while Grandma brought out the tray of cookies and placed it on the coffee table in front of the couch. They all took seats, and after everyone had a cup of tea and a cookie, Sara decided to ask a few questions about the Lancaster Amish.

"When I stopped for lunch at a restaurant in Bird-in-Hand today, I heard someone mention how they looked forward to the mud sale that would take place in the spring of next year." Sara looked at Grandpa. "What is a mud sale anyhow?"

Grandpa leaned slightly forward, with both hands on his knees. "Local volunteer fire companies in Lancaster County raise funds through what they call 'mud sales.' Many of the items available at these auctions are sold outside during the spring when the weather is normally wet."

"Which, of course, makes the ground muddy," Grandma interjected. "That's why the auctions are called mud sales."

"What kind of things do they auction off?" Sara questioned.

Grandpa spoke again. "Everything from furniture, tools, building materials, farming equipment, garden items, livestock, and Amish buggies to a variety of quilts."

Sara reached for another cookie. "I'd like to learn how to make a quilt someday."

Grandma's eyes brightened. "Then I shall teach you. Maybe during the cold winter months, when there isn't so much work to be done outside, we can set up my quilting frame and I'll teach you and Michelle how to make a simple nine-patch quilt for your beds."

Sara smiled, but inside she fumed. *Why does Michelle, who isn't a family member, have to be included in everything?* It seemed as if Grandma — and Grandpa too — thought of her as one of their granddaughters. This irked Sara, but she kept her thoughts to herself. If she said what she truly felt, her grandparents might think she was a terrible person. *They may even choose Michelle over me. I'll bet the pretender would like that. Truth be told, she's probably hoping I'll move back to New Jersey so she can have my grandparents all to herself.* Sara's spine stiffened. *Well, that's not going to happen. Even if I do move out of Grandpa and Grandma's house to a place of my own, I'll be living somewhere in Lancaster County.*

When Michelle arrived home — feeling as if this truly was her home — she put Peanuts in the stall and rubbed her down real good. "You sure have a nice, heavy winter coat already." Michelle patted the mare's neck. "But it's not that surprising, with the cold weather we're having."

95

Michelle continued grooming Peanuts, while talking to her. She understood the horse's hard work and wanted to reward the animal with some proper care in return.

When Michelle left the mare's stall, she took a few minutes to pet Rascal and Sadie, who had eagerly greeted her.

"You two go play now or take a nap," Michelle instructed the dogs after she'd given them what she felt was enough attention.

Sadie slunk away, but Rascal remained by Michelle, pawing at her leg.

She bent down and patted the dog's head. "All right, pooch, go find something else to do."

Rascal gave a pathetic whine, and Michelle lifted her gaze to the ceiling. "Some dogs would do anything to get attention." She gave Rascal another few pats, then sprinted out of the barn.

When Michelle entered the house a few minutes later, she heard Willis and Mary Ruth talking to Sara. Their voices came from the living room. She stepped partially into the room. "Hi, I'm home."

"Come join us." Mary Ruth pointed to the coffee table. "There are still a few cookies left, and I'd be happy to fix you a cup of tea if you'd like."

"No, that's okay. I don't wanna interrupt,"

Michelle replied. "Besides I was planning to help Willis with any chores he needed to get done this afternoon. Is there anything I can get started on?"

"You're not interrupting," Willis said with a shake of his head. "And we can get to those chores later. Please, come have a seat."

Feeling like a fifth wheel on a buggy, Michelle came fully into the room and sat on one end of the couch. She glanced over at Sara, seated on the other end, and smiled. "How's your day been going so far?"

"Okay." Sara didn't look at Michelle.

"Sara got a job working at the flower shop in town," Mary Ruth said.

"Have you had any job offers?" Sara asked, barely glancing in Michelle's direction.

"Not yet. But after I left the Kings' place this morning, I stopped by several restaurants in the area to see if they were hiring." She frowned. "So far, nothing. I'll keep trying until I find a job though."

"What kind of work are you looking for?" Sara asked.

"I've done some waitressing in the past." Michelle lifted her shoulders. "But I'll do most anything if it pays well enough. I'd even wash dishes — although it's not my first choice."

Sara made no comment, but Willis and Mary Ruth both encouraged Michelle to be patient. "The right job for you will open soon," Willis said.

Michelle didn't understand why she hadn't found anything yet. She'd been here a whole month without a single interview. *I need to get out there again tomorrow and make an effort to find something, even if I have to look outside of Strasburg. I can't sit around here mooching off the Lapps any longer. There must be some restaurant in Lancaster County that needs help and would be willing to hire me.*

"Look what Sara made for us." Mary Ruth held up a coin purse, and then motioned to the key ring lying on the end table next to Willis's chair.

"How nice." Michelle didn't want Willis to think she wasn't interested, so she picked up the gift and looked it over. "Oh, this reminds me. I'll be right back."

Running outside to the buggy, she felt a pang of jealousy creep in. *Sara has a job, and I don't. The Lapp's are impressed with her little gifts. I hope they'll like what I got them today.*

Michelle retrieved the poinsettia Ezekiel's mother sold her this morning. While it wasn't homemade like Sara's gifts, it was home grown and would add a little pre-Christmas feeling to the inside of the house.

"While Michelle is outside, I have something else I want to give you." Sara got up and brought the bag she'd left in the hall into the living room. "Here you go."

"I can't imagine what else you could be surprising us with." When Grandma peeked inside, her fingers touched her parted lips. "Look here, Willis. Isn't it lovely?" She took the plant out of the bag and held it up.

Grandpa nodded agreeably. "Bet it would look nice on the dining-room table."

Grandma rose to her feet and gave Sara a hug. "Thank you, Sara. I've never seen a poinsettia this big before, and it's such a beautiful deep red."

"You're welcome. I'm glad you like it. After I got the job at the flower shop, I couldn't resist getting a poinsettia for you. The store is filled with them."

"It's sure a beauty." Grandpa offered Sara a wide grin.

At that moment, Michelle burst into the living room. "I have something for —" She stopped talking as she looked at the beautiful poinsettia Sara had given them. It was twice the size as the one Michelle held. "I — I had hoped to surprise you with this," she stammered. "But I see that you already have a much nicer one."

Before Grandpa or Grandma could say anything, Michelle set the poinsettia on the coffee table and dashed out of the room. Her footsteps could be heard bounding up the stairs, followed by the slamming of her bedroom door.

"Oh dear." Grandma looked at Grandpa with eyes widened. "I'd better go see if she's all right."

CHAPTER 9

Michelle was glad when Sara left for her job the following morning. This gave her a rare moment to talk to Mary Ruth privately. She needed to apologize for her rude behavior last evening when she'd run out of the room after seeing the poinsettia Sara had given her grandparents. Michelle had even skipped supper last night — partly because she was still upset, and also because she'd developed a headache.

As Michelle approached the sink, where Mary Ruth stood washing the breakfast dishes, her throat felt like it was filled with a wad of cotton. Picking up the dish towel, she tried to swallow. "I owe you an apology, Mary Ruth. I shouldn't have been envious of the poinsettia Sara gave you and Willis. It was childish of me to hide out in my room last night too. Will you forgive me for ignoring you when you knocked and called out to me through the bedroom door?"

Mary Ruth smiled as she turned to look at Michelle. "Of course I accept your apology. I am concerned though about the competition going on between you and Sara. I had hoped the two of you might become friends by now, instead of vying for our attention and trying to one-up each other."

Michelle lowered her gaze. "It's not jealousy of Sara, for she is your granddaughter. I still feel that I owe you and Willis something to make up for my deception. And whenever I try to do anything nice for you, Sara always does something better." She lifted her head. "Besides, I don't see how Sara and I can ever be friends. Simply put — she doesn't like me, and probably never will."

Mary Ruth shook her head. "Never say never. If you show Sara you are friendly and try to be kind, I'm certain in time she will warm up to you."

"How much time?" Michelle's forehead wrinkled.

"I don't know, but Willis and I have been praying for both of you."

"Thanks. Truth is, I need a lot of prayer right now, and it's not just about my situation with Sara."

"What is it?" Mary Ruth questioned. "Or

is it something you'd rather not talk about?"

Michelle heaved a sigh. "I think it's something I *need* to talk about."

"I'll dry my hands, and we can sit at the table while you tell me what's troubling you."

"That's all right. I can talk and dry the dishes as you wash."

"Okay then." Mary Ruth resumed her chore. "I'm all ears."

"I am trying to decide whether or not I should join the Amish church."

Mary Ruth dropped her sponge into the soapy water, sending bubbles halfway up to the ceiling, while a few foamy suds landed on her nose. "Goodness." She giggled, using her apron to wipe the soapy blob off.

Michelle joined the carefree moment, laughing and smacking her hands together to pop a few little bubbles floating in front of them.

"Are you truly serious about joining the Amish church?" Mary Ruth asked, once their laughter subsided.

Michelle gave a decisive nod. "Ezekiel plans to join in the spring, and he wants me to take instruction classes with him in preparation for baptism."

"Is becoming Amish something you truly

want to do?" Mary Ruth picked up the sponge.

"I — I think so. But I know it'll be a challenge, and I'm not sure if I am up to it."

"You seem to have adapted well to our Plain lifestyle." Mary Ruth pushed up her damp sleeve. "I've never heard you complain about not having electricity or all the modern conveniences that are not found in our home. You've also learned how to drive a horse and buggy."

"True, but that's not the part I am concerned about."

"What then?"

"In addition to learning how to speak Pennsylvania Dutch fluently, I'd be required to learn German so I can understand the sermons that are preached during church."

Mary Ruth sponged off a spatula, rinsed the object well, and placed it on the drying rack. "Willis and I can help you with that."

"Do you think I'm smart enough to learn both languages? I was never at the top of my class in school, and I didn't get good grades. Truth is, compared to most of the other kids, I felt stupid."

"You're not stupid, and that's in the past. You've already learned several words from our everyday language, and I have no doubt of your ability to learn more." Mary Ruth's tone was reassuring.

Michelle pulled the dishcloth across one of the clean plates. She tried to envision herself in Amish clothing and living a wholesome lifestyle, like the woman she wished was her grandmother. *But maybe I'm like my own mother — a liar and a person people don't trust.* Michelle felt as though she were sinking in deep despair, unable to handle this rising challenge. "There's something else, Mary Ruth." She set the dry plate aside.

"What is it, dear one?"

"I don't feel worthy of becoming Amish. My life has been full of imperfections, and everyone in this area knows how I deceived you and Willis when I pretended to be your granddaughter." Michelle's posture slumped. "I still haven't completely forgiven myself, and there may be some in your church district who have not forgiven me either."

"It's in the past, Michelle. You prayed and asked God to pardon your sins, and you've apologized to us too. If you feel led to become Amish, then I think you should pursue it." Mary Ruth offered Michelle a sweet smile and gave her a hug. It felt reassuring. "And thank you for opening up and sharing your feelings with me," she added. "You are on a new path with your life, and Willis and I will be praying for you."

Tears welled in Michelle's eyes. "Danki for listening, and for the good advice. I will pray about the matter a few more days before giving Ezekiel my decision."

Sara had only been working at the flower shop a few hours when she realized how much she was going to like her new job. She inhaled deeply. How pleasant it was to be surrounded by so many beautiful floral arrangements. Even though it was chilly November outside, it smelled like springtime inside the store.

Several people had come in already this morning, and Sara kept busy waiting on customers and answering the phone to take orders. With Christmas less than a month away, business would no doubt be thriving from now through the end of December.

"Have the poinsettias I ordered come in yet?" Sara's boss, Andy Roberts asked, stepping up to the counter where she stood. "The poinsettias we have are selling fast, and the same holds true for the Christmas cacti. Hopefully the plants I ordered will be here soon."

"I haven't seen any sign of a delivery truck yet."

"No, it won't be a truck. The people I order many of my flowers from are Amish. They either deliver them with their horse-and-market buggy, or sometimes will hire a driver who owns a van."

"Oh, I see. It's nice you're able to buy flowers and plants locally."

Dragging his fingers through his thinning gray hair, Andy nodded. "I appreciate the fact that there is a greenhouse in the area that can provide me with flowers pretty much all year. I also like that it's Amish-owned, because they are easy to work with. I've never been dissatisfied with the quality of their flowers and plants." He motioned to the back of the store. "Welp, I'd better get busy and help my wife with making the arrangements. Karen wouldn't appreciate it if she got stuck with all the work while I stayed out here yakking all day. Let me know if you need anything," Andy called as he ambled toward the back room.

Sara looked around the shop again. Since she had been so busy, she hadn't noticed how few poinsettias were actually left in the store until Mr. Roberts mentioned it. She was glad she bought the beautiful one yesterday, because right now only a couple of small ones remained.

A few minutes later, a tall Amish man

entered the store. He was slender and had a full beard that was gray, which was in sharp contrast to his mostly light blond hair. With only a few wrinkles on his face, Sara figured he might be in his late forties, but the beard made him appear older.

"May I help you?" she asked when he stepped up to the counter.

He nodded. "Came in to buy a bouquet of flowers for my wife's birthday." His blue eyes twinkled under the lights in the store. "I've been doin' that on her birthday every year since we got married, and sometimes I get Mattie flowers for no occasion at all."

"I'm sure she appreciates your thoughtfulness." Sara opened the cooler to show him what was available. "These are the bouquets that have already been made up. Do you see anything your wife might like?"

His forehead wrinkled as he rubbed one hand down the side of his black trousers. "Don't think so. What else have you got?"

Sara glanced toward the back room. "I'll go get one of the owners and see if they can make something up that would be more to your wife's liking."

"Okay." The man reached under his straw hat and scratched the side of his head. "Are you new here? Don't recall seeing you before."

"Today's my first day on the job," Sara explained. "And I am new to the area. Now, if you don't mind waiting, I'll be right back."

"Don't mind a bit."

Sara hurried to the back room, and was pleased when Karen said she would be right out.

Sara returned to her place behind the counter in time to see Ezekiel King enter the store.

"Sure didn't expect to see you here." Ezekiel gave Sara a wide smile. "I'm guessin' because you're behind the counter that you're not one of the customers."

"You're right. I started working here this morning," she responded. "What brings you into the flower shop, Ezekiel?"

"Came to deliver some poinsettias."

"Oh, so you're the delivery they've been waiting for."

"Yep. This florist and a couple others in Lancaster County buy their Christmas flowers from our greenhouse." Ezekiel glanced at the Amish man who stood waiting in front of the counter. "Hey, Mr. Fisher. How are you?"

The other man shuffled his feet. "Do I know you?"

"Not personally, but I met you once when I stopped by your bulk-food store in Gordonville. My folks have a greenhouse here in Strasburg."

"I see." Mr. Fisher's attention turned to Karen Roberts when she came out of the back room. As he explained to her what he wanted for his wife's bouquet, Ezekiel continued his conversation with Sara.

"I'm glad you were able to find a job so quickly. Michelle's been lookin' for a month now and hasn't found a single waitressing position."

Hearing Michelle's name caused Sara to think about how Michelle responded last evening when they'd both given Sara's grandparents a poinsettia. After seeing the look of disappointment on Michelle's face, and then watching her run out of the room, Sara realized the reason for the young woman's disappointment. *I probably would have felt the same way if I'd given Grandpa and Grandma the smaller plant. But she should have gotten past it, instead of staying in her room all evening and ignoring Grandma when she knocked on her bedroom door, wanting to talk. It just showed Michelle's immaturity.*

"Did you hear what I said?"

Sara jerked her head. "What was that, Ezekiel?"

"I asked if you would hold the door while

110

I bring in the poinsettias."

"Oh yes. Certainly."

Before they reached the door, a thunderous crash sounded outside on the street. Watching through the glass doors, Sara saw that a car had been rear-ended. Both drivers appeared to be okay, as they got out of their vehicles. But soon, a shouting match ensued.

Sara looked at Ezekiel with raised eyebrows and motioned to the angry man. "I wonder why he's so mad. Look at all the dents already on the side of his car. That's worse than the new one he's pointing to on the front fender of the other's man vehicle."

The taller man, dressed in a gray business suit, stood shaking his head as he pointed to the spot on his car that had suffered the damage. It was easy to put two and two together on what had happened. Apparently, the well-tailored man had made a quick stop and the other guy couldn't brake quickly enough.

"I wonder how long this will take." Sara continued to watch.

Ezekiel shrugged his shoulders and pointed to the police car pulling up. Quickly, the officer directed both guys to move their vehicles off the road.

"Guess it's safe to go out now," Ezekiel

commented. "A little excitement — the kind we don't need. But at least no horse and buggy was involved. That happens all too often."

As Sara held the door, she watched while Ezekiel unloaded a box full of poinsettias from his driver's van. Most of them were the traditional red, but a few were an off-white, while a couple of others had a pink-ish hue. It would be fun to place them around the store among the other displays. Meanwhile, she heard Mr. Fisher say he had some errands to run and would be back later to pick up his wife's bouquet.

Sara didn't know Mattie Fisher, but she couldn't help feeling a bit envious of the woman. *Being married to a man who brought flowers on her birthday every year must make Mrs. Fisher feel very special.* It wasn't only the idea of getting a pretty bouquet Sara envied; it was the thought of having a man care about her so much that he'd go to extra lengths to make her birthday special.

Not like Dean, who was so into his work and recreational sports that he sometimes forgot Mama's birthday and even their wedding anniversary. Sara bit her bottom lip until she tasted blood. *I wish I knew what my real father was like. Of course, if he didn't care enough to marry Mama when she was preg-*

nant, then he probably wouldn't have been a good husband either.

Chapter 10

Clarks Summit

Brad headed down the hall toward the cafeteria. All was quiet except for the rhythmic sound of his footsteps on the polished floor. It was hard to believe today was the last day of November, and also the last day of classes for this week. In just a few short weeks, he would be leaving the seminary for a much-needed Christmas break. It would be good to take some time away from his studies and all the pressures he faced in order to finish his masters of divinity degree. There was so much to learn before he could apply for a church. Sometimes, his head felt like it was spinning. Expository preaching, Christian leadership, and biblical counseling were all classes he was expected to take. Although Brad was eager to shepherd a flock of his own, the idea frightened him a bit. What if he wasn't up to the task? Would the congregation relate to him, and he to them? If it was a small church, how much responsibility would be placed upon him?

Brad remembered one church he and his parents had attended when he was boy. It had been small and without enough willing people to do all the jobs. That meant poor overworked Pastor Jenkins was responsible not only for preaching and shepherding the flock but also directing the music, hauling neighborhood children to Sunday school in his van, and taking care of a good deal of the janitorial duties.

As Brad sat at one of the lunch tables inside the cafeteria and took out the sandwich he'd packed this morning, his thoughts drifted toward home. Except for a lingering cough, Mom's bout with the flu was behind her. Fortunately, Brad's father didn't get sick and was able to take time off work to care for Mom during the worst of her illness. Apparently Dad's immune system was stronger than hers.

Brad looked forward to being with his parents for Christmas, but he was also eager to spend part of his holiday break in Lancaster County. It would be good to see everyone he knew there again. Many of the folks he'd worked for, like Willis and Mary Ruth Lapp, were almost like family and made him feel as if he had a second home.

"Mind if I sit here?" Holding a tray full of food in one hand, Elliot Whittier looked down at Brad.

"Be my guest." Brad motioned to the empty chair across from him.

"I see you brought your own lunch," his friend commented as he took a seat.

"Yeah. It's cheaper than buying a hot meal every day." Brad unwrapped his tuna fish sandwich, then thumped his stomach. "It'll fill the empty hole, I guess."

"Today it looks as if the kitchen staff is working in slow motion." Elliot chuckled. "Guess they're in need of some time off too." He shook some ketchup on his hamburger. "So how are you liking it here?"

"It's okay. Just a lot harder than I thought it would be."

Elliot nodded and licked a blob of ketchup off his finger. "I know what you mean. There's a lot more to becoming a minister than meets the eye."

"That's for sure."

"With all the studying I have to do, it's putting a crimp on my social life." Elliot's brows furrowed as he took a bite of his burger. "I'm worried my girlfriend, Mindy, might break up with me if I don't find the time to take her out pretty soon. At the rate things are going, we may never get married."

Brad reached for his bottle of water. "Didn't realize you were engaged."

"We're not officially. I'm waiting until I complete seminary to propose to her." Elliot tipped his head, looking curiously at Brad. "Think you'll ever get married? I mean, having a wife is not criteria for pastoring a church, but it would sure make it easier to share the burden with a good helpmate at your side."

Brad shrugged his shoulders. "If I found the right woman, I would consider marriage. But that's not a concern for me at this point, since I currently have no girlfriend. And to be honest, I don't know where I'd find the time to date anyone right now." He smiled. "So for now, it's best that I concentrate on my studies and keep my nose in the books."

Strasburg

Despite the chill seeping into the buggy, Michelle's face felt like she'd been in the sun too long. She was heading down the road toward the Kings' place, ready to give Ezekiel her answer. After praying about it these last few days, Michelle had made her decision about whether to join the Amish church or not. She hoped it was the right one, because many doubts still swam around her head about the future.

From past experience, it seemed that so far, every decision she'd made in her life turned out to be wrong. Yet through it all, she'd persevered. Giving up was not in her nature. When Michelle left Lancaster County after leaving a note for the Lapps admitting she had pretended to be Sara, she'd been tempted to give up. But after reading some scripture, she had fallen under conviction and felt as if God had given her a sense of purpose. She certainly hadn't expected that part of the purpose would be returning to Strasburg with Ezekiel to face Willis and Mary Ruth. And the last thing Michelle ever expected was to be living in their home again by invitation.

"Your owners are such good people." Michelle spoke out loud as she shook the reins a bit to get Peanuts to go faster. The mare whinnied as though in agreement.

One thing about taking a ride in the buggy, it gave her mind something else to focus on while moving along at a slower pace. Michelle kept rehearsing what she wanted to say to Ezekiel about her decision.

She rolled her shoulders to release some tension. Michelle hoped Ezekiel was at home or in the greenhouse, for if she didn't speak to him today, she might lose her nerve.

Ezekiel was heading to the house to get the ham sandwich Mom had put in the refrigerator for him, when a nickering horse pulling a buggy trotted into the yard. He recognized Mary Ruth's mare, and was pleased when he saw Michelle in the driver's seat of the buggy.

Ezekiel's gaze rested on her, picturing his girl being Amish. Michelle adjusted so naturally to driving a horse and buggy. He felt sure she could become Amish if she chose to. *But I shouldn't get my hopes up,* Ezekiel chided himself. He wondered if she'd come here to give him her answer about taking classes to join the church.

Ezekiel turned away from the house and hurried over to the hitching rail near their barn. After Michelle got the horse stopped, he secured Peanuts to the rail. Then he went around to the driver's side to help Michelle out, but by the time he got there, she'd already stepped down.

"I'm glad to see you." Ezekiel resisted the urge to pull her into his arms. With customers coming and going from the greenhouse and family members taking turns up at the house to eat their lunch, hugging Michelle in broad daylight wouldn't be appropriate.

"I'm glad to see you too." She looked up at him, then glanced off to the left when two fluffy cats darted out of the barn.

"Would you like to come inside and have lunch with me? We can share my ham sandwich."

Michelle shook her head. "I ate at the Lapps' before Willis and Mary Ruth took off with his horse and buggy for town. They had several errands to run."

"Okay, well, at least come inside out of the cold. We can talk while I eat my lunch."

With only a slight hesitation, Michelle began walking toward the house. Once inside, she took off her jacket and hung it over the back of a chair at the kitchen table. "Is anyone else here right now?" she questioned.

"You mean, any of my family?"

"Yeah."

Ezekiel shook his head. "It's my turn for lunch, while everyone else works in the greenhouse. When I get back to work, Mom and Amy will come up and eat."

"Something smells really good in here." Tipping her head back, she sniffed. "There's a hint of cinnamon in the air."

"Mom baked homemade sticky buns this

morning. Would you like one with something hot to drink?"

"No thanks. Since you're busy today, I won't take up much of your time." Michelle took a seat at the table. "I'm here to give you my answer about joining the Amish church."

Ezekiel's hands felt clammy, and he resisted the urge to pace. "I'm glad you've reached a decision." He sat down in the chair beside her, rubbing both palms against his pants legs. "Can I just say something before you give me your answer?"

"Of course."

"No matter what you have decided, it won't make any difference in the way I feel about you." Ezekiel swiped his tongue across his parched lips. "Even if we can't be together as boyfriend and girlfriend, I'd like to still be your friend." He leaned back in his chair.

She gave him a dimpled smile. "Is that all you wanted to say?"

"Jah."

"Okay, now it's my turn." Michelle touched her pink cheeks and exhaled. "After much thought and prayer, I've come to the conclusion that I do want to join the Amish church. So if you'll promise to help me through the transition, I'll take the necessary classes with you."

"I'm so glad." Ezekiel glanced around to be sure none of his family had come into the house. Then he leaned closer to Michelle and gave her a quick, but meaningful kiss. "You won't regret it, I promise. We will do this together, and I'll support you in every way."

Michelle gave the side of his face a gentle stroke with her thumb. "Danki."

He felt an unexpected release of tension throughout his body. "You're welcome."

They sat smiling at each other, until Michelle pushed back her chair and stood. "I need to let you eat so you can get back to work. Besides, I promised to do a few chores for Willis and Mary Ruth while they're shopping in town. So I'd better be on my way."

"Okay. I'll see you on Sunday. Oh, and don't forget to get there early. Our first class will begin thirty minutes before the church service starts."

"Don't worry. I'll be there in plenty of time."

After Michelle headed out the door, Ezekiel got up and watched out the window until her horse and buggy were out of sight. Then he closed his eyes and sent up a heartfelt prayer. *Thank You, Lord, for giving*

Michelle the desire and courage to pursue an Amish way of life. I also want to thank You for giving me hope that I might have a lifelong future with her.

Ezekiel turned from the window and went to the refrigerator. He felt ever so thankful she had agreed to take classes in readiness for church membership. Once they'd both gotten baptized and became members, Ezekiel would be free to ask Michelle to marry him.

Since no one else was home and Sara didn't have to go to work until the afternoon, she decided to go back to the basement and look at the old jar filled with paper notes again. She was eager to find out what some of the others might say. Maybe something in one of them would give her a clue as to who the author of those notes might be.

Slipping on a sweater and holding the battery-operated lantern, Sara made her way down the creaky wooden steps, holding tightly with the other hand to the shaky handrail. As her feet touched the cement floor, the shelf where the laundry soap, bleach, and stain removers were kept came into view. A pile of old rags lay on another shelf, along with a box of matches and several rolls of paper towels.

The groan of a shifting wooden beam, and an unidentifiable scratching noise, set shivers up her spine. *Sure hope I don't encounter any mice down here.*

Sara held the light in front of her, shining it to the right, to the left, down on the floor, and up toward the ceiling. She didn't like dark, damp places, but her desire to find what other messages were in that old jar took precedence over her fears.

Sara made her way over to the shelves. "Eww . . ." After walking into a clingy web, she wiped her face, then ran her fingers through her hair and down over her clothing. "I hope there was no spider in that web." The idea of it crawling on her somewhere made Sara cringe.

When she reached the shelf where the empty canning jars were located, Sara held the lantern higher until the antique jar came into view. The old, bubbled glass was a light seafoam green. The lid on top of the jar looked like tarnished silver. Funny she hadn't noticed those details when she'd seen the jar before. *Could this be a different one, or am I seeing the jar more clearly today?*

After unscrewing the lid, and laying it on the wooden table near the antiquated washing machine, Sara shook the jar, in an attempt to read a different message than she

124

had the last time.

Sara reached in and took out a piece of paper that had been folded twice. After smoothing out the creases, she read the message out loud. "Life's situations can become an opportunity for transformation."

Transformation to what? Sara wondered. Who wrote this, and what does it mean?

She pondered the words a few more seconds before taking out and reading another slip of paper. This one had a Bible verse on it: " 'To whom ye forgive any thing, I forgive also: for if I forgave any thing, to whom I forgave it, for your sakes forgave I it in the person of Christ.' "

There it was again — that word "forgiveness." Sara pursed her lips. *I don't see why it's so important for people to forgive. When a person's done wrong, it's only human to feel angry or hold a grudge. I am not doing anything mean, or trying to punish those who have hurt me, so I don't understand why I need to forgive.*

Hearing footsteps from the room above, Sara hastily put the papers back in the jar, closed the lid, and returned the jar to its shelf. She was certain Mary Ruth and Willis couldn't be back from town this soon, so it must be Michelle she'd heard upstairs. *Maybe I'll stay down here with the cobwebs and spiders awhile longer. It would be better than facing her right now.*

CHAPTER 11

During supper that evening, Sara toyed with her chicken and dumplings as she listened to Michelle tell Grandpa and Grandma about her visit with Ezekiel and how she'd decided to prepare for joining the Amish church in the spring.

Why is she doing this? Sara wondered. *What reason could Michelle possibly have for becoming Amish? She must have some ulterior motive — something that goes beyond wanting to be with her boyfriend.*

Sara picked up her glass of water and took a drink. *By becoming Amish, Michelle might hope she can get even closer to Grandpa and Grandma, and perhaps even gain something from them. But what could it be? Their attention? Love? Support? Or could she be hoping to someday receive an inheritance from their estate?* From what Sara understood, the imposter didn't own anything but the clothes on her back. *Yes, I'll bet she is after something.*

Sara's jaw clenched as she set her glass down a little too hard, and some water splashed out by her plate. She grabbed a napkin and wiped it up before anyone noticed her annoyance. *If Michelle goes through with her plan to join the Amish church, it'll drive an even bigger wedge between us.*

Sara breathed deeply, trying to squelch her agitation as she listened to more of Michelle's plans. *Wish I didn't feel this way. Am I jealous because Michelle got to know my grandparents first and she spent all those weeks with them, as they drew close to her? I have the right to feel this way. It should have been me instead of Michelle they picked up at the bus station in Philly that day. I am the real granddaughter, and yet here she is.*

It perturbed Sara whenever she heard Michelle speak Pennsylvania Dutch, and more so, seeing how much it pleased Grandma and Grandpa. It was obvious that in spite of Michelle's deceitfulness, she had managed to worm her way into their hearts.

Sara's fingers dug into her palms. *I have Mom to blame for this. It's because of her that I feel so defeated and mistrusting. If only she'd been honest with me.*

Feeling a need to get the topic off Michelle and onto something else, Sara mentioned the accident she and Ezekiel had witnessed in front of the flower shop yesterday. "You should have seen how angry one of the men got. I thought for a while he might hit the other guy."

"That isn't the way an Amish man would have acted, is it?" Michelle looked at Sara's grandfather.

He shook his head. "Hopefully not. Getting angry and shouting at someone when an accident occurs is not the way to handle things."

"Nor is it the Christian thing to do," Grandma put in.

"Some people, like my ex-boyfriend, are full of anger, and you never know what might set them off." Michelle's voice cracked. "I never should have gotten involved with Jerry. He was a loser and an abuser. I'm glad to be shed of him."

Grandma placed her hand on Michelle's arm and gave it a few pats. "You've been through a lot, but that's all in the past. You have a new future to look forward to now."

If the pretender was telling the truth, and not making things up in order to prey on Grandma and Grandpa's sympathies, then Sara couldn't help feeling a bit sorry for her, because no one deserved to be abused. But if Michelle made up the story about the angry boyfriend in an attempt to get pity, then shame on her.

It was hard to know what to believe where the auburn-haired woman was concerned. Sara wished she could come right out and question Michelle's motives. But she wouldn't say anything in front of her grandparents. She would, however, keep a close eye on Michelle and make sure she didn't do anything to hurt Grandpa or Grandma ever again.

As they continued with supper, Mary Ruth glanced at her husband, wondering if he had noticed Sara's demeanor at the table this evening. Their granddaughter was clearly uneasy around Michelle and had not been her friendly self since she returned here before Thanksgiving. *No doubt our precious granddaughter feels threatened by Michelle's presence in this house, even though I have tried to reassure Sara that our love for her hasn't changed because Michelle's come back and is here with us.*

Willis didn't appear to notice Sara's pinched expression when Michelle shared her news about joining the Amish church. He seemed pleased with the idea and kept his focus on the chicken dumplings rather than paying attention to Sara's response to the information Michelle had shared with them. Nor had he said much, other than his one comment when Sara changed the subject to the accident that had taken place outside of the florist's.

Mary Ruth forked a piece of tender chicken into her mouth. *Is my husband oblivious to what's still going on between Sara and Michelle? Maybe men don't take note of such things, the way we womenfolk do.*

She glanced at Willis again, but he didn't seem to notice. *Or maybe he's choosing to ignore it, hoping things will work out between the young women without our further interference. I've spoken to Sara once and he talked with Michelle, so it's time for me to take a step back and give the situation to God.* Mary Ruth blotted her lips with a napkin. *If Sara's attitude toward Michelle doesn't improve by Christmas, I will talk to her again, because this can't go on indefinitely.*

Clarks Summit

Seated at the table in the kitchen of his apartment, Brad reflected on when he was a boy and had visited this area with his folks. Clarks Summit, with its four dams called Cobbs, Fords, Interlaken, and the Summit Lake Dam, was a great vacation spot. He recalled how his family liked to come up on a warm sunny day and visit one of the four reservoirs to cool off. His mom would pack up food for lunch, and Dad brought a portable barbecue along with some folding chairs.

While eating his supper, Brad decided to check in with his parents to see how things were going. He had been praying for them and hoped things had improved.

"Hey, Mom, how are you doing?" Brad put his cell phone on speaker so he could eat his evening meal and talk at the same time.

"Better. My cough's subsiding, and I have more energy."

"Good to hear." Brad twirled some noodles on a fork and slurped up some spaghetti, then washed it down with milk from his glass.

"Are you eating, dear? I don't want to interrupt your supper."

"No, it's okay. My phone's on speaker so I can eat while I'm talking with you, no problem."

"Did you have a nice Thanksgiving?"

"It was all right. I ate at a local restaurant. It wasn't like your good home-cooked meals, but I survived."

"Sorry you had to be alone. It was a bad time for me to get the flu."

"It's okay, Mom. You didn't get sick on purpose."

"That's for sure. So how are things going there with your studies?" she asked.

"The course I'm taking now is tough, but I'll get through it." Brad put another forkful of spaghetti in his mouth and ate it before speaking again. "I'm sure looking forward to Christmas break though. I need some downtime and a chance to rest my tired brain. Also, it'll be nice to spend a little time with you and Dad."

There was a pause. His mother cleared her throat. "Umm . . . About Christmas . . ."

"What about Christmas, Mom?"

"I heard from my sister today, and she's scheduled to have a hysterectomy two days before Christmas."

"So you're going to Seattle to be with her." Brad finished his mother's sentence.

"Yes, I need to be there. As you know, your aunt Marlene has been all alone since her husband died a year ago, and she can't take care of herself when she comes home from the hospital. I will probably need to stay for several weeks past Christmas."

"I understand. Will Dad be going with you?"

"He will, but only for part of the time. He'll stay through the holiday, but when he needs to return to work, he'll fly home." Her voice faltered. "I feel terrible about leaving you alone on Christmas. You'd be welcome to go with us to Seattle, but I'm sure there are other places you'd rather be for the holidays."

Brad took another drink from his glass. "Actually, I had planned on spending some of my Christmas break in Lancaster County. I'm sure if I let them know ahead of time that I'll be in the area, my Amish friends Willis and Mary Ruth Lapp will invite me for Christmas dinner. At least I hope that's the case, because I'd sure like to see them again."

"Are you sure it's not their granddaughter you're eager to see? From what you mentioned in one of our phone calls this past summer, you and Sara were sort of dating."

"We did see each other socially a few times," he admitted, "but she's not the right girl for me."

"How do you know?"

Brad lifted his gaze to the ceiling. *I shouldn't have told Mom anything. Now she'll pester me to death if I don't tell her everything — or at least what I think she wants to know.*

"For one thing, Mom, I don't believe Sara's a Christian."

"Ah, I see. You were wise not to get serious about her then."

"Yes. Besides, I had a hunch she was interested in a young Amish man in Strasburg. Sara hung out with Ezekiel quite a bit." Brad reached for a napkin and wiped his mouth. "Before I left for seminary, I wrote Sara a letter saying goodbye and that I wished her well and would be praying for her."

"Sounds to me like your dad and I raised a smart man. With your plans to become a minister, the last thing you need is to be married to a nonbeliever. But then, I have to ask: Would Ezekiel be interested in her if she doesn't believe in God? And also, if Sara is not a Christian, how is it she would be interested in an Amish man? Aren't most Amish people Christians?"

"The ones I know sure are. But that's something Ezekiel will have to work out with her, if he's interested."

"Oh, sorry, Brad. Your dad just came in the door, so I need to get supper on the table. I fixed his favorite spaghetti with marinara sauce."

Brad chuckled. "That's what I'm eating right now too. Only my meal isn't homemade. It came out of a can."

"Oh my. Those meals in a can aren't that healthy."

"I know, but I have a lot of studying to do yet this evening, so I didn't have time to cook anything from scratch."

"Someday you'll meet the right woman who will not only cook you well-balanced meals, but she'll also be a helpmate in your ministry."

"Yes, if I'm meant to get married, God will send the right woman, and I will know it without a doubt. And now, Mom, I'd better let you go or I'll soon hear Dad grumbling."

She snickered. "Take care, Brad, and safe travels to the Lancaster area when you go. Oh, and please stay in touch."

"I will, and you do the same. Please let me know when you get to Seattle, and I'd appreciate a report on how Aunt Marlene is doing. And remember," he added, "I'll be praying for your sister, as well as for you and Dad, as you travel to Washington state."

When Mom hung up, Brad clicked off his phone. As he grasped his fork to finish his meal, a vision of Sara popped into his head. He had to admit he'd been attracted to her pretty auburn hair, blue-green eyes, and slender figure. But looks weren't everything, and unless she'd come to know the Lord since he last saw her, Brad would not allow himself to get involved with Sara again. He would, however, call and leave a message for the Lapps, letting them know he planned to be in their area over Christmas vacation. He also needed to call his friend, Ned Evans, whom he had shared an apartment with while attending college in Lancaster before coming to seminary. Hopefully, Ned wouldn't mind if he stayed with him for two weeks. It would be like old times.

CHAPTER 12

Strasburg

Michelle gazed at the plain blue dress lying on the end of her bed. It was hard to believe the frock was hers. For the last two weeks Mary Ruth had been giving Michelle sewing lessons, and last night she'd finished hemming the Amish dress she had made mostly by herself. It would be the first of several, because one plain dress in her closet was not enough.

Michelle was still amazed at the idea of having to sew dresses to be used for different occasions. She would need clothes for church, work, and someday maybe her own wedding attire.

I shouldn't jump too quickly on that idea, she told herself. *I've got a lot to overcome first, and Ezekiel hasn't proposed to me yet either.* She giggled and stifled it with her hand. *But it's hard not to get excited, especially at the thought of accomplishing my goal.*

Since Michelle had made up her mind to join the Amish church, she figured it was best if she wore Amish clothes from now on. No more makeup, jewelry, or ponytails for her either. During the day, Michelle's hair would be worn in a bun at the back of her head, with a white, heart-shaped covering on top. For work around the house or chores outside, Michelle would wear a dark-colored scarf on her head. Only at night would her hair be let down.

For some reason, images of Michelle's biological parents, Herb and Ginny Taylor, popped into her mind. *If my real parents could see me now, wouldn't they be surprised? But then, with the kind of life they lived, maybe they're no longer alive.* Her mouth twisted grimly. *I know one thing: they couldn't have cared less when that woman from child services took me and my brothers away. They all but shoved us out the door. And what's even worse, we ended up in different foster homes, never to see each other again.*

It angered Michelle whenever she thought of her so-called parents and how they could have ruined her life if she'd continued living with them. "But you didn't get the chance to mess up my brother's and my lives any more than you did." Michelle spoke as if they were standing right in front of her.

Thinking of Ernie and Jack made her feel sad. *I pray they're okay. It's not likely, but maybe someday our paths will cross.*

Switching her thoughts back to the current situation, Michelle didn't mind the idea of wearing Amish dresses, or even using a horse and buggy as her main mode of transportation. What bothered her most was the language barrier. Although Mary Ruth, Willis, and Ezekiel had promised to work with Michelle on learning the Pennsylvania Dutch language, she still doubted her abilities.

I wonder if Sara will ever decide to join the Amish church, Michelle thought as she slipped the dress on over her head. *Since her mother grew up in an Amish home, I would think she might be inclined in that direction.* Sara had never mentioned the idea in Michelle's presence, but then Sara said as little as possible to Michelle.

Michelle put the blind up and stood a few feet from the window. Seeing her image reflected in the glass, she used it like a full-length mirror. It wasn't fully daylight yet, so she could see herself pretty well. Michelle turned at different angles to see how she looked in the Amish dress. It might take a little getting used to, but she liked it. *It fits me well, like it was custom made, and it feels comfortable to wear.* Michelle slipped on the apron and tied it in the back.

Mary Ruth had done a wonderful job helping her measure correctly and making sure it all went together as it should. At times it was still difficult for Michelle not to call Mary Ruth "Grandma," because she made her feel like part of the family.

The fact is Sara has that complete right, not me. Sighing, Michelle picked up her brush and worked through all the tangles in her hair. Then she pulled her hair back into a bun, making sure the sides were twisted the way Mary Ruth and other Lancaster Amish women wore theirs. *I wonder if others will think I fit in.* She glanced at her reflection in the mirror on her dresser and shook her head. *Why am I filled with so much self-doubt? If only I could be more confident, like Sara. She seems so self-assured.*

Hoping to keep her nervousness from showing, Michelle drew a quick breath, opened her bedroom door, and started down the stairs.

Sara took out a frying pan and put just enough coconut oil in the bottom to keep the eggs she would soon be frying from sticking. She'd come down earlier than usual to help start breakfast, wanting a few moments alone with her grandmother before Michelle showed up. "Since I've only been working at the flower shop two weeks, it's going to be a while before I have enough money saved up to rent an apartment in town," she said, looking at Grandma, who had taken a pan of biscuits from the oven. Her glasses had steamed over from the moist, hot pan of food.

Grandma's nose crinkled as she squinted at Sara over the top of her glasses. "And you know, dear one, we've had this discussion before. You should realize by now that your grandpa and I would be disappointed if you moved out of our house anytime soon. We haven't had a chance to really get to know you." Grandma took out some flour for making gravy.

It hadn't taken Sara long to learn that biscuits and gravy were one of Grandpa's favorite things to have with his scrambled eggs. "I won't be moving anytime soon. I promise."

Grandma's mouth opened like she was about to say more, but Michelle entered the room. Sara's grandmother placed her hands against her cheeks and made a little gasping noise. "*Ach,* Michelle — you look so Amish in that dress." She glanced at Sara, while gesturing to Michelle. "Didn't she do a nice job making it?"

Without speaking, Sara nodded. It was hard to understand why Grandma and Grandpa got so excited over every little thing Michelle did.

She reached for the egg carton near the stove. *I still feel sometimes that they care more about Michelle than they do me. Is it because they've known her longer, or is it her personality they enjoy?*

When Grandpa came in from outside, Sara put her thoughts to rest until he made a comment about Michelle's dress. "Well now, don't you look nice this morning, Michelle. If I was basing it on your appearance only, I'd believe you were already one of us."

"Danki." Michelle's cheeks reddened. "I hope I don't look too *lecherich.*"

Grandma shook her head. "Of course you don't look ridiculous. You look like a pretty young Amish woman."

Sara resisted the urge to give a negative comment and kept her focus on the eggs she'd begun breaking into the pan. This morning, she would scramble them as they cooked. To her way of thinking, Michelle was looking for a compliment — something to make her feel good about herself. *Well, she's not going to get any compliments from me.*

Sara wished she could find something about Michelle that she liked, but the longer they both lived here, the more things the imposter did to irritate her. And the way her grandparents had accepted Michelle without question made it even more difficult for Sara.

Grandpa removed his straw hat and placed it on a wall peg. "Not to change the subject or anything, but I just came from the phone shack, and there was a message from Brad Fuller."

Michelle turned her head in Grandpa's direction. "What did he say?"

"Said he'll be in the area for Christmas and wants to spend some time with us while he's here." He looked over at Grandma. "If Brad doesn't have any other plans, should we invite him to eat with us on Christmas Day?"

"Of course." Grandma bobbed her head. "It will be nice to see him again and find out how things are going with his ministerial studies." She turned toward Michelle. "I imagine Brad will be *verschtaunt* to see that you're back living with us again and have decided to become Amish."

Michelle shook her head. "He won't be

144

surprised that I'm living here, because as far as he knows, I never left."

"Oh, that's right." Grandma gestured to Michelle's dress. "But he won't expect to see you wearing that, and Brad will likely be pleased when he learns of your decision to join the Amish church."

"I hope so." Michelle moved slowly across the kitchen. "I'm looking forward to seeing Brad again, because I have so much to tell him about how I've changed since we last saw each other."

The discussion going on caused Sara to recall the letter she'd gotten from a man named Brad. She assumed it was the same person they were talking about and couldn't help wondering what he was like. Sara had made no mention of the letter to Michelle, since she'd thrown it away when she returned to her duplex back in October. And she saw no reason to bring it up now.

"You're sure in good spirits today, Son," Ezekiel's mother commented as she placed a bowl of oatmeal in front of him and took her seat at the table. "What's that big smile you're wearing about?"

"Jah," Dad put in. "For the last couple of weeks I've heard you whistling a lot. This morning, during chores, it sounded like you

145

were serenading the horses." He chuckled.

A wave of heat rushed to Ezekiel's face. He wished he didn't blush so easily. "One reason I'm happy is because I'll be seeing Michelle this evening. We're going out to supper." He shifted his position on the chair. "But the main thing that has put me in a good mood is the decision Michelle made two weeks ago."

Mom tipped her head. "What was that?"

"To go Amish. She took her first instruction class with me a week ago, Sunday."

"I didn't realize she was part of that class," Ezekiel's sister Amy interjected.

"Neither did I." Mom's fingers moved slowly as she touched the neckline of her dress. "What is her reason for wanting to join our church?"

"She feels it's the right thing for her — same as me." Ezekiel touched his chest. "After my encounter with those fellows up in Harrisburg who roughed me up, I realized the English world that I'd thought I wanted to be a part of is not for me."

"Are you sayin' that all English people are bad?" Ezekiel's twelve-year-old brother Henry questioned.

"No, not at all. There are many good people among the English." Ezekiel reached for the bowl of brown sugar and added some to his oatmeal. "It was when those guys were calling me names and making fun of me being Amish that my eyes were opened. I'm not ashamed of my heritage, and I don't want to separate myself from the people in my life who are special to me."

"Since you haven't joined the church yet you wouldn't be shunned if you went English," Abe said.

"I know that. I just wanna be Amish. Is that all right with you?" Ezekiel spoke louder, to make sure he had gotten his point across.

Dad held up his hand. "Okay, boys . . . Let's not start a discussion that might end up in an argument this morning." He looked over at Ezekiel. "Before we pray and start eating, I would like to ask you a question."

"Sure, Dad." Ezekiel sat with both hands in his lap.

"Is Michelle hoping you will marry her? Is that why she's so eager to join our church?"

Feeling like a bird trapped in a cage, Ezekiel's gaze traveled from his mother, to his three siblings, and then back to his father. "I — I don't believe that's the reason she wants to become Amish, since I've made no mention of marriage to her." He reached up and rubbed the back of his ever-warming neck. "But the truth is, I do want to marry her. And someday, when the time is right, I will propose marriage."

All eyes widened, and his mother's mouth turned down at the corners. "Oh Son, I hope you'll give that some serious consideration. Michelle was not raised Amish, and she doesn't think the way we all do." Deep wrinkles formed across Mom's forehead. "But my biggest concern with your interest in her goes well beyond that."

Ezekiel leaned slightly forward. "What do you mean?" He was glad none of his siblings had joined the conversation. They all sat quietly in their seats.

"That lie she told to the Lapps about being their granddaughter . . ." Mom blinked her eyes. "If Michelle is capable of hurting two kind and generous people like Willis and Mary Ruth, then there's no telling what she might say or do to disappoint you or someone else."

"People can change, you know," Ezekiel said. "And I firmly believe that Michelle has had a change of heart. She's apologized to the Lapps, and also confessed her sin to God. So don't you think you oughta give her a chance, just like the Lapps have done?"

Mom took a drink of water and set her glass back on the table. "Whether she's changed or not remains to be seen." She looked over at Dad. "Should we say our prayers?"

"Of course." Dad bowed his head, and everyone else did the same.

Ezekiel's silent prayer was only a few words: *Lord, I pray that you will help my folks — particularly Mom — see Michelle for the wonderful person she truly is.*

CHAPTER 13

"Oh look! It's snowing!" Michelle pointed out the living-room window. "I hope it sticks and we end up with a white Christmas. Isn't this exciting?" She glanced in Sara's direction, but the Lapps' granddaughter didn't look up from the book she was reading as she lay stretched out on the couch. Today was Monday — Sara's day off from working at the flower shop — and she'd acted kind of tired all morning.

Michelle pursed her lips. *Didn't Sara hear what I said, or is she ignoring me on purpose? How much longer will she carry a grudge against me?* In Michelle's eyes, it seemed like nothing she said or did around Sara was right. *Guess I should be used to it, but by now, I'd hoped for a different outcome.*

Michelle pressed her nose against the window's cold glass and blew her breath, watching it steam up. *I won't let Sara bring me down.* Michelle encouraged herself with the pleasure of watching the lightweight feathery snowflakes float slowly to the ground. Then she drew a smiley face before wiping the glass clean.

Ever since Michelle had announced that she wanted to become Amish and had begun wearing plain clothes, Sara's attitude toward her had become even colder. It didn't make sense. *Why should she care that I've decided to join the Amish church?* Michelle asked herself.

Sighing, she moved away from the window. "Think I'll go down to the basement and tell Mary Ruth it's snowing. I also want to see if she needs my help with the laundry."

"I already asked, and she said no." Sara lifted her head from the pillow. "But go ahead if you want to. Maybe she'll accept *your* help."

Ignoring Sara's sarcastic tone, Michelle left the room and headed for the basement. Whether Mary Ruth allowed her to help with the laundry or not, at least her company would be more pleasant than Sara's.

Before going downstairs, Michelle stopped in the kitchen to get a drink of water. Leaning against the counter, she took a deep breath. *Sometimes I wish I could move out and get a place of my own. It's hard being in*

151

the same house with Sara.

Without coming out and actually saying so, Sara had been relentless in reminding Michelle how she felt. Her actions spoke louder than words. Sara's grandparents had accepted Michelle's apology, but it was obvious Sara was not ready to forgive Michelle for what she had done.

I need to get a job before I can move out. But since I have no car or horse and buggy, I'd have to find a place to live in that's close enough to walk to my job and to wherever church is being held, since I'm now taking classes with Ezekiel. Guess I'll have to stay put awhile longer and quit feeling sorry for myself.

Michelle's thoughts went to the first Sunday class she'd taken with Ezekiel. The group consisted of ten young people, made up of mostly young women, but there were four men who were no doubt ready for marriage. One fella seemed older than the others. He was there with a younger woman whose resemblance to him was uncanny. Michelle figured she must be his sister or cousin. She liked how the classes and church were held on Sundays. It wasn't as bad as she'd thought it would be either. The instructional lessons were based on what the Amish called the Dordrecht Confession of Faith. It was an important statement of the Amish faith that had been written in the Netherlands in 1632. The ministers who were present during the class encouraged the youth and exhorted them to study the complete articles of faith and the scriptures that supported each one. Two articles per Sunday were used, as well as Bible stories of faithful patriarchs. On that first Sunday, those in the class learned about article 1, "Of Faith in God and the Creation," as well as article 2, "Of the Transgression by Adam of the Divine Command."

The one thing that stood out the most in Michelle's mind was that without faith it was impossible to please God, and that those who came to God must believe there is a God and that He is a rewarder of those who seek Him.

Reflecting on her desire to please God, Michelle decided that she needed to pray for her parents, and perhaps even make an effort to contact them. While she had no desire to go back home, letting them know where she was and what her plans were for the future would be the right thing to do. There was also a chance that if she talked to her mom or dad, they might know what happened to Ernie and Jack.

On the second Sunday of classes, they

were taught article 3, "Of the Restoration and Reconciliation of the Human Race with God," and article 4, "Of the Coming of our Redeemer and Savior Jesus Christ."

It was also a comfort knowing Ezekiel was taking the classes. While Michelle understood most of what had been said, it had been more difficult to deal with some of the curious stares from the others in the class.

I'm not giving up, she told herself. *People can stare all they want.* Michelle sighed, allowing her thoughts to return to the present. *Guess I feel the same about Sara and won't surrender to her either. Maybe someday she'll understand the situation I was in that made me do that deceitful thing.*

Before heading downstairs, Michelle glanced out the kitchen window and a smile formed on her lips. *I hope it keeps snowing. It's so pretty when everything gets covered in white.*

As Brad entered the town of Strasburg, the sight of several horse and buggies heading in the opposite direction brought a smile to his lips. He was definitely back in Amish country, and happy to be on his way to the Lapps'. While Christmas was still a few days away, he'd decided to stop by their place to say hello and deliver a gift before heading over to Ned's apartment. Willis and Mary Ruth's home wasn't too far out of the way, and he was eager to see how they were doing. The couple had always treated Brad with genuine warmth. He couldn't help being drawn to their open-hearted kindness.

"I'd say the world would be a better place if there were more people in it like Willis and Mary Ruth Lapp," Brad said out loud, before slowing down to avoid hitting a dog. Fortunately, after he honked his horn, the mutt moved out of the way.

"People should keep their dogs in the yard," he muttered. "It's not safe for them to get out in the road."

After driving several more blocks, Brad turned his vehicle off the main road and headed farther out to the country. Snowflakes had begun to fall, and he turned on his windshield wipers to whisk them away. The roads were still bare, and hopefully would remain that way until later when he headed to Ned's place.

"Snow for Christmas would be kind of nice." Grinning, he sang "Jingle Bells," followed by "White Christmas." By the time Brad reached the Lapps' driveway, he was definitely in the Christmas spirit.

He parked his van near the barn, got out, and started for the house. Then, remembering the Christmas cactus he'd picked up before leaving Clarks Summit, he ran back to the vehicle. Brad had opened the door on the passenger's side when Willis stepped out of the barn.

"Howdy, Brad. Sure good to see you." Willis stepped up to Brad and gave him a hearty handshake. Snowflakes landed on Willis's hat, turning the brim and top white.

"It's great to see you too." Brad looked around. "Are Mary Ruth and Sara inside?"

"Yes, and so is Michelle. I have a few more things to take care of in the barn, but why don't you go ahead to the house? When I come in we can sit down and talk awhile."

"Sounds good." Brad had no idea who Michelle was or why Willis had mentioned her. He assumed she must be a friend or some relative he hadn't met before. "Before I go in though, do you need some assistance with your chores in the barn? I'd be happy to help with anything."

Willis shook his head. "Thank you, but it's nothing I can't handle myself. Besides, you've been driving a few hours and probably should relax awhile. You go on ahead. I'm sure the ladies will be glad to see you."

"All right then. I'll see you in a bit." Carrying the cactus, Brad made his way up to the house. He stepped onto the front porch and knocked on the door. When it opened, a beautiful young woman with long blond hair looked at him with a curious expression. He figured she must be Michelle.

"May I help you?" she asked.

"Yeah, I'm here to see Sara and Mary Ruth. Willis said they were both in the house."

The young woman tilted her head to the right. "I'm Sara, and Mary Ruth is in the basement with her other houseguest. Would you like me to call her?"

Brad scratched the side of his head. "You said your name is Sara?"

"That's right."

"Are there two women named Sara here today?"

"No, just one." She pointed to herself. "I'm Sara Murray — Willis and Mary Ruth's granddaughter."

"Huh?" With a jerk of his head, Brad's mind raced, searching for answers but finding none. This made no sense. Had Willis set this up to play a trick on him? Mary Ruth's husband was full of wit, but how could he have known Brad would be stopping by here today? As far as Willis knew, Brad wasn't coming to their house until Christmas Day.

The pretty blond's blue eyes seemed to

bore into him. "The Lapps are my grandparents, but since it appears you don't believe me, I'll get my grandmother. Please, wait here on the porch." She closed the door so quickly, Brad felt a *whoosh* of air.

He shuffled over to the wooden bench on the covered porch, set the plant on the small table next to the bench, and sat down. *Wish I would've brought a pair of gloves with me.*

Pulling his coat collar up closer around his neck, then blowing on his cold hands, Brad felt more confused than ever. *How can that woman's name be Sara Murray? It has to be some kind of a joke.*

After a few minutes, the front door opened. This time, he was greeted by Mary Ruth. "Oh dear. I'm sorry you were left out here in the cold. When Sara said someone was waiting on the porch to see me, I had no idea it was you." She stepped out, and when Brad stood up, Mary Ruth gave him a hug. "We didn't expect you until next week, on Christmas Day."

"Right." Brad bent down and picked up the cactus. "I came into town a few days early, and since I'd bought this for you, I decided to drop by before going to my friend Ned's place."

She looked up, offering him one of her sweet smiles. "I'm glad you did. Now please come inside out of the cold. The way it's snowing right now, the flakes are beginning to blow in on the porch."

"Yeah, you're right." Brad followed Mary Ruth into the house and handed her the plant. The house was pleasantly warm and just as inviting as he remembered. It made him wish the snow would fall a little harder so he could stay.

"Thank you, Brad. This is a lovely cactus, and it was so thoughtful of you." She placed it on the table in the entryway. "Come into the living room now. Sara is waiting there, and I'd like to introduce her to you."

Brad raised his eyebrows but remained silent. *Why would Mary Ruth need to introduce me to Sara? After all the time I spent with her this summer, I should know Sara pretty well by now. Could Mary Ruth be in on the little charade Willis set up?*

When Brad entered the living room, he was surprised to see the blond-haired woman who had claimed to be Sara sitting on the couch.

"Brad, this is our granddaughter Sara." Mary Ruth gestured to the young woman, then motioned to him. "Sara, this is Brad Fuller. As we mentioned before, he will be our guest for Christmas dinner."

"But I thought . . ." He quickly ended his

comment. Holding his earlobe between his thumb and index finger, Brad gave it a tug. He was about to ask if Mary Ruth was teasing him, when a woman with auburn hair, wearing an Amish dress and a white *kapp* on her head, entered the room.

"Oh Brad, you came early." She came slowly toward him.

He stared at her in disbelief. It was Sara — the one he'd gotten to know this past summer.

"I need to confess something. My name isn't Sara Murray — it's Michelle Taylor." Her eyes glistened with tears as she pointed to the blond-haired woman. "She's the real Sara, and I–I'm an imposter. At least, I was when you thought I was her."

Brad's muscles tightened and his head jerked back. He was speechless. Apparently this was no joke. He, however, felt like a fool. How could this woman who'd pretended to be the Lapps' granddaughter have pulled the wool over his eyes? *I'm a smart man,* Brad told himself. *I should have sensed she was lying to me. And what about the Lapps? How did they feel when they found out the truth?*

From the affection Brad saw on Mary Ruth's face as she looked at Michelle, he realized there was no displeasure. If he were being honest with himself, Brad had to admit there had always been this feeling about the young woman named Michelle that hadn't seemed right. It was as though she'd been hiding something, yet he couldn't discern what it was. He'd let his guard down and had foolishly been taken in by her. He should have gone with his gut instinct and asked the right questions or probed deeper into her personal life.

Brad pressed his lips tightly together, lest he say the wrong thing. Now it all made sense. He felt a mixture of betrayal and anger. And on top of his frustration with Michelle, here sat the real Sara Murray, and he had no idea what to say to either of them. The way Sara sat with her arms folded, he doubted she wanted to talk at all. But Brad couldn't leave until he had some answers. Not only about the reason Michelle had lied to him, but he wanted to know why she was dressed in Amish clothes.

CHAPTER 14

Sara sat on the couch, too stunned to say a word. *So this is the same man who sent that letter to Michelle, thinking she was my grandparents' granddaughter. Brad was completely in the dark about Michelle's deceit. No wonder he looks so confused and somewhat disturbed. Poor guy.*

"I — I should go," Brad mumbled, shuffling toward the front door. "I need time to think about all of this."

"Wait, Brad. Please let me explain." Michelle's voice shook as she clasped his arm.

He stopped walking. "Think I've heard enough."

Grandma stepped forward. "Brad, I think you ought to at least hear her out before you go."

He sank into the closest chair. "Okay, Michelle, you have my undivided attention."

Sara could tell by the way his knee bounced that he'd rather be anyplace but

162

here. She couldn't help feeling sorry for him. The unsuspecting man had been duped, just like she and her grandparents had. But now it was time for him to hear the full story — or at least, Michelle's version of it. *When the pretender finishes telling her side of things, maybe I'll jump in with my part of the story.* She clasped her hands tightly together. *Or maybe it would be best if I kept quiet and let her do all the talking. No matter what Michelle says, unless Brad is gullible, he will surely see her for what she is.*

Sara still couldn't get over all the drama Michelle had caused by pretending to be her. *Why couldn't she have just told Grandma and Grandpa she wasn't their granddaughter when she met them at the bus station in Philly?*

Turning her attention fully on Michelle, Sara watched as she sniffed, then swiped at the tears on her reddened cheeks. She was either fully embarrassed to be forced into confessing her misdeed to Brad, or Michelle had become an actress.

Sara noticed Michelle's obvious discomfort as she leaned slightly forward with her arms held against her chest. No doubt she was using these few extra minutes to think about what she wanted to say.

"My real name is Michelle Taylor, and I'm

no relation to Mary Ruth and Willis. I was at the bus station in Philadelphia, needing a place to go, when I met the Lapps, and they assumed I was their granddaughter." Michelle took a seat in the recliner. It was the one Grandpa usually sat in. Then more explanation spilled forth.

"Desperate to get out of Philly, I went along with it and came here with them, pretending I was the woman they'd been looking for." She paused and drew a shaky breath. "I'm sorry for deceiving you, Brad. What I did was wrong, and I hope, like Mary Ruth and Willis did, that you'll find it in your heart to forgive me."

Sara glanced at Brad, waiting for his reaction. Would he be as forgiving as her grandparents had been, or would this man put Michelle in her place? She hoped it would be the latter.

"I forgive you, Michelle." Brad spoke softly. "But I wish you had told me the truth on your own during the time we spent together this past summer."

"I — I wanted to, and I almost did on one occasion, but I was afraid of your response. I was worried it would ruin our friendship, and I was afraid you would tell the Lapps." Michelle blotted the tears on her cheeks. "Also, I'd gotten in so deep with my trail of lies, I didn't know how to get out without hurting someone." She looked at Sara's grandmother. "Especially Mary Ruth and Willis. During the time I was living here, I came to love them and almost felt as if they were actually my grandparents. In the end, it seems I hurt everyone." Michelle glanced in Sara's direction.

Sara grimaced at the sour taste in her mouth. She pressed her lips together to keep from blurting out what she thought. *Nice performance, Michelle.*

"We felt love for Michelle too — when we believed she was Sara, and yes even now," Grandma put in.

Sara could hardly hold her composure. *I knew it. I bet they love her more than me.*

"When did you tell them the truth?" Brad's question was directed at Michelle.

"A few months ago. I had been intercepting Sara's letters, and when her last one came, saying she'd be coming here soon, I realized it was time to go." Michelle lowered her gaze, fingering the ties on her head covering. "I couldn't face Mary Ruth and Willis with the truth, so I took the coward's way out and left a note on the kitchen table, confessing what I'd done. Then I asked one of their drivers to take me to Harrisburg. And that's where I lived till Ezekiel came and talked me into coming back here."

"After she apologized, we invited her to stay with us again." Mary Ruth smiled as she gestured to Michelle. "Now she is preparing to join the Amish church."

Brad's eyebrows lifted. "So that must be why you're wearing an Amish dress."

Michelle nodded. "Ezekiel and I are both planning to join the church in the spring. We've already started taking classes." Her tone was enthusiastic. "He and the Lapps have been helpful with teaching me how to speak the Pennsylvania Dutch language."

"Michelle is a good learner. I think she'll do just fine becoming Amish like us." Mary Ruth's face seemed to radiate with joy.

Sara sat, biting her tongue through all this "Michelle" time. *Please give me strength . . . Oh, how I want to say what's really on my mind about the pretender. I'd like Brad to know how she has pushed her way into my grandparents' lives.* Sara hoped he wasn't taken in by Michelle's sob story.

Brad rubbed the back of his neck. "Well, this is certainly a surprise. I'm happy for you, Michelle."

"Does that mean I'm forgiven for deceiving you?"

"Of course, but I'll admit, I am disappointed you didn't come and talk to me about this when I was here during the sum-mer."

Michelle dropped her gaze. "I know."

At that moment, Grandpa entered the room. "My chores are done." He grinned at Brad. "Now we can sit and visit awhile. I'd like to know how things have been going for you these last few months." He looked at Grandma. "But before we do that, why don't the two of us go to the kitchen and get some coffee and something sweet to serve?"

Grandma rose from her seat. "That's an excellent idea, Willis."

Sara was on the verge of asking if they wanted her help, when Brad turned to her and said, "Sorry if it seemed as though you were being ignored or left out of the conver-sation since I got here. I'd like the chance to visit with you too."

"Maybe some other time. I have a few things I need to do in my room." She fled the room and raced up the stairs. She needed time by herself to process things. Apparently Brad was taken in by Michelle, like her grandparents were. Sara wondered if there was anything she could have said to make him see what Michelle was really like.

Upstairs in her room, Sara went to the window and opened it, sucking in some much-needed air. Snowflakes blew in onto the window ledge, while others melted onto the floor. She'd never expected Brad would show up, or that he'd be sucked in by Michelle and her excuses.

Sara stood, immersed in thought, continuing to calm herself as she breathed in the fresh, crisp air the opened window allowed. As the snowflakes continued falling and a squirrel scampered through the backyard, she watched this tranquil moment while using her fingers to rub circular motions around her throbbing temples. *I hope Brad finds out for himself what a fake Michelle is. She can't fool everyone forever. Sooner or later the imposter is bound to trip up and someone will finally see through her.*

As Brad sat in the living room, enjoying coffee and some of Mary Ruth's delicious sticky buns, his thoughts went to Sara. She was a beautiful young woman, with shiny blond hair that reminded him of spun gold. But she had been anything but cordial. In fact, throughout his conversation with Michelle, Sara seemed agitated. Could there be something about him she disliked, or was she upset with Michelle for stealing her identity? If that was the case, he couldn't blame her, but then why would she be living here at the Lapps' with Michelle? For that matter, it seemed strange Mary Ruth and Willis would invite Michelle to live here, knowing she had impersonated their granddaughter. Not to mention that the real Sara was here too.

Licking his fingers, Brad reached for another sticky bun.

Michelle giggled and handed him a napkin. "Here, looks like you need this."

"Thanks." Brad's answer was stiff as he watched Michelle's smile slowly fade and her eyes look downward.

He shifted on his chair. *Wish I had a chance to talk to Sara privately. I'd like to know what her thoughts are about Michelle. If she's holding a grudge against her, I might be able to help — or at least offer some support if she needs it.*

"Say, Brad, didn't you hear what I asked?"

Willis's question pulled Brad's thoughts aside. "Uh no. Sorry, I must have spaced out." He turned his attention to Willis. "What did you ask?"

The older man held out the plate of sticky buns. "Wondered if you'd like another one of these."

"No thanks, I'd better not." Brad thumped his stomach. "I've already had two, and if I eat another I'll be too full to join my friend

Ned for lunch."

"You could stay and eat here," Mary Ruth suggested. "We'd be happy to have you share our noon meal."

"I appreciate the offer, but I should get going. Ned will probably be wondering why I haven't shown up yet." Glancing out the window, Brad set his coffee cup down and stood. "The snow hasn't let up, so it's probably good I'm leaving now. I'll be back for Christmas dinner though." He grinned at Mary Ruth. "Wouldn't want to miss out on your holiday meal, which I am sure will be delicious."

"You don't have to wait until Christmas to come over," Michelle interjected.

"That's right," Mary Ruth agreed. "Feel free to come over any day you like."

"How about tomorrow?" Willis poured himself another cup of coffee. "Sara will be working at the flower shop in town, but the rest of us will be around."

"I can't say for sure whether I'll be by tomorrow, but it will be soon, I promise." Brad's face radiated heat as he noticed Michelle watching him intently. It looked as if she might say something, but she sat quietly with one hand on her hip.

Brad said his goodbyes, put on his jacket, and went out the door. When he climbed into his van and waited for the engine to warm, he saw Michelle rush out of the house with a shawl around her shoulders, as she ran toward the barn.

I hope she's okay. Brad thought to himself. *I probably should have stayed and talked to her more. She's been through quite an ordeal and had a lot of guilt to deal with before she admitted the truth to Mary Ruth and Willis.*

Brad rubbed his hands in front of the vent, where the heat was now flowing. He waited a few minutes longer to see if Michelle would come out of the barn. *Should I go in and talk to her — see if she's upset?* He thumped the steering wheel. *No, I'd better go. If Michelle went there to be alone, she might not appreciate me barging in.*

Brad put the van in reverse and turned toward the road. *Maybe tomorrow I'll take a ride into Strasburg and see if I can find the flower shop where Sara works. If I go shortly before noon, I might be able catch her before she takes a lunch break. There are a few questions I'd like to ask.*

CHAPTER 15

Lancaster, Pennsylvania

"Where you headed, sleepyhead?" Ned asked when Brad grabbed his jacket and slipped it on.

"I'm going to Strasburg. Thought I mentioned it last night before we went to bed."

"If you did, I don't remember." Ned combed his fingers through his thick brown hair. "But then you didn't have a lot to say after you got here. Figured you were tired from the trip, so I didn't ply you with a bunch of questions about how things were going at the seminary or in your personal life. Oh, and since you slept in so late, you totally missed breakfast, and I was going to make you a good one too." He pointed to the frying pan sitting on a hot pad near the stove. "Before you walked into the kitchen, I was about to come knocking on your door. Didn't think you'd want to sleep all day."

"Yeah, I was kinda out of it."

"Did you sleep okay on that new mattress in the other bedroom?"

"It was fine." Brad managed a weak smile. As tired as he was, he hadn't gotten much sleep last night, thinking about the situation with Michelle and Sara. A ton of questions reeled through his head, none of which he had the answer to. Brad saw no point in telling Ned any of that though. "Since I'll be here till New Year's, we'll have a chance to get caught up with each other's lives." He zipped up his jacket.

"Good point." Ned smiled.

"It's okay. I'll be eating lunch soon. And hey, I'll take a raincheck on that breakfast."

"You got it." Ned headed to his desk. "Welp, I have some bills to pay, and I need to get them done and in the mail before noon. You have a nice day, and I'll catch you later."

Brad waved and went out the door. He was eager to get to Strasburg, although unsure of what he would say when he saw Sara.

Strasburg

Michelle opened her closet door and looked at the English clothes still hanging there. *I should put these in boxes and give them to a thrift store.*

173

She pulled a blouse off the hanger and held it up to see what shape it was in. This was one of her favorite tops. She enjoyed wearing it for special occasions.

Michelle placed the blouse on the bed and stood back. *But I need to move on, and the only way to do that is to purge all of these English clothes.*

She went back to the closet and removed the rest of her clothes from their hangers. After folding them into piles, she put the items in plastic bags, ready to be taken to the thrift store.

Now I need to get busy and make more Amish clothes. Michelle slid the hangers to one end of her closet. She then headed for Mary Ruth's sewing room and took a seat at the treadle machine. As Michelle worked on another plain dress to add to her wardrobe, it felt as if she might be getting the hang of things. *Maybe I won't need to call on Mary Ruth for help so much anymore.*

She'd never expected to enjoy such a simple pleasure as sewing a dress, much less be able to make it herself. She didn't remember her biological mother sewing. And even though Michelle had seen her foster mom at the sewing machine a few times, she'd never volunteered to teach Michelle how to sew.

When the thread snapped, and Michelle paused to rethread it, her thoughts went to Brad. When he'd stopped by yesterday and she apologized for hiding the truth of her identity, he'd forgiven her. But had he really? Or did Brad only say so to make himself look good in Mary Ruth's eyes? Since his goal was to become a preacher, how would it look if he'd refused to accept her apology?

Then there was Sara. Even though she'd been acting a little more civil lately, Michelle felt sure it was for her grandparents' sake. Who knew what Sara really thought?

Michelle picked up the piece of material again and stitched the first seam. *Why don't things ever work out for me? Every time I'm with Ezekiel, he offers me hope. But when he isn't around to offer reassurance and someone even looks at me with disapproval, my doubts surface.* She suspected she no longer had Brad's approval and felt sure he was disappointed in her.

Yesterday, when Michelle had rushed out to the barn, she'd gone straight to the prayer jar she previously found there, hoping for some reassurance. After reading a few verses of scripture that an unknown person had written and put in the old jar, Michelle found a measure of comfort. In particular,

2 Corinthians 5:17 spoke to her: *"Therefore if any man be in Christ, he is a new creature: old things are passed away; behold, all things are become new."* It reminded her that since she had accepted Christ, she was a new person, forgiven of her sins, and could begin anew. It didn't matter what others thought of her or how they responded. She just had to keep that verse in her heart and hold her head up high. But Michelle needed to take each day as it came and spend much time in prayer.

With Christmas coming next week, customers had flowed in and out of the floral shop all morning. Right now, however, with the noon hour approaching, there seemed to be a letup of shoppers.

Sara's stomach growled, and she glanced at her watch. *This might be a good time to get something to eat.*

With food on her mind, she thought about the promise she'd made this morning to bring supper home from one of the local restaurants in town. Grandma seemed pleased, and Grandpa said it would be good for Grandma to take a night off. Since her grandparents liked chicken potpie, Sara knew the family-style restaurant that Karen Roberts had recommended would be the perfect place.

Sara was glad for the opportunity to do something nice for her grandparents. And bringing home a meal would be something Michelle hadn't done, at least.

About to head into the back room to tell Andy and Karen she was leaving for lunch, Sara paused when the shop door opened and Brad stepped in. *I wonder what he's doing here.*

As Brad approached, Sara offered him what she hoped was a pleasing smile. "I'm surprised to see you. Did you come to buy flowers for someone?"

He shook his head. "Came to see you."

"How did you know where to find me?"

"It was mentioned yesterday that you worked at a flower shop here in Strasburg, and since this is the only one in town, I figured it had to be the right place." He moved closer to Sara. "If you haven't eaten yet, I'd like to take you out for lunch so we can get better acquainted."

"I'm surprised you didn't invite Michelle to join us. I gather the two of you are pretty good friends." Sara hoped her sarcasm wasn't too obvious.

Brad's gaze flicked upward. "As you may already know, I did some work for your grandparents this summer. They also called on me to drive them some places. So Michelle and I became friends while she was living with the Lapps."

"You mean, when you thought she was me?"

He gave a nod. "But if she hadn't been there pretending to be Sara Murray, then it would have been you I'd have gotten to know." His gaze was so steady, she felt as if his blue eyes were holding her captive.

Looking away, Sara mumbled, "Be that as it may, we didn't get to know each other this summer, and I'm not sure there's any point in us going out to lunch today."

"Have you already eaten?"

"No."

"I haven't either, and if you'll let me, I'd like to treat you to lunch. In addition to getting better acquainted, I want to ask a few questions about Michelle."

"I doubt I'll be able to tell you anything you don't already know, but if you'll wait a few minutes, I'll tell my boss I'm taking my lunch break now." Sara didn't know why she'd agreed to go, but at least this would give her a chance to let Brad know what she thought of Michelle. Sara had a feeling he might be interested in Ms. Taylor, and it would be too bad for him if he got caught in her trap, the way Ezekiel had.

Brad's lips parted slightly, as a slow smile spread across his handsome face. "I'm more than happy to wait for you."

"Okay." Curling her trembling fingers against her moist palms, Sara hurried toward the back room. *Sure hope having lunch with him is not a mistake. What if Brad repeats everything I say to Michelle?*

As Brad sat across the table from Sara at Isaac's Famous Grilled Sandwiches, he admired her beauty. Since she'd made no mention of a husband and didn't wear a wedding ring, he assumed the Lapps' granddaughter must be single. *But if Sara is married, then wouldn't her husband have come with her to see Willis and Mary Ruth?* Brad looked at her intently. *She could be in a serious relationship or even engaged.*

Don't know why I'm even thinking such thoughts, he reprimanded himself. *I'm here to talk about her situation with Michelle, not concern myself with her relationship status.*

"So tell me a little about yourself." He clasped the mug of hot chocolate he'd ordered to go with his Gooney Bird turkey sandwich on pumpernickel bread. "I'd also like to know how it is that Michelle ended up pretending to be you for so long."

179

"There's not much to tell about me. I'm single, and I grew up in Newark, New Jersey, with my mother, stepfather, and later a half-brother." Sara pulled a napkin from the holder between them and blotted her lips. "And as far as how Michelle ended up pretending to be me . . . I figured you would have asked her that question."

"I only know the little bit she told me, but nothing from your perspective."

"What exactly do you want to know?" Sara bit into her avocado and roasted red pepper salad.

Brad scratched his head. He thought he'd just told her what he wanted to know. *Maybe I didn't explain it well enough.*

"For starters . . . Is the story Mary Ruth and Willis told true, about not knowing they had a granddaughter named Sara until they received a letter from you in June? Or maybe it was late May," he amended.

"It was June, and yes, the story they told is true. I wrote to them after I found a note in my mother's Bible soon after her death. The letter didn't give me a lot of information — only that I had grandparents living in Strasburg whom she had never told me about. It also gave their name and address." Sara paused to take a sip of hot tea. "Mama also said she hoped I would get the chance to meet them some day."

"Did your mother tell you that your grandparents were Amish?"

She shook her head. "I had no idea until the day I first met them in October."

"After you found your mother's letter, why did it take you so long to meet Willis and Mary Ruth?" Brad's curiosity piqued.

"I wrote to Grandma and Grandpa right away, saying I wanted the chance to get to know them." Sara set her cup down. "I explained that I would like to come sometime after I finished my summer business classes. I also mentioned that I may take the bus to Philadelphia." She pursed her lips. "I waited to hear back from them, and when they didn't respond, I wrote again."

"How did Michelle come into the picture?"

"From what Grandma told me, they thought my first letter said I'd be arriving at the bus station on June fifth, and that I wanted them to pick me up." Sara drummed her fingers on the table. "So they went there, and when they saw Michelle, they mistook her for me."

Brad frowned. "I can't believe she went along with it, knowing she wasn't their granddaughter."

"It was a devious thing to do. And to make

181

things worse, once Michelle was settled in at Grandma and Grandpa's, she intercepted all the other letters I sent them throughout the summer months." Sara's brows lowered. "The imposter even went so far as to write me a letter, pretending to be Grandma."

"What did it say?" Brad felt fully drawn into the story and was eager to hear more.

"She said they were really busy and asked me to postpone my visit until fall." Sara's fingers trembled a bit, as she placed her hands on the table. "I thought it was kind of strange, but of course I waited, and the day I finally arrived, which wasn't by bus after all, Michelle met me at the door. She said the Lapps weren't home and that I should go inside and wait for them. Then, the great pretender made a run for it." She blinked rapidly. "Of course I had no way of knowing at that point who she was or what all had transpired."

"Whew, that's quite a story." Brad shook his head. "It's hard to believe that —"

"Oh, it's the truth all right. I have no reason to lie about it." Sara looked at Brad with a piercing gaze. "Unlike Ms. Michelle, I am not one to make up stories."

He held up his hand. "Never said I didn't believe you. I'm just shocked, hearing how it went and struggling to figure out why Michelle was so deceitful."

"It's not hard to understand, if you think about it."

"What do you mean?"

"She's trying to steal my grandparents from me." Sara grimaced. "And I'm sure she has an ulterior motive."

"Like what?"

She shrugged. "I haven't figured that out yet, but I will . . . You can count on it."

Brad sat quietly, trying to piece everything together. According to Michelle, she was genuinely sorry for what she'd done and had turned over a new leaf. But what if Sara was right and Michelle did have an ulterior motive for worming her way into Willis and Mary Ruth's lives? Even though Brad wouldn't be in the area for more than two weeks, he planned to look into this further and hopefully find out more. Maybe he'd been too quick to forgive and look the other way when Michelle asked his forgiveness. If she was using Willis and Mary Ruth for some underhanded reason, she needed to be stopped, and soon.

CHAPTER 16

"I don't see why you have to eat dinner at the Lapps' today," Ezekiel's mother said when he slipped on his jacket and started for the back door. "Our family should be together on Christmas Day."

Ezekiel halted and turned to look at her. "I told you a week ago that I wouldn't be here for the afternoon meal today."

"Jah, but I thought . . ."

"What?" Ezekiel's fingers dug into his palms. "Did you think I would change my mind and stay home today?"

Her nose crinkled. "Christmas is a time to be with one's family, and I would think you'd want to spend the holiday with us."

"Figured you wouldn't mind, 'cause I ate the Thanksgiving meal here. Plus, I was here last night with all of you when some of my aunts, uncles, and cousins came over. I realize that I've never missed a Christmas here at home, but today, I wanna be with my *aldi.*" Ezekiel paused for a breath. "Since we've been so busy in the greenhouse these past few weeks, I haven't had the chance to see Michelle much lately."

Mom opened her mouth in readiness to say more, but Dad cut her off.

"Let the boy alone," he spoke from across the room, where he sat at the table with a cup of coffee. "Don't you remember how many holiday meals I ate at your folks' house when we were courting?"

Ezekiel's eyes widened, waiting for his mother's response. She remained silent. He couldn't believe his dad had stuck up for him and seemed to understand that he wanted to spend time with his girlfriend. If Dad was okay with him courting Michelle, maybe eventually Mom would be too.

Brad was eager to get to the Lapps' house, but he kept his speed down since there was snow and ice on the road in many places where it had not been melted by the sun.

Ned left early to be with his family, but under his little three-foot Christmas tree, Brad had found a package for him. Grinning, he reached up and touched the red woolen scarf around his neck. "That Ned — always thinking of others."

Even though he'd dropped off a cactus

the day he arrived, Brad didn't want to go to the Lapps' empty handed, since they'd asked him to join their Christmas gathering and meal. So yesterday he'd gone to the local bakery and bought an assortment of cookies to bring for dessert. He looked forward to the meal, not to mention seeing Sara again. He hoped he might also have a few minutes alone with Michelle so he could ask some questions and hopefully find out if she was up to anything, as Sara suspected. He had stopped by the Lapps' two days ago, but Michelle wasn't home. Mary Ruth said she was out, seeking a job at one of the local restaurants.

With a houseful of company today, Brad figured he may not get the chance to speak to Michelle privately, but it wouldn't stop him from making observations.

When Brad pulled his van into the Lapps' yard, he spotted a horse and buggy at the hitching rail. He turned off the engine and got out of his vehicle, then joined Ezekiel by the horse. "Merry Christmas." He reached out to shake his friend's hand. "Nice to see you. How are you doing?"

"I'm doin' well, and Merry Christmas to you too." Ezekiel grinned, returning Brad's firm handshake. "It's good to have you back

186

in the area. How long are you planning to stay?"

"Just through the holidays. I'll be returning to the university in Clarks Summit on New Year's Day. I have a long ways to go before my studies are done."

"Well, I'm glad you're here." Ezekiel removed the bit from his horse's mouth. "Since I'll be here awhile, I'm takin' Big Red to the barn. Want to come along, or are you anxious to get up to the house?"

"Can't say I'm not eager to get in out of the cold or enjoy the delicious aroma that's no doubt coming from Mary Ruth's kitchen, but I'll take a walk to the barn with you." Brad was glad for the opportunity to talk to Ezekiel alone. Maybe he could offer some answers concerning Michelle.

When they entered the barn, Brad breathed in the aroma of sweet hay in the air. A couple of horses were already in the stalls, munching away on their supper.

Ezekiel put Big Red in an empty stall, wiped him down, and made sure the horse had something to eat and drink. Brad pet Sadie and Rascal as he waited until Ezekiel finished, then he asked his first question.

"I heard you've decided to join the Amish church, and that Michelle's planning to as well."

"You heard right." Leaning against the horse's stall, Ezekiel smiled. "I had an experience up in Harrisburg when I went there looking for Michelle. It made me realize that living the English life isn't for me." His face sobered. "Not to say all English are bad. I just came to the conclusion that I need to appreciate my heritage and don't have to be embarrassed about the way we Amish choose to live. My family means a lot to me too which also helped in making the decision."

Brad's head moved slowly up and down. "Makes sense to me. I am a little curious though why Michelle, who led us to believe her name was Sara, decided to join the Amish church."

"You know, she's sorry for that." Ezekiel's gaze dropped for a few seconds, before he looked directly at Brad. "Has she explained things to you yet?"

"Some. But I'm not sure I have all the facts."

Ezekiel brushed some stray pieces of hay from his jacket. "What do you wanna know?"

Brad figured he may as well be direct. "Why would she have let the Lapps believe she was Sara? Has she told you that?"

Ezekiel nodded. "Michelle's had a rough

life. When she was a kid, she and her brothers were taken from their abusive parents, and she lived with foster parents until she struck out on her own when she turned eighteen. To this day, she still doesn't know where her two brothers ended up. Can you imagine that?"

"I'm sure it's been tough, but what happened when she left her foster parents?"

"Michelle went from town to town and worked at whatever jobs she could find." Ezekiel licked his lower lip. "Then she got involved with an abusive man and lost her job in Philadelphia about the same time. There was one thing Michelle was sure of — she could not tolerate his abuse. She was desperate and went to the bus station to buy a ticket so she could get away from the boyfriend and start over in some other place."

Brad leaned against the wooden beam near him. "Is there more to the story?"

Ezekiel nodded. "While Michelle was at the station, the Lapps showed up, thinking she was their granddaughter. You have to remember, the Lapps didn't know they had a granddaughter until Sara wrote the first letter. So when they saw a young woman with the same auburn hair as their daughter's, they were convinced she was Sara.

Then, because Michelle was desperate to get away, on impulse, she went along with it and let them believe she was Sara." Brad's head tilted while he mentally weighed this information.

"Didn't she realize the truth would eventually come out?"

"Sure, but like I said, she was desperate." Ezekiel reached across the stall gate and gave Big Red's head a few pats. "I'm not condoning what she did, but I wanted you to understand what drove her to making a poor decision."

"Many people make wrong choices because of their circumstances, but lying, and even telling half-truths are never right." Brad joined Ezekiel in petting the horse. "So what is Michelle's reason for joining the Amish church? Is it to please you? I've known for some time that you were interested in her."

Ezekiel's cheeks reddened. "I can't deny it. Ever since the first day I met her — when I saw her fall in the mud — I was attracted. 'Course I didn't let on right away."

"She's interested in you too, I presume." Brad couldn't help smiling.

"Yeah. In fact, we've begun courting."

"I see." The word *courting* seemed a bit old-fashioned to Brad, and he was on the verge of posing another question, when the Lapps' son, Ivan, entered the barn with his sons, Benjamin and Peter. *Well, at least I found out the reason Michelle did what she did, even though it wasn't right. Because of her deceit, the Lapps were hurt, and most of all, Sara.* Brad looked out the barn doors toward the house. *I need to reach out to her in support.*

With the exception of Michelle's presence, Sara couldn't recall a better Christmas. Even though there was no tree, adorning ornaments, twinkling lights, or other decorations in her grandparents' cozy home, it didn't deter the spirit and festivity of the day. Except for Brad's Christmas cactus and the two poinsettias she and Michelle had given to her grandparents, one would think it was a normal family gathering. Nonetheless, Sara felt the overwhelming joy of this holiday celebration. Last week, when she'd brought the chicken potpie home for supper, she'd felt the same joy, seeing the twinkle in Grandma's eyes as she thanked Sara for her thoughtfulness.

This morning had started with a hearty breakfast. Afterward, preparation for the family meal began. Even before that, Grandma had put the ham in the oven for a slow bake. The aroma of the meat as it slowly warmed up made Sara's mouth water in anticipation.

Grandpa and Grandma had insisted Sara and Michelle should not give them any Christmas presents. Grandma said just having them both here was gift enough, and Grandpa agreed. So Sara and Michelle said they didn't want any gifts either.

Michelle wore another new outfit — a teal green dress with a black apron she had made, while Sara donned a pretty satin red blouse and black skirt. She wore a simple heart-shaped necklace, but decided to leave her earrings out for today.

Now as Sara sat at her grandparents' extended dining-room table, she tried to keep her focus on the playful banter going on between Grandpa and Uncle Ivan. The love and respect they felt for one another was obvious, even with their kidding and poking fun at each other's corny jokes. Every now and then Sara glanced at Brad, and each time she did, she noticed him staring at her. Sara wished she could get in his head and know what he was thinking. Did he find out something more about Michelle? If so, would he share it with her?

Before they'd sat down to her grandmother's delicious ham dinner, Brad had sought Sara out and asked if he could take her to lunch again — tomorrow if she was free. She'd agreed to go — partly because he was good looking and charming, but mostly because she wanted to talk more about Michelle. Sara hadn't mentioned it when she and Brad ate lunch at Isaac's restaurant the other day, but she hoped that Brad might persuade Michelle to move out of their house. Giving the pretender the cold shoulder sure hadn't worked.

Sara looked to her left, where Michelle sat, giving Ezekiel a dose of her cow eyes. Throughout most of the meal, their conversation had been to each other. Michelle was obviously smitten with him. A person would have to be blind not to notice her love-sick actions. Could she be using her relationship with Ezekiel to find favor with Grandma and Grandpa?

I wouldn't put anything past her, Sara thought. *Everything about today would be perfect if Michelle weren't here.* Sara forked a piece of succulent ham into her mouth. *She's not even part of the family, and yet here she sits at our table, sharing Christmas dinner as though she too is Grandma and Grandpa's granddaughter.*

Sara wondered how long she would have to endure this ongoing trial with Michelle.

And how did this current test benefit her anyway? Sara felt sure she was in the right and Michelle was in the wrong. Sara thought she'd forgiven the imposter, but deep down, she hadn't.

Sara's only hope was for Michelle to either find a job and move out on her own or marry Ezekiel and settle into a home with him. Sara needed a chance to be with her grandparents without Michelle always around. Michelle needed to make a life of her own. The whole idea that the pretender was even living here was ridiculous. As far as Sara was concerned, Grandma and Grandpa's generosity went too far. She didn't want to see them get hurt again. But if Michelle was up to no good, there might not be anything she could do to stop it.

CHAPTER 17

"Thanks for agreeing to meet me for lunch today, even though we just saw each other yesterday," Brad said when he and Sara took seats at Strasburg Pizza the day after Christmas.

She nodded. "I'm glad I could. Things are slow at the flower shop today, so there was no problem with me going out for lunch."

"What kind of pizza do you like? Or would you rather have a cold or hot sub sandwich?"

"I only have an hour lunch, so I'd better choose something that can be made up quickly." Sara perused the menu. "Maybe I'll go with a readymade pizza slice topped with veggies."

Looking down at his menu and back at her, he asked, "Is that all you want to eat?"

"Yes." Placing both hands against her stomach, she laughed. "Think I ate enough yesterday to fill me for a week."

He grinned. "Same here. That grandma of yours is some cook. The ham was sure delicious. I can still remember the juiciness of it."

A muscle jumped in Sara's cheek as she flicked her gaze upward. "For your information, Mr. Fuller, Michelle and I helped with the meal."

"I kinda figured you did." He scrubbed a hand over his face. "Sorry about that. It was all great."

"Never mind, it's okay." Sara changed the subject. "It feels sort of funny working the day after Christmas. I used to work at a dentist's office in New Jersey, and my boss always closed the day after Christmas, to give everyone two days off."

"Did you mind going to work today?" Brad asked.

"No, not really. I am a little tired, but I like working here, so it wasn't too hard to come in."

"I understand." He heaved a sigh. "It will be hard for me to get back into the swing of things once I head back to school. I'll have to get my brain into study mode again."

"Do you really plan to become a minister?"

Brad nodded. "It's been a dream of mine for a long time. I'm looking forward to the day I get to pastor a church full-time."

"I see." Sara looked around the pizza shop. "Sure is busy in here for the day after Christmas."

"Yeah. I suspect a lot of the restaurants have plenty of customers today. This is a hectic day for the stores, with customers returning gifts and hitting all the after-holiday bargains."

"I never got into doing that." Sara shook her head. "I don't mind a good sale, but it's the crowds I can't deal with."

"I'm with you on that."

A commotion at a nearby table caused Sara and Brad to look in that direction.

"I didn't order a pizza!" The man yelled when the waitress brought his order. "You were supposed to bring me a steak sub and fries. I have to be back at work in twenty minutes, so now I'll have to take my lunch to go. That is, if you can get it to me in time."

"I'm sorry, sir," the young waitress apologized. The poor thing looked as if she was on the verge of tears. "It's my first day on the job. I'll get the right order for you, and it will be on the house."

"Well, that's more like it." The guy leaned back in his chair.

Sara looked back at Brad and whispered,

"That man seems a bit frazzled."

"Bet he works in a store" — Brad winked — "and is dealing with Christmas returns."

Sara giggled. "He must be having a bad day."

A waiter came, interrupting their conversation. Sara ordered a slice of vegetarian pizza, along with a small tossed green salad, and a glass of water.

"I'll have the same as her." Brad smiled up at the waiter. "Only, make that two slices of pizza instead of one."

The young man nodded. "Do you want water too?"

"Nope. Think I'll go with an orange soda."

"Okay. I'll return with your drinks shortly."

When their waiter moved away from the table, Brad leaned closer to Sara and said, "When Ezekiel arrived at your grandparents' yesterday, I went to the barn with him while he put his horse away."

Sara tipped her head with a quizzical expression.

"I asked Ezekiel some questions about Michelle." Brad paused to collect his thoughts. "He explained Michelle's reasons for pretending she was you."

"Oh? And what would those be?"

Brad repeated everything Ezekiel had told him.

Sara's forehead wrinkled. "She's not the only person with problems from the past. And certainly, not everyone goes around lying to get what they want or uses their own misfortune to gain something from someone. At least, I never would. I believe Michelle's reason for impersonating me goes deeper than having an unhappy childhood and needing a place to live." She blew out a quick breath. "I truly believe Michelle is after something."

"What do you think she wants?"

Before Sara could respond, their waiter was back with the water and soda. "Your pizza should be out shortly." He looked at Sara. "Would you like your salad before the pizza comes out?"

She shook her head. "It's fine if you bring them at the same time."

"Okay." He hurried from the table.

"Now, back to my question . . . What do you think Michelle wants?" Brad asked.

"For one thing, she's vying for my grandparents' love and attention. I think she would like them to care more about her than they do me."

Brad was about to refute that statement, when Sara spoke again. "I also think Michelle may be hoping for something — like an inheritance when they die someday. She probably wants to join the Amish faith to get in their good graces."

With elbows on the table, Brad clasped his fingers together. "For their sake, as well as yours and Ezekiel's, I hope that's not true. Ezekiel is obviously in love with Michelle, and he believes her intentions are good."

"I'd like to think so, but I have a knack for reading people." Sara lifted her chin. "In my opinion, Michelle is not to be trusted, so I'm keeping an eye on her."

Their meal came then, so Brad decided to drop the subject and talk about something else. His intuition told him that Sara had some deep issues of her own to resolve, but he wouldn't bring that up now. Maybe some other time, if he gained her confidence, he could delve into Sara's personal life. One thing was for sure: he'd like to know where she stood spiritually.

"I have a favor to ask," Sara said when she and Brad finished their lunch.

He looked at her intently. "What is it?"

She wiped some crumbs off her slacks and set her napkin aside. "Since you knew Michelle from the time you worked for my grandparents, I was wondering if you could persuade her to move out of their house."

His brows furrowed. "Why would I do that?"

"Because she has no right to be there."

"She might not have the right, but Willis and Mary Ruth must want Michelle there, or they wouldn't have invited her to stay in their home."

Sara poked her tongue along the inside of her cheek. "You're on her side, aren't you?"

He shook his head. "I'm not taking anyone's side. I just think this is something you should discuss with your grandparents, not me, an outsider."

"You're not really an outsider. You're Michelle's friend, and Grandma and Grandpa's too."

"True, but unless they ask for my opinion, I won't voice my thoughts, let alone tell them what to do."

"Okay, no problem. I'll take it up with Michelle myself." With a huff, Sara pushed her chair aside and stood. "I need to get back to the flower shop so Mr. and Mrs. Roberts can take their lunch break."

Brad jumped up. "As soon as I pay the bill I'll give you a lift."

"Don't bother. The shop's not that far. I'll walk." Without giving him a chance to respond, Sara rushed to the front of the restaurant and slipped out the door.

"Christmas went well, don't you think?" Willis asked when he came into the kitchen for lunch.

Mary Ruth nodded and placed a loaf of bread on the table. "It's sure quiet around here today, with Sara working at the flower shop and Michelle out looking for a job."

Willis chuckled as he took a seat at the table. "You like lots of action around you, jah?"

"Not necessarily action, but it is nice to have someone to talk to."

He pointed to himself. "Don't you enjoy talking to me?"

"Course I do, but you spend a good deal of the day doing chores and taking care of the hogs. And when you're here in the house, you find a newspaper or magazine to read. I feel kind of left out at times."

Willis got up and came around to the side of the table where Mary Ruth stood. "I'll try to do better in that regard." He gave her a hug. "After all, neither of the girls will be livin' here forever, so I may as well start spending more time with you now."

She smiled up at him. "You're such a good

husband. What would I ever do without you?"

He tweaked the end of her nose playfully. "I hope when the good Lord decides to take us, we both leave this earth together."

She flapped her hand. "Go on now, and sit yourself back down. Let's have no talk of death or dying. I'm sure you're *hungerich,* and so am I, so let's eat ourselves full."

When Michelle arrived back at the Lapps', her spirits soared. She'd been hired as a waitress at one of the busiest restaurants in Ronks. Amish and English folks both liked to eat there, and while she was waiting to be interviewed at one of the back tables, she'd noticed how a constant flow of customers kept the other waitresses on their toes. Michelle would be working five days a week, with Mondays and some Saturdays off. It was a good thing she'd kept the comfortable shoes she'd worn while working at the restaurant in Harrisburg.

I'm not sure Sara will like it with me having Mondays off too, but, oh well . . . She'll just have to get used to it. Michelle would miss spending her days with Mary Ruth and Willis, but it would be nice to have money she could contribute to their expenses. With a steady paycheck and tip money, she also hoped to open a savings account at the local bank. Of course, her first paycheck would be used to pay back the money she'd taken from their coffee can of emergency cash when she'd run off to Harrisburg in October.

"Sure wish I could undo the past," she murmured as she unhitched Peanuts and led her into the barn.

Woof! Woof! Woof!

Michelle looked down at Rascal, pawing at her leg, and shook her finger. "Not now, pup. I need to put Mary Ruth's horse in her stall."

Woof! The dog's tail wagged so fast it looked like a blur.

"Go in the yard. I'll play fetch-the-ball when I'm done here."

Rascal let out a pathetic whine, then slunk out of the barn.

Michelle shook her head. *That mutt always wants my attention. Poor thing. I haven't spent much time with Rascal lately. I'll have to pay him more attention on my days off, and Sunday afternoons too.*

Peanuts nickered softly as she led the mare into her stall for a thorough rubdown. When Michelle was done, she left the stall and started for the barn doors. "Okay, now it's Rascal's turn. I'm sure he's ready to play."

Michelle had no more than stepped outside, when Sara's car came up the driveway. The next thing she knew, Rascal, barking wildly, raced toward the vehicle. Normally, he wasn't prone to car chasing, but for some reason, he was today.

"Sara, stop!" Michelle clapped her hands and hollered, "Come here, Rascal. Get away from that car!"

As though seeing it in slow motion, Michelle watched in horror as Sara's car hit Rascal, knocking the poor pooch to the cold, snow-covered ground.

CHAPTER 18

Sara's hands shook so badly, she could hardly open her car door. In the six years she'd been driving, she had never been involved in an accident or hit an animal. Sara had seen Rascal running toward her car, but the driveway was slippery, and when she turned the wheel to avoid hitting the dog, he'd gotten in the way.

Her heart pounded, and her legs felt like two sticks of rubber as she made her way to Rascal's lifeless form. She knelt on the snow-packed ground beside him, hoping to see the extent of his injuries.

"You hit my dog! Oh no . . . Oh no . . . Rascal!" A shrill voice seemed to come out of nowhere.

Sara looked up through a film of tears and saw Michelle running toward her. "I — I didn't do it on purpose. The ice . . . The snow . . . The dog . . ."

Michelle dropped down beside Rascal,

calling his name over and over while stroking his head. The poor dog did not respond.
"No, no. He can't be dead," she wailed.
"He's the only dog I've ever owned." Her
voice shook with raw emotion. "He's not
even a year old yet."

"M—maybe he's not dead. He could just
be unconscious." Even as the words came
out of her mouth, Sara feared they weren't
true. So far, Rascal had not made a sound
— not even a whimper — or so much as
moved a muscle. Even if the dog was still
alive, he'd most likely been seriously injured.

While Michelle remained in the snow,
stroking her dog's head, Sara clambered to
her feet. "I'll go get Grandpa. He will know
what to do."

Michelle didn't even look up.

As she started for the house, Sara glanced
back. She almost wished she hadn't. It was
a pitiful, heart-wrenching sight to see Michelle bent over her beloved pet. Even worse
was when she put her ear to the dog's body
to see if there was a heartbeat. "Oh please,
God," Sara murmured, looking up toward
the sky. "Don't let her dog be dead."

Being in shock herself, and moving on a
slippery surface, Sara hurried on. She found
her grandmother in the kitchen, putting a
meatloaf in the oven.

"Oh Sara, I didn't realize you were home." Grandma closed the oven door and turned from the stove. "How was your day at the flower shop? Was business slower than usual now that Christmas is over?"

With so many questions being thrown at her at once, Sara could hardly speak. Her day at work and how many customers came in didn't matter at all. Sara's only concern was the poor dog lying on the cold ground next to her front tire — not to mention Michelle's reaction to what had happened to her dog.

Grandma tilted her head. "Sara, your face is as pale as goat's milk. Is anything wrong? Please tell me, did something happen outside?"

Tears spilled onto Sara's cheeks. "I — I hit Rascal. Michelle is outside with him, but I think I killed him." Sara swallowed, fearing she might get sick.

Grandma's eyes widened. "Oh no. I'm sure it was an accident, for I know you didn't hit Rascal on purpose." She gave Sara a supportive hug.

She remained in Grandma's embrace, while more tears escaped her eyes. Then, regaining her composure, Sara stepped away, drying her tears. "Thank you."

Sara's gaze darted to the window, then

back to her grandmother. "Where's Grandpa? We need him to help us."

"He's in the living room, probably taking a nap. I'll go get him." Grandma moved from the kitchen much faster than usual.

Sara wasn't sure if she should go back outside and wait, or remain in the kitchen until Grandpa came out. She opted for the latter, needing his support and not knowing if Michelle would accept her apology.

As Michelle held Rascal's head in her lap, deep sobs poured forth from the depths of her soul. She knew without anyone telling her that the dog was dead, for there was no sign of life in him at all. While Michelle sat with Rascal, a memory slipped in from when he was a puppy, and why she had chosen the runt. Rascal had been a lot like her, struggling to survive. Besides being the smallest in the litter, he'd had to squirm his way in between the larger puppies in order to get some milk. Michelle could not refuse such a little fighter.

Michelle smiled briefly, but then the next wave of tears began. "Oh Rascal, I truly am sorry," she sobbed, as a sense of guilt overcame her. "All you wanted to do was play when I came into the barn, and I made you wait. Today I refused to play, and it cost you your life."

If only you hadn't run at Sara's car. If she'd only seen you in time and stopped her vehicle, you wouldn't be slipping away from me now. Michelle felt horrible and full of regret. Minutes ago, Rascal was full of life and wanting a little attention. *If I'd only taken some time to play ball with my devoted friend, he would still be here now.* All the rehashing and *if only*s made her feel even worse.

Michelle closed her eyes, holding out hope that her suspicions were wrong. She hadn't felt this helpless and full of despair since she and her little brothers were separated. But at least Ernie and Jack hadn't been killed, only taken away and never seen again. Once Rascal was buried, she would never see him again either.

Rascal's mother approached from the barn and slinked slowly up to Rascal. Michelle could hardly stand watching poor Sadie sniff over her puppy. Then the collie lay down between the pup and Michelle, resting her head on Michelle's leg.

"Oh Sadie." Michelle cried even harder when the collie let out a sad whimper. Reaching out and pulling Sadie closer, Michelle buried her face in the collie's neck and found a slight thread of comfort in the warmth of the dog's fur. Sadie whined again, as if she understood.

Hearing voices, Michelle looked up and saw Willis and Sara come out of the house and plod toward her through the snow.

"Let me see how badly he's been hurt." Willis knelt down and checked Rascal over. Then he put his hand in front of the dog's mouth and listened for breath with his ear. "I'm so sorry, Michelle." His voice sounded flat, almost monotone. "Rascal is gone."

She sniffed deeply. "I — I think I already knew. I listened for a heartbeat, but he hasn't drawn a breath. Even so, I didn't want to give up hope."

"I apologize. As soon as I saw him running at the car, I should have stopped." Sara put her hand on Michelle's trembling shoulder. "I didn't realize how icy the driveway was either. Oh Michelle, I am so sorry."

"I'll go to the house and get a box to put him in." Grandpa rose to his feet. "There's a patch of ground out back by the burn barrel where the ground isn't so frozen. I'll bury him there."

Michelle could only nod as tears coursed down her cheeks. She'd given no response to Sara's apology and couldn't even think to do that right now. All she wanted was to get away from this horrible scene and

211

mounting grief. She needed to be with Ezekiel and seek comfort from him.

"Can I take the horse and buggy out again, Willis?" she asked, hiccuping as she tried holding back more tears. "There's someplace I need to go."

His eyebrows squished together as he tugged on one ear. "Well, yes, but Mary Ruth has supper in the oven."

Michelle stood, brushing snow off her dress. "I couldn't eat anything right now. I need to see Ezekiel."

"I can drive you over," Sara offered. "Please let me do that for you. You're in no condition to take the horse and buggy out right now."

"I'm fine."

Willis eyed Michelle. "If you're determined to go by yourself, then go ahead and take the horse and buggy. I'll ask Mary Ruth to keep some of the meatloaf warm for you."

"Don't bother. I wouldn't be able to eat it." Michelle watched as Sadie followed Willis to the house. Then, looking Sara straight in the eyes, she said, "In case you didn't know, Rascal was a gift from Mary Ruth and Willis for my birthday last June." Unable to say any more, Michelle took off for the barn to get Mary Ruth's horse. The thrill of finding a job today was long forgotten.

After securing Peanuts to the reins, Michelle pulled the carriage from the buggy shed and wheeled it so she could easily back the horse up to it. Peanuts nickered and stomped with an eagerness to go somewhere. This usually made Michelle happy, but right now her whole body felt numb.

She moved to the front of the horse. The mare's soft eyes, full of life, looked back at her. Warm tears dribbled down Michelle's face. Her heart felt as though it was breaking. Michelle stroked the horse's soft muzzle. *I hope Ezekiel is done for the day at the greenhouse and hasn't gone anywhere. I really need his support.*

Sara walked slowly back to the house. At this moment, she felt as if the weight of the world rested on her shoulders. She'd said she was sorry, but Michelle had not accepted her apology. *Doesn't she realize I didn't do it on purpose? It's not like I set out to run over her dog. If Michelle hadn't been here impersonating me this summer, she wouldn't be going through this right now.*

The more Sara thought about it, the more upset she became. She felt guilty enough without facing Michelle's accusing look and her refusal to acknowledge Sara's apology or her offer to drive Michelle to Ezekiel's. Trying to justify the situation by saying it was Michelle's fault as much as hers didn't give Sara vindication.

She kicked at a clump of snow as she neared the porch. *If I could undo what happened, I surely would.*

She stepped near the threshold of the door and paused, remembering her conversation with Brad at noon. Sara was set then to have it out with Michelle, but how could she now? Hopefully, Michelle would find the comfort she needed in the arms of her Amish boyfriend.

Ezekiel had come out of the greenhouse and was getting ready to head for the house, when a horse and buggy entered the yard. He was surprised when it pulled up to the hitching rail and Michelle got out. Ezekiel hadn't expected to see her this evening.

The minute he saw her tear-stained face, Ezekiel knew something was wrong. "What is it, Michelle? You look *umgerennt.*"

Her chin trembled. "I am very upset. My dog just died, and it's Sara's fault."

Ezekiel gasped. "Oh no! What happened?"

Sniffling, and practically choking on sobs, Michelle told him everything that had occurred. "I couldn't stay and watch as Willis buried Rascal. And I can't be around Sara right now. I needed to be with you, Ezekiel."

He pulled Michelle into his arms and gently patted her back. "I don't think Sara did it on purpose. It sounds like an unfortunate accident."

She pressed her face against Ezekiel's chest. "Sara said she was sorry."

"Did you accept her apology?"

"No, I could barely look at her without feeling anger."

"There are many passages in the Bible about forgiveness. Can you think of one?"

"I — I can't remember where it's found, but as I recall, there's a verse that says: 'For if ye forgive men their trespasses, your heavenly Father will . . .' " Michelle's voice trailed off.

" 'Will also forgive you,' " Ezekiel finished the quotation. "It's found in Matthew 6:14. And the verse after that says, 'But if ye forgive not men their trespasses, neither will your Father forgive your trespasses.' "

Although crying so hard her sides ached, Michelle knew what she must do, no matter how difficult it was. For without forgiveness, no healing would come.

CHAPTER 19

When supper was over, and the dishes were done, Sara volunteered to take the empty canning jar the green beans had been in down to the basement. Michelle still hadn't returned, and Sara figured she'd probably stayed at Ezekiel's parents' house for supper.

Although Grandma's meatloaf had tasted good, Sara hadn't had much of an appetite. How could the day after Christmas turn so tragically wrong?

When Grandpa came inside after burying Rascal, he'd looked so sad it made Sara feel even worse. She'd never owned a pet, but was learning quickly how much they could be part of one's family. *Maybe I should have helped Grandpa when he buried Michelle's dog.* But Sara couldn't bring herself to do so. How could she, when it was her fault? A few minutes alone in the basement might help, especially if she took down that old jar again and read some of the messages inside. It could even take her mind off the current situation and the guilt she felt.

Holding a flashlight in one hand, and the clean jar in the other, Sara made her way slowly down the basement stairs. When she reached the bottom, she found the battery-operated lantern and clicked it on. After putting the canning jar away, she reached up behind the antique jars and took down the one filled with notes. Taking a seat on a wooden stool, she poked her fingers in, pulled out a slip of paper, and read Matthew 7:1 silently: *"Judge not, that ye be not judged."*

Sara flinched. Ever since she'd arrived at Grandma and Grandpa's and found Michelle living here, she had been judge and jury. Michelle was guilty of impersonating her. She had openly admitted it and even apologized. But Sara had not forgiven her, and at every turn, she judged Michelle for every little thing she did.

Maybe I shouldn't judge her. Michelle might not be the horrible person I've made her out to be. Sara tapped her foot. *Even if she is up to no good, the Bible says I should not judge her.*

Sara drew a deep breath and reached in for another piece of paper that quoted Matthew 5:44: *"But I say unto you, Love your enemies."*

She swallowed hard as tears sprang to her eyes. *I have seen Michelle as an enemy, but the Bible says I'm supposed to love her.*

Sara squeezed her eyes shut. *How am I supposed to do that? How can I love Michelle when she's trying to take my grandparents from me?*

She opened her eyes and was about to put the papers back in the jar, when she heard footsteps coming down the stairs. Hurriedly, she crammed the papers back in, but before she could make a move to return the jar to its shelf, someone spoke.

"Mary Ruth said I would find you down here."

Sara jerked her head. Michelle stood not more than a foot away. Barely able to respond, she murmured, "I — I came down to put the empty bean jar away."

Michelle pointed to the antique jar in Sara's hand. "I see you found one of the mysterious prayer jars."

Sara's mouth opened slightly. "Y–you know about this?"

"Yes, and there's another one on a shelf in the barn." Michelle offered Sara a weak smile. "Some of the notes I found inside those jars helped me a lot. They made me

218

realize what I was doing was wrong."

Sara sat quietly, unsure of what to say. Finally, she asked another question. "Do you know who wrote the notes, or why they are in this jar?"

Michelle shook her head. "I've wondered if Mary Ruth might have written them, but I was hesitant to ask. Thought if she is the author, it might be too personal or she wouldn't want to talk about it."

Sara nodded slowly.

Michelle moved closer and touched Sara's shoulder. "I want you to know that I forgive you. After talking about it with Ezekiel, and thinking things through, I realized it wasn't your fault. I'm also to blame for not paying attention to my dog. Rascal shouldn't have been chasing your car, and the snow and ice only made things worse. Will you forgive me for not accepting your apology before?"

Tears welled in Sara's eyes. She was overwhelmed with relief. "There's nothing to forgive on my end, but I appreciate knowing you don't hold me responsible."

Michelle pulled Sara into a hug, and Sara did not resist. It was the first time since she and Michelle had been living here that Sara had good feelings toward Michelle, and a great load was beginning to lift.

■ ■ ■ ■

"I got a job today," Michelle announced as she sat in the living room that evening with Willis, Mary Ruth, and Sara. The mood had been somber up until now.

Mary Ruth's eyes brightened as she set her knitting needles aside. "That's *wunderbaar*!"

"Jah, congratulations," Willis said with a twinkle in his eyes.

Sara nodded as well. "Where will you be working, and what will you be doing?"

"It's at Dienners Country Restaurant in Ronks, and I'll be waitressing." Michelle pulled her fingers along the top of the black apron she wore over her plain dress. "From what I hear, it's a favorite restaurant with Amish as well as English people. And the best news of all is that I'll be starting tomorrow." She looked over at Willis. "I can still help you with chores before and after I get off work and also on my days off."

He smiled. "We'll see how it goes."

"What are your days off?" Mary Ruth questioned.

"Sundays, Mondays, and some Saturdays — same as Sara. Of course, I would never work on Sunday, even if the restaurant was open that day." Michelle quickly added.

"How will you get to work each day?" Mary Ruth picked up her knitting needles again. "You could drive the horse and buggy to Ronks, because there's a hitching rail outside the restaurant, but it wouldn't be good to leave the horse there all day."

"You're right," Michelle agreed. "I'll have to hire a driver to take me to work in the mornings. Once the spring weather takes over I can walk home from there. The three-and-a-half-mile jaunt might do me some good." Michelle patted her stomach and giggled. "Your good cooking is catching up with me."

"There's no need for that." Sara shook her head. "I'll drop you off at the restaurant before going to work at the flower shop. Then I can pick you up again when I get off in the afternoon. Ronks isn't that far from the flower shop."

"It's nice of you to offer, but my hours might not coincide with yours."

Sara shrugged. "It doesn't matter. If you end up working a later shift, I can always come back here after I leave work and then go to Dienners and pick you up when your afternoon shift ends." She gave Michelle a reassuring smile. "It's not that far away, and it won't take long by car. Maybe ten minutes, if that. We can work something out, so don't worry about a thing."

Alone in their room that night, Mary Ruth sat down on the bed beside her husband. "Things are looking up, don't you think?"

Closing the book from the page he'd been reading, Willis pushed his glasses back in place. "What'd you say?"

"I said, 'Things are looking up.' "

He squinted at her. "In what way?"

"For one thing, after many weeks of searching, Michelle has finally found a job."

Willis tugged his left ear. "Jah, that's a good thing."

She nudged his arm. "And could you believe how well Sara and Michelle got along this evening? There were no curt remarks on either side, and what a surprise when Sara offered to give Michelle a ride to and from work."

He moved his head slowly up and down. "It was unexpected — that's for sure. I wonder what brought on the change."

Mary Ruth turned her hands palms up. "I have no idea, but it's an answer to prayer. It's sad what happened to poor Rascal today, but maybe this tragedy turned into something positive."

"Jah, even poor Sadie seems lost right

now, so she'll need some extra attention for a spell."

"I'm sure she misses her puppy as much as Michelle does." Mary Ruth looked toward the window. "Do you think we should have brought Sadie inside and let her sleep in Michelle's room tonight, or even here in ours?"

"Sadie is in the barn where she's used to being. She might be lonely, but she'll be okay."

"I hope things keep going like they are between the girls. I enjoy their company so much, and to see them getting along better is such a blessing." Mary Ruth placed both hands on her chest.

He patted her arm. "We need to pray that what happened between Sara and Michelle tonight will continue on in the days ahead."

"I wholeheartedly agree." Mary Ruth removed her head covering and prepared for bed. Michelle had gone up to her room early this evening, leaving them alone with Sara in the living room. Mary Ruth had been tempted to ask about her granddaughter's change of heart but had decided it was better to hold back. If either Sara or Michelle wanted to talk with her about it, she felt sure they would. In the meantime, she'd keep praying and showing them love.

■ ■ ■ ■

After coming upstairs, Sara stood in front of the mirror on her bedroom wall, holding one of her mother's old heart-shaped head coverings by its ribbon-strings. She'd found it, along with several other items in the cedar chest at the foot of her bed.

I wonder how I would look wearing this. She pulled her hair back into a bun and pinned it in place, then set the kapp on her head. With the exception of the jeans and rose-colored top she wore, Sara almost looked Amish. *Could I be happy wearing plain clothes all the time?* she wondered. *Michelle seems to be, and she has no Amish heritage.*

Leaving the kapp on, Sara moved away from the mirror and took a seat on the bench near the window. She bent down to remove her shoes and socks. Wiggling her bare toes, she closed her eyes and tried to picture what her mother must have looked like when she lived here as a teenager. *Was Mama unhappy being Amish, or did she run away from home only because she felt guilty and couldn't face her parents with the truth about being pregnant?*

Sara had so many unanswered questions she wished she could ask her mother right now. And of course the biggest question of all was, *Who is my father?*

Her eyes snapped open. *Will I ever find out, and if I were to meet him, would he welcome me as his daughter? How would I react if I did find him? He'd be a stranger to me.* Sara inhaled and blew out a shallow breath. *Maybe it would be best if I never find the answer. I should probably forget about trying to find my father.*

CHAPTER 20

Lancaster

"So what's on your plate this morning?"

Brad grinned at his friend from across the table and pointed to his poached eggs.

Ned groaned. "Very funny. I meant what do you have planned for today?"

"I know. Just kidding." Brad snickered. "Well, let's see. First thing after breakfast I plan to make another trip to Strasburg." He added some salt and pepper to his eggs. "Since Sara will be at work today, it'll give me a chance to talk to the Lapps privately. Of course, if Michelle is there, that might make it more difficult to say what's on my mind."

Ned's eyebrows rose. "How come you don't want Michelle to hear what you're saying?"

"Because it concerns her and Sara and how they've been acting toward each other."

"Oh yeah, that's right. You did mention

them being at odds."

"It's worse now than ever." Brad shook his head.

"Did something else happen?"

"Sara still resents Michelle for pretending to be her, and she feels that Michelle has been taking advantage of Willis and Mary Ruth Lapp. She also believes Michelle has an ulterior motive."

"Do you think she does?"

"I don't know." Brad paused to eat a few bites of his eggs. "Sara asked if I would suggest to Michelle that she move out."

"Wow. Did you agree to that?" Ned slathered a blob of peanut butter on his toast.

"No way. Sara got irritated and said I was siding with Michelle." Brad grimaced. "I guess many people often look for someone to blame when something doesn't go their way."

Ned bobbed his head. "You're right. When I was a kid and my little brother fell out of a tree, our sister blamed me because I wasn't watching Dennis. I can remember the incident as though it happened yesterday — probably because I felt so guilty."

Brad nodded with understanding. "The problem with guilt is until we let go, our thoughts can be consumed with it — sometimes to the point of it making us sick or affecting our relationships with others."

"I agree." Ned finished the rest of his toast and swiped a napkin across his face. "I'd better go. Don't wanna be late for my dental appointment." He pushed back his chair and stood. "I hope things go well when you talk to the Lapps."

"Same here." Even though Brad had prayed when he'd first sat down at the table, he closed his eyes and offered another petition to God. "Please fill my mouth with the right words when I speak to Willis and Mary Ruth. And give all three of us wisdom to know how to help Sara and Michelle realize they need to set their differences aside."

Ronks, Pennsylvania
"It was nice of you to drive me to work this morning, but don't feel that you have to do it every day if our schedules conflict." Michelle looked over and smiled, as Sara pulled her car into Dienners' parking lot.

"Not a problem. I'll do it whenever I can, especially because we'll be getting into the coldest part of winter soon." Sara turned off the engine. "Since we're here a few minutes early, I'd like to talk to you about something."

"Sure, what is it?"

Sara cleared her throat. "Well, shortly after

I came to visit my grandparents for the first time, I received a letter from Brad."

"Oh? I didn't realize you had known him before."

"I didn't. The letter was obviously meant for you, because he knew you as Sara."

"Oh yeah." Michelle's cheeks colored. "What did his letter say?"

Sara tapped her chin. "I can't remember word-for-word, but the gist of it was that he wanted to let you know he had settled in at the seminary in Clarks Summit."

Michelle nodded. "That's right. Brad told me he would be going there in one of our earlier conversations. Did he say anything else I should know about?"

"He said he hoped you had gotten the note he'd brought by the Lapps' before he left. Oh, and there was a Bible verse included with his letter." Sara paused, wondering if she should say more.

"What else?"

"Umm . . . Brad also mentioned that he hoped you would write him sometime and as soon as he had a free weekend he'd like to come here for a visit."

Michelle pursed her lips. "I see."

"Was there more?"

"He asked you to give his love to your

grandparents and said he was praying for you."

"You mean, *your* grandparents."

"Yes, but he thought they were yours."

Michelle's head moved up and down. "I really messed up, didn't I? Everyone in this Amish community would have been better off if I hadn't let them think I was you."

"It's in the past and can't be changed." *Then why can't you forget about trying to find out who your father is?* The little voice in Sara's head reminded her that, despite her best intentions, she had not left her past behind, and may never unless she found the answer she sought.

"Do you still have Brad's letter?" Michelle asked.

Sara shook her head. "I didn't think I would ever see you again, so I threw the letter away."

"Oh, I see." Michelle gave one of her head covering strings a tug. "Guess it really doesn't matter, since he didn't say anything I don't already know." She sucked in her bottom lip, and then let her mouth relax. "There was a time when I thought I might be falling for Brad, but I quickly realized we weren't suited and that I had no future with him." She smiled. "Ezekiel and I are meant to be together, even if his mother doesn't think so."

"Maybe Belinda will change her mind."

Michelle shrugged. "I hope so, because I can't imagine what it would be like if Ezekiel and I ended up getting married and there was still tension between his mother and me."

Sara gave Michelle's arm a light tap. "Well, as my mother used to say, 'Remember to take one day at a time.' "

"Good advice." Michelle looked at her watch. "Oh goodness. I better get inside. My boss wanted me here a little early to go over some things I need to know. Don't want to start off on the wrong foot my first day."

"I heard a car pull into the yard," Mary Ruth shouted from the kitchen. "Would you please see who it is, Willis? I would do it, but I'm in the middle of rolling out pie dough."

"Jah, okay," he called back.

Mary Ruth was putting the dough into the pans when Willis entered the kitchen with Brad. "This is a nice surprise." She gestured with her head. "If you'd like to take a seat at the table, I'll make some coffee as soon as I get the pie shells in the oven to lightly brown."

"Sounds good." Brad took a seat, and Willis did the same.

"Too bad the pies aren't baked yet," her husband commented. "I could go for something a little sweet right about now."

"Not a problem," Mary Ruth assured him. "There are plenty of peanut butter *kichlin* in the cookie jar. Feel free to get some out for our guest, as well as yourself."

Willis didn't have to be asked twice. He got right up and walked over to the ceramic jar on the counter. Soon he and Brad, both with smiling faces, were nibbling on cookies.

"Delicious!" Brad smacked his lips. "Did you make them, Mary Ruth?"

She shook her head. "Michelle did."

"Speaking of Michelle, where is she today?" He glanced around as though expecting her to join them.

"She should be in Ronks by now." Mary Ruth smiled as she poured pumpkin filling into the lightly browned pie shells, ready for further baking. "She got hired as a waitress at Dienners, and this was her first day on the job."

"That's good to hear. I imagine Sara's working today too?"

"Sure is." Willis spoke before Mary Ruth

had a chance to respond to Brad's question.

"Good to know. I'm glad neither of them is here right now."

Mary Ruth returned the pies to the oven and turned to face Brad. "How come?"

"Because I don't want them to hear what I'm about to say." Brad reached for another cookie.

Mary Ruth placed a pot of coffee on the stove, then took a seat across from Brad. "What is it you wanted to tell us that the girls aren't supposed to hear?"

He rested both arms on the table. "Sara has talked to me about Michelle and how she feels about her pretending to be your granddaughter all those months. She is clearly upset, not only with that, but about Michelle living here with you." Brad's gaze went from Mary Ruth to Willis. "Has she spoken to either of you about it?"

"We have talked, but not specifically about that." Mary Ruth shook her head. "We have noticed the tension between Sara and Michelle . . . until last night, that is."

"What happened last night?"

"We have no idea," Willis spoke up. "They just acted more civil toward each other."

"You probably don't know this, but something unfortunate happened yesterday,"

Mary Ruth added.

Brad remained silent as she explained what happened to Michelle's dog. As Mary Ruth described the outcome, Brad's expression changed from curiosity to a look of disbelief.

"And then last evening, after Michelle told us she found a job, Sara offered to give her a ride to work," Willis interjected.

Brad's eyes widened. "That's really something. Never expected to hear this kind of news when I came over here. Wonder what brought on the change, especially after what happened to Rascal."

Mary Ruth got up to get the coffeepot. "I have no idea, but I am ever so grateful. Sara is our flesh-and-blood granddaughter, and we love her dearly, but we also care about Michelle."

Willis bobbed his head as though in agreement.

"I understand." Brad accepted the cup of coffee Mary Ruth offered him. "It sounds like an answer to prayer."

"Yes, indeed." Mary Ruth poured coffee for herself and Willis and took her seat at the table. "I only hope whatever good has transpired between the girls will last."

Each time Brad entered the Lapps' house,

he appreciated the warm and inviting feeling, and this morning had been no different. He'd enjoyed talking with Willis and Mary Ruth, and was especially happy to hear of the turnabout with Sara and Michelle. He felt sure it couldn't have been anything he'd said to Sara that had influenced her, but it didn't matter. He was just glad things were going better between the two young women.

Driving back to Ned's apartment, Brad thought about Sara. He wasn't happy with the way things had ended the last time he was with her. Here it was Thursday already, and he only had five more days before he had to be back at the university.

"I have to work it in somehow to see Sara before I go back." He spoke out loud. "I wonder what she's doing on New Year's Eve. Think I'll stop by the flower shop sometime tomorrow or the next day and see if she has any plans."

CHAPTER 21

Ronks

Michelle shivered as she stood outside Dienners, waiting for Sara to pick her up. It had been a busy day at the restaurant, and her feet ached from being on them for the breakfast and lunch shifts. Even her comfortable shoes didn't seem to help her feet today. She had only agreed to work two shifts every day to make more money. The morning shift started at seven, and the afternoon shift ended at three. Since Sara started at eight and left her job in Strasburg at four, it meant Sara went in early and Michelle stayed at Dienners an hour after quitting time, waiting for her ride. While Sara's offer to take Michelle to and from work was generous, this wasn't the ideal situation.

Sure wish Sara and I worked the same hours. Michelle blew on her hands, getting colder by the minute. *Maybe Sara's boss would be willing to change her work schedule*

*to match mine. But then I guess he wouldn't
need her to come to work that early every day.*

If Michelle had a car of her own, she could drive herself, but that would defeat the purpose of trying to live a Plain life while waiting to join the Amish church.

Michelle thought about all the frustration it caused Ezekiel when his folks found out he'd bought a truck. Things were much better between him and his parents since he'd decided to join the church and sell the vehicle. At least now, and even after Michelle and Ezekiel became members, they would be allowed to ride in other people's cars.

A horn honked, drawing Michelle's thoughts aside. She looked to the left and spotted Sara's car pulling into the parking lot, so she hurried that way.

"How was your first day on the job?" Sara asked after Michelle took a seat on the passenger's side.

"It went fine, and I made some good tips, but boy, am I ever tired." Michelle reached down and rubbed the calf of her right leg. "It's been so long since I waitressed that I forgot what it was like to be on my feet for so many hours." She looked over at Sara and smiled. "I'm glad I don't have to walk home, and I appreciate you going out of your way to pick me up."

"It's no bother. I am happy to do it," Sara replied. *Since I hit your dog, it's the least I can do.*

"How did your day go?" Michelle asked.

"It went well, but things were kind of quiet. Only a few people came into the shop to buy or order flowers."

"Bet it will get hectic again close to Valentine's Day." Michelle slipped off her shoes and wiggled her toes near the heat vent.

Sara nodded as she pulled out of the parking lot. "Andy and Karen Roberts already warned me about that. They said it would be even more demanding than Christmas, with folks flocking into the store to buy flowers. But I think I'll be up to the challenge. And it will likely be one of the times I'll need to work longer hours."

"You're a strong woman, Sara. I envy you for that," Michelle said.

"What makes you think I'm strong?"

"Oh, I don't know. Maybe strong isn't the right word. I guess confident might be a better way of putting it."

"I'm not as confident as you might think."

"Really? It doesn't show."

"Maybe not outwardly, but inside I am

sometimes a ball of nerves." Sara clicked the blinker on as she prepared to turn the next corner.

"Never would have guessed it. To me you appear so self-assured."

Sara shook her head. "When I first came to Strasburg to meet my grandparents, I was full of anxiety — afraid they might not like me."

Michelle groaned, rubbing her feet. "I felt the same way when I met them. Only my situation was different. I knew if they found out I was pretending to be you, they'd probably never speak to me again — not to mention that I would have had to move out."

"But Grandpa and Grandma did, and they even welcomed you into their home."

"True. Their love and forgiveness was more than I deserved."

"Is there anyone in your life you have not forgiven?" Sara asked as they approached Strasburg.

Michelle sat quietly for several seconds before she answered. "For a long time, there was. My parents were abusive, and when my brothers and I became wards of the state and got shipped off to different foster parents, I was angry. I told myself I would never forgive our mom and dad for what they did to us, even if they got down on their knees and begged."

"What about now? Would you forgive them if they asked?"

"Yes, and I already have. In fact, I wrote them a letter the other day. Wanted my folks to know where I am and said I've forgiven them for the abusive things they did to me and my brothers while we were living with them."

Strasburg

Sara didn't respond until they arrived at her grandparents' place. After she turned off the car's engine, she turned to face Michelle. "It had to be difficult for you to forgive your parents."

"From a human standpoint it was."

"Well, I want you to know that I have forgiven you for pretending to be me, but there are some people in my life I can't forgive right now. Truthfully, I'm not sure I ever will."

"With God's help you can."

Sara's chin trembled. "If there is a God, then He shouldn't allow people to keep secrets or treat others unfairly."

Before Michelle could put on her shoes and offer a response, Sara hopped out of the car and hurried to the house. Just thinking about the people in her life who had done her an injustice gave her a headache. And the idea of forgiving them seemed impossible.

The minute her granddaughter entered the house, Mary Ruth knew something was wrong. Grimacing, Sara held her head and mumbled something about needing to go to her room to lie down.

Should I go after her? Mary Ruth wondered as Sara raced up the stairs. *Maybe she's sick or had a rough day at work. Oh, I hope nothing's happened between her and Michelle again.*

Mary Ruth was almost to the stairs when Michelle came in. "I don't know what happened with Sara," she said breathlessly. "We were talking in the car one minute, and then after we drove into the yard, Sara got out and took off for the house. Makes me wonder if she got upset about something I said."

Mary Ruth moved closer to Michelle. "What did you say to her?"

"We were talking about forgiving others, and Sara said if there's a God, He shouldn't allow people to keep secrets or treat others unfairly." Michelle's brows drew inward. "I was about to tell her that we are not puppets, and if other people do things to hurt

241

us, it's not God's fault, because He gave everyone a free will. But I never got the chance to express that, since Sara hurried away."

Mary Ruth nodded slowly. "When Sara came in, I could tell she either wasn't feeling well or was upset about something. Apparently it was the latter."

"I guess so." Michelle gestured to the kitchen. "Can we go in there and talk more?"

"Of course. I'll fix some hot tea and you can tell me how things went with your job."

When Michelle entered the kitchen behind Mary Ruth, she filled the teakettle with water and placed it on the stove."

"Danki, but you didn't have to do that," Mary Ruth said.

"I was happy to heat the *wasser.* You and Willis certainly do enough for me. Besides, I enjoy helping out."

Mary Ruth smiled. "You're very kind." While she and Michelle waited for the water to heat, they took seats at the table.

"Where's Willis?" Michelle asked. "Is he out in the barn or taking a nap in his easy chair, like he often does this time of the day?"

"Neither. Our driver Stan picked Willis up after lunch and drove him to a chiropractic appointment. I'm guessing it took longer than expected. Either that, or they stopped afterward to run a few errands."

"At least we don't have to worry about them getting stuck in bad weather." Michelle glanced out the window. "The roads were perfectly clear on the way home, and there's no snow in sight."

"That's good to hear." Mary Ruth rose from the table. "Supper is in the oven, but it'll be at least an hour before we eat. Would you like an apple or some cheese and crackers to tide you over?"

"No, thanks. The only thing I need right now is something for my sore feet. I'm not used to being on them all day, but I'm sure after I've worked at the restaurant awhile I'll toughen up." Michelle gave a shallow laugh.

"I have some liniment you can rub on your feet and legs. And a warm soak in the tub might help as well."

"Good idea."

Mary Ruth leaned slightly forward. "Now about Sara . . . Do you think she still hasn't forgiven you for letting Willis and me believe you were her all those months?"

Michelle shook her head. "She said she's forgiven me, but I believe there is someone from Sara's past she hasn't forgiven."

"Did she say who?"

"No, but she did say there were some people in her life she can't forgive right now. She also said she wasn't sure she ever could."

Mary Ruth rapped her knuckles on the table. "I wonder if those people might be her parents. Perhaps she hasn't forgiven her biological father — whoever he is — for not coming forward and standing by her mother when she was pregnant. Or maybe she's holding a grudge because her mother didn't tell her about us when she was alive."

"But Sara knows about you now, and she ought to realize how much you love her."

"That is true."

The teakettle whistled, and Michelle jumped up to get it. Mary Ruth remained at the table while Michelle fixed their cups of tea. *I wonder how my granddaughter would respond if I brought up the topic of her not knowing about us until she read her mother's letter. I won't go barging up to Sara's room to say anything now, but when I am alone with her sometime and feel the time is right, I will bring up the subject. Hopefully she'll be willing to discuss it. And if Sara is holding resentment toward Rhoda, I pray she will forgive her, for that is the only way she will ever feel a sense of peace.*

■ ■ ■ ■

Still wearing her coat, Sara held her temples as she paced her bedroom floor for the umpteenth time. *I need to clear my head and stop beating myself up about who my father is. And I don't want to think about forgiveness right now either. Maybe some fresh air will help.*

Sara went downstairs and stopped in the kitchen, where Michelle sat with Grandma, drinking tea. *It figures they'd be together. They've probably been talking about me.*

"I'm going outside for some fresh air," Sara announced.

"Would you like a cup of cinnamon tea?" Michelle asked, her feet propped up on an empty kitchen chair.

"No, thanks. Maybe later." Sara reached for the doorknob, just as Grandpa came in.

"Oh good, you're back!" Grandma got up and greeted him as he stepped into the kitchen. "I didn't hear your driver pull in. How did your appointment go?"

"Feel good as new again." Grandpa rolled his shoulders and neck with apparent ease. "But before I forget — I checked for phone messages out in the shed, and Sara, there is one for you."

"Okay, thanks Grandpa. I'll go out and see who it's from."

As she walked out onto the porch, Sara took a deep cleansing breath of the cool crisp evening air. This time of year, the atmosphere seemed so clean and fresh. Not like the heat of summer when the weather turned hot and humid.

Sadie barked and ran up to greet Sara, wagging her tail. "Hey, girl. How are you doing?" Sara stopped to pet the collie's head. "Bet you're lonely, huh? Well, come on and keep me company while I see who left me a message."

As if she understood what Sara had said, Sadie barked again, ran ahead, and sat waiting for Sara outside the phone shed.

Sara pulled open the door and left it partially open. When she sat on the chair inside, Sadie came in and plopped down on top of Sara's feet, which felt pretty nice. "You can keep my feet warm for me." Sara smiled, feeling a bit better from being with the dog.

Pushing the answering machine's Message button, she was surprised to hear a message from her stepfather. Dean didn't say much, just asked Sara to give him a call.

"That's strange. I wonder why he didn't call my cell phone." Sara looked at Sadie, as though expecting an answer. "Of course, since arriving, I've rarely used my cell or checked it regularly for messages."

Sara punched in Dean's number, and he answered on the second ring. "Hello, Dean. I got your message."

"Hi, Sara. Just wanted to call and see how your Christmas went. I got your card and had planned to call to wish you a Merry Christmas, but Kenny and I went out to dinner that evening and didn't get back till late. Now here it is, almost New Year's."

"Well, thanks." Sara was surprised by his call and felt a little guilty for not calling him or Kenny on Christmas. "Umm . . ." She shifted the receiver to her other ear, glancing down at Sadie.

"How have you been, Sara? We haven't talked in a while."

"I'm doing fine. How are things going there?"

"Okay. The people who rented your half of the duplex are nice, and I haven't had any trouble with them paying the rent on time."

"That's good." Sara mentioned her new job at the floral shop, and told Dean a few things about her grandparents. "Oh, by the way — how is Kenny doing?"

"Fine. He's in his room right now, doing

homework and counting the days until he graduates from high school this spring."

"Hard to believe he'll be graduating."

"Yeah, it sure is."

"Well, I won't keep you, Sara, but before we hang up, I wanted to run something by you."

"What is it?" Sara asked.

"Would you mind if Kenny and I came to visit you sometime? Maybe when the winter weather is over and the roads will be safer. We could come some weekend, since I don't want Kenny to miss any school. I think it's past time for him to meet his grandparents, don't you?"

"Sure." Sara was stunned hearing Dean wanted to visit, but now it made sense. Kenny had every right to get to know Grandpa and Grandma, and they him.

"We may only come to visit for a few hours and go back on the same day. Or if we want to spend a little more time, we could get a hotel and stay overnight."

"Um . . . Okay. Give me a call when you think that might be."

"Sounds good. And don't forget, Sara, you can call me anytime you want. We shouldn't let so much time go by before we talk again."

"Yeah, you're right." Sara was anxious to

end the conversation. "Sorry, Dean, but it's cold out here in the phone shack, and I need to go."

"Certainly, Sara. You take care now, and I'll talk to you again soon."

"Okay. Tell my little brother I said hi."

"Will do."

After Sara's stepfather said goodbye, she sat in the phone shed awhile, in spite of the cold. *Maybe I should have talked with him longer. It's really not that cold, and I am wearing a coat.* She glanced down at the dog. *Not to mention my feet are plenty warm, thanks to Sadie.*

It was nice Dean wanted to stay in touch, even if they'd never been close. Of course, the main reason for him coming to Strasburg would be for Kenny, not Sara. She tapped her knuckles on the table where the telephone sat. *No surprise. Dean's always thought more about Kenny's needs than mine. But I guess that's because he's his biological father.*

Coaxing Sadie along, Sara left the phone shed and walked back toward the house, feeling worse than she had before. She could not handle more guilt right now. *Guess I should have called Dean a few weeks ago, at least to wish him and Kenny a Merry Christmas, but I didn't want to ruin my own*

Christmas having to hear all about whatever Dean had bought for Kenny. While Sara would not have admitted it to anyone, she didn't care that much about seeing her stepfather, although it would be nice to see her brother. If Dean really cared about Sara, he would have taken more of an interest in her when she was a girl, growing up.

CHAPTER 22

The following day, Brad decided to stop by the flower shop in Strasburg to see Sara again. It was after twelve when he got there, but he hoped he wasn't too late to take her out to lunch.

When Brad entered the store, he saw no sign of Sara. An older woman with light brown hair, sprinkled with gray, sat behind the counter. As he approached, she smiled. "Good afternoon. May I help you, sir?"

"Umm . . . yes . . ." Brad glanced around. "Is Sara working today?"

"Yes, she's in the back room having lunch." The woman pointed over her shoulder. "Did you need to speak with her, or is there something I can help you with?"

"My name is Brad, and Sara and I know each other." He shifted his weight. "I'd like to talk to her if possible."

The woman rose from the stool. "I'll tell her you're here."

As he waited for Sara, Brad walked around the shop, looking at all the plants and flowers for sale. Some were kept in a refrigerated cooler, but most, like the indoor plants, had been set in various locations throughout the store.

Think I might pay for one of these plants or a bouquet of flowers and have it sent to my aunt. She'd probably enjoy looking at it while she's recuperating from her recent surgery. Brad thumped his head. *I should have thought to do that sooner.*

As he was contemplating which arrangement to choose, Sara came out of the back room, along with the woman who had been behind the desk.

"Hi, Brad." Sara offered a friendly smile. "Mrs. Roberts said you wanted to speak to me."

He gave a quick nod. "I'd hoped to take you out for lunch again, but I guess I got here too late."

"Yes, I'm almost done and will be back working behind the front desk again soon." She moved a little closer to him. "I'd offer to share my lunch with you, but I only brought half a sandwich today and it's nearly gone."

"That's okay. I'll pick up something to eat after I leave here." Brad's voice lowered when he saw Mrs. Roberts looking at him. No doubt she was listening in on their conversation.

He jammed his hands into his jacket pockets, feeling nervous and nearly tongue-tied all of a sudden. "Have you, uh, made any special plans for New Year's Eve?"

"No, I haven't. I'll probably spend the evening with my grandparents, and if they are too tired to stay up till midnight, I'll most likely go to bed too."

"What about Michelle? Won't she be there?"

Sara shook her head. "I heard her mention to Grandma that she will be doing something with Ezekiel that evening. I believe they'll be getting together with some of his friends. Come to think of it, Michelle said their get-together would be at his cousin Raymond's house."

"Do you think your grandparents would mind if I stole you away for at least part of New Year's Eve?" he asked. "There's going to be a Christian concert in Lancaster that evening, and I thought it would be fun to go."

She dropped her gaze to the floor, and then looked up at him again. "It sounds interesting, but let me check with Grandma and Grandpa first and see if they would mind if I go."

"Okay, sure. You have my number, so give me a call and let me know as soon as you've talked to them."

"I will." Sara cheeks turned slightly pink. "Guess I'd better go back and finish the little bit that's left of my lunch. Thanks for coming in, Brad. I'll talk to you soon."

When Sara disappeared into the back room, Brad stepped up to the counter. His stomach growled while he picked a nicely colored bouquet for his aunt. "This should brighten up her day."

After he wrote a message for the card to accompany the flowers being sent, Brad checked his phone where all his addresses were stored. "And here is the address I'd like them to be sent to. My aunt lives in Seattle, Washington, so I hope it won't be a problem."

"No, we are an FTD florist, so we can schedule a delivery anywhere in the United States. Is there any particular day you want these to arrive?" Mrs. Roberts asked.

"As soon as you can send them would be nice." Brad clutched his stomach when it growled loudly again.

"Sounds like you'd better eat some lunch." She grinned.

"Yep, that's where I'm heading next."

Brad paid for the purchase. "Okay. Well, thanks for taking care of that."

"Thank you for shopping here. Have a nice day."

Walking out the door, Brad's thoughts went to Sara again. He hoped the Lapps wouldn't object to her going to the concert with him, because he looked forward to being with her again, on a real date.

Sara couldn't believe she was actually considering going to a Christian concert with Brad. *I'm not a religious person,* she told herself as she finished her lunch. *I may not even enjoy the music.* Sara drank the last of her bottled water. *But I would like to spend New Year's Eve with Brad.*

It made no sense that she'd be attracted to a man of God — preparing to go into the ministry, no less. She stared at her empty bottle. *Brad's not my type. We have nothing in common, really. Then why do I feel so drawn to him? Does Brad feel it too? Is that why he seems to be interested in me?*

It wasn't Brad's good looks that drew her to him either. It was his soft-spoken, gentle, caring way. He clearly was concerned about people and their problems. Everything about him seemed genuine. He was the real deal, not fake or trying to be impressive.

255

She still hadn't told him things were better between her and Michelle or why. *Maybe if we go out on New Year's Eve I'll bring up the subject.*

Sara gathered up her things and looked at her watch. It was time to relieve Karen so she could take her lunch break. So for now, Sara would put all thoughts of Brad Fuller out of her mind and concentrate on greeting customers and placing orders. After she picked Michelle up at Dienners later this afternoon, Sara would stop by the grocery store and get something for tonight's supper. She had told Grandma this morning during breakfast that she'd cook this evening's meal. Unfortunately, Sara had no idea what to fix. Maybe Michelle would have some idea. After all, she knew Sara's grandparents better than she did, since she'd lived with them longer.

Ronks

Michelle glanced at the clock. Just another thirty minutes and her shift would be done for the day. The lunch crowd had dispersed a few hours ago, and only a few customers had come in since then. But that was normal for this time of the day. In another hour, people would be coming in for supper, but Michelle would be gone by then. It was another chilly day, with fresh snow on the ground, so she would wait inside until closer to when Sara picked her up a little after four thirty.

An elderly Amish couple had just come in and been seated, so she went to take their orders. Michelle had noticed as they'd walked to the table that the woman used a cane, while the man supported her as she held onto his arm.

"If you have any questions about the items we serve, let me know." Michelle handed each of them a menu.

Since Michelle wore Amish clothes, they must have assumed she could speak their language, for they responded to her in Pennsylvania Dutch.

A warm tingle swept up the back of Michelle's neck, and then across her face. "Sorry, but I only know a few Amish words," she explained.

The woman tipped her head back, looking curiously at Michelle through her thick-lensed glasses. "Aren't you Amish?"

"N–no, not yet." Michelle tried not to stutter. "I want to become Amish though, and I'm taking classes to join the church."

The woman blinked rapidly. "Seriously?"

Michelle gave a brief nod.

"So you didn't grow up in an Amish home?"

"No."

"Then why would you want to join the Plain faith?" For the first time, the man spoke as he squinted his gray-blue eyes at Michelle.

With the way the couple looked at her, Michelle felt like she'd said something wrong. *Are they just curious or don't they approve of an English person becoming Amish?* Michelle hoped they didn't question her much longer. Was it really that unusual for an English person to want to become a member of the Amish church?

She pulled her shoulders straight back and lifted her chin. "I don't need modern things to make me happy, and I appreciate the simple lifestyle of the Amish people."

"Leaving your progressive world behind and becoming one of us Plain folks will be difficult." The man's gnarly fingers shook as he pointed at Michelle. "Very few people have done it, because it's not an easy road unless you are born into it and raised without modern-day conveniences."

"I understand." Hoping they wouldn't ask more questions, she gestured to their menus. "Would you like to choose something from there, or do you prefer to serve yourselves from the buffet? I believe the dinner items have recently been set out."

"We'll choose from the items on the buffet." The Amish man looked at his wife. "Right, Vera?"

She gave a brief nod.

"What would you both like to drink?" Michelle wondered how the woman would manage the buffet while holding a cane. She wasn't about to challenge this feisty couple, and thought they probably had things figured out on how to fill their plates.

"Water is fine for me," Vera replied.

"Same here," her husband said. "Oh, and I'd also like a cup of coffee. What about you, Vera. Do you want some *kaffi?*"

"No, just water this time." When she shook her head, the ties on her head covering swished back and forth.

"Okay then. While I get your drinks, feel free to go to the buffet." Michelle was about to walk away when the man spoke again.

"You don't have to join the Amish church to simplify. You can put some of our principles into practice and still remain English."

"Yeah, I know." Michelle wished this topic hadn't been brought up again. It felt as if the man thought her decision to become Amish was wrong. Was he hoping to talk her out of it? And if so, for what reason?

Michelle didn't even know these people. She couldn't imagine why they would care whether she joined the Amish church or not.

Michelle pressed the order pad against her chest as she felt another uncontrollable rush of heat. "Will there be anything else?"

The man opened his mouth, as if to say something, but his wife spoke first. "No, that will be all. Thank you."

With relief, Michelle hurried away. *Will other Amish people react to me like that couple did?* she wondered. *Am I foolish to believe I can become one of them and that I'll be accepted? Maybe I haven't thought things through clearly enough. It might be good if I talk to Mary Ruth or Willis about this.* While they hadn't said anything to discourage her, the Lapps might believe Michelle was making a mistake taking steps to become Amish.

CHAPTER 23

Strasburg

"Are you sleeping?" Mary Ruth stood near her husband's chair and nudged his arm.

He opened one eye and grinned at her. "Nope. Just restin' my eyes."

"If your eyes need resting, maybe the rest of you does too. Should we call it a night and head for *bett*?"

He yawned and put his recliner in an upright position. "Can't go to bed yet, Mary Ruth."

"Why not?"

"Cause we haven't had any of those apple dumplings you made earlier this evening." He winked at her. "It wouldn't seem right to break tradition and not eat an apple dumpling on New Year's Eve."

Chuckling, she swatted his arm playfully. "Very well then. Shall we go to the kitchen, or would you rather I bring them out here?"

"Let's eat 'em in here. I'll stoke up the

logs in the fireplace and we can sit on the sofa together while we enjoy our sweet treats." Willis winked a second time. "It'll be just like the old days when you and I were courting."

Mary Ruth smiled, remembering their first New Year's Eve as a young couple. She had invited Willis to her house for supper and to play board games with her family. About an hour before midnight, her parents said they were tired and went off to bed. Her siblings, Alma, Thomas, and Paul, all married and a few years older than her, had already gone home, which left Mary Ruth and Willis alone to greet the New Year. Since Mary Ruth had made apple dumplings earlier that day, she brought some out to serve her special beau. Willis ate two, and said she was a fine cook, and then he added that after they were married, eating apple dumplings should be a New Year's tradition. Mary Ruth wasn't sure if he was kidding or not, but every year since then she had made apple dumplings to serve on New Year's Eve.

Pushing her reflections to the back of her mind, Mary Ruth went to the kitchen. When she returned a short time later with their treat, she was pleased to see Willis had a nice fire going. The warmth of it permeated all of the living room and offered additional light as well.

"Here you go, Willis." She placed the tray of apple dumplings on the coffee table, along with two mugs of hot cider.

"Danki." He took a seat on the couch and patted the cushion beside him. "Sit here beside me and we can eat together as we enjoy the fire."

Mary Ruth willingly obliged, then handed him a bowl with one of the dumplings and a spoon. "Seems kind of quiet here this evening without Sara and Michelle."

Just then, the hefty log in the fireplace popped loudly in the roaring blaze, sending sparks up the chimney. "Well it *was* quiet, that is. Guess I spoke too soon." Mary Ruth giggled. "Don't you just love the sound of a crackling fire and the smell of logs burning?"

"Sure do." Willis nodded. "I'm enjoyin' our time alone together too. And no doubt the girls are having a good time tonight with friends their age, rather than hangin' around us old folks."

"Jah, it is good for them to do some fun things with others." Mary Ruth reached for her mug, blew on the hot cider, and took a cautious sip. "Now that they both have jobs, I hope neither of them decides to move out." She heaved a deep sigh. "It would be so lonely here without them."

"I'm sure if they do move out, they will stay in the area. They both seem happier here now."

"I think so too." She set her mug back on the coffee table and turned to face Willis. "Even though Michelle isn't really our *grossdochder,* I feel like she's part of our family."

"I agree." Willis picked up his mug of apple cider. "I hope once Michelle finishes her instruction classes, she'll feel ready to join the church and won't have any doubts."

"Michelle talked with me last evening about an incident she had at the restaurant on Friday. She was upset because of it."

"What happened?" Willis asked.

"Michelle waited on an Amish couple, and when they started speaking Pennsylvania Dutch to her, she couldn't understand what they had said. With the clothes Michelle was wearing, the couple must have assumed she was Amish."

"Ah, I see. Bet it was kinda awkward for her."

"Jah. And after Michelle explained that she was learning to be Amish, they started questioning her decision, and she had the impression they were trying to talk her out of it." Mary Ruth paused for a breath. "It sounded like Michelle handled it well, but I could tell it rattled her a bit."

"She will be tested in many ways, but if Michelle truly wants this, her strength won't let those uncertainties get in the way." Willis gave his earlobe a tug — a habit he'd had since she'd known him. "And after hearing how she conducted herself, I am confident that she'll be okay. Michelle's a strong girl."

"I want to remain optimistic too." Mary Ruth sighed once more. "And what about Sara? Do you think she'll ever want to become Amish?"

He shrugged. "I'm guessing not, but that will be her decision."

Mary Ruth didn't voice her thoughts, but secretly she hoped their English granddaughter might also choose to join the Amish church. While it wouldn't make up for losing their one and only daughter to the English world, it would certainly be a comfort to have Sara become part of their church.

Michelle had never been too interested in card games, but Dutch Blitz, the one she was playing now with Ezekiel, his cousin Raymond, and Raymond's girlfriend, Anna, held her interest. It had taken her a while to catch on, but once she did, the game became fun. While some English folks might not agree, Michelle thought game playing, and even just talking, was more enjoyable than watching TV. Sometimes, like now, she felt as though she were meant to be Amish. Other times, such as when she attended Amish church and couldn't understand everything being said, Michelle wondered if she would ever truly fit in with the Plain people.

If trying to learn everything wasn't challenging enough, the incident at the restaurant the other day had increased her reservations. Even with all the Amish couple's negative comments, Michelle thought she'd handled their questioning pretty well. Talking about it with Mary Ruth last night had eased some of her tension. At least for tonight she was being accepted, and all the laughter, fun, and games helped her relax. At moments like this, with Ezekiel by her side, Michelle felt as if things were finally looking up. Even Raymond's parents, before heading to bed, had joined their conversation and included Michelle in all that had been said. It was too bad Ezekiel's mom and dad hadn't accepted her so easily. She wondered if she would ever win them over.

"Anyone care for more potato chips and

onion dip?" Raymond asked, pulling Michelle out of her ruminations. "Mom said there's more in the kitchen."

Anna shook her head. "I've snacked way too much this evening. Don't think I could eat another bite."

"And I'm fine with the bowl of pretzels still here on the table." Ezekiel looked at Michelle. "How about you?"

"I'm with Anna." Michelle put one hand beneath her chin. "I'm full up to here."

Ezekiel snickered, then reached under the table and clasped her other hand. "I think my aldi likes to *iwwerdreiwe.*"

Michelle felt a tightening in her chest. *Here we go again . . . another Amish word I don't understand.* "I know *aldi* means 'girlfriend,' but what does *iwwerdreiwe* mean?" she asked.

"It's the Pennsylvania Dutch word for exaggerate," Ezekiel explained.

Exasperated, she let go of his hand. "I was not exaggerating. I really am too full to eat anything else."

"But you said you were full up to here." He touched a spot just below her chin.

She gave a huff. "Okay, so I embellished it a bit."

Anna's pale blue eyes twinkled as she smiled at Michelle from across the table.

"And in the process, you learned a new Pennsylvania Dutch word."

Michelle bobbed her head. "True. Sometimes I wonder though if I'll ever be able to carry on a full conversation in your language."

"Aw, sure you will. It'll just take time and practice." Raymond picked up the deck of cards. "Is everyone ready for another game? If we get started now, we'll likely be done before the clock strikes midnight and we ring in the New Year."

"Sure, let's get to it." Ezekiel gave Michelle's arm a gentle nudge and said in a low voice, "I can't think of anyone I'd rather ring in the New Year with than you."

Michelle's cheeks warmed as she whispered back, "Same here."

Lancaster

"What did you think of the concert?" Brad asked when he and Sara got into his minivan.

Sara's fingers twisted around the straps of her purse. "It was different than I thought it would be."

He tipped his head. "In what way?"

"When you said Christian concert, I expected to hear a lot of church hymns and such."

268

Brad smiled, slowly shaking his head. "It was a contemporary Christian concert, with a variety of musicians." He touched his chest. "And I, for one, enjoyed every group that performed tonight."

"Yeah, it was good." Sara didn't want him to think she wasn't interested in his kind of music or that she had no specific religious inclinations. She enjoyed Brad's company and hoped she could see him again the next time he visited Lancaster County.

Offering him what she hoped was a pleasant smile, she said, "I enjoyed being with you tonight. Thanks for inviting me to spend New Year's Eve with you."

"You're welcome. I enjoyed being with you too." He started the engine. "Are you hungry? Should we go somewhere for a bite to eat?"

"Would any place be open this late?"

"Oh, I'm sure since it's New Year's Eve some of the restaurants will be open till after midnight."

"I'm okay with that, but if you'd rather, we could just go back to my grandparents' house and have something to eat there." Sara giggled. "If I know Grandma, she probably made something yummy for her and Grandpa to eat this evening. And no doubt, she made plenty to go around."

"Okay, let's go there then. It'll be quieter and easier to visit." Brad pulled his vehicle out of the parking lot.

"Maybe by now Ezekiel has brought Michelle home. They might want to join us in the kitchen for a midnight snack."

"Yeah, that'd be fine too."

"Speaking of Michelle" — Sara looked over at Brad — "the two of us are getting along much better now."

"Well, that's good to hear." Brad sounded relieved. Sara sensed he'd been worried about her strained relationship with Michelle.

"After Michelle revealed some things about her life, I have a better understanding of her." Sara heaved a sigh. "And you will be happy to know that I have gotten over the fact that Michelle pretended to be me. I can't change what happened, and neither can she, so we may as well try to get along."

Brad reached over and squeezed Sara's hand. "I am glad to hear it."

"There's something else." Sara's gaze lowered as she explained about killing Michelle's dog. "Michelle forgave me for that too."

"I'm sure she knew you didn't do it on purpose."

"Yes, but I think she may have wondered

at first."

"Thanks for sharing this with me, Sara." Brad turned the radio to a station playing Christian music. "The burden of what you were both feeling should be lifted now."

Sara nodded. "It is." *But I am carrying some other burdens I haven't told you about.*

As they headed back to Strasburg, Sara leaned her head against the passenger's headrest. The roads were bare and wet, but as they left the outskirts of Lancaster, snow flurries began. At first they came down lightly, but by the time they reached Strasburg, the wind had picked up and thick snowflakes came in flurries. It looked like the beginning of a blizzard.

"Maybe you should just drop me off and head back to your friend's place in Lancaster," Sara said as they turned onto her grandparents' driveway, now covered in snow. "I wouldn't want you to get stuck or slide off the road in this unpredictable weather."

"Not to worry. I'm sure it'll be fine. The last time I listened to the weather report, nothing was mentioned about a storm," Brad said. "Besides, I had snow tires put on the van before I came down here for Christmas break. But if it makes you feel any better, I'll leave right after midnight, when the

New Year begins."

Sara smiled and touched his arm. "Okay, Brad. Now let's go inside."

CHAPTER 24

Strasburg

"It looks like my grandparents must have gone to bed," Sara said when she and Brad entered the dimly lit house. She was thankful a battery-operated light had been left on in the living room.

"Maybe I should go," Brad responded. "I wouldn't want to wake them."

"It's okay. Their bedroom is near the end of the hall, and if we go out to the kitchen our voices are less likely to be heard."

"Sure, no problem." Brad followed Sara to the kitchen. She noticed the gas lamp hanging from the ceiling had been lit as well, giving plenty of light for them to see.

"Oh, yum. Look what Grandma left for us." Sara hung her coat on a wall peg before pointing to a tray of apple dumplings on the counter. She picked up the note lying beside them and read it to Brad. "Sara and Michelle, please help yourselves to these apple dumplings and feel free to share them with your dates." She looked at Brad. "Would you like one with a glass of milk or maybe some hot apple cider? It won't take long to heat it on the stove."

"Hot cider sounds good. And if those dumplings taste half as scrumptious as they look, I may have to eat two." Brad gave her a dimpled grin and draped his jacket over the back of a kitchen chair. "That is, if there's enough for me to have seconds."

She poked his arm playfully. "There are eight of the tasty morsels here, so if you're still hungry after eating one, I think a second helping can be arranged."

Brad formed a steeple with his hands and pressed them to his lips. "Thank you, ma'am."

Sara's heart skipped a beat as she gazed at his smiling face. His eyes appeared to be filled with an inner glow — almost as though it came from deep within his soul. Sara hadn't known Brad very long, but as near as she could tell, there wasn't a phony bone in this man's body. Too bad he was going back to his ministerial studies tomorrow. Sara wished she had the opportunity to spend more time with Brad so she could get to know him better. Being around him made her feel more relaxed than she had in a long time. Of course, her grandparents had that effect on her too, just not in the same way.

Pulling her thoughts aside, Sara took out two bowls for the apple dumplings and told Brad to help himself. As he was doing that, she got out the apple cider and poured enough for two cups into a kettle. While it heated, she put spoons and napkins on the table, and then suggested they both take a seat.

While Sara and Brad waited for the cider to heat, they ate the apple dumplings and visited.

"Yep, this is every bit as good as I thought it would be." Brad smacked his lips. "And I'm 100 percent sure I'll want another." He glanced at the stove. "Gotta have a dumpling to go with the cider, right?"

She snickered. "Yes, of course, and I'm not surprised you would want more than one apple dumpling."

When the cider was warm enough, Sara poured the golden liquid into their mugs. "Here you go, Brad." She placed his on the table in front of him, picked up Brad's bowl, and dished up another apple dumpling.

"Aren't you gonna have seconds?" He looked at her expectantly.

"One's plenty for me." Holding her cider,

Sara took the seat across from him and took a cautious sip. "When do you think you might come down this way again?"

"Maybe some weekend, if the weather co-operates." He blew on his cider and took a drink. "Wow, this is as good as the dumplings. Is it homemade?"

"Yes. My grandpa has an old-fashioned cider press. I wasn't here to watch him make this batch of apple cider, but he told me about it."

"Maybe next year you'll get in on it."

"I hope so. Even if I have my own place by then, it'll be somewhere in the area." Sara drank more of the cider. "After all the years I went without knowing I had maternal grandparents, I am determined to stay close to them so we can spend as much time together as possible."

Brad nodded slowly. "That's understandable."

"What about you? Where do you see yourself living once you finish your ministerial training?"

He shrugged his shoulders. "That all depends on where the Lord sends me."

"What do you mean?" She set her mug down.

"I will put my name in with the denomination I belong to. When a position opens, and I'm called for an interview, I'll do a lot of praying, because when I take a church, I may need to relocate to a different state."

Sara leaned her elbows on the table. "How would your family feel about that?"

"Mom and Dad probably wouldn't like it, especially since I am their only child. But they understand my need to answer God's call, so no doubt they'd give me their blessing."

She looked down at her empty bowl. "It must be nice to have parents who are so accepting."

"Yeah, it's great. Mom and Dad have a strong faith in God, which makes it easier for them to agree with my decision to become a minister." Brad's forehead wrinkled a bit. "Dad wasn't on board with it at first though. He's a chiropractor and wanted me to follow in his footsteps."

"I guess that's not uncommon. My stepfather has already made it clear that he wants my brother, Kenny, to learn the plumbing trade when he graduates from high school this coming spring."

"Is your brother all right with that?" Brad asked, taking a spoonful of dumpling.

"I guess so. I haven't heard anything to the contrary."

"Well, some kids do end up taking after

their dads, but I'm not one of them." Brad gestured with his hand, and pointed above. "Gotta do what the Lord tells me to do and go wherever He leads."

Sara heard the whinny of a horse outside. She jumped up from the table. "I bet that's Ezekiel bringing Michelle home."

"Are you sure you still want to come in for a while?" Michelle turned on the buggy seat to face Ezekiel, even though it was dark and she couldn't fully see his face. "The snow's coming down harder, and it could get worse before you leave for home."

"I'm not worried. Big Red does fine in the snow. He could probably take me there even if I wasn't guiding him with the reins." Ezekiel spoke with an air of confidence. "He's even gotten used to all the places I've taken him to deliver honey to my regular customers."

"Okay then, I'll fix us something to eat and drink. I see smoke coming out of the chimney, so how 'bout we sit by the fire to ring in the New Year?"

"Sounds pretty cozy."

Michelle opened the door on her side of the buggy. "I'll secure your horse to the hitching rail." Before Ezekiel could comment, she hopped down. Of course, her feet sank into the snow, sending a chill all the way up her legs. "Brr . . . it's so cold." She hurried to get Big Red tied to the rail, then made her way to the house.

Ezekiel stepped onto the porch behind her. "You didn't have to take care of my *gaul.* I would have done it, Michelle."

"No problem. I wanted to help." She gestured to the van parked near the house. "That must be Brad's, but it looks like he left his lights on. They're barely glowing. I wonder what time the concert got out, and how long he's been here."

"I better go turn them off, or he'll end up with a dead battery." Ezekiel pulled his jacket collar tighter around his neck.

"Okay, I'll wait for you here on the porch." Michelle blew out a breath and watched the cold vapor vanish into the blustery air. Jumping up and down didn't help. Her toes were beyond warming.

When he returned, Ezekiel stamped his feet on the mat by the door. "I couldn't turn off the lights. The van door is locked."

"Let's go inside and let Brad know. Maybe he can still start it up."

"Yeah, let's hope." Ezekiel gave his belly a thump. "If there's anything good to eat, I hope Brad and Sara left some for us."

Michelle bumped his arm with her elbow.

"You would think something like that." She opened the door, and they both stepped into the house. "There's a light coming from the kitchen, so they must be in there."

Ezekiel pushed open the door, and Michelle stepped in first. Sure enough, Sara and Brad sat at the table. "Whatcha up to?" she asked.

Sara looked over her shoulder. "We're enjoying some of my grandma's yummy apple dumplings. Why don't you grab bowls and join us?"

"There's cider in the refrigerator that you can warm on the stove too," Brad interjected. "And boy, is it ever good."

"Before I delve into those dumplings, I wanted you to know that your van lights are on, Brad." Ezekiel pointed toward the kitchen window. "They look pretty dim. I was gonna turn 'em off, but the doors are locked."

"Oh, great." Brad thumped his head. "Thought I'd shut those off. The last thing I need is a dead battery." He leaped out of his chair and, without bothering to put on his jacket, raced out the back door.

While Michelle dished up dumplings for her and Ezekiel, he heated the cider and poured some into mugs. Then they both sat at the table.

"How was your evening?"

"How was the concert?"

Michelle giggled when she and Sara spoke at the same time. "Our evening was good." Michelle looked over at Ezekiel. "I learned how to play a new card game I'd never heard of before."

"Glad to hear it. The concert was nice too." Sara glanced at the door, as though watching for Brad.

"I noticed smoke coming from the chimney when Ezekiel and I rode in. Maybe once Brad comes inside, we can go to the living room and sit by the fire."

"Sounds like a good idea. Brad will need to warm up, since he left his coat hanging on the chair." Sara pointed, then she looked back at Michelle. "It was snowing pretty hard when we got here. How are things now?"

"Still snowing and blowing. Looks like it's turning into a blizzard," Ezekiel responded.

A few minutes later Brad returned, hair covered in snow and wearing a disgruntled expression. "My car won't start. Think the battery must've been weak, 'cause it's definitely dead." He went over to the sink and brushed the snow off his head. "On top of that, the snow's coming down so hard there's hardly any visibility. Since there's probably no place to get a new battery at this hour, guess I'll have to call a tow truck to come get the van. After it's towed, I'll give my friend Ned a call and see if he can give me a ride back to his apartment."

"I have a better idea," Michelle spoke up. "Why don't you and Ezekiel spend the night here? That way Sara and I won't have to worry about either of you."

Ezekiel shook his head. "I'm sure I can make it home fine with my horse and buggy."

"It might be a good idea if you did stay the night." Sara touched Brad's arm. "Since it's New Year's Eve and snowing like crazy, it might even be hard to get a tow truck to come out here." She gestured toward the living room. "One of you can sleep on the couch, and the other can take the downstairs guest room. I'm sure if Grandma and Grandpa were awake, they'd say the same thing."

Michelle bobbed her head. "Sara's right. By morning, the weather will hopefully have improved and at least the main roads been cleared. Then Ezekiel can go home, and Brad, you can call a tow truck, or maybe your friend could bring you a new battery."

Ezekiel rubbed his chin. "I don't know. I'd have to call my folks and leave a message so when they check their answering machine in the morning they'd know where I was and wouldn't worry. Oh, and I'd also need to put Big Red in the barn. Sure can't leave him hitched to the rail all night with the snow comin' down so hard, not to mention no food or water for the poor animal."

"You can borrow my cell phone to make the call. Then I'll help you take care of your horse." Brad reached into his shirt pocket and pulled out his phone. He looked over at Sara and smiled. "Guess we'll take you up on the offer to spend the night. If I can't get a new battery right away or the roads present a problem, I may have to rethink how I'll get back to school tomorrow. Hopefully, everything will look better in the morning."

CHAPTER 25

Mary Ruth yawned as she padded down the hall toward the kitchen to get some coffee going and start breakfast. A few minutes ago, when she looked out their bedroom window, she noticed several inches of snow now blanketed the ground.

Approaching the living-room archway, Mary Ruth stopped short when she heard a sound she'd come to know well over the years. Someone was snoring, and it wasn't Willis. She'd seen her husband go into the bathroom a few seconds ago, so the heavy breathing, coupled with snoring, couldn't be coming from him. Perhaps because of the snow, Michelle had brought Sadie inside, instead of leaving her in the barn where she usually stayed.

Mary Ruth pursed her lips. *Could the dog be making all those familiar sounds?* Sadie had been known to snore as loud as any human being. Many afternoons when relaxing on the porch, Willis and Sadie would both end up napping. At times, Mary Ruth couldn't distinguish her husband's snoring from the dog's.

Poking her head into the room, she was surprised to see it wasn't Sadie cutting z's at all. Ezekiel King, fully clothed except for his shoes, was spread out on the couch with a blanket draped over him. He'd obviously spent the night.

But why? Mary Ruth tapped a fist against her lips. *When Ezekiel brought Michelle back from the gathering at Raymond's last night, had he been too tired to go home? Or had the roads gotten so bad from the snow that he decided to stay here instead?*

Knowing she would find out soon enough, Mary Ruth tiptoed out of the room and went straight to the kitchen. After lighting a gas lamp and lifting the window shade, she watched as a current of wind blew swirls of snow through the yard, swishing up and momentarily blinding the wintery scene. Her eyebrows lifted. *I wonder if this weather is the reason Ezekiel spent the night.* Looking farther out on the yard, she saw Ezekiel's carriage covered with snow. Not far from it, Brad's van was parked, also blanketed in snow. *Did he spend the night here too? If so, where is he now?*

Mary Ruth didn't have to wait long for an answer, for a few minutes later, Sara entered the kitchen. "I'm glad you're up. We had some overnight guests you weren't expecting," she announced.

Mary Ruth bobbed her head up and down. "I saw Ezekiel sleeping on the couch, and since Brad's van is parked outside, I assumed he must be here too."

Nodding, Sara pushed a lock of hair away from her face. "When he brought me home last night, I invited him in for a snack."

"I see." Mary Ruth leaned against the counter, waiting for Sara to continue.

"Then when Ezekiel and Michelle showed up, Ezekiel informed Brad that his van lights were still on but quite dim. So Brad rushed outside and discovered his battery was dead." Sara paused and cleared her throat. "Since it was late and snow had started coming down hard, we invited the guys to spend the night. Ezekiel took the living-room couch, and Brad is in the downstairs guest room. I hope you don't mind."

"Course not." Mary Ruth shook her head. "Staying the night was the sensible thing to do."

Sara's lips parted in a slow smile. No doubt she felt relief.

Mary Ruth filled the coffeepot with water.

"Let's get some breakfast going. I imagine most anytime now, everyone will file into the kitchen, eager to eat."

Sara was about to go knock on the guest room door, when Brad stepped into the kitchen. Everyone else waited at the table. "Sorry for holding up breakfast." He reached up, pinching the bridge of his nose. "I was on the phone with my buddy Ned. He's going to pick up a battery for my van at the Walmart in Lancaster and bring it out to me. Then, once I get my rig running, we'll go to his place so I can pack up my things before heading back to the university."

"Are you sure the roads are clear enough to drive on this morning?" Sara's grandpa asked. "Looks like we had a pretty good snowfall last night. You might hit ice or snow all the way up to Clarks Summit."

"I agree." Sara's chin jutted out. "It could be dangerous. Maybe you should stay another day."

Brad peered out the kitchen window. "My tires are good. I should be fine." He scrubbed a hand over his face as he looked over at Sara. "If I didn't have to go back to class tomorrow, I'd stay longer, but I can't afford to get behind in my studies."

She slowly nodded. "You will call and let us know when you get there, I hope."

"Of course. I'd planned to do that anyway."

She smiled and gestured to the empty chair next to Ezekiel. "My grandma outdid herself fixing breakfast this morning. Please, join us."

"Now, Sara," Grandma said, "I can't take all the credit for this meal. You and Michelle made part of it." She pointed to the platter of ham and eggs.

"Everything looks delicious, so thank you ladies, one and all." Brad gave a thumbs-up and took a seat.

When Grandpa lowered his head for prayer, everyone else did the same. Sara wondered what her grandparents would think if they knew she only sat with her eyes closed out of respect, but never offered a single word in prayer. What was the point? If God was real, He wouldn't care about anything she had to say.

Soon after Brad left, Michelle stood on the porch, watching Ezekiel hitch his horse to the buggy. She hoped he wouldn't be in trouble with his parents for staying out all night. Had they received his message? Would they blame her for him not coming home last night?

It wasn't my fault, she reminded herself. *It was the blizzardlike conditions that made Ezekiel decide to stay overnight.*

Michelle waved as Ezekiel got into his buggy and headed out of the yard. With head held high, Big Red snorted and plodded through the snow as though it was nothing. Truth be told, Ezekiel probably could have made it home last night. But Michelle was glad he'd stayed. In addition to spending a few more hours with Ezekiel, she didn't have to worry about him being out on the road in bad conditions — not to mention dealing with any drivers who might have had too much alcohol to drink as they celebrated the New Year.

A chill ran through her body as she reflected on one particular New Year's Eve, when she was ten years old. Her parents had gone out for the evening, leaving her alone to care for her brothers. Michelle hadn't minded so much, since it allowed her and the boys a few hours of peace, without the threat that one of their parents might blow up at them. What she didn't like, and still remembered, was when Mom and Dad arrived home. He was in a drunken stupor, and she wasn't much better. They were both out of sorts, shouting all kinds of obscenities at each other, and ready to take their anger out on Michelle. Fortunately, Ernie and Jack were in bed, or they might have suffered the physical abuse Michelle had gotten later that night.

Her hand went instinctively to the middle of her back, where many welts had remained for several days after Dad used a thick, heavy strap on her. As far as Michelle could tell, she had done nothing to deserve such severe punishment. Her only crime was when she'd suggested Dad and Mom go to bed.

"Don't be tellin' me what to do, sister. You ain't the boss around here," he'd hollered with slurred words. While Dad went to get the oversized strip of leather, Mom shuffled off to bed. It was obvious she couldn't have cared less about her children's welfare.

The back door opened, causing Michelle to jump. She turned and saw Mary Ruth looking at her.

"What's wrong?" the woman asked, gently touching Michelle's arm. "Have you been crying?"

Michelle sniffed and swiped at the tears she hadn't realized were on her cheeks until now. "It–it's nothing," she murmured, rubbing her arms. "I'm just cold, is all."

"You should have put on more than a

sweater to come out here." As usual, Mary Ruth's voice was soothing.

Silently, Michelle followed Mary Ruth inside. She wished she could shut the door on her memories as easily as she closed the door on the winter's cold. Would things from her past always be there to haunt her? If Michelle could erase all the painful recollections, she surely would. Truth was, maybe she still hadn't forgiven her folks.

Ezekiel looked at the snowy scene around him, as Big Red trotted down the newly plowed road. It was New Year's Day, and traffic was low, but it was hard to enjoy the quiet beauty with the thoughts of what might be awaiting him once he got home.

He hadn't expected anyone to answer when he called his parents last night, but no doubt by now, they would have gone to the phone shed and listened to his message. Would they understand his reason for staying at the Lapps'? Ezekiel figured they wouldn't be satisfied until they heard the whole story, especially Mom. Instead of rehearsing what he would tell his folks, Ezekiel leaned back, letting his horse continue to lead.

Sure wish Michelle was sitting here beside me right now. Ezekiel looked over at the empty seat next to him, where she sat on the way to and from his cousin's last night. Glancing out at the snow-covered hills, Ezekiel tried to redirect his thoughts by absorbing the untouched splendor. Before it was shoveled or plowed, the fresh fallen snow was pristine, hiding imperfections under a blanket of white. *Sorta like our sins when we accept Christ into our life,* he acknowledged. *But the Lord doesn't just cover our sins — He removes them.*

A short time later, Ezekiel guided his horse up the driveway. With no encouragement, Big Red trotted right up to the hitching rail. Once in the barn, after attending to the gelding and making sure he had plenty of feed, Ezekiel headed for the house.

After stomping his shoes on the rug by the door, he walked into the kitchen. The smell of maple syrup still lingered from breakfast. *I bet Mom fixed pancakes this morning.*

"*Guder mariye,* Ezekiel. It's nice of you to finally come home." His mother's remark startled him. Then her tone changed to concern. "You had me worried to death. Where were you all night, Son?"

"Mornin', Mom." Ezekiel took off his jacket and hung it on the peg, then balanced his hat on top of that. Running his fingers through his slightly damp hair, he sat down at the table. "I left a message on the answering machine explaining that I was staying at the Lapps'."

His mother's eyes opened wider and she gave a little gasp. "For goodness' sake."

Ezekiel figured Mom wouldn't take it very well, so he continued to explain. "When I took Michelle home, she invited me in. It wasn't midnight yet, and we wanted to see the New Year come in together." Ezekiel paused to take a quick breath. "Brad's van was there, and he'd left his lights on."

"What does that have to do with anything?" Her eyes narrowed.

"Nothing really, except his battery was dead, and because of the weather turning worse, we figured the chances were slim for him getting a tow truck to come." The next part, Ezekiel knew, would be difficult. "To make a long story short, Michelle suggested Brad and I spend the night and wait till the roads cleared this morning. Sara agreed. Neither of 'em wanted to worry about us being out on the unplowed roads."

"Oh, so you caused us to worry instead." Mom gave the top of her apron a tug, as though it was the source of her discomfort.

"So I'm guessing you didn't get my message?"

She shook her head. "Were the Lapps in agreement to you staying there overnight?"

"They were already in bed when we got there." Ezekiel watched his mother's muscles tense. *Why is she making such a big deal of this?*

Mom stood with her hands on her hips. "Do you have any idea how much I fretted? I got no sleep waiting for you to come home last night." She went to the stove and poured herself a cup of coffee but didn't offer any to Ezekiel. "I'm sure you didn't have one bit of trouble sleeping." She turned to face him. "And just where did you sleep, Ezekiel?"

"Mom, I have no idea what you are insinuating." Ezekiel felt a headache coming on as his frustration built. "But if it makes you feel any better, I slept on the Lapps' couch in the living room, and Brad took the guest room down the hall. Willis and Mary Ruth were in their bedroom, and the girls were upstairs in their rooms."

"Well, I don't think it was —" Mom looked toward the kitchen door as Ezekiel's dad came in from outside.

"Oh, there you are, Son. Glad to see you made it home okay." He hung his hat and jacket on an empty peg next to Ezekiel's.

"Do you know where our son has been all night?"

"Why yes, Belinda. I just came from the phone shed, checking messages, and I learned where Ezekiel was last night. I heard him and Big Red go past the shed when I was listening to his message too. Why do you ask?"

"Why?" Mom's eyebrows lifted. "And you're okay with him staying all night at the Lapps'?"

"Jah. Our son is home, and he's safe and sound." Dad gestured to Ezekiel. "It was a good decision, with the way the weather turned last night."

"Danki, Dad." Ezekiel got up from the table and gave his father's shoulder a couple of thumps. In times past, both Dad and Mom had been hard on him — especially where Michelle was concerned. It was nice to have Dad stick up for him this morning. "Think I'll go check on the beehives to make sure they're still in an upright position."

Looking down at the floor, Mom cleared her throat. "Would you like me to fix you some breakfast, Son?"

"No, thanks. I already ate." Ezekiel grabbed his boots and put them on. After slipping on his jacket and hat, he headed out the door.

Ezekiel had always respected his parents, but Mom was going a bit overboard this morning. *I would think by now she'd trust my decisions. After all, I am an adult.* He inhaled the cold crisp air, which helped to clear his head. *I realize Mom is just concerned, but is this how it will always be with her — never having anything nice to say about Michelle and always assuming the worst of her?*

Ezekiel felt ready to marry Michelle. In fact, he'd marry her tomorrow if possible. But until the classes were done and they'd joined the church, he would patiently wait. Michelle thought taking the classes would be a big test for her. Little did she know the bigger challenge would be his mother — not only for Michelle, but him as well.

CHAPTER 26

By the end of January, the weather had improved from what it had been earlier in the month. If not for the temperature drop every evening, it seemed as if spring had arrived early this year. But Sara figured the warmer weather would be short lived and was only giving everyone a little tease of what was to come.

Things were going well at work, and they were gearing up for the flowers that would be sold before and on Valentine's Day. Sara was glad to be keeping busy at work, as well as at her grandparents' home. It took her mind off other things plaguing her lately. The fact that no one she had asked in her grandparents' church district knew who her biological father might be was one of the things disturbing Sara. But even more upsetting was that her mother had chosen to hide the truth from her, and also from Grandma and Grandpa. Sara had asked

Dean once if Mama ever told him who her real father was, but his answer was no.

Sara tapped her pen on the hard surface of her desk. *I wonder if Dean does know the truth and is keeping it from me because he promised Mama he wouldn't say anything.* Sara had always known her stepfather was devoted to his wife, even though she felt certain he'd never truly accepted Sara as his daughter. *But then, maybe Dean knows nothing and never pushed Mama to reveal the name of my father.*

Since Sara's mother was no longer living and Sara couldn't confront her with this, she'd come to realize she might never know the truth. The more Sara thought about it, the more bitter she felt, so it was best if she kept her mind on other things.

Sara's thoughts turned in another direction. Last night she'd received a phone call from Brad. In fact, he had called her at least once a week since returning to ministerial school. In the most recent conversation he'd mentioned the possibility of making another trip to Strasburg soon — maybe some weekend in March. Sara looked forward to seeing him again.

Brad must be at least a little interested in me, she thought, *or he wouldn't have kept in touch at all. I just wish . . .*

Sara's introspections were pushed aside when the door opened and a middle-aged Amish man entered the shop. In December, he'd come to the flower shop to buy a Christmas plant for his wife. As Sara recalled, his name was Herschel Fisher.

"Good morning." He stepped up to the counter.

Sara smiled. "Morning. May I help you with something?"

"Yes, please. I'd like to buy more flowers for my wife."

What a thoughtful man. "Are you looking for a bouquet of cut flowers, or did you have a houseplant in mind? We have several nice African violets that are blooming right now."

Herschel pulled his fingers down the side of his bearded face. "You know, a blooming houseplant might be kind of nice. It will last a lot longer than fresh-cut flowers."

Sara bobbed her head and stepped out from behind the counter. "I'll show you what's available." She led the way to the area where the houseplants were located. As Herschel looked them over, she stood back and let him decide. Finally, after several minutes' deliberation, he chose a dark maroon violet with several lacey blooms.

Sara went back to the counter, rang up his purchase, and placed the plant inside a small cardboard box.

Herschel thanked her, picked up the box, and started across the room. When he reached the door and grasped the handle, she called out to him: "Tell your wife if she follows the watering directions that I put on the little card inside the box, the plant should do well and keep blooming for a good many years."

The Amish man turned his head, blinked his eyes at Sara, and was gone.

Sara's throat tightened. *Oh to have a man who loves me so much that he regularly buys flowers, even when it isn't a special occasion.*

Clarks Summit

Brad sat in the school cafeteria, staring at his unfinished bowl of tomato soup, and thinking about Sara. Ever since he'd left Strasburg on New Year's Day, she'd been on his mind. He reflected on the events of New Year's Eve and how he'd been tempted to kiss her when the Lapps' grandfather clock struck twelve. But reason won out, and he'd only given Sara a brief hug, wishing her a happy new year.

It's funny, Brad thought, *but when I believed Michelle was Sara, I was attracted to her. Then, when I realized she wasn't a Christian, I backed off. Now I find myself interested in the real Sara.*

Truth was, Brad had no idea whether Sara was a believer or not. So why was he even considering trying to develop a relationship with her?

In his conversation with Sara last night, Brad had mentioned going to Strasburg to see her sometime in March. Even just a weekend there would give him a little more time to get to know her better. Maybe he'd find the courage to ask where she stood spiritually. If Sara was not a Christian, he would definitely need to curtail the feelings he was beginning to have for her.

"Is this seat taken?" A pleasant female voice cut into Brad's contemplations.

"Uh, no. Be my guest." He smiled at the pretty, dark-haired woman smiling down at him.

She pulled out a chair and sat down, placing her lunch tray on the table in front of her. "Hi, my name's Terri Conners. I don't believe we've met."

Brad held out his hand. "Brad Fuller. Nice to meet you, Terri."

Her long eyelashes fluttered as she gave him a dimpled grin. "Same here."

For lack of anything better to say, Brad picked up his spoon and ate the rest of his nearly cold soup. When he finished, he was surprised to see Terri watching him with a curious expression.

"Was I slurping?" he asked.

"A little bit."

Brad grabbed a napkin and wiped his mouth. "Sorry about that."

Her hand fluttered in Brad's direction. "No problem. I have three brothers, so I'm used to hearing a little slurping at the table. Besides, there really is no other way to eat soup."

He suppressed a snicker. "So where are you from, and what brought you to this university?"

"I was born and raised in Maine, and I came here with a scholarship. This is my second year." Terri took a sip of the chocolate milk on her tray. "My goal is to become a youth minister." She gestured to Brad. "How about you? What's your plan for after you graduate?"

"My goal is to take a church and minister full-time."

"Senior pastor or someone's assistant?" she asked.

"I don't know for sure. It all depends on what I'm offered." Brad wadded his napkin into a ball. "But even if I end up starting out as someone's assistant, I hope to move up the ranks someday."

She drank more milk and blotted her lips. "I'm a preacher's kid, so I know firsthand how tough the ministry can be. But the rewards outweigh the struggles and the often difficult tasks."

Brad reflected on her words a few seconds before responding. "I'm sure it won't be easy, but I can do all things through Christ."

"Yes." Terri's blue eyes sparkled with enthusiasm. "I cling to that verse in Philippians too."

Brad watched as she peeled back the covering on a small container of applesauce.

After taking a bite, she asked Brad another question. "What do you do when you have some free time? Is there anywhere you like to go?"

"I enjoy going to Strasburg when I get the chance. In fact, last summer I did some work for the Amish in that area."

"I've always wanted to see Amish country." Terri finished her applesauce. "What kind of work have you done for them?"

"Sometimes they hired me to drive them to appointments or some store that was too far from their home to take a horse and buggy. Other times, I was asked to help out with chores around someone's farm."

"Interesting. Maybe I'll take a drive down that way sometime, when I don't have my nose in the books."

Nodding, Brad rubbed the back of his neck. It was nice to talk with someone who shared his beliefs and understood about life in the ministry. He admired Terri for wanting to be a youth pastor. To him, that would be a bigger challenge than being a senior pastor of a megachurch. He hoped she was up to the task.

Ronks

Michelle hurried toward the kitchen to turn in someone's dinner order. The restaurant had been busy ever since she'd begun her first shift shortly before noon. Michelle had been asked to work the lunch and dinner shifts this week. Since her schedule didn't coincide with Sara's, she'd hired Stan to take her to and from work. She hated spending money on a driver — especially when she still owed the Lapps some of the money she'd stolen from them last October. She didn't have much left to pay back, but the sooner Michelle got it done, the better she'd feel about it.

In addition to the temperature being colder in the evenings, walking home from work when it was dark outside wasn't a good idea. Otherwise, she wouldn't have minded one bit. Come spring, if Michelle still had a job here, she planned to walk to and from work every day. By then the days would be getting longer, and it wouldn't be dark when she walked home. The exercise would be good for her too, and she wouldn't feel obligated to Sara. While their relationship might not be considered a close friendship as such, they had reached a mutual understanding, and for that, she felt grateful. It was a far cry from the tension between them a few months ago.

Michelle's thoughts went to Ezekiel. How appreciative she felt for his friendship and the relationship they'd been building. He was kind, helpful, understanding, humble, and everything she'd ever wanted in a man. Ezekiel was nothing like some of the self-centered, commanding jerks she had dated in the past.

On New Year's Eve, they'd kissed a few moments before midnight, and Ezekiel wished her a happy new year at the stroke of midnight. Michelle sensed that he had wanted to kiss her again, but he didn't. With Brad and Sara in the room, Ezekiel probably felt a bit awkward.

If he asked me to marry him right now, I'd say yes, Michelle told herself as she moved in the direction of the dining room. *But I need to be patient and try not to put the buggy*

before the horse. Besides, we need to finish
the classes we're taking so we can both join
the church.

Michelle straightened up a pile of menus
that could easily have fallen to the floor.
Maybe Ezekiel has no plans of ever propos-
ing. He might see me as nothing more than a
friend.

Michelle's thoughts took her back to the
evening when Ezekiel came all the way up
to Harrisburg to convince her to return to
Strasburg and face Willis and Mary Ruth.
He'd expressed his love for her then. And if
he truly did love her, then surely a marriage
proposal would eventually come.

Michelle entered the dining room, and
was about to approach one of the tables in
her section, when she saw a familiar face.
Heart pounding, and hands shaking, she
stopped walking and stood as though glued
to the floor. Her old boyfriend Jerry sat at a
table next to a young woman with short,
bleached-blond hair. Since they sat in the
section Michelle was responsible for, she
had no choice but to wait on them.

Glancing at the clock on the far wall, Michelle's teeth clamped down on her lower
lip. *Oh, how I wish it was quitting time. I'd be*
out that door in a flash.

CHAPTER 27

As Michelle stepped up to the table where Jerry and the blond woman sat, her mouth felt so dry she could barely swallow, let alone speak an intelligent sentence. Holding her ordering pad in front of her as though it were a shield, all she could do was stand there, looking at Jerry. At first glance, she realized his curly brown hair had been cut a bit shorter and neater. And instead of his normal attire of jeans and a T-shirt, Jerry wore a neatly pressed, dark-green buttoned shirt and tan-colored casual pants. She was surprised to see that he even wore a tie.

Squinting until his eyes appeared as mere slits, he stared back at her. "Michelle?"

She gave a slow nod.

Jerry's eyes opened wide. "What are you doin' here, and how come you're wearing that weird getup?" He pointed to Michelle's plain dress and apron.

Finally able to find her voice, she

squeaked, "I work here, and I am wearing these clothes because I'm Amish. Or at least I will be sometime this spring." *If things go well, that is,* Michelle silently added.

With an obnoxious snort, Jerry turned to the woman in the chair beside him. "Can you believe that, Nicki? My old girlfriend's crossed over into an old-fashioned world of pioneer living."

His friend didn't hold back her own snicker. In fact, she seemed anxious to join in with Jerry's ridicule as she maintained steady eye contact with Michelle.

Michelle couldn't help noticing all the makeup this girl wore on her face, especially around her eyes, which were outlined in dark black pencil. The young woman's lashes were so thick with mascara, they clumped together. Her wrists were covered by several inches of bracelets, and numerous earrings dangled from both ears. The blond even wore a small loop in her nose.

Michelle thought back to when she wore makeup and jewelry, but she hadn't worn either in a good many weeks. Even when she wore makeup, it was never as much as this blond wore. Michelle did not miss wearing it either. *The poor girl probably doesn't realize she is covering up all her natural beauty.*

Aside from over-done jewelry and too much makeup, the blond was dressed like a model. What Michelle could see of her outfit, a pretty silk sleeveless blouse and nice black pants, made Jerry's new girlfriend look like she'd stepped out of a fashion magazine. Michelle also caught sight of the matching black jacket draped across the back of Nicki's chair.

Nicki sneered at Michelle, probably eager to hurl a few insults her way. To Michelle's surprise, *pathetic* was the only word the young woman said. Then, glancing at Jerry, they both laughed.

After taking his girlfriend's hand, Jerry looked back at Michelle and shook his head. "Never thought I'd see you again, much less lookin' like a frumpy ole housemaid. How in the world did you end up here in the middle of Amish country, and who'd you let talk you into crossin' over?"

Michelle was tempted to tell Jerry that none of it was his business, but in order to show she had changed since leaving him, she forced a smile, pulled her shoulders back, and held her head high. "It's a long story, and I'm sure you would be bored if I shared it."

With a smirk, he leaned in her direction. "Try me."

"I'd rather not." Michelle held her ground, staring right back at him. She was not going to let her ex-boyfriend get control of anything like he had done in the past. "Now if you came here to eat supper, what would you like to order? You can either get something off the menu, or choose whatever you want from the buffet." She gestured in that direction, trying, at the same time, to keep a composed demeanor. She wanted it to appear as though she was holding her own with this situation, but inside, Michelle was anything but calm.

"So, what do you want, babe?" Jerry nudged the woman beside him, who kept her gaze on Michelle, as if sizing her up and down. No doubt Nicki saw Michelle as nothing more than a country bumpkin.

Nicki glanced at the menu, squinting as she slid her finger down the items listed. Then, leaning over and holding the menu in front of her face, she whispered something to Jerry.

Michelle rolled her eyes as she waited impatiently. *She's probably talking about me.*

Jerry's friend set the menu down. "I'll do the buffet. It'll be quicker, and we don't wanna be late for the musical we came down here to see." She leaned closer to Jerry. "Do we, hon?"

"No we don't, babe." Jerry planted a kiss on Nicki's lips.

Musical? Ignoring the kiss, Michelle shifted the ordering pad from one hand to the other. Since when had Jerry become so refined? In the short time Michelle had dated him, he'd never invited her to go anywhere nice. Not unless the local pool hall or a drive to the store to get beer and frozen pizza could be considered nice. Hopefully, with Nicki, Jerry was cleaning up his act, but it was doubtful. And if he was, the guy still had a long ways to go.

Michelle stuck her pencil behind one ear, just under her white head covering. It was difficult to be patient as she waited for Jerry to decide what he wanted to eat.

"Guess I'll choose something from the buffet too, little miss Plain Jane." Jerry wrinkled his nose. "And if you care to know, I'm well rid of you, Michelle. I'm actually glad you split when you did, 'cause I was about done with our relationship anyways." He pointed at her head covering. "Seeing this new getup of yours, I sure wouldn't be seen with the likes of you now."

"Good to know." Michelle put on her cheeriest smile. "Thank you for sharing that information with me, Jerry. I appreciate your kindness." She started to walk away, but turned around in time to see Jerry's expression turn from thinking he'd worn her down to one of astonishment. Perhaps he'd underestimated her.

"Can I bring you two anything to drink other than water?" Michelle asked.

"I'll have a glass of beer." He looked at his date. "Better make that two. My girl here likes a little brew. Right, sweetie?"

Nicki snickered. "That's right, Jerry."

Michelle lifted her gaze to the ceiling. "This restaurant is run by a Christian family, and they don't serve alcoholic beverages."

"No beer, huh?" He grunted. "That's really stupid. Bet they lose a lot of business because of that old-fashioned decision."

"We should have gone to the place you took me to back in May," Nicki muttered.

Looking around at the crowded restaurant, where nearly every table was occupied, Michelle was tempted to argue with Jerry, but she didn't see the point. It wasn't worth the waste of time. Besides, this kind of talk was nothing new. Jerry thought he was right about everything.

"Maybe instead of coming here, you should have taken Nicki to that place you went to in *May*." Michelle stressed the word

May to make sure Jerry heard it, loud and clear.

Michelle's steady stare on his face could have bored a hole in a piece of rock, and she found pleasure in seeing that the once-domineering Jerry had to look away. Michelle didn't flinch and almost laughed when he loosened his tie and tugged at the collar around his throat, which must have felt too tight.

I cannot believe this guy. That two-timer was seeing Nicki last spring, when he was still with me. Wouldn't I have surprised Jerry if I'd agreed to move in with him? Guess he knew I meant it when I kept telling him no.

Michelle found strength in holding her composure. Jerry didn't like to be turned down. He may have controlled her once, but not anymore. "Is there something else either of you would like to drink?" she asked.

Jerry flapped a hand in her direction. "Naw, I'll stick with H₂O."

Michelle looked at his girlfriend. "How about you?"

"I'd like a glass of root beer, please." The smirk on her lips remained. "You do serve that here, don't you?"

"Of course. I'll get your beverages while you're helping yourselves to the buffet." Michelle turned and hurried away. *At least one of them has a few manners — even though Nicki saying please is the only good manner she's shown. I hope that poor woman knows what she's in for, dating a creep like Jerry. Wish I could warn her. Who knows, he could be cheating on her too. But then even if I did alert Nicki, she probably wouldn't believe me. Hopefully, the pretty little blond will come to her senses before it's too late, and run as far away as possible from Jerry. People like him don't change overnight.*

Strasburg

As Sara did the supper dishes with her grandmother that evening, she thought about the two photo albums she'd found after her mother died. She had been meaning to share them with Grandpa and Grandma but wanted to bring the albums out when Michelle was not around. Since Michelle was working the dinner shift at the restaurant, this was the perfect opportunity. The pictures inside the scrapbooks were of Sara as a child and also some of Mama. These special mementos were for her grandparents' eyes only. Michelle was an outsider, not part of this family. Sara saw no reason to share the photos with her.

"Would you and Grandpa like to join me

in the living room after we finish the dishes?" Sara looked over at her grandmother. "I have something special I'd like to show you."

With a curious expression, Grandma nodded. "Why, certainly. Your grandpa went out to the barn to do a final check on the animals, but as soon as he comes in, we can gather in the other room."

"Sounds good." Sara picked up another glass to dry. Since Grandma and Grandpa had no photographs in the house, she hoped they wouldn't object to looking at the album she had brought with her from New Jersey.

Half an hour later, Sara sat in the cozy but plain living room with her grandparents. Holding the albums in her lap, she'd taken a seat on the couch and asked them to sit on either side of her.

Firewood crackled and popped from the warm blaze Grandpa had built in the fireplace soon after he'd returned to the house.

"The day I found my mother's old Bible I came across these two books filled with photos," Sara began. "Since Mama is in many of the pictures, I thought you might want to see them."

Tipping her head to one side, Grandma looked at Grandpa as though seeking his

315

permission. With only a slight hesitation, he gave an affirmative nod.

Sara's fingers trembled as she opened the first album. It began with a few pictures of Mama holding Sara when she was a baby. Even though Sara was still hurt by her mother's deception, seeing the photos again made her long for what she had lost.

Grandma's eyes teared up as she pointed to the first photo. "Look, Willis, it's our *dochder,* dressed in English clothes. And see here . . . Rhoda is holding a *boppli.*" She looked at Sara then gestured to the baby on Mama's lap. "Is that you?"

"Yes. And on the next several pages there are more pictures of Mama and me in different stages of me growing up."

Sara's grandparents looked at every page in both albums. By the time they reached the last set of photos, Grandma's handkerchief was wet with tears. Grandpa too looked like he might break down crying. It tugged on Sara's heart to see how moved they were after seeing all these pictures of their only daughter.

Grandma sniffed and wiped at the wetness on her cheeks. "Oh, how I wish we could have seen our precious girl before she died." Using her fingertips, she made circles across her forehead. "It doesn't seem fair."

Then, picking up the first album again, Sara's grandma flipped slowly through the pages one more time, sometimes stopping to run her finger over certain photos.

"If only Rhoda had come home or at least contacted us through the years." Grandpa reached across the back of the couch and patted Grandma's shoulder.

Seeing the pain these two dear people had endured caused Sara to choke up. *Oh Mama, you did a terrible thing when you ran away from home.* Her nose burned with unshed tears, but she refused to give in to them, because she'd already done enough crying when her mother died. Sara still held the second album in her lap. She sat staring at one of the pictures on the last page where her mother sat beside Dean on the sofa. It had been taken soon after they were married. *Oh Mama, how could you have hurt the ones you supposedly loved?*

Even though Sara loved her mother, she wasn't sure she could forgive Mama for the lie she'd lived all those years. Keeping her past a secret from Sara was bad enough, but losing contact with such loving parents was unimaginable.

At that moment, Sara made up her mind that as long as Grandma and Grandpa were still alive, she would be there for them.

Sara's grandparents deserved her love and undivided attention.

Grandma handed the first album they'd looked at over to Grandpa so he could view the pictures again. It was understandable why that one held their interest more, since Sara's mom had only left a few weeks prior to when many of those early photos were taken. Except for the English clothing she wore, their daughter, no doubt, looked the same as they remembered.

Sara's grandparents grew quiet, presumably both deep in thought. *No one, and nothing, shall ever come between us,* Sara determined in her heart. *I will be here for Grandma and Grandpa for as long as they need me.*

CHAPTER 28

When Michelle entered the kitchen the fol
lowing morning, she felt guilty seeing Sara
and Mary Ruth had already made breakfast.
"Sorry for sleeping in. I should have been
here to help." She took a pitcher of Mary
Ruth's homemade grape juice from the refrigerator.

Mary Ruth smiled. "It's okay. Sara and I
managed without your help today. You
looked tired when you came home last
night, so I thought you might want to sleep
awhile longer this morning."

Michelle sighed. "I was tired and stressed.
My afternoon went okay, but something
happened during the dinner shift that really
shook me up."

"What was it?" Sara asked. "Were they
super busy at the restaurant?"

"Nothing out of the ordinary." Michelle
pulled out a chair and sank into it with a
moan. "My ex-boyfriend Jerry showed up

with a new girlfriend. At least I thought she was new. Turns out he'd been dating her at the time he was seeing me."

Mary Ruth's brows wrinkled. "Who is Jerry?"

"He's a guy from Philadelphia who I should never have gotten involved with." Michelle's lips curled. "He was an abusive control freak, and I'm glad I got away from him when I did."

Mary Ruth stepped behind the chair where Michelle sat and placed her hands on Michelle's shoulders. "I am sorry you had a rough day. Did this Jerry fellow threaten to harm you in any way?"

"No, but he made fun of the way I was dressed, and when I told him I planned to join the Amish church, he said he was well rid of me." Michelle crossed her arms. "Even though the girl he was with acted kinda rude, I actually felt sorry for her. I'm sure she has no idea what Jerry is really like. In fact, she went along with his belittling comments, and seemed to enjoy it. He pretended to be charming when we first met, but it didn't take long until his true colors were brought to light. His apologies and promises that never held true made the next ones seem less believable." Michelle shook her head. "I was such a fool."

"Unfortunately, there are many people like your ex in this world." Sara's eyes appeared cold and flat. "They treat others with no respect — like they don't amount to anything at all."

Michelle wasn't sure if Sara was generalizing or referring to someone in particular. But it was obvious that Michelle wasn't the only one with an unhappy past.

Since it was Saturday, and Sara didn't have to work, shortly before noon she decided to go down to the basement. Grandpa had dropped Grandma off at one of her friend's for the day, and then he went to town to run several errands.

When Michelle said she wanted to get some sewing done, Sara saw this as a good opportunity to go down to the basement to read more of the notes in the prayer jar she'd found.

Beginning her descent into the darkness of the basement, it only took a moment for Sara to realize she'd forgotten a flashlight or a lantern. She refused to go into the musty cellar with no light to guide her down the worn, wooden steps, so she turned around and returned to the kitchen. At moments like this, Sara wondered if she would ever adjust to her grandparents' simple life of no electricity in their home. Normally, it didn't bother her so much, but sometimes she missed the ease of simply flipping a switch to turn on an overhead light.

Once she had a flashlight in hand, Sara headed back down the stairs, feeling a little more secure. While she wasn't afraid of the dark, Grandpa and Grandma's basement seemed kind of creepy — not to mention that Sara needed to see where she was going. She certainly didn't want to trip over something or run into an icky spider's web. Just thinking about those horrible eight-legged creatures gave her the willies.

At the bottom of the steps, Sara flashed the beam of light around the basement, searching for the battery-operated light Grandma kept near her antiquated washing machine. Sure enough, it was on the small table beside the washer.

Sara clicked it on, and a beam of light illuminated the area. Grandma kept the part of the basement where she washed clothes clean and organized. But some other areas were cluttered with boxes filled with all kinds of items. Looking past them, Sara aimed her flashlight in the direction of the shelves where the empty canning jars were kept. Climbing up on a stool, it didn't take long until she spotted the jar full of papers

— the one Michelle referred to as a prayer jar.

The fact that two prayer jars existed — one here and one in the barn — fascinated Sara. Since neither she nor Michelle knew who had written the notes inside the jars, the mystery of it kept calling to her.

Sara took the jar down and seated herself on the stool. Unscrewing the old lid, she reached inside and pulled out one of the notes. It was different than the ones she'd read before. *"Turn your cares into prayers."* Five simple words, but not possible for Sara. She had too many cares in this world, and no amount of praying would remove them. If things went wrong, it was her responsibility to make them right whenever she could. The challenge of fixing other people's mistakes proved difficult, but at least she could try. One thing Sara had learned over the years was to take responsibility for her own actions and make the best of the hand she'd been dealt. Although she would never admit it out loud, there were times when she felt as if her world had spun out of control, and she was powerless to stop it.

Sara folded the piece of paper, put it back in the jar, and took another one. This one quoted Proverbs 28:26: *"He that trusteth in his own heart is a fool: but whoso walketh wisely, he shall be delivered."*

Sara shifted on the stool. It was hard to sit still. *So I'm a fool if I trust in my own heart, huh?* She crossed her right leg and bounced her foot up and down. *How's a person supposed to walk wisely if they don't trust in their own heart, which I assume means, thoughts?*

Grandma's religious. I'll bet anything she's the one who wrote these messages. Sara wished she felt free to ask her grandmother about them, but bringing up the prayer jars she and Michelle had found might be like opening Pandora's fabled box. For now at least, she would keep quiet about the prayer jars. Maybe someday, if the time was right, she would ask Grandma about them.

When Sara came up from the basement, she went to Grandma's sewing room to see how Michelle was doing. Seeing no sign of her there, Sara headed for the kitchen.

Michelle wasn't in that room either, but she had left a note on the table saying she'd gone over to the Kings' place to see Ezekiel.

I wonder how long she'll be there. Sara glanced out the kitchen window. *I hope she gets back before Lenore shows up to make greeting cards with us.*

Truthfully, Sara had gotten so caught up reading prayers, quotes, and Bible verses from the prayer jar in the basement she'd almost forgotten about Lenore coming over today. It wasn't until she saw the package of cardstock on one end of the kitchen counter that she remembered Lenore had called a few days ago to set things up. Until Sara's mind became preoccupied with other things, she'd been looking forward to getting together with her cousin. It would be fun to learn more about creating one-of-a kind greeting cards using rubber stamps, colored pencils, pretty ribbons, and several other decorative items. There was nothing plain about the cards Lenore and many other Amish made to share with others.

Sara tapped her fingers on the edge of the counter. *I wonder if Karen Roberts would be interested in buying some of the cards Lenore makes to sell in the flower shop.* Sara made a mental note to mention it when she went to work next week.

Since it was almost noon, and Michelle wasn't back yet, Sara fixed a sandwich and ate lunch. When she finished eating, she washed her dishes and made sure the table was clean. Following that, she took a seat and waited for Lenore to arrive.

At one o'clock, Sara heard a horse and buggy pull in. Hoping it might be Michelle, she hurried to the back door and opened it.

The horse at the rail was not Grandma's, so she knew it wasn't Michelle, because Peanuts was Michelle's favorite horse to drive. And since Grandpa had given Grandma a ride to her friend's using his horse and buggy, Michelle wouldn't have taken his rig either.

Sara watched as Lenore stepped down from the carriage and secured her mare. She did it with ease — as though she'd been doing it all her life.

Sara rubbed her arms to ward off the chill. The brief spring-like weather they'd enjoyed had vanished, and the cold winter temperatures were back. At least there'd been no recent ice or snow to deal with on the roads. Sara had never enjoyed driving in the snow and sometimes wished she lived where it was warm all year long, like Florida, the Bahamas, or Hawaii.

"Do you need any help?" Remembering her manners, Sara called to Lenore, as she removed a cardboard box from her buggy.

"No, I just have this one thing to carry. But thanks for offering." Lenore walked briskly across the yard and soon stepped onto the back porch. "Hello, Sara. It's good to see you again."

"It's nice to see you too." Sara opened the door wider. "You can set the box on the

326

kitchen counter. I have the table cleared off and am more than ready for us to make some cards."

Lenore's dimples deepened when she smiled at Sara. "I've been looking forward to this time for the three of us to make cards and enjoy each other's company." She set the box down. "I hope you and Michelle will have as much fun making cards as I do."

Sara slipped her hands into her jeans pockets. "Unfortunately, Michelle is not here right now. When I came up from the basement earlier, I found a note she'd left, saying she was going over to Ezekiel's. She may have forgotten about our plans to make cards today."

Lenore's brows furrowed a bit, but then relaxed. "That's okay. The two of us can have just as much fun making cards."

Sara bobbed her head. "Definitely. Oh, before we start, have you had lunch yet? I've already eaten, but I can fix you something."

"I ate before I came over, but thank you just the same." Lenore opened the flaps of the box and took out several items — scissors, cardstock, rubber stamps, ink pads, glue, glitter, and some colorful ribbons. Once she'd placed all the supplies on the table, they both took a seat.

"Before we get started, would you mind if I ask you a question that has nothing to do with stamping or creating beautiful cards?" Sara figured since she and her cousin were alone, this was a good time to see if Lenore knew anything about Sara's biological father.

Lenore smiled. "Sure, go ahead. What do you want to know?"

Sara moistened her lips. "It's about my mother."

"As I've mentioned before, I never met your mother." Lenore rubbed the tiny mole on her left arm.

"Yes, but I thought maybe your father may have said something."

"About what?"

"My mother. I am interested in who she used to hang out with."

Lenore massaged her forehead, as though deep in thought. "One time, I did overhear him talking to my mother about his sister."

Sara sat up straighter, her interest now piqued. "What did he say?"

"As I recall, Dad and Mom were discussing how, even after several years, Grandma couldn't deal with the sadness she felt over Rhoda leaving home."

Sara pushed against the back of her chair. "Yes, I am aware of that. What I need to know is whether your dad knew of anyone Mama might have been dating."

Lenore gave a slow nod. "I was just going to say that while talking with Mom, Dad said something about the English kids his sister liked to hang around with. He said one young fellow Rhoda talked to a lot worried him, because he was afraid the young man might influence her to go English and never join the Amish church."

"When I asked Uncle Ivan if he knew who my father was, he said no." Sara's jaw clenched. "I wonder why he never mentioned this English man to me."

Lenore lifted one hand, turning her palm upward. "I have no idea. Maybe you should ask him."

Sara gave a determined nod. "I most definitely will." This new bit of news her cousin had shared made Sara wonder if Uncle Ivan might be hiding something from her. It made no sense, but maybe, for some particular reason, he didn't want Sara to know who her real father was.

CHAPTER 29

Michelle had just finished the morning shift and was preparing the tables for the lunch crowd, when a man with dark, curly hair entered the restaurant. At first glance she thought Jerry had come back, but a second look told her otherwise. This man was older and had the beginnings of a beard.

Michelle blew out a quick breath. *What a relief! I'm not ready for another encounter with my ex-boyfriend today, or any day for that matter. I don't even like calling him my ex-boyfriend. I certainly wasn't his girlfriend.*

Saturday, when she'd gone to the Kings' to see Ezekiel, Michelle had been disappointed because they were busy at the greenhouse and he couldn't talk to her for more than a few minutes. She'd managed to tell Ezekiel briefly about her encounter with Jerry, and he had been sympathetic. Michelle wished she could have gone into more detail about what had transpired.

Hopefully, Ezekiel would have been pleased with how she'd handled the situation.

After Michelle left the greenhouse, she'd stopped by one of the restaurants in Strasburg and eaten lunch. Other people had been eating by themselves that day, but it was hard not to feel sorry for herself as she sat there all alone.

Sometimes Michelle truly felt as if she were alone. After all, she had no family anymore, and her only real friend was Ezekiel. At times, she wasn't even sure about him. Lately, they seemed to be drifting apart. Was it because he was so busy, or had Ezekiel lost interest in her?

After lunch, Michelle had gone back to the Lapps' and discovered Lenore was there. That's when Michelle realized she'd forgotten that she, Sara, and Lenore were supposed to make greeting cards together.

I sure messed that up, Michelle berated herself. By the time she'd arrived, they were almost done. So instead of joining them, Michelle had gone to her room, saying she had a headache, which wasn't a lie.

Yesterday hadn't gone much better. The class she and Ezekiel had taken before Sunday service started seemed even more difficult to understand this time. After church, Ezekiel had said he wanted to take

Michelle for a buggy ride, but he couldn't because he and his family had been invited to his aunt's home for supper and to play board games that could last well into the evening. Ezekiel had invited Michelle to go along, but she'd declined, sure that her presence would not be appreciated, since she was not a family member. "And I probably never will be," Michelle muttered under her breath.

"What was that? Were you speaking to me?"

Michelle's face heated when she turned and saw Linda, one of the other waitresses, standing behind her. "Sorry about that. I was talking to myself."

Linda snickered. "No problem. I do it sometimes too." She gestured to the front door, as several people entered the restaurant. "Looks like we might have another good crowd here today." Leaning close to Michelle's ear, she whispered, "More tips for us, right?"

Smiling, Michelle nodded. More tips were exactly what she needed. With any luck, by the end of this week, she'd have enough money to pay the Lapps the remainder of what she still owed.

Paradise, Pennsylvania

After Sara got off work Monday afternoon, she headed for the general store owned by her uncle Ivan. Since Andy and Karen had closed the flower shop a bit earlier today because of dental appointments, Sara had plenty of time to stop by Ivan's place of business. Afterward, she should still make it to Ronks in plenty of time to pick up Michelle when she got off work. Sara hoped Uncle Ivan wouldn't be too busy to talk to her, because she needed some answers.

A heavy rain had begun to fall, so after Sara pulled into the parking lot, she grabbed her umbrella. Hurrying toward the store, Sara tilted the umbrella back to glance at the sky. The ceiling of clouds had lowered, and ice pellets, mixed in with drops of rain, hit her face. She nervously bit her lip, watching the sleet melt as it made contact with the steps leading to the door. *I hope this doesn't turn icy before I leave. Slippery roads make me anxious.*

When Sara entered the store, she saw only a few customers browsing around, but there was no sign of Uncle Ivan. Stepping up to the counter, where her aunt Yvonne sat, she said hello and then asked if Ivan was in the store.

"It's good to see you, Sara." Aunt Yvonne

motioned to the back of the building. "My husband's in the storage room, opening several boxes of books that came in recently."

"Would it be okay if I went there? I need to ask him something."

Her aunt smiled. "Certainly. I'm sure he won't mind at all."

Sara hurried in the direction her aunt had pointed. It didn't take long to find the storage room, since the door was partially open. She spotted Uncle Ivan kneeling on the floor beside one of the many cardboard boxes.

"Hi, Uncle Ivan." Sara spoke quietly, so as not to startle him. "Sorry to bother you, but I was wondering if you have a few minutes to talk."

"Course I do." He rose to his feet, gave her a hug, then gestured to the folding chairs on the opposite side of the room. "Let's take a seat so we can be more comfortable."

After they both sat down, he turned to her and smiled. "It's good to see you, Sara. I believe this is the first time you've been in our general store."

"Actually, I was here a few weeks ago when Grandma and I were out shopping one day. I think you were running errands at the time."

"I see." Ivan motioned toward the back door. "How's the weather out there? I've been back here quite a while and haven't had a chance to look outside."

"It started raining a few minutes ago, but there's sleet mixed in."

"Well, be careful when you go back out on the roads. You never know what the unpredictable weather's gonna do. You don't want to be caught on glazed-over roads." He reached around and rubbed a spot on his back. "I'm curious — what brings you to our store this afternoon?"

"I wanted to talk to you about my mother." Sara crossed her ankles, then uncrossed them. She hoped her uncle wouldn't suspect she was nervous about bringing up this conversation.

"What about Rhoda?"

"Well, last Saturday Lenore and I were together, making some greeting cards. During the course of our conversation, we talked about my mom."

He sat quietly, as though waiting for her to continue.

"Lenore mentioned she'd overheard you talking to your wife once about how Mama had run around with some English kids, and one fellow in particular. So, I thought maybe . . ."

Uncle Ivan held up his hand. "First of all, my daughter should not have been listening in on our conversation."

I should have worded it differently. Sara chose her next sentence carefully, in defense of Lenore. "I don't believe she was intentionally eavesdropping. Lenore happened to overhear what you said."

"Be that as it may, the conversation was between me and Yvonne, and she certainly had no right to repeat what she'd heard."

"While that might be true, what's been said has been said." Sara leaned forward in her chair. "Is it true that my mom ran around with some English fellow?"

Ivan nodded. "Rhoda had several English friends."

"Could the man you mentioned to your wife be my biological father?"

He shrugged his broad shoulders. "Anything's possible, but I only saw Rhoda with him a couple of times. And she never admitted to me that they were seeing each other socially or had developed a serious relationship." Ivan's forehead wrinkled. "Of course, during my sister's running-around time, she didn't share much of anything of importance with me."

"Do you know the man's name, or where

he was from?"

Her uncle shook his head, then paused and gave his earlobe a tug. "Now that I think more about it, I did hear her call him Ricky one of the times I saw them together. Yeah, I think that was his name, but I have no idea where he was from."

"What was his last name?"

"I don't know; Rhoda never said."

Sara released an exasperated breath. At this rate she would never find out who her father was. Should she give up her search or keep asking around?

She jumped when Ivan spoke again. "I'm glad you stopped by, Sara, but it's getting late. Under normal circumstances, I'd invite you to stay and join us for supper later on, but I'd feel better if you were on your way home."

Sara glanced at her wristwatch. "I guess you are right. Michelle gets off work soon, and I need to pick her up. Then we'll head straight home. I'm sure Grandma will have supper started by then." Her fingers curled into the palms of her hands as she walked with her uncle to the door. *Surely someone has to know who Mama became serious about. And if a man named Ricky was the one, then there has to be a way to find out his last*

*name and where he's from. The question is,
Who else can I ask?*

Strasburg

As pellets of ice bounced off the windshield, Sara drove slower.

"How was work today?" Michelle asked.

"It went okay. My employers closed the store early today, so before I came to get you I dropped by my uncle Ivan's store in Paradise."

"I've only been there once. Did you get some shopping done?"

"No, I didn't go there to shop." Sara kept her gaze on the road ahead, as the nasty weather had worsened.

"Why did you go there then?"

"To ask Uncle Ivan if he knew anything about a certain man my mother was seen with during her running-around days. I'm still hoping to find out who my biological father is." Sara gripped the steering wheel tighter. "I get so frustrated when I ask people about it and no one seems to know anything."

"Maybe you're not supposed to find out." Michelle sighed. "If I had a choice of having a father or not, I sure would have been better off not knowing mine. Of course," she admitted, "I'm saying that in hindsight now."

Sara's eyes opened wide. Gripping the steering wheel, she yelled: "Hold on!" The wet roads had caused the car to slide when Sara hit the brakes. The next thing she knew, they'd ended up in a low-lying ditch.

"Sara, are you okay?" Michelle held onto the grab handle above the passenger door.

"Yeah. How about you?" Sara's fingers hurt when she tried to open them after clamping onto the steering wheel so tightly.

"I'm not hurt. Just shook up a bit."

Sara turned her head and looked out the back window. "I hope I didn't hit that cat."

"What cat?" Michelle also turned to look. "I don't see anything."

"A gray cat darted out in front of us. I'm surprised you didn't see it." Sara's hands shook. "The last thing I need is to kill another animal." She clamped her hand over her mouth. "Michelle, I'm sorry. I didn't mean to say it like that." Weeks had gone by since Rascal's death, and Sara's comment had even startled her. She did not want to stir up any emotions from that day. Especially when things were going better between her and Michelle.

"It's okay. Guess we better see if any damage was done to your car."

"I agree." Sara realized she had to deal with the situation at hand, but she felt grateful Michelle wasn't offended by her previous comment.

They got out of the car and went around to look at the front, and then the back of vehicle. There didn't appear to be any damage, but Sara's car was wedged in the ditch, with the back right tire suspended in midair.

Sara groaned. "This is not good."

"How about you get into the car, and I'll try to push you out." Michelle went back to the front seat to retrieve her gloves, then walked to the back of the car again. The ditch had water lying in it, and even though shallow, Sara could see Michelle's feet had gotten quite wet.

"Okay, I'm going to ease on the gas," Sara hollered, after sliding into her seat.

"Go ahead. I'm ready."

Sara watched in the rearview mirror as Michelle put her hands on the right side of the trunk and started pushing. The car didn't budge.

"Try again." Michelle motioned.

Sara put her foot on the accelerator, but her vehicle still did not move. "Let's try to get a rocking motion going," she shouted through the open window. "That might work."

"Okay!" Michelle worked with Sara, and they managed to get the car rocking back and forth. Unfortunately, the ditch would not let go of Sara's vehicle. To make matters worse, each time Sara eased harder on the gas, the left tire sprayed Michelle with mud.

Walking to the driver's side, Michelle wiped her face. "This isn't working. We're really stuck."

"We'd better lock up the car and walk the rest of the way home," Sara suggested, looking toward the sound of horse's hooves *clip-clopping* on the pavement.

A few minutes later, an Amish buggy, heading in the opposite direction pulled up on the other side of the road. The driver got out and secured his horse to a fence post nearby. When he walked across and joined them, Sara recognized him right away.

"Do you need some help?" When he looked at Sara, his brows rose slightly. "Don't you work at the flower shop in Strasburg?"

"Why yes. And you're Herschel Fisher." Sara looked at Michelle. "Mr. Fisher is a customer at the flower shop."

"Nice to meet you." Michelle glanced at her soggy-looking feet, then back at Mr. Fisher. "We're stuck. We tried rocking the car, hoping to get it out of the ditch, but I don't have enough strength to even budge the vehicle."

"Let me help you." Herschel looked at Sara. "Just ease on the gas when I tell you." He turned to Michelle. "You'd better stand back out of the way."

Michelle did as she was told. All it took was Herschel's strength, and after a few pushes, Sara's car was out of the ditch.

She sighed with relief. "How can I ever thank you, Mr. Fisher?" Sara noticed his clothes were sprayed with mud too.

"No thanks is needed."

She got out of the car and handed him and Michelle paper towels.

"Yeah, thanks, Mr. Fisher. Without you, we would still be stuck." Michelle wiped her face with the towel.

Herschel touched the brim of his hat. "I'm glad I happened along when I did." He told the girls goodbye and hurried back to his buggy. When he reached it, he turned and shouted, "Be careful driving. The roads might get icy as the temperature starts to dip."

"We don't have far to go. Thanks again." Sara joined Michelle in the car. When she turned the heat up, Michelle tossed her gloves on the floor and held her hands toward the vent. "Boy, I'm glad he came along when he did."

"Me too." Sara looked out her side mirror, watching Herschel's buggy as it got farther away. "The next time that nice man comes into the flower shop, I'm going to pay for whatever he purchases."

"Good idea." Michelle bobbed her head. "This incident has made me realize how much I appreciate the Amish people in this community. Most that I know are always willing to help when someone has a need."

"You're right," Sara agreed. "Everyone is like family — willing to be there for each other. I admire that so much."

Michelle gave Sara's arm a light tap. "Maybe you should think about giving up your English ways and becoming Amish."

Sara glanced at Michelle, then focused back on the road. "It's a nice thought, but I think not."

CHAPTER 30

On Valentine's Day, at Mary Ruth's request, Michelle walked out to get the mail. She had done this every day when she'd first lived with the Lapps so she could intercept any letters the real Sara might have sent.

I should never have deceived them like that. Michelle kicked a clump of dirt in the graveled driveway. *If I could only go back in time, I'd make it all right.*

It wasn't good to dwell on the past or berate herself for things she couldn't change, but sometimes the memory of her lies plagued her. She'd been forgiven, and for that she was thankful, but perhaps she still hadn't pardoned herself.

Michelle's breath expelled in a frosty vapor as a shiver went through her. The morning air was nippy, this second Thursday of February. She looked up toward the sky. Every day last week had been cloudy and dreary, but today the clouds were finally peeling away. Behind them she enjoyed the large patches of crystal-blue sky and the warmth of a brilliant sun. In certain areas where cloud formations still mingled, translucent rays of light scattered over the ground below.

Michelle hugged her arms around herself. Even though February was a cold month, this weather was invigorating. But spring would start next month, and she was eager for warmer temperatures too. Today being Valentine's Day made the sun's appearance even more special.

When Michelle reached the mailbox, she pulled out a stack of mail that included several advertisement flyers, as well as envelopes that appeared to be bills. One letter was addressed to Sara and postmarked, *"Clarks Summit."*

She smiled. *I bet this is from Brad. He's the only person we know who lives up there.* She turned the square envelope over and studied it a few seconds. *I wonder if this is a Valentine's Day card.*

Michelle thumbed through the mail once more to see if any envelopes were addressed to her. Finding none, she closed the mailbox flap and started back toward the house. As she approached the Lapps' home, she stopped walking and stood looking up with her mouth slightly open. On the frosty roof, someone had written a message for her: MI-CHELLE . . . LOOK IN THE BARN.

Now who would climb all the way up there and leave me a message like that? Surely Willis wouldn't have done anything so dangerous. His wife would have a conniption if he took a chance like that.

Michelle hurried into the house, dropped the mail on the table, then ran all the way to the barn. She'd barely gotten inside, when Ezekiel stepped out of the shadows, causing her to jump.

"Ezekiel, you about scared me to death! What are you doing here at this time of day? Shouldn't you be helping at the green-house?"

"I will be, but we don't open for another hour or so. I have plenty of time to get back by then." He moved closer. So close, she could feel his warm breath on her face. "I came to bring you a Valentine's Day present."

Confused, Michelle tipped her head. Ezekiel held no present in his hands. But then, seeing him here on this cold, raw morning was gift enough in itself.

"Didn't you see the *botschaft* I left on the Lapps' roof for you?" he asked.

"I did see the message, which is why I

346

came running out to the barn. I just didn't realize you were the one who wrote it." Pleased that she'd understood the Pennsylvania Dutch word Ezekiel had spoken, Michelle poked his arm. "What were you thinking, pulling a stunt like that? The roof is high, not to mention slippery from the frost. How did you even get up there? Don't you realize how dangerous it could —"

Ezekiel wrapped his arms around Michelle's waist and stopped her words with a kiss so sweet she forgot all the questions he had not yet answered. When the kiss ended, she pulled back slightly, looking up at him with a heart full of love. "So you are my Valentine's Day present?"

He shook his head. "Not really. I'm just the messenger and deliverer of the gift."

"What gift?"

Ezekiel took hold of Michelle's hand. "Come with me, and soon you will see your Valentine's Day surprise."

She followed him willingly toward the back of the barn, where a gas lantern hanging from the rafters had been lit. When they reached a small wooden barrier, Ezekiel stopped and pointed inside. "Happy Valentine's Day, Michelle. I hope you like her."

Sleeping in a pile of straw lay the cutest little auburn-haired pup.

"The puppy's an Irish setter, and she's seven weeks old today." Ezekiel slipped his arm around Michelle's waist. "I know she won't replace Rascal, but the puppy needs a loving owner, and I believe you're the one she's meant to have."

Tears slipped from Michelle's eyes and rolled down her cheeks. "Oh Ezekiel, danki." She stepped over the enclosure, bent down, and scooped the pup into her arms. "I'm gonna call her, Val — short for —"

"Valentine's Day." Ezekiel finished Michelle's sentence. "When I went to look at the puppies, this cute little thing was the only one left out of a litter of fourteen. I wasn't going to let her get away." He reached out to rub the dog's ears, covered with wavy fur. "When I saw the pup's auburn fur, it reminded me of the color of your hair — not to mention that auburn is kind of a reddish color, appropriate for Valentine's Day."

Holding securely to her new pet, Michelle stepped back over the barricade and kissed Ezekiel's cheek. "It's all so perfect. This is the best Valentine's gift anyone has ever given me. Not that I've had many presents on Valentine's Day."

He returned the kiss on Michelle's lips. "And you are the best aldi any man could ever want. I love you with all my heart."

"I love you too, Ezekiel."

At that moment, the puppy woke up and licked Michelle's chin. Hints of Val's sweet-smelling breath reached her. Chuckling, she stroked the dog's silky head. One thing she would teach little Val when she was old enough to learn would be not to chase cars. Michelle couldn't risk losing another dog.

Sara had just entered the kitchen to help Grandma with breakfast, when Michelle came into the room, holding a bundle of auburn-colored fur in her arms and smiling ear to ear.

"Look what Ezekiel gave me for Valentine's Day." She held the puppy up and then draped the little thing over her shoulder as if it were a baby.

"What a *siess hundli*!" Sara's grandma exclaimed. "And what a thoughtful gift Ezekiel gave you this morning."

Michelle nuzzled the pup with her nose. "You're right, Mary Ruth. She is a sweet puppy."

"Have you chosen a name for her yet?" Sara questioned.

"Yep. Since I got the puppy on Valentine's Day, I decided to call her Val."

"Now that's appropriate," Grandpa interjected when he entered the kitchen. "I went out to the barn a short time ago, and just before Ezekiel left, he told me how he'd surprised you with the hundli. And that's not all." He grinned at Michelle. "That beau of yours told me how he climbed up on our roof this morning and wrote a message for you in the frost."

"Jah, I couldn't believe he would do such a thing. I'm not sure I want to know how he got up there either. Oh, and speaking of messages — there's an envelope for you on the table, Sara." Michelle motioned with her head. "It's postmarked Clarks Summit, so it's probably from Brad." A slow smile spread across Michelle's face. "I bet he sent you a Valentine card."

"I wouldn't be surprised if that fellow's not sweet on you, Sara." Grandpa's bushy brows jiggled up and down.

With trembling fingers, Sara looked through the stack of mail. When she came to the one in question, she tore it open. Her shoulders slumped, however, when she saw a "thinking of you" card with a verse of scripture on the inside. She read: " 'They that trust in the Lord shall be as mount Zion, which cannot be removed, but abideth for ever.' Psalm 125:1."

Sara pursed her lips. *I wonder what that's*

*supposed to mean. What exactly is Brad try-
ing to tell me?*

"Is it a Valentine's card?" Michelle asked.

Sara shook her head. "Just a 'thinking of
you' card." Unable to hide her disappointment, she moved over to the stove to heat
up the frying pan in readiness for the bacon
Grandma had taken from the refrigerator.

"Uh-oh." Michelle giggled, holding little
Val away from her shoulder. "Looks like this
little *schtinker* just initiated me."

Sara turned toward Michelle and noticed
a wet area forming on the front of her dress.

Michelle switched arms and cuddled her
puppy. "I'll take the cutie back to the barn.
Then I'll come back in and change clothes
before I sit down to breakfast."

"There are some cardboard boxes in the
basement. If you like, you can put your
puppy in that and keep her inside while we
eat," Grandma suggested.

"Sounds like a good idea, but I'd better
get her introduced to Sadie." Michelle put
her jacket back on. "Wish me luck."

It was wrong to feel envious, but Sara
couldn't help feeling a bit jealous of Michelle. Her boyfriend cared so much about
her that he'd not only given her a puppy,
but he had risked life and limb to leave Michelle a message on Grandma and Grand-

351

pa's frosty roof this morning. Every day when Michelle looked at her puppy, she'd be reminded of how much Ezekiel loved her.

Sara hadn't heard a word from Brad in two weeks, and now just a note with a scripture she didn't understand? *The least he could have done is send me a Valentine card. Of course,* Sara thought, when reason won out, *I am not Brad's girlfriend, so why would he have even thought about me in relationship to Valentine's Day? We haven't known each other very long, and to him I'm only an acquaintance. For all I know, he already has a girlfriend. I'm just fooling myself to think he might be interested in me.*

As the bacon began to sizzle, Sara reflected more on the situation. It was too soon to really know how she felt about Brad, but for some reason, ever since she'd met the would-be preacher, he had been on her mind.

Clarks Summit
As Brad prepared for his first class, his thoughts went to Sara, as they often did since he'd returned from Strasburg on New Year's. Had she received his "thinking of you" card by now? If so, Brad wondered what her reaction was to the verse of scripture he'd included. It was the one God had

placed on his heart to include.

He glanced at the calendar on his cell phone. It was Valentine's Day, and he'd remembered his mother with a card and a dozen pink carnations — her favorite flower. He'd ordered it from a local florist, and the flowers had been delivered to his aunt's place in Seattle, where he assumed Mom was still helping out. Brad had also sent Aunt Marlene another bouquet, because she loved the first one he'd sent while recuperating and he didn't want her to feel left out.

Brad had toyed with the idea of sending flowers to Sara but dismissed the idea. Not only would it be an added expense, but she might get the wrong idea.

He looked at his watch and saw he still had enough time to get to the university. Maybe he'd opt for a bowl of cereal this morning since it wouldn't take long to eat.

When he went to get a bowl, his cell phone rang. Seeing it was his parents' number, he answered right away.

"Hi, Brad, it's Mom."

"Hey, Mom, how you doing? I was just thinking of you and Aunt Marlene."

"I'm well. Just wanted to call and let you know I'm home. But first, and most importantly, happy belated birthday, Brad." She sighed. "I was going to call last Friday on your birthday, because I thought I'd be home by then. Unfortunately, your aunt came down with a bad cold, and I had to stay an extra week. Sorry we missed Christmas together, and now your birthday came and went too."

"It's okay, Mom. I've been so busy I have hardly had time to think about it." Brad looked at his watch again and saw he only had half an hour until his first class started. Since he hadn't talked to his mother since Aunt Marlene's surgery, he'd just skip breakfast so he could talk longer to her. "How is Aunt Marlene doing since I last talked to you?"

"She did well after some convincing to lay low. You know how your aunt is — nothing keeps her down. Anyway, she healed well from her surgery, and luckily her cold only lasted a few days, so I was able to come home yesterday." She paused, and then added, "I want to thank you for the beautiful pink carnations you sent me. They were delivered to her house two days before I left. And your aunt liked her flowers too."

"Good to hear. Glad I sent them early."

"Yes, I'm sitting here looking at a picture of them now. You remembered pink carnations are my favorite. Unfortunately, I couldn't bring them home in my suitcase."

"I'm glad you got to enjoy the flowers for a few days. Hey, how's Dad doing? Did he manage okay while you were gone?"

"He said so. I'm sure he enjoyed the peace and quiet." She paused again, then asked, "Did you get your friend anything for Valentine's Day?"

"Are you referring to Sara?"

"If that's the one you told me about the last time we talked, then yes."

"No, Mom, we're still just friends, so it wasn't appropriate to send something to her for Valentine's Day." Brad looked at his watch one more time. "Sorry, Mom, but I'm gonna have to go. I have fifteen minutes to get to my first class."

"Okay, Brad. Have a good day. Oh, and I'll fix you something special for dinner when we see you next time."

"No problem, and tell Dad I said hi."

As Brad put on his coat, he thought about his mother's question. *I need to get to know Sara better before giving her any gifts,* Brad told himself as he gathered a stack of books and put them in his backpack. Since spring break would be coming up next month, he hoped to make a trip to Strasburg and stay with Ned again. Of course, the main reason Brad planned to go to Lancaster County was to see Sara. In the meantime, he would keep in touch through letters and phone calls as time allowed. If it was meant for them to develop a relationship that went beyond friendship, Brad would know. Hopefully, Sara would too.

CHAPTER 31

Strasburg

"I can't believe it's the third Saturday of March already." Mary Ruth pointed to the calendar on her kitchen wall. "With this warmer weather we're having, it'll soon be time to plant my garden. And did you notice" — she added with enthusiasm — "the hyacinths are almost ready to bloom?"

"Jah, I did see that." Smiling, Michelle washed their breakfast bowls. It was nice to see Mary Ruth get excited about something as simple as planting a garden and seeing flowers bloom. "You can count on my help again this year," Michelle volunteered. With the exception of the pesky gnats that would no doubt plague her as they had last summer, she too looked forward to planting seeds, pulling weeds, and harvesting a bounty of organically grown produce.

"I'm also willing to help you in the garden on my days off, Grandma," Sara said, reaching for another juice glass to dry. "From the time I was a young girl, I helped Mama in her garden, so I've had a little experience."

"Thank you, Sara. I will take all the help I can get. And as I may have mentioned, your mother always liked to have her fingers in the dirt." Mary Ruth stared across the room, as though reliving something from the past. "I remember how excited she got, especially when she was a little girl and saw the seeds she helped me put into the soil sprout and turn into mature plants."

"Speaking of help, I promised I would help Willis feed the hogs this morning." Michelle rinsed out the sponge and let the water out of the sink. "As soon as we finish with that chore, I'll be in the barn with Val." Michelle looked at Sara. "Wanna join us?"

Sara laid her dishcloth aside. "Feeding the hogs or playing with your puppy?"

Michelle shrugged. "Both if you want to."

Sara wrinkled her nose. "Think I'll pass on feeding the hogs, but I would like to play with your cute little pup again."

"Okay. I should be done helping Willis in half an hour or so. I'll see you in the barn as soon as I'm done." Michelle slipped on a pair of black boots, grabbed a lightweight jacket, and went out the back door.

■ ■ ■ ■

With a relaxed posture, Mary Ruth looked at Sara and grinned. "That young woman is going to make a good Amish wife someday. She doesn't mind doing the most unpleasant chores."

"I believe you are right. Michelle seems to have found her niche." Sara glanced out the kitchen window. "I, on the other hand, have no idea where my life is supposed to take me." She turned to look at Mary Ruth. "Some days I feel like I'm floundering."

Mary Ruth's brows furrowed. "Oh dear, I had no idea you felt that way. Is it because you're living here without access to electricity and other modern things? Because if that is the case, and you'd rather be out on your own, your grandpa and I will understand." She paused and massaged a sore spot on her thumb knuckle where she'd bumped it while opening a drawer. "Of course, we love having you here, and if you choose to stay, it would make us very happy. But if you decide to move out, we will not pressure you to stay."

Sara's forehead wrinkled slightly as she reached back to tighten the pink rubber band holding her ponytail in place. "I enjoy living here with you and Grandpa, and for now, at least, I'd like to stay. I have access to electricity at the flower shop, and I'm able to use my laptop and charge my cell phone whenever there's a need."

Mary Ruth closed her eyes briefly, then opened them again. "I'm so glad, dear one. Meeting you, and having you living with us has meant the world to your grandpa and me. I hope that no matter what the future holds, we never lose contact with each other." She gave Sara a hug. As they held each other in a meaningful embrace, Mary Ruth sent up a silent prayer. *Thank You, Lord, for bringing Sara and Michelle into our lives. In different ways, they have brought us* so *much happiness. I thank You for the friendship I see blossoming between them. The girls may not realize it, but they need each other, so this is truly an answer to prayer.*

When Sara entered the barn, she found Michelle kneeling on the floor, alternating between petting Sadie and the little Irish setter.

Sara couldn't help but smile when Sadie licked the pup's head. "I think Val may have found a surrogate mother," she said, kneeling beside Michelle.

"Yeah. Sadie has had a bit of practice. She

was a good mother when she gave birth to a litter of puppies back in June." Michelle stroked Sadie's head, then Val's. "Ezekiel knew what he was doing when he gave me this puppy. She's not only good medicine for me, but also for Sadie. Having Val to play with helps us not to miss Rascal so much."

Sara reached out and stroked the pup's silky ears. "I bet even when she is fully grown she'll be cute — or at least beautiful — with all that shiny auburn hair."

"I believe you're right." Michelle pointed in the direction of the shelf where the antique canning jars were set. "Changing the subject . . . I was wondering if you have read anything from either of the prayer jars lately."

"Just the one in the basement, but that was several weeks ago."

"Should we get the jar in here down and read a few notes now? I could use a little inspiration."

"Sure. I'm always in need of encouragement." Sara stood, and Michelle did the same.

Val whined for a few seconds, but then the pup settled down when Sadie nuzzled her head with her nose.

"Sadie makes a good babysitter," Sara said

as they walked to the other side of the barn.

Michelle snickered. "I sure never expected Willis and Mary Ruth's dog to take such an interest in my little hundli. Figured she might either be jealous or treat Val like she's a nuisance. But so far, it's all been good."

"All puppies can be an annoyance at times, but their cuteness usually outweighs their mischievous ways."

"That's for sure." Michelle climbed up on a stool and took down the glass jar filled with inspirational writings. Then Sara sat beside her on a bale of hay.

Michelle pulled a slip of paper from the jar and read the message out loud. "Broken people are made whole by God's love." She looked over at Sara. "I can sure relate to that quote."

Sara shrugged. *How does she want me to respond? Am I supposed to admit that I'm broken? Is that what Michelle wants to hear?* Truth was, Sara could barely admit that fact to herself.

"Okay now, it's your turn." Michelle handed the jar to Sara.

Sara pulled out a slip of paper that had been slightly torn on one corner. The words were still legible though. She read it silently, wondering once again who had written these notes. This one in particular really captured her attention.

"You look bewildered." Michelle bumped Sara's arm. "What's it say?"

"Leave the past where it belongs — which is in the past. Look forward to the future that has been planned for you." Sara pressed her lips together, then opened them again. "I'm not sure why, but this makes me think of something my mother said to me once."

"What was it?" Michelle asked.

"Mama told me a person might believe their life is taking them in one direction, and then something happens to turn their world upside down." Sara's voice wavered. "I — I didn't understand what she meant until my world was upended when I found out she'd been hiding a secret from me since I was born."

"You mean about the fact that she ran away from home and you had grandparents whom you grew up knowing nothing about?"

Sara gave a slow nod as she folded her arms tightly across her chest. "I loved my mother — don't get me wrong, but I'm still struggling with her deceit, and I can't seem to forgive her for that. Since I am her only daughter, I would think I'd be the last person she'd want to deceive."

Michelle placed her hand on Sara's arm,

giving it a gentle squeeze. "I know all about the struggle to forgive people who have hurt me." She looked at the jar Sara held. "Finding the prayer jars was a turning point for me. I can honestly say that my life has changed since reading the notes I discovered — especially the Bible verses that pointed me in the direction of accepting Christ as my Savior and learning the importance of going to God in prayer whenever I have a need. Have you done that, Sara? Have you asked Jesus to forgive your sins and come into your heart?"

Sara's body tensed and she found it difficult to swallow. "No, I — I haven't."

"Would you like to do it right now?" Michelle's voice was gentle, and Sara sensed her concern. "I'd be happy to pray with you."

Sara reached back and fiddled with the end of her ponytail. "I appreciate your concern, but I'm not ready to commit to anything right now. *Or forgive Mama for keeping the truth of my heritage from me all these years,* she silently added.

Sara felt relief when she heard a vehicle pull up outside. The look of disappointment she'd seen on Michelle's face when she refused her help had almost made her cave in. "That must be Brad. When he called me the other night, he said he'd be coming here today." She handed the jar back to Michelle, leaped to her feet, and raced out the barn door.

When Brad stepped out of his van, and saw Sara walking toward him, he felt an adrenaline rush course through his body. Although she wore a pair of jeans and a plain sweatshirt, he thought Sara looked even more beautiful than the last time he'd seen her. She wore her hair in a ponytail today, showing more of her beautiful face. Her blue eyes seemed more vivid than he'd noticed before too.

Brad had to calm his breathing as he stepped forward and gave her a hug. "It's good to see you again, Sara."

"It's nice to see you too." Her dimpled smile made him feel like hugging her again. But he didn't want to appear too forward, so he held himself in check. Besides, they had an audience now, since Michelle had just stepped out of the barn.

Brad smiled and waved. "Hey, Michelle. How's it going?"

"Good. Real good. Come see what Ezekiel gave me for Valentine's Day." She gestured to the barn.

"You'd better go see." Sara took hold of

his hand. "I promise you won't be disappointed."

Eager to see what gift Ezekiel had given Michelle, Brad went willingly with Sara. Michelle was way ahead of them, and by the time they entered the barn, she met them near the door with a red-furred pup in her arms.

"This is Val," Michelle announced, rubbing the dog's floppy ears. "Since she was a Valentine's Day gift, the name I chose for her seems appropriate."

Brad reached out his hand and stroked the pup's other ear. "She's a cute little thing. Irish setter, right?"

Michelle nodded. "By the time she's fully grown, she'll probably be bigger than Sadie."

As if on cue, the collie padded out from the back of the barn, wagging her tail.

"Well, hello there, girl." Brad bent down to pet Sadie, while Sara looked on. "And what does she think of your little furry intruder?" he asked, directing his question to Michelle. He had to grin to himself when Sadie sat down, making herself comfortable on his foot.

"Much to my surprise, Sadie actually likes Val."

"It's true," Sara chimed in. "Michelle and

I were both surprised to see how well Sadie took to the puppy."

"That's great." Brad smiled at Michelle. "It was a thoughtful gift your boyfriend gave you. The pup's a keeper, and so is your guy."

Her cheeks reddened. "I agree. Ezekiel has always been good to me."

Brad glanced at Sara. "So are you ready to do something fun today?"

"Yes, I am." Sara rubbed her hands together. "What did you have in mind?"

"We could attend the mud sale going on in Manheim. Or how about staying local and taking a ride on the Strasburg Rail Road?" Brad scraped a hand through his hair. "But you know what I'd really like to show you this morning?"

"What's that?" Sara's brows raised slightly.

"The Biblical Tabernacle here in Lancaster County."

"Tabernacle?" She glanced at Michelle, then back at Brad.

"Yes. It's a full-scale replica of the tabernacle we read about in the Old Testament."

"And it is inside the Mennonite Information Center," Michelle interjected. "I've never been there, but I've heard it's quite interesting. Ezekiel and I have talked about going to see it sometime. You should go see it with Brad, Sara."

"Okay, sure . . . why not?" Sara's tone was less than enthusiastic. Brad wondered if she'd agreed to go only because he'd suggested it. However, once Sara got there and saw the uniqueness of it, he felt sure she would be glad they went.

CHAPTER 32

Lancaster

As Sara stood next to Brad, inside a large building with a contoured ceiling, she listened to their guide give details about the brazen altar and ark of the covenant, while pointing out the replica of it.

Brad looked over at Sara and whispered, "Even for people who know their biblical history, this presentation is fascinating."

People like you, not me. Sara nodded.

"Now as you look into the holy place, you will see a full-size wax figure representing the high priest," their female narrator said. "The priest presided over the altar of incense, and his robes had precious stones embedded in gold on the breastplate he wore."

Sara also learned that the golden candlestick and table of shewbread were made to scale. There was an authentically researched design of the veil, showing how, in biblical times, it separated the people from the presence of God. All this information was new to her, but she made no mention of it to Brad.

When the presentation was over, at Brad's suggestion, they wandered into the area where various religious books were sold. Brad picked out two books, and asked if Sara wanted anything, but she declined, saying, "Not at this time."

"If it's about the cost, I'd be happy to buy it for you."

She shook her head. "It's not that. I just have plenty of books already that still need to be read." *Liar.* Sara's conscience pricked her. While she did have a few unread books in her room, none of them were of a religious nature.

After Brad paid for his purchases, he suggested they go to Miller's restaurant on Route 30 between Ronks and Paradise. "They have a good variety of food there." He thumped his stomach. "So we won't leave hungry. And since I invited you on this date, the meal will be my treat."

"Sounds good, but I can't guarantee you'll get your money's worth. I'm not a big eater."

"No problem. While they're known for their smorgasbord, they have a great salad bar, plus lots of other lighter choices." Brad opened the door for Sara and stepped outside behind her. When they got to his van, he opened the passenger's door for her and waited until she fastened her seatbelt to close it.

Sara had never been out with anyone as polite as Brad. She appreciated his consideration and the extra attention he gave her. He was attractive and pleasant to talk to but probably not her type. But the truth was she wasn't sure what kind of man would be good for her. Sara knew one thing for sure — Brad would make a wonderful husband for a lucky woman someday.

Between Ronks and Paradise

"Wow, you weren't kidding about all the food they serve on the buffet here." Sara's eyes widened. Looking around the dining room, where the food stations were located, she could hardly take it all in. Even the dessert bar caught her attention, although Sara was sure she'd never be able to eat anything from it.

"This restaurant is not as big as the Shady Maple Smorgasbord up in East Earl, but it offers more than enough food for most people." Brad pulled out a chair for Sara and waited until she was seated at their table before taking the seat across from her.

When a waitress came, they both ordered iced tea, and Brad told her that he and Sara would be eating from the buffet.

After the young woman left, he looked across the table at Sara and smiled. "If you don't mind, I'd like to pray before we get our food. Would it be okay if I pray out loud, or would you prefer we pray the Amish way?"

Sara took a sip of water. "The Amish way is fine for me. After living with my grand-parents these past four months, I've gotten used to their way of praying silently. Besides, my mother used to offer silent prayers too."

"No problem. We can pray the Amish way." Brad bowed his head, and Sara did the same. Sara would never have admitted to Brad, or anyone else for that matter, that she rarely prayed. And on the few occasions Sara had whispered a prayer, she wasn't sure it was even heard. If God was real, He seemed too far away to hear anyone's prayers. And if He did listen to people's prayers, why would He care about hers? Sara really had no connection to God. How could she when He'd taken the only person she'd ever loved? It was one more thing Sara had to feel bitter about.

Sara opened her eyes, to see if Brad had

finished praying. Seeing that his head was still bowed, she dropped her gaze as well, allowing more thoughts to swirl in her head.

Is it Mama's betrayal that bothers me the most, her untimely death, or not knowing my real father? Her fingers tightened around the napkin in her lap. *Maybe the root of my bitterness stems from having a stepfather who has never cared much for me.*

Sara couldn't change a single thing about her past, and stewing about it didn't help. Yet there were moments, like now, when Mama's deception and Dean's lack of attention cut through Sara's soul like a piercing arrow.

When she heard a slight rustle, Sara looked up, and was relieved to see Brad's eyes were open. No doubt he'd prayed a meaningful prayer. *It's a good thing he doesn't know my thoughts were elsewhere. Brad probably wouldn't want to go out with me again if he knew how I feel about my mother, not to mention my stepfather.*

Sara forced a smile, hoping her pent-up emotions wouldn't show on her face. How many times had she gone over all this in her head? As time went on, her resentment had increased. She'd been getting along better with Michelle these days, so why couldn't she forgive the other people who had hurt her and move on?

Brad pushed his chair back and stood. "Should we help ourselves to some food?"

"Sure." Sara followed as he led the way to the buffet stations. It would be good to focus on eating rather than reminiscing about the past or trying to dissect her feelings.

Sara helped herself to the salad bar, then added a few chilled steamed shrimp, a piece of carved turkey, and some mixed cooked vegetables to her plate. Normally, she didn't eat this much for lunch, but all this appetizing food was too tempting to ignore. Of course, she would probably pay the price for it later when she was too full to eat whatever Grandma fixed for supper.

Back at the table, Brad pointed to his full plate of food and rolled his eyes. "I'd planned on having at least one piece of pie, but after I eat all this, I doubt I'll have enough room for dessert."

"I hear you. This is a lot of food."

As they ate, they talked about Michelle's new puppy and how happy and content she seemed these days.

"She's certainly not the same young woman I met last summer. She seemed so distraught and like she was hiding something," Brad commented. "Once Michelle admitted her deceit, and sought forgiveness from the Lord as well as the Lapps, she became like a new person."

Sara wasn't quite sure how to respond. "I guess you're right. She has changed, but I thought it was mostly due to her decision to join the Amish faith."

"I don't believe she would have ever made that decision if she hadn't become a Christian." Brad leaned forward, looking at Sara with a most serious expression. "How about you, Sara? Are you a Christian?"

Sara fiddled with the spoon lying next to her plate. Between the things Michelle said to her this morning, and the information she and Brad heard about the Biblical Tabernacle, Sara felt as if she was being pressured to become a Christian. This unexpected question from Brad was the final straw.

What am I supposed to say in response? I don't like it when people lie, yet I feel like I'm being backed into a corner.

Sara took a drink of iced tea, stalling for time. After a few uncomfortable seconds, she set her glass down and forced herself to make eye contact with him. "Yes, I'm a Christian." Her conscience prodded, *No, you're not,* but she pushed the thought aside. *What other choice did I have? If I had* admitted *I'm not a Christian, Brad most likely would not want to see me again.*

A slow smile spread across his face. "That's good to hear." No doubt, he was relieved to know the woman he was having lunch with wasn't an atheist, at least.

Sara's conscience stabbed her again. *Listen to me. I'm no better than Michelle used to be. She pretended to be me, and now I'm pretending to be a Christian. Guess that makes me a liar and a hypocrite. I am professing to be something I'm not so I can have a relationship with a man who truly is a Christian, in every sense of the word.* Staring down at her napkin, Sara wadded it into a ball. *My heart has been hardened toward God, and I'm not sure it will ever soften.*

"Will you excuse me for a minute?" Sara could barely meet Brad's eyes. She needed a bit of space and didn't want to continue this conversation, so she found an excuse to escape. "I need to get a little more dressing for my salad."

"Sure, I may need to make another trip to the buffet myself, but I'll finish what I have here first."

"Okay then. I'll be right back." Sara hurried across the room and didn't look back. *I should have been honest with Brad, but I didn't have the nerve.*

■ ■ ■ ■

Brad watched as Sara made her way to the salad bar. From the way she hurried off, it seemed like she may have been anxious to leave the table. *Sure hope I didn't say anything to upset her.* To be truthful, Brad wasn't sure Sara had enjoyed herself today. He'd found the tabernacle replica fascinating, but most of the time during the tour Sara had appeared distant, almost detached, when their guide explained things. It seemed as if her mind was somewhere else.

As he took a swallow of iced tea, Brad came to a conclusion. *Some people aren't biblical history buffs like me. Guess I should have taken Sara to the mud sale in Manheim or rode the Strasburg Rail Road train ride through part of Amish country.* His shoulders rose and fell. *I should have let Sara decide what she wanted to do, instead of deciding it for her.*

Brad looked up in time to see Sara coming in his direction, and at the same moment, another familiar person came into view, and she was making her way toward him.

Just as Sara got to the table with a small

container of salad dressing, a lovely dark-haired woman stepped up to their table and greeted Brad like an old friend. "Well, fancy seeing you here, Brad."

"Terri, what a surprise." Brad looked at Sara. "This is Terri Conners. She attends the same university I do. Terri, this is my friend, Sara Murray."

"Nice to meet you," Sara and Terri said in unison.

"Do you mind if I join you?" Terri gestured to the empty chair at their table.

"No problem." Brad stood up and pulled out the chair for her.

"I'm glad I ran into you here, and you were so right." Terri's arm brushed Brad's as she leaned closer to him. "Amish country is incredible. There's so much to see and do. I wish now that I'd come here sooner."

Is this young woman just a friend of Brad's, or could she be his girlfriend? Sara tapped her foot under the table.

"I met Terri in the school cafeteria one day. We got to talking about places to visit, and I told her about Lancaster County." Brad explained, looking at Sara. "Terri's studying to be a youth minister. She's in her second year of school."

Terri directed her attention to Sara. "I'm a preacher's kid, born and raised in Maine."

She turned back to Brad. "But I tell you, after spending a few days in this arca, I could move here in a heartbeat."

"Have you done much sightseeing?" Brad asked.

"Yes, I have. One day I visited an Amish farm, and afterward the tour group even got to see the house. I, along with a bunch of other tourists, then sat down to the most fabulous home-cooked meal. We were seated at a long table and talked among ourselves as we ate." Terri kept her focus on Brad, glancing only briefly in Sara's direction. "Afterward, I even got the chance to ride in a horse and buggy. That was sure fun."

"My grandparents are Amish," Sara spoke up.

Terri eyed her with a curious expression. "But you're not Amish?"

Sara shook her head. The last thing she wanted was for Terri to start asking more questions, so she quickly changed the subject. "Brad and I toured the Biblical Tabernacle earlier today."

"I was there yesterday. Too bad we didn't end up there at the same time. It would have been nice to hang out with someone I know." Once more, Terri directed her comment to Brad. "Wasn't the made-to-scale tabernacle interesting?"

"It sure was."

Sara sat quietly listening to the two of them describe what they liked best about the tour. This pretty, dark-haired woman had such an easy time talking with Brad, and he seemed equally comfortable with Terri.

Sara felt almost invisible as she picked at the rest of her salad. *Am I imagining it, or is Ms. Conners interested in Brad?* She stirred restlessly. *I have no claim whatsoever on Brad, and I probably shouldn't care, but I do. But then Terri's obviously a Christian — a much better fit for him.*

CHAPTER 33

Strasburg

Brad lounged in a chair on the Lapps' front porch, waiting for Sara to get her purse, which she'd forgotten on the way out the door. This was his last day of spring break, and he'd invited her to attend church with him in Lancaster. Sara seemed hesitant when he'd first extended the invitation, saying she usually went to Amish church with her grandparents. But when Willis reminded Sara this was their off-Sunday and they were planning to visit their son Ivan's church district in Paradise, she agreed to go along with Brad.

It surprised him, since Ivan was Sara's uncle. He figured she'd want to go with her grandparents. For whatever her reason, Brad was glad Sara was willing to attend church with him.

Running a finger down the crease in his dark gray dress slacks, Brad thought about

381

the previous week. He'd spent as much time with Sara as possible — stopping by the flower shop a few times, in addition to taking her out for dinner on three occasions. Brad had also been invited to the Lapps' for supper on two evenings. Each time Brad and Sara were together, he found himself more drawn to her. Sara seemed more relaxed this week than last, which made him regret having to leave even more. He wished he didn't have to return to the university so soon. If it were possible, he'd stay in Strasburg permanently.

But Brad couldn't lose sight of his goal to preach, which meant more studying in preparation for the ministry. He'd decided to return to Strasburg for the summer months and already looked forward to that. He hoped to drive and work for the Amish again and might take an online class or two, rather than attending summer classes at the university. Brad felt confident that by the end of the summer he would know if Sara was the woman God had in mind for him.

I'm relieved Sara is a Christian, and I'm glad I found the courage to ask. My only other concern is whether she'd be willing to take on the role of a pastor's wife.

Brad sat up straight. *I'm moving way too fast. I haven't given it enough time to know if*

Sara and I are even right for each other.

When the front door opened, and Sara stepped onto the porch, Brad jumped up. "Ready to go?"

With a nod, she clasped his extended hand. Being with Sara and heading for worship service on this blue-skied Sunday morning felt exactly right. Brad looked forward to summer and enjoying more days like this.

Lancaster

What am I doing here? I feel so out of place. Sara glanced around the rural church Brad had taken her to this morning. The polished wooden pews had been arranged neatly in rows. On the back of each pew a wooden shelf held a Bible, songbook, and several welcome cards. Along both sides of the room were three stained glass windows, with another one on the wall behind the baptistery at the front of the sanctuary. In front of the pulpit sat an ornate-looking table with a large Bible on it that was flanked by two white candles.

Also near the front of the room and to the left a bit sat a grand piano, as well as a keyboard, where two female musicians sat. In addition to a drummer, three other men sat on the platform with guitars.

Four attractively dressed people — two men and two women — stepped forward with microphones to lead the singing. The first four songs were lively choruses — quite a change from the drawn-out hymns sung in German Sara had become used to hearing during Amish worship services. A good portion of the congregation clapped as they sang — another thing that would not be done in the Amish church.

The fact that Sara could not understand any of the words written in the Amish *Ausbund,* or know what the ministers said when they preached in German, might be why she felt more comfortable attending Amish church. Sara disliked the idea that she was being preached at, so not understanding the bishop and ministers' words was a benefit.

After the choruses, the song leader asked everyone to be seated. Two men passed the offering plates around, and then more singing followed — this time, several hymns.

As Sara stood next to Brad, following the words in her songbook, she gave him a sidelong glance. His joyful expression as he lifted both hands and sang with honest enthusiasm said it all. Brad was a committed Christian, in every sense of the word. He needed no hymnal to read the lyrics.

This devout man knew all the songs by heart.

I should break things off with him, Sara thought. *I am not cut out for a religious life, which seems to be his whole world.*

Sara looked around at the congregation, as nearly everyone lifted their voices in praise to the Lord once again. She turned her head, glancing at the pews toward the back of the church and stifled her intake of breath. Terri Conners sat two rows behind them.

Sara lowered her gaze, turned around, and joined in with the singing. *I cannot believe Terri Conners is here too. Did she follow us, or did Brad tell her he'd be attending here today?*

When the singing ended and they were seated again, Brad reached for Sara's hand and gave her fingers a gentle squeeze. Her hand remained in his until the pastor stepped up to the pulpit and asked everyone to open their Bibles. Brad let go of Sara's hand and opened his Bible. Sara was amazed at how quickly he found the passage of scripture the minister said he would be preaching from. If Sara had been asked to find the book of Acts, it would have taken her forever.

Sara thought about her mother's Bible,

which she'd rarely looked at since finding Mama's note telling Sara about her grandparents. *I wonder how well my mother knew the scriptures. Was she as well versed with them as Grandpa and Grandma are, or did the Bible mean little or nothing to Mama, as it does to me?*

Sara clutched the folds in her skirt, tuning out the pastor's words, although Brad seemed fixated on the message. *If my mother had a connection with God, then why wasn't she honest enough to tell me about her past, while she was still alive — and more importantly, about my father?*

Sara's mother had grown up in a home where devotions and prayer prevailed. And until she'd run away from home, she had no doubt attended Amish church. *Why then,* Sara wondered, *didn't Mama talk about spiritual things with me?*

Why? Why? Why? Sara's lips tightened as another wave of bitterness rose in her soul. Try as she might, Sara couldn't push the feelings aside. *If Mama had professed to be a Christian, and acted like one by being honest, then I might be a Christian too.*

The whimper of a baby pushed Sara's thoughts aside. Holding the fussy infant in one arm and a diaper bag in the other, the young woman in front of them slipped quietly from her pew. Sara watched her go out the back of the church and couldn't help noticing Terri again.

Sara thought of a plan. *Somehow, Brad and I are going to get out of this church without running into her.*

When the pastor mentioned another verse, this one from John, Brad turned back several pages in his Bible.

Sara tried to be attentive and listen to what the middle-aged man behind the pulpit had to say, but her mind wandered all over the place.

Before Brad leaves for Clarks Summit, I should tell him I can't see him anymore. Her stomach tightened as she bit the inside of her cheek. Another option would be to keep seeing Brad and continue letting him think she was a Christian. *But what about Terri Conners? Should I get out of the way so she can move in on Brad?* It was obvious to Sara that was what the young woman wanted.

When the service ended, and Brad took Sara's hand again, she lost her resolve. She would continue with the facade a little longer. Later down the road if their relationship became serious, she would admit to Brad that she wasn't a believer. It would be a test to see what kind of a man he was. For to Sara's way of thinking, a true Christian should not be prejudiced against someone who wasn't.

Since the service had ended, Brad assumed Sara would get up, but she remained on their pew. "Are you ready to go?" he asked.

"Yes. Just thought it would be good to wait for the elderly parishioners to leave before we rush out. I noticed most of them were sitting up front."

"You've made a good point." Brad glanced at the older people slowly making their way to the aisle. One man, who was stooped over, walked with a cane. Another elderly couple walked arm in arm, as if to steady the other. *These good folks are probably long-time members of this church, and they deserve to be treated with respect. I'm glad Sara pointed it out.*

"It looks like most of the church has cleared out now." Sara got up and entered into the aisle.

At the door, the pastor greeted Brad and Sara and welcomed them to his church. As Brad explained to the preacher about his interest in ministry, he realized Sara had already stepped out the door. He shook the clergyman's hand and hurried after her.

It was hard to read Sara's thoughts as they

walked to the parking lot. She hadn't said a word since they'd left the church.

They were almost to Brad's van, when someone called his name. He turned around.

"Brad!" Terri waved her arms.

He waved back in response, and holding Sara's hand, he led her over to where Terri stood by her car.

"I can't believe the way we keep bumping into each other." Terri grinned at Brad. "Are you heading back to school today?"

"Yes, but there are still a few people I want to say goodbye to, so I'll be leaving a bit later."

"I hate to ask, but would you mind if I followed you back to Clarks Summit? I've been staying at a bed-and-breakfast near the entrance to Highway 222 and need to check out by noon. I can wait for you in the parking lot there."

"Sure, I guess that would work." Brad glanced at Sara, quietly fiddling with her purse straps.

"Thank you, Brad." Terri touched his arm. "I figure you'd know a better way to get back to Clarks Summit. I ended up taking a longer route when I came down here, and I'd like to save on gas when I travel back."

"Okay, Terri, I'll see you soon."

As Brad walked with Sara back to his van, he sensed something was troubling her and wondered if it had anything to do with Terri. *Or maybe,* he thought, *Sara didn't enjoy the church service today.*

"Are you okay? You've been kind of quiet since the service let out." Brad said, once he'd started the van.

"I'm fine."

"Did you enjoy the church service?"

Sara nodded. "It was nice. A lot different than Amish church, that's for sure."

"What church did you attend when you lived in New Jersey?" Brad left the parking lot and pulled out into traffic.

"Umm . . ." More toying with her purse. Was she nervous about something?

"I assume you and your family had a home church."

"Yes. Yes, of course. It was a few blocks from our home." Sara turned her head to the right, looking out the passenger's window.

Something didn't seem right. She'd been aloof — almost distracted since Terri showed up. Brad was on the verge of saying something, but changed his mind. All he wanted was to enjoy Sara's company before it was time to return to Clarks Summit. If

Sara was upset about something, surely she would have said so.

Paradise

As Michelle sat on a backless wooden bench in the basement of the home of Lenore's parents, she reflected on the conversation she'd had with Sara in the barn last week. Sara seemed like a good person, and because she had forgiven Michelle for impersonating her, Michelle assumed Sara was a Christian. To hear Sara say she was not a believer had been a surprise.

Michelle's brows furrowed. *If Sara could forgive me, then why not her mother? A lot of parents have done worse things to their kids than keeping the truth about their heritage from them. Ask me. I should know.*

Michelle had prayed for Sara every day since their discussion in the barn. She'd been tempted to talk to Sara's grandparents about it, but didn't follow through. If Sara found out Michelle had divulged the information she'd shared with her, it could ruin the bond they'd begun to form.

Michelle's thoughts shifted gears. *I wonder if Sara enjoyed the church service she and Brad went to.* Brad was an upright person, and his being around her was good for Sara — especially in a spiritual way. Perhaps he could get through to her when no one else could.

She glanced over at Lenore, sitting beside her, so straight and tall. The attention of the Lapps' granddaughter appeared to be fully focused on her grandfather, who'd begun preaching the second sermon of the day. Michelle had no doubt as to whether the pleasant schoolteacher was a Christian or not. Everything about Lenore spelled peace, love, and joy — all the attributes of a person who loved the Lord and set an example for others. It was hard to believe Lenore wasn't being courted by anyone. She had the makings of a fantastic wife.

Michelle remembered how, when she'd first met Lenore, she had been surprised to learn that she often attended church in her grandparents' district. But then she'd found out that many Amish people visit neighboring church districts on their off-Sundays, as she and the Lapps were doing today. Willis had even been invited as a guest minister to preach one of the sermons.

Michelle stirred restlessly. *I hope when I get baptized next Sunday and become a church member, my actions will let others know I am a Christian.*

While the Amish people she knew did not go around testifying and preaching their faith to people outside of their Plain community, they tried by their actions and deeds to be an example of what it meant to be a Christian.

"The world will know us by our actions," Willis had said in one of the messages he'd preached. Michelle felt thankful for Ezekiel's interpretation of the sermon that day, since she still struggled to understand the German language spoken during church. The everyday Pennsylvania Dutch dialect had been easier to grasp, and for the most part, she understood it and could speak a good many sentences now. How thankful she was for Ezekiel's and the Lapps' patience in teaching her those Amish words.

Next Sunday, church would be held at the home of Ezekiel's parents, where the baptism would take place. As much as Michelle wanted to become Amish, she still struggled with the question, *Am I ready to take this most serious step?*

She closed her eyes briefly and lifted a silent prayer. *Dear Lord, please give me a sense of peace about this, for getting baptized and becoming a church member is a life-long commitment — to You and the Amish church.*

CHAPTER 34

A week later, Strasburg

Throughout the first sermon, preached by Willis Lapp, and now with the second one started by one of the other ministers, Ezekiel's thoughts should have been focused on the man's words, rather than someplace else. While he felt certain that joining the Amish church was the right thing for him, he still had some concerns. Saturday evening, Ezekiel, Michelle, and the eight other baptismal candidates met with the ministers one last time. The preachers had taken turns reading the articles of faith and answering any questions the young people had. It was their final opportunity to change their minds about joining the church.

Ezekiel had been relieved when Michelle didn't back out. He'd been worried at first, but she seemed as sure as he was that becoming a church member was the right thing for her. What concerned him the most was when the ministers reminded the male candidates that, by becoming members, they were also agreeing to serve in the church as a minister or deacon, should the lot ever fall upon them. Ezekiel wasn't sure he could handle such a big responsibility, and he hoped he would never be faced with it in the years to come. But if the time should ever come and his name was chosen, he would trust the Lord for the wisdom and strength to perform his duties.

He glanced across the way at Michelle. She sat looking down at her hands clasped together in her lap. No doubt, she felt a bit anxious this morning too.

Michelle's stomach churned like a blender at full speed. In a few minutes she, along with the other candidates for membership, would kneel before the bishop to answer the questions he would ask each of them. This was the most exciting yet frightening thing Michelle had ever done. More so than her high school graduation, after which she'd decided it was time to leave her foster parents' home and branch out on her own. Any doubts she may have had about making this lifelong change had passed when she entered Ezekiel's parents' house this morning and took her seat on one of the benches. Michelle was not the same person she used to be. She was fully committed to the Lord now, and would soon be committed to the Amish church as well.

Today was a special day for those seeking membership. Many of the candidates' family members and friends had come to the service. Michelle wished her brothers could be here too. *If Ernie and Jack knew about my decision to become Amish, what would they think? Would they make fun of me, like Jerry and his girlfriend did when I waited on them at the restaurant? Or would my brothers support my decision and say they were happy for me?*

Michelle looked over at Ezekiel, wondering what he might be thinking right now. Was he nervous? Excited? She couldn't be certain, although the way his right knee kept bouncing up and down, he had to be feeling one of those things.

Ezekiel hadn't spoken up yesterday when asked if he had any reservations about joining the church. So Michelle had no doubts about his readiness to make the commitment with her today.

When the second sermon concluded, the bishop asked the candidates to leave their seats and kneel in front of him. Michelle's heart pounded as he asked the group of young people their first question. "Can you confess that you believe Jesus Christ is the Son of God?"

Michelle, along with the others, replied: "Yes, I believe Jesus Christ is the Son of God."

The second question came: "Do you recognize this to be a Christian order, church, and fellowship under which you now submit yourself to?"

Everyone replied affirmatively.

"Do you renounce the world, the devil, with all his subtle ways, as well as your own flesh and blood, and do you desire to serve Jesus Christ alone, who died on the cross for you?"

Tears welled in Michelle's eyes as she and the others answered, "Yes."

Then the final question came. "Do you also promise before God and His church that you will support these teachings and regulations with the Lord's help, faithfully attending the services of the church and helping to counsel and work in it, and will not forsake it, whether it leads to life or death?"

"Yes." Michelle's throat tightened to such a degree that she could barely swallow or get the words out. Her heart was filled with unspeakable joy. It seemed as if she had been waiting for this blessed occasion all of her life.

Sara stood with the others in the congregation as the bishop offered a prayer. Michelle, Ezekiel, and the eight other young people remained in their kneeling position.

Following the prayer, everyone in the congregation returned to their benches, except for the bishop and deacon, who continued to stand in front of those who were knelt before them.

Sara watched with curiosity as the bishop went down the line, holding his cupped hands on top of each candidate's head. Then the deacon poured water into the bishop's hands three times, as the bishop spoke: "Upon your faith, which you have confessed before God and many witnesses, you are baptized in the name of the Father, the Son, and the Holy Ghost."

After each person had been baptized, the bishop offered his hand and a holy kiss of peace to the males. His wife did the same for the females. Lastly a benediction was given: "You are no longer guests and strangers, but fellow citizens with the saints and of the household of God."

Michelle is doing what she believes is right for her, Sara mused. *But I am more certain than ever that I could never become Amish.* Hearing the bishop's questions and the candidates' answers, Sara knew if she'd been on her knees with the others, she would have had to either deny a relationship with Christ or pretend to be a believer, like she had with Brad.

Sara's fingers curled into the palms of her hands. *I am nothing but a hypocrite, pretending to be one thing, when I'm really something else.* Sara had never liked being lied to, yet her life had become a big fabrication. She felt trapped in her own web of lies and saw no way of escape. She understood now how easy it must have been for Michelle to deceive her grandparents. No doubt the imposter had convinced herself that she was doing it for the right reasons.

And what is my reason for pretending to be a Christian? Sara asked herself. *Do I really care for Brad, or is just a passing fancy?* Sara had never been caught up in a lie before, but now she couldn't seem to help herself.

She weighed in again on a week ago, when Brad's friend Terri kept showing up. While Brad had not admitted having feelings for Terri, Sara was almost certain the young ministerial student had eyes for him. She'd even been tempted to ask Brad if he'd ever taken Terri on a date.

Sara hoped she'd been able to hide her feelings from him, just as she hoped he didn't suspect she wasn't truly a believer.

She hadn't heard anything from Brad this week, other than a phone call letting her know he had made it back to Clarks Summit last Sunday afternoon. It hadn't been a lengthy call, and he'd said he needed to call his parents too. Sara suspected by the tone of Brad's voice that he was tired after the long day, so she'd told him to get some rest and that she hoped he would have a good week.

While Sara was glad to hear he'd arrived okay, other doubts kept feeding into her brain. Were Brad and Terri seeing each other during or after school? Did they meet for lunch every day?

Feeling the need for a breath of fresh air to clear her head, when the service ended and people began to set up tables for the meal, Sara left the house. She needed time alone, to think about her situation.

After the meal, as Mary Ruth helped some of the other women clean up, she thought about Sara.

She could not forget the look on her granddaughter's face when she and Willis hugged Michelle and said how happy it made them to see her get baptized and become a church member.

Sara had remained quiet during the meal too, responding only when spoken to. Was she jealous of the attention they'd given Michelle, or could Sara's mind be elsewhere today?

There seemed to be an unnatural stillness about Sara as she stood off to one side, watching other family members and friends walk up to Michelle and offer a hug or handshake. Could Sara be jealous of the attention Michelle was receiving? Or might Sara be wishing that she too had joined the Amish church today? If so, she'd given no indication of that. Even though their granddaughter had chosen to continue living with them, she seemed satisfied with her English way of life. Sara obviously did not want to give up owning a car, her cell phone, or her laptop.

Mary Ruth's eyes watered as she wiped off the last of the tables. *If Rhoda hadn't run away from home and joined the Amish church herself, Sara would no doubt have joined by now too.* But Mary Ruth knew that if Sara ever contemplated joining their faith sometime in the future, it would be a decision she would have to make for herself. Neither Mary Ruth nor Willis would try to sway their granddaughter one way or the other.

In contrast to Sara's disinterest in becoming Amish, Michelle fairly beamed as church members and friends went up to welcome her. She especially lit up when Ezekiel's mother gave her a hug and whispered something in her ear. Belinda must have said something kind, for Mary Ruth was sure the moisture on Michelle's smiling face was from happy tears. Hopefully, Ezekiel's mother had accepted Michelle and felt good about the decision Ezekiel's girlfriend had made to become Amish.

Mary Ruth was glad that, no matter what Sara might be feeling, she had at least greeted Michelle after the service and given her a hug. Mary Ruth let out a deep sigh. *I am ever so happy for Michelle,* she thought. *She has come a long ways, and it was pure joy to watch her get baptized and know that she is now one of us.*

Mary Ruth glanced out the window and saw Sara standing against one of the trees in the Kings' backyard, her chin resting on her fist as though deep in thought.

"Well it looks like everything is about cleaned up." Belinda King approached, holding a garbage bag in her hands.

Mary Ruth nodded. "It was a good day, jah?"

"Yes, it was, and I couldn't be happier for my son today. Also, Michelle has proven to be more than I gave her credit for," Belinda added. "I told her earlier that I am sorry for ever doubting her motives. It's obvious now that she is truly committed to the Amish way and also to my son."

"We are also happy for Michelle and Ezekiel," Ivan said as he and Yvonne joined the conversation.

Lenore had been talking with Michelle and Ezekiel, and the three of them came over when they saw the small group forming.

"Where's Sara?" Michelle asked.

"Yes, I want to say goodbye to her before we leave," Lenore interjected.

"I saw her outside in the yard." Mary Ruth gestured to the window.

"I'll see if I can find her." Lenore gave Mary Ruth a hug. "I love you, Grandma."

"I love you too, sweet girl."

Lenore turned to her parents. "After I say a few words to Sara, if I can find her, I'll wait for you in the buggy."

"Okay, we'll be there shortly." Ivan shook Michelle's and Ezekiel's hands. "Again, we welcome both of you to the church."

Yvonne nodded, then gave Michelle a hug and shook Ezekiel's hand.

Mary Ruth's heart swelled, seeing Michelle's sweet expression as she thanked Sara's aunt and uncle for their warm greetings.

"Okay, Mom," Ivan said, "We need to see if Benjamin and Peter have already headed for home. It's a good thing they came in Peter's carriage, because my buggy isn't big enough for the five us now that our *kinner* are grown."

Mary Ruth chuckled. "That's how it is when the children grow up."

"We have to catch Dad and say goodbye to him too, but I promise, we'll be seeing you both soon." Ivan and Yvonne gave Mary Ruth a hug, and headed out the door.

"Family is everything, isn't it?" Belinda smiled as she watched Ivan and Yvonne depart.

"Jah, it certainly is." Mary Ruth stole another look out the window and noticed Lenore walking around, obviously looking for Sara.

Mary Ruth gathered up her things before looking for Willis and Sara. It was time to go home. Later today when things quieted down, she would spend some time with her English granddaughter.

CHAPTER 35

The echo of Big Red's hooves hitting the pavement rang in Ezekiel's ears. His fingers, nose, and even his face tingled with anticipation. He was on his way to the Lapps' to pick up Michelle for a Sunday evening buggy ride, and he'd never felt more nervous. They had both become Amish today, and now it was time to ask Michelle a most important question.

"Don't know what I'm gonna do if she turns me down." Ezekiel spoke out loud. "I've never cared for anyone the way I do Michelle." He wiped a sweaty hand on his pants leg. "She's all I could ever want. Can't imagine spending the rest of my life without her."

Big Red's ears perked up, and he trotted a little faster. Did the horse sense how eager Ezekiel was to see his girlfriend?

The closer he came to the Lapps' place, the more anxious Ezekiel became. He swallowed a few times, his mouth turning dry. He would have his answer — and soon.

Michelle went to the living-room window and peeked out.

"Are you watching for Ezekiel?" Willis asked from his easy chair across the room.

"Jah." She turned to look at him. "He said he'd be here by six thirty."

Willis winked at Mary Ruth, who sat in the chair closest to him. "I'd have to say, this young woman is as *naerfich* this evening as she was in church this morning when she got baptized."

"I'm not nervous," Michelle defended herself, but she smiled, knowing Willis was only joking with her. "I'll admit, I am eager to see Ezekiel and go for a ride in his buggy."

"It's not like you've never ridden in his rig before." Willis's brows moved up and down as he gave her a playful grin.

His wife shook her finger at him. "Now, Husband, you should stop tormenting the poor girl. Some people don't appreciate your teasing, you know."

Willis's smile widened as he looked back at Michelle. "You know I'm only kidding, right?"

"Of course, and it doesn't bother me one bit." Michelle glanced over at Sara, slouched on the couch, hugging a throw pillow in front of her. Sara hadn't said much to any of them since they'd arrived home after the church meal. An hour ago, Sara mentioned having a headache, but when Mary Ruth suggested Sara take an aspirin and go upstairs to take a nap, Sara declined.

Michelle wished she could speak to Sara privately, but with Mary Ruth and Willis in the room, it wasn't a good idea. Michelle hadn't said anything to either of them about the conversation she'd had with Sara in the barn last week. She didn't know whether they were aware of the bitterness their granddaughter felt about her mother's deception. If they knew, it might be something they didn't want to talk about. *I wonder if Willis and Mary Ruth know Sara's not a Christian. Bet if they did, they'd really be concerned.*

The whinny of a horse brought Michelle's attention to the window again. She smiled as she watched Ezekiel's horse trot into the yard and head straight for the hitching rail.

With a quick goodbye to the Lapps and Sara, Michelle grabbed her black shawl and hurried out the door. Before Ezekiel even had the chance to tie Big Red to the rail, she opened the passenger's door and climbed into the buggy.

He looked over at her with a big smile. "*Guder owed,* Michelle."

With her heart beating a staccato, Michelle replied, "Good evening, Ezekiel."

"Ready for a nice long ride?"

"Jah. I'm more than ready."

Ezekiel backed the horse up, turned the carriage around, and headed out the driveway and onto the main road. They had only gone a short distance when he pulled over at a wide spot in the road, halting Big Red.

"What's the matter, Ezekiel? Is there something wrong with your gaul?"

"Nope. My horse is fine and dandy." Ezekiel reached across the seat and took Michelle's hand. "I'm not sure I'll be fine though — least not till I ask you a question."

"Oh? What is it?"

He leaned closer, and his voice trembled a bit. "I — I love you, Michelle. And I was wondering . . . That is, would you be willing to marry me in the fall?"

Overcome with emotion, all she could do was nod. Then as tears slipped from under Michelle's lashes, she finally found her voice. "I love you too, Ezekiel, and I'd be most honored to become your wife — as soon as tomorrow if it was possible."

She could hardly wait to share this good

news with Mary Ruth and Willis. Michelle felt certain they'd be happy for her and Ezekiel. She wasn't sure about Ezekiel's parents though. Today, they'd said they were glad she had joined the church, but what if they didn't approve of her as their son's wife? If they didn't give Ezekiel their blessing, would he change his mind about marrying her?

Clarks Summit

As Brad sat at a table inside a family restaurant, he reflected on his week at school, and how glad he'd been when the weekend finally came. It felt good to be free of his studies for a while and not have a textbook staring back at him. He'd called Sara last night, but only reached her voice mail. The last time they'd talked, the evening after he had gotten back from Strasburg, she'd seemed kind of distant. He figured she was either preoccupied or might be irritated about something.

Brad had hoped to try calling again, but the week ended up more hectic than he had anticipated. He'd delved into his studies each day when classes were over until he couldn't keep his eyes open. Even when Brad took lunch in the cafeteria, he had one of his textbooks open.

One afternoon, Brad had seen Terri sitting at the far end of the room with her nose in a book. *Does Sara believe there might be something going on between me and Terri?* He'd thought he'd made it clear the day he left for Clarks Summit that he had no interest in Terri other than friendship. Each night before Brad fell asleep, Sara was the only one on his mind.

Brad drummed his fingers on the table, waiting impatiently for his food to arrive. He glanced at his cell phone. *I wish Sara would return my call. Should I try calling her again? I'd like to hear how Michelle's baptism went today.*

Brad was about to punch in her number, when his phone buzzed. Hoping it was Sara, he answered without checking the caller ID.

"Hello."

"Hi, Brad. Your dad and I haven't heard from you since you went back to school after your spring vacation. We've been wondering how you're doing."

Staring into his cup of coffee, Brad offered his mother a heartfelt apology. "Sorry, Mom. I've been really busy, but then that's no excuse. I should have called to see how things are going with you and Dad this week."

"It's all right. We understand your studies

come first right now."

Brad dropped his arms to his sides. He'd taken the time to call Sara but had neglected his own parents. He felt like a heel.

"Are you still there, Brad?"

"Yeah, Mom. I'll try to keep in better touch."

"How was your trip to Lancaster County? Did you get to see the young woman you told us about?"

"Yes. Sara and I spent a fair amount of time together. I'm eager to see her again."

"Is there something you're not telling me?" Mom made a little *hmm . . .* noise. He could almost picture the look of curiosity on her face.

"What do you think I'm not telling you?" Brad asked.

"Is there something serious developing between you and Sara? That is her name, right?"

"Yes, Mom, but I'm not certain yet about the direction my relationship is going with her. Like I told you the last time we talked, for now, Sara and I are just friends."

"Well, don't rush things, Brad. Remember to pray about the direction God would have you take, and He will direct you down the right path."

"Yeah, good advice."

"Don't forget, we still want to get together with you. We owe you a birthday meal."

"Okay, Mom, we'll work something out."

The waitress came with Brad's meal, so he politely told his mother that his food was here and he needed to go. "I'll be in touch soon," he added. "Take care, Mom, and tell Dad I said hello."

When Brad clicked off the phone, he bowed his head and said a silent prayer. *Heavenly Father, please give me wisdom and a sense of direction where Sara is concerned. If it's not meant for us to be together, let me know.*

Strasburg

"Would you like a cup of hot chocolate, Sara?" Grandma asked, getting up from her chair. "I'm going to fix one for your grandpa and me."

Sara pulled herself into an upright position. "That would be nice. Can I help you with it?"

Grandma shook her head. "It won't take me long. Please, stay here and rest. You look awfully tired this evening."

Sara didn't argue. She was tired; but more than that, her depressed spirit weighed in on her like a heavy blanket. The battery in her cell phone had died last night, and she wouldn't be able to charge it until she got to work tomorrow morning. But Sara's depression wasn't because of that. It was on a much deeper level. She had convinced herself that Brad was interested in Terri Conners, even though he'd assured her they were only friends. She also couldn't seem to stop thinking about the lie she'd told Brad. Only Michelle knew the truth, but Sara wished now she'd never admitted her lack of Christianity.

She lay down again, pushing her head against the throw pillow. *What if Michelle uses that information to put distance between me and my grandparents? But what would be her reason for doing such a thing?* Sara closed her eyes and tried to squelch the negative thoughts.

Several minutes later, Grandma entered the room. "Here we go."

Sara opened her eyes and sat up, watching as her grandmother placed a tray on the coffee table. In addition to three mugs of hot chocolate and napkins, the spicy smell of sliced gingerbread on a plate reached Sara. Grandma handed one of the mugs to her and gestured to the gingerbread. "Please, help yourself."

Sara took the smallest piece and ate it. "Yum . . . This is delicious, Grandma."

"Thank you." Grandma smiled and handed a mug to Grandpa.

"Danki, Mary Ruth." He took a sip. "Ahh . . . This sure hits the spot."

Taking her own mug, Grandma seated herself on the end of the sofa. "Today was a special day indeed." She looked over at Grandpa.

"It was a nice baptismal service," he agreed.

"I'm so happy Michelle joined our church." Tears welled in Grandma's eyes. "We had always hoped our daughter would get baptized, but Rhoda had other ideas. Unfortunately, she did not want to be Amish." With a wistful expression, she looked over at Sara. "If your mother had joined the church and remained here with us during her pregnancy, you might be Amish now too."

Is Grandma trying to make me feel guilty because I've shown no interest in becoming Amish? Sara drank some of her hot beverage, cringing when she burned the end of her tongue. *Or is Grandma having a few moments of wishful thinking that have more to do with my mother than me?*

CHAPTER 36

"I have some good news to share with all of you," Michelle announced Monday morning at the breakfast table. She clasped her hands tightly together, hardly able to contain her excitement.

Mary Ruth leaned forward, eyes all aglow. "What is it, Michelle? I'm always eager to hear *gut neiichkeede.*"

"Same here," Willis agreed. "There's too much bad news in our world today, so we need something positive to focus on."

Michelle couldn't hold back a smile. "Last night, when Ezekiel took me out for a ride, he proposed marriage."

Mary Ruth clapped her hands. "Now that certainly is good news."

"I hope you said yes." Willis reached for a piece of toast and spread apple butter on it.

Michelle nodded. "A year ago, I would never have imagined I could be this happy."

"April fools, right?" Sara said without smiling.

"No, I would not tease about something this important." Michelle's stomach fluttered as she looked at Sara. *I wonder what made her say such a thing. Isn't Sara the least bit happy for me?*

"Well then, I guess if it's true, congratulations are in order. I hope you and Ezekiel will be happy." Although Sara spoke with sincerity, her words seemed as if they were forced.

"We will be happy. I feel it right here." Michelle clasped both hands against her chest. "We're going to plan for a November wedding." She paused to add a spoonful of honey to her bowl of baked oatmeal. "I would have told you when I got home last night, but everyone had gone to bed, and I didn't want to wake you."

Mary Ruth reached over and placed her hand on Michelle's arm, giving it a few tender pats. "Since you have no family living in the area, I hope you will allow us to help with the wedding."

Willis bobbed his head agreeably. "My fraa is right. We want to help you make all the arrangements, and I'm sure Ezekiel's parents will help too."

"Ezekiel and I will talk more about it

416

when he picks me up after work this evening," Michelle said. She'd be working the afternoon and evening shifts at the restaurant today and wouldn't be riding with Sara. Earlier, Willis had offered to take Michelle to work, as he had some errands to run this afternoon. Since Ezekiel would be picking her up in his horse and buggy, Michelle didn't have to hire a driver.

With the exception of Sara's little April Fool's comment, Michelle's week had started out well. Now if she could just figure out a way to help Sara see the need to forgive her mother, everything would be nearly perfect.

Soon after they finished eating, Sara left for work and Mary Ruth began washing the breakfast dishes.

"I'll go out and get the mail," Michelle offered. "Oh, and I can also stop at the phone shack to check for messages."

"That'd be great." Willis picked up the newspaper lying on his end of the table. "That'll give me time to check the news before I go out to feed the hogs."

"I'll help you with that chore as soon as I get back to the house," Michelle said.

He waved a hand. "No, that's all right. I can manage on my own this morning."

"Okay then. I'll be back shortly with the

mail and a list of any phone messages you may have received."

Michelle opened the back door and stepped outside. Her mood matched the beautiful weather. But even had it been a dreary day, her spirits would not be dampened.

Last month, spring had officially arrived. Michelle could hear it with the birds singing from the trees where leaves slowly sprouted. A sunny, blue sky greeted her, and as Michelle stood breathing in the fresh air, she lifted her head and looked up. *Thank You, Lord, for all the good things that have come into my life. I feel so undeserving, but I am grateful that You are a generous, loving God. Please be with Sara today and soften her heart toward things of a spiritual nature.*

When Michelle finished praying, she hurried down the driveway to the mailbox. She was surprised to discover that it was empty. Normally, the Lapps had at least a few pieces of mail. Maybe the mailman hadn't been by yet. Or perhaps on this rare occasion, he had no mail for them at all.

"Oh well . . . no mail means no bills." Michelle had quoted that more than once when she lived on her own. It was always a relief when bills didn't come, because money was sometimes scarce.

Pushing the memory aside, Michelle headed back up the driveway and stepped into the small wooden building that housed the Lapps' telephone. She had no more than taken a seat on the folding chair to check the answering machine, when the phone rang. She quickly reached for the receiver before the answering machine kicked in. "Hello."

Clarks Summit

Brad was surprised to hear Michelle's voice. "Hey there. I didn't expect anyone to answer. Figured I'd have to leave a message, like usual."

Michelle explained that she had entered the phone shack to check for messages when it rang.

"Ah, I see. Guess that's bound to happen once in a while."

"Yes. Call it good timing."

"So how are you doing?"

"Couldn't be better. Yesterday morning, Ezekiel and I got baptized and became members of the Amish church. It was a meaningful day for me."

"I can imagine. And that's really fantastic. I'm happy for both you and Ezekiel."

"Something else special happened on Sunday."

"What was it?"

"Ezekiel came by in the evening to take me for a buggy ride, and he surprised me by asking if I would marry him."

"Wow! What was your response?"

"I said yes, of course." She giggled.

Brad heard the excitement in Michelle's voice. She had certainly changed from the troubled young woman he'd first met. "Congratulations! When will the wedding take place?"

"We hope to be married in November, and Ezekiel and I would be pleased if you could come to the wedding."

"You bet. Wouldn't miss it for the world." Brad paused briefly, looking at his watch. "Say, I don't mean to change the subject so quickly, but I have a class starting in half an hour. I need to ask though — how's Sara? I tried calling her over the weekend, but all I got was her voice mail."

"That's because her cell phone battery went dead."

"I see. I thought it was strange that she hadn't responded to my messages and wondered if everything was all right."

"Sara will probably call you when she gets to work and is able to charge her phone."

"Okay, but if I don't hear from her by this evening I'll try calling again."

"I've been praying for Sara, and it would be good if you did too."

Brad's brows furrowed. "What do you mean? Is there a problem?"

"Sara seemed despondent all weekend, and I have to wonder if it had anything to do with a discussion the two of us had last Saturday."

"If you don't mind me asking, what was it about?"

"Sara mentioned her mother, and how she resents the fact that she didn't find out about her Amish grandparents until after her mother died," Michelle replied. "She's holding resentment and feels bitter about this."

Brad scratched his head. "I did notice Sara wasn't her cheerful self when we were together the last time. I thought it might have something to do with me running into a friend from the university."

"No, I believe it had more to do with me asking Sara if she was a Christian."

"What'd she say?"

"Sara admitted that she is not a Christian, and even though I offered to help her become one, she showed no interest."

Squeezing his eyes shut, Brad rubbed the middle of his forehead. This made no sense.

"Brad, are you there?"

"Yeah. I'm just trying to process what you said." He lifted his hands and stared at his palms as though they held some answers. "Are you sure Sara said she was not a Christian?"

"I'm positive. It was right before you came to pick her up for your date."

It felt like someone had punched Brad in the stomach. *Why would Sara lie to me about being a Christian? Did she tell me she was because she thought that's what I wanted to hear?* He blew out his cheeks as he released a puff of air. *If she's not a believer, we can't have a relationship that goes beyond friendship.*

In addition to Brad taking to heart the scripture found in 2 Corinthians 6:14 that read, *"Be ye not unequally yoked together with unbelievers,"* he was preparing for the ministry. The last thing he needed was a wife who didn't share his beliefs.

Strasburg

"Good morning. Did you have a nice weekend?" Karen asked when Sara entered the flower shop.

Sara nodded briefly. "How was yours?"

"Ours went well. Saturday was busy here at the store, but Sunday we were able to relax awhile. Then while I got a few things done around the house, my hubby mowed the lawn."

"Sounds like a busy weekend." Sara put her purse under the counter and plugged her cell phone into the outlet on the wall behind her.

"It was, but we like to stay busy." Karen shook her head. "I'm not the kind of person to sit around doing nothing, and neither is Andy. So on that note, I'd better return to what I started before you came in. We just got several orders for a funeral service, so there are a lot of flower arrangements to be made yet. You know where we'll be if you need anything," Karen called over her shoulder as she headed for the other room.

"Will do."

Before looking over the books, Sara did a walk around the shop, making sure everything was in place. Then looking at her watch, she glanced out the door before flipping the metal sign over, from CLOSED to OPEN.

Looking up and down the sidewalk, she noticed that, except for a little traffic as people headed to work, all looked quiet.

Maybe being around all these cheerful colors will brighten my mood, Sara thought, inhaling the flowery scent of the store. *I certainly need something to get me out of these doldrums I've been in lately.*

Once Sara got her cell phone charging, she checked her voice mail for messages. She saw that there were two from Brad and one from her brother, Kenny. *I wonder what Kenny wants. He rarely calls.*

Returning Kenny's call could wait awhile, so Sara decided to call Brad first and let him know that her battery had been dead. She would have to leave a message, since at this time of the morning he was probably in class.

Sara picked up her phone, and was about to punch in Brad's number, when the phone rang. The caller ID showed it was Kenny.

That's odd. I wonder why he would be calling me at this time of the day. I would think Kenny would be in school right now. She swiped her thumb across the screen to answer. "Hi, Kenny. I'm surprised to hear from you on a school day." This was Kenny's last year in high school, and in a little over two months he'd be graduating. Sara hoped he hadn't done something foolhardy, like dropping out when he was this close to finishing.

"I–I'm calling about Dad. He was in an accident on the way to work this morning, and he's in the hospital." Kenny's voice trembled. No doubt he struggled with his emotions. "My friend Shawn's mother brought me to the ER. I'm here now, waiting to find out more about Dad." His voice had dropped to just above a whisper.

Sara's fingers touched her parted lips as she gasped. "Oh no. How bad is he hurt?"

"Real bad. He may not make it, Sara. Can you please come? I need you here with me. I can't go through this alone."

Sara's thoughts became so fuzzy she could barely think. She'd never heard Kenny in this state of mind and knew things must be very serious. She would have to explain the situation to her boss, and ask for time off. Even if it meant losing her job, Sara had to go. Her brother needed her. He had no one else. "Try not to worry, Kenny. I'll be there as soon as I can."

Sara clicked off the phone. As she made her way to the back room, a sinking feeling in the pit of her stomach grew heavier with each step she took. *What will happen to Kenny if Dean doesn't make it? He's too young to be on his own.*

CHAPTER 37

Mary Ruth pushed her feet forcefully against the floor to get the rocking chair moving faster. She'd been concerned about Sara ever since she came home from work early and announced that she'd gotten word of her stepfather having been in a serious accident on his way to work. She hadn't given many details, because she didn't know much, but Sara had quickly packed her suitcase and informed them that she was heading for New Jersey.

"You'd better be careful with that rocking chair or it might topple over backward." Willis shook his finger at Mary Ruth, before taking a seat in his recliner. "I can tell you're *brutzich.*"

"You're right. I am fretful." Mary Ruth slowed the rocker. "I wish Sara would have let me go with her when I offered. Someone should be there for her during this difficult time."

"Sara explained that she might be in Newark for several days or even weeks," Willis reminded Mary Ruth. "She didn't want to take you from the work you have to do around here. Besides, Sara's brother will be with her."

"True, but she's there to offer him *dreeschde,* and if her stepfather doesn't make it, she will definitely need someone to comfort her."

"Let's cross that path when the time comes." Willis reached for his Bible lying on the end table beside his chair. "In the meantime, we need to read a few passages of scripture and lift Sara, her brother, and Mr. Murray up in prayer."

Newark

Sara's body felt numb as she sat beside her stepfather's hospital bed. Kenny stood nearby with folded arms, staring at his father's battered body. The doctors and hospital staff had done all they could, but Dean hadn't woke up from his unconscious state. Short of a miracle, it didn't look like he would make it through the night. Sara hoped Dean would live — if for no other reason than for Kenny's sake. The seventeen-year-old boy needed his father.

Sara glanced at her watch. She had arrived shortly after lunch, but already it felt much later than one thirty. So many feelings raced through her as she watched for any sign of movement from Dean.

She thought back to the last time they had talked, right before the New Year. *Dean called to wish me a belated merry Christmas and happy New Year. I should have called him on Christmas Eve or made time to call on Christmas Day. Isn't that when people are supposed to put aside their feelings and try to forget any differences, even if it's only for one day?*

Sara looked at Dean, and her eyes grew moist as she remembered him saying he wanted to bring Kenny to Strasburg to meet his grandparents. It was unlikely now that it would ever happen.

You need to pray. A little voice in Sara's head nudged her to do so. She swallowed hard. *Why bother. I prayed for Mama, and she died anyway. I always tried to be a good daughter, but God never answered any of my prayers.*

Sara recalled her grandpa saying in a message he'd preached several weeks ago and later translated for her: *"Prayer isn't a business transaction. We don't give something to get something in return."*

Sara's fingers tightened and bit into her

palms. *If that is the case, then why bother asking God for anything at all?*

Feeling the need for some fresh air and exercise, Sara left her chair. "I'm going down the hall to take a walk," she whispered to Kenny.

He nodded slowly, then turned toward the window.

Sara slipped from the room, and made her way past the nurse's station. When she came to a door identified as the chapel, she stepped inside. Sara felt relieved to find it empty. She needed time to be by herself and think.

The room reminded her of the church Brad had taken her to, only much smaller. She noticed two rows of padded chairs facing the front of the room, where a cross hung on the wall next to a stained glass window. Sunlight shone through, casting a warm glow of colorful patterns on a table below the window. A white cloth had been draped over the table, and a black Bible lay on top. A padded kneeling bench sat in front of the table, which Sara assumed was for those who wanted to pray. Sara wasn't sure she wanted to pray, but what else could she do for Dean right now? *How can such a beautiful sunny day have turned so tragic?* she asked herself.

Walking slowly to the front of the room, Sara picked up the Bible and took a seat on a chair in the first row. Holding the book against her chest, she bowed her head and offered a simple prayer: *Dear God, if You're listening, please heal Dean's injuries. And if You choose to take him, please give me the right words to help Kenny deal with his loss.*

Sara heard someone come into the room, and she opened her eyes. When she turned her head, she realized it was Kenny. "How'd you know I was here?"

"I didn't. Came here to pray." He sank into the chair beside her. "I'm scared Dad's not gonna make it, Sara."

Words wouldn't come, so she simply set the Bible aside and took hold of her brother's hand.

"I wish he'd wake up so we could talk to him." Kenny's chin trembled, and Sara saw moisture in his aqua-blue eyes. "Things haven't always been that great between me and Dad. I — I need to tell him I'm sorry for something I said last night."

"Do you want to talk about it?"

He nodded. "I told Dad I wanted to go to college and major in music, instead of becoming a plumber after I graduate in June." Kenny pulled a hanky from his pocket and blew his nose. "Dad got really

430

upset and said he wasn't gonna waste his money on a college education that might take me nowhere. He said learnin' the trade he'd learned when he was my age was a sure thing."

"How did you respond?"

"I got mad. Said if it was you wanting to go to college, I bet he'd pay for it, no questions asked."

Confused, Sara let go of Kenny's hand and reached up to rub the bridge of her nose. "That's not true. He didn't pay for the business classes I took at the community college."

"No, but he wanted to. Remember when he offered you the money?"

"Yes, but I thought it was for Mama's sake that he volunteered."

Kenny shook his head. "Nope, it was his idea. Dad's been behind the decision you made."

"Really? He's never said so."

"Yeah he has . . . just maybe not to your face. But when I came up with an idea like teaching music, he gave me no encouragement at all." Kenny looked at Sara with a most serious expression. "He may not have said so, but Dad's always cared about you. There've been times when I thought he even loved you more than me."

"No way, Kenny. I've never gotten that impression at all. And just so you know — I didn't expect anything from your dad. In fact, I had always planned to pay for my education. Someday, if the opportunity arises, I'd like to have my own business to run."

"What kind of business?"

Sara shrugged. "Maybe a floral shop like the one where I've been working. Only, if it were mine, I would incorporate some craft items, homemade cards, and maybe even beaded jewelry, like I enjoy making. Even though I didn't mind the job I had previously, I've known all along working as a part-time receptionist was not for me. It did help pay for school though. And your father helped as well, by not charging me a high rent."

Kenny's eyes widened. "I never knew that before."

"Guess I didn't think to mention it." Sara placed her hand on his arm. "And you aren't the only one having regrets." She went on to tell her brother about the phone call she'd received from his dad right before the New Year. "He wanted the two of you to come and see me, and meet your grandparents, but it never happened, and now I wish it had, Kenny. I have to ask myself —

was I so busy I couldn't have called him a few times just to chat? All these years, I don't ever remember actually sitting and talking with Dean. I completely shut him out."

"I lived in the same house with him, but after Mom died, we drifted apart." Kenny wiped his nose. "Guess we both have regrets where Dad's concerned."

Sara remained silent, taking in all Kenny had said. Things she'd assumed about Dean could not be further from the truth. Her brother seemed deep in thought too, for he was just as quiet. It did Sara good to have this conversation with her brother. Although surprised by what each had revealed to the other, a little weight seemed to lift off Sara's shoulders. She now saw Kenny in a different light than she had before.

"Kenny, I have to admit . . . I didn't realize you wanted to get a degree in music."

"That's 'cause I never told you." He sniffed. "You know I like to sing and play the guitar, right?"

"Yes, but I thought you did it for your own pleasure."

He bobbed his head. "I do, but I'd like to teach music someday — to elementary school kids or someday even in a high school setting."

"Sounds like a good goal — definitely something to work toward."

"Try telling that to Dad." Kenny's shoulders drooped. "If it meant the difference between life and death for Dad, I'd give up my goal to teach music."

Sara had to bite her lip in order to hold back the sob rising in her throat. In all the years since her little brother was born, she had no idea there had ever been any problem between Dean and Kenny, or that Dean actually cared for her. And all this time she'd been holding an unnecessary grudge against him — not to mention the negative feelings she'd kept bottled up about Mama.

Despite her best efforts, tears sprang to Sara's eyes. *What an ungrateful stepdaughter I have been. And I haven't been much of a sister to Kenny either.*

She reached into her purse and fumbled around for a tissue. What her fingers touched instead was a folded piece of paper. She pulled it out and read the message out loud: " 'For if ye forgive men their trespasses, your heavenly Father will also forgive you.' Matthew 6:14."

The tears came even harder, almost blinding Sara's vision. This was the same note she had read in one of the prayer jars she'd found at her grandparents' place. She had no idea how it had gotten in her purse.

Sara turned to face Kenny. "We need to get back to your dad's room, but before we go, I'd like to offer a prayer."

He nodded in agreement.

Sara reached for his hand again and bowed her head. "Lord, my brother and I have had some issues with bitterness and an unforgiving spirit. I ask You to forgive us for the sins we have done in the past, and please take our resentment away. Also, be with our dad — for Dean truly is the only father I have ever known. If it's Your will, we ask that You heal his body. But if You choose to take him, Lord, then please give Kenny and me a sense of peace and clear direction for the remainder of our lives. Amen."

"Amen," Kenny repeated.

They opened their eyes at the same time and stood. Knowing they both needed some comfort and reassurance right now, Sara gave her brother a hug. And he hugged her back just as hard.

"Let's go back to Dad's room now and sit by his bed. Maybe if we pray hard enough, he will wake up."

CHAPTER 38

Ronks

Michelle stood outside the restaurant that evening, waiting for Ezekiel to pick her up. It had been difficult to concentrate on her job today, thinking about Sara and her stepfather. Learning about his accident had put a damper on Michelle's happier mood this morning, when she was excited to tell everyone about Ezekiel's proposal.

Michelle could still see Sara's panicked expression when she'd returned home from the flower shop before Willis had taken Michelle to work. After explaining about Mr. Murray's situation, Sara said she needed to go to New Jersey right away. When Sara rushed upstairs to pack, Michelle had slipped a note from one of the prayer jars into Sara's purse. Knowing how Sara felt about her stepfather, Michelle hoped the verse might speak to Sara's heart. Throughout Michelle's workday, whenever Sara came to mind, she sent up a prayer on her behalf, as well as for Sara's stepfather and brother.

Hearing a distinctive *clippity-clop* sound, Michelle looked down the street. As a horse and buggy drew closer, she realized it was Ezekiel. With no hesitation, she hurried out to the parking lot and waited for him to pull in. Right now, she needed to be with her future husband.

"How was your day?" Ezekiel asked after Michelle got into the buggy. Since it was dark inside the carriage, she couldn't see his face clearly. But Ezekiel's upbeat tone let her know he was in good spirits this evening.

"Everything at the restaurant went okay, but things aren't so good for Sara right now."

"What happened?"

Michelle explained the situation, including the part about the Bible verse she had put in Sara's purse. "I am hoping when she finds the slip of paper it will tug at her heartstrings and she'll let go of her bitterness." Michelle touched her chest. "I know all about feelings of resentment and how they can eat a person up. But after I found the Lord and asked Him to forgive me for the wrongs I had done, I was able to forgive

437

those who had hurt me so deeply."

Ezekiel reached across the seat and clasped Michelle's hand. "Same for me. The bitterness I once had toward my folks has been released, and now we're gettin' along much better. It's not always easy to forgive, but God requires it of us. I hope for Sara's sake that she is able to resolve things with her stepfather."

Strasburg

When Ezekiel pulled Big Red up to the Lapps' hitching rail, Michelle asked if he wanted to come in for a while.

"Sure, but I can't stay too late. I need to go to bed early. We're having a sale at the greenhouse tomorrow, and Dad wants me to be there an hour earlier than usual to help him set up for the event."

"No problem. I'm sure Willis and Mary Ruth will want to go to bed early as well. When Sara left for Newark, they both looked pretty distraught, so I'm sure they are tired."

Once Ezekiel had his horse secured, they headed for the house. They found Mary Ruth and Willis in the kitchen, drinking tea and eating banana bread.

"Pull up a chair and join us." Willis motioned with his head.

"Would either of you like a glass of milk or some hot tea?" Mary Ruth asked.

"Milk sounds good to me." Ezekiel smacked his lips. "And so does a slice of that bread."

"I'll get the milk." Michelle went to the refrigerator, while Ezekiel took a seat across from Willis, and Mary Ruth sliced more bread.

"Have you heard anything from Sara?" Michelle directed her question to Willis, since he was often the one who went out to the phone shack to check their voice mail.

"Jah, but just once," he replied. "She left us a message saying she arrived at the hospital in Newark shortly after lunch, but we've heard nothing since."

Michelle placed the milk and two glasses on the table before sitting down. "I wonder if Brad knows about Sara's stepfather."

Mary Ruth's lips puckered. "He probably isn't aware, unless Sara called him."

"She may not have." Michelle stood. "Think I'll go out to the phone shack and give him a call. It would be good if he knew so he can be praying." Michelle grabbed her sweater, along with a flashlight, and went out the back door.

■ ■ ■ ■

Clarks Summit

Brad was about to call it a night, when his cell phone rang. He recognized the Lapps' number, so he answered right away.

"Brad, it's me — Michelle."

"Oh, hi. How are you doing?"

"I'm fine, but Sara isn't. Have you heard from her today, Brad?"

"I haven't. Is she sick?"

"No. Her stepdad was in an accident on his way to work this morning. When Sara's brother called to tell her about it, he said his dad had been seriously injured, and it didn't look good. So Sara packed a bag and headed for Newark."

Brad rubbed his furrowed brow. "Wow, that's too bad. I'll certainly be praying for Sara's dad."

"Sara and her brother need prayer too."

"Yes, of course. I'll pray for all of them. Please let me know if you hear anything more."

"I will. Take care, Brad."

"You too. Bye, Michelle."

Brad clicked off his phone and sat staring at the stack of study books on the table. *What should I do? Should I call Sara and let her know I heard about her dad and that I'm praying for him?* This was certainly not the time to discuss the lie Sara had told him about being a Christian. She needed his support, not a lecture, right now.

Newark, New Jersey
Sara and Kenny had been sitting beside Dean's bed most of the day. The good news was he was still alive, but he hadn't opened his eyes or spoken to them.

Glancing out the window, Sara noticed the sky had turned dark but some light filtered in from the parking lot. She checked her watch. It was almost nine o'clock, and she was exhausted. No doubt her brother was too. Kenny's friend, Shawn, and his parents, had come to the hospital a few hours ago. They weren't allowed into the room, since Dean's condition was critical and only family members could visit. So Kenny had met them in the waiting room, while Sara remained here, praying for a miracle. Now, as the two of them sat quietly, she'd begun to think that miracle might never come.

Thoughts of Sara's mother came to mind. In the chapel when she'd forgiven Dean, she'd also set her bitterness toward Mama aside. The past was in the past, and it couldn't be changed, so why keep harboring resentment? Sara's mother must have had her reasons for keeping her past a secret. She had relinquished her pain and bitterness to God. She had accepted His Son as her Savior too.

Sara's cell phone buzzed, and she pulled it out of her purse. Seeing it was Brad, Sara told Kenny she'd be right back, and then she slipped quietly from the room.

"Hello, Brad," Sara said, once she was in the hall. "S–something terrible happened today." Her voice faltered.

"I know. I just got off the phone with Michelle. She told me your stepdad was in an accident. How's he doing?"

"Not well. Kenny and I have been with him most of the day, but he hasn't responded to either of us."

"I'm sorry, Sara. I've been praying for all of you and will continue to do so."

"Thanks. We need all the prayers we can get."

"If there is anything I can do for you, please let me know."

"Okay. Thanks for calling. Bye, Brad."

When Sara returned to Dean's room, she was surprised to see that his eyes were open. Kenny stood near the bed, and it appeared as if his dad was trying to speak.

Sara hurried over to join her brother. "Dad," she murmured, barely able to get the words out. "We've been praying for you."

"Th–thank you." Dean spoke softly, and then he closed his eyes. A few seconds went by before he opened them again. "I–I'm not gonna make it, am I?"

Gently, Sara placed her hand on his arm, unable, at first, to respond. She glanced over at Kenny. The poor kid was on the verge of tears. Then somehow, she found her voice. Sara wanted to remain positive for Dean and her brother.

"Dad, you hang in there." She smiled at him. "We still have that visit to Strasburg to plan for." Even as the words slipped out, Sara knew deep in her heart the trip Dean had wanted to make would never happen.

"There's something I need to tell both of you." Dean spoke in a raspy voice.

Kenny shook his head. "It's okay, Dad. No need to talk. Save your strength."

"No, no . . . I — I need to say it." In a desperate plea, he beckoned them to lean closer. "I have money set aside for both of you." He paused and drew a shallow breath. "Use it to pursue your dreams." Dean reached out a feeble hand, and Kenny clasped it. "You should both decide what to

443

do with the house. There is no mortgage. It's paid in full." His voice faltered, and then he rallied again. "After your mom died, I — I transferred the deed to both of your names."

When Sara looked at her brother and saw the tears streaming down his face, it was nearly her undoing.

"It was wrong of me, Son, not to support your hopes all these years and wanting you to do what I thought was best. I take it all back now, and I'm sorry. Please go after whatever makes you happy." Then he looked at Sara. "Same goes for you, honey. If your dreams lie in Strasburg, follow them."

All Sara could do was nod, and grip his arm tighter.

"Sing for me, Kenny. Sing me a song." Dean's voice grew faint again. It was as if he had used all the strength he had left to tell them what they needed to know once he was gone.

"What would you like me to sing, Dad?" Kenny's voice shook with emotion.

"Anything. It will help me not to be afraid."

Kenny picked up the Bible the hospital chaplain had left when he'd come into the room earlier. A song printed on a piece of paper had been tucked inside. Kenny had showed it to Sara after they returned from the chapel earlier.

"This song is called 'Near to the Heart of God.' " Kenny stood at the foot of his father's bed and lifted his face to the ceiling. " 'There is a place of quiet rest, near to the heart of God, a place where sin cannot molest, near to the heart of God. O Jesus, blest Redeemer, sent from the heart of God, hold us, who wait before thee, near to the heart of God.' "

Kenny's voice grew stronger with each stanza. By the time he reached the second verse, goosebumps had erupted on Sara's arms. Although Kenny had told her in the chapel that he liked to sing, she had no idea he was this good. Her brother's voice was so clear and pure, it sounded almost heavenly. And his vibrato was nothing short of amazing.

" 'There is a place of comfort sweet,' " Kenny continued, " 'near to the heart of God, a place where we our Savior meet, near to the heart of God.' " As he sang the last stanza with even more emotion, Sara could hardly breathe.

" 'There is a place of full release, near to the heart of God, a place where all is joy and peace, near to the heart of God.' "

Through a film of tears, Sara looked at

Dean. His eyes were closed, and he had a peaceful smile on his lips. His chest was motionless however. He did not appear to be breathing.

Sara pushed the call button for the nurse to confirm what she already knew. The man who had raised her and Kenny had slipped quietly from this world into the next. "Oh Daddy," she sobbed. "I never knew how much I loved you until now."

She put her arms around Kenny and held him close, as the two of them wept. Sara thought about Michelle and how she'd lost contact with her brothers. She couldn't imagine how difficult it must be for Michelle not to know where her brothers were, not to mention her needing their support during difficult times.

At that sad and most difficult moment, Sara determined in her heart that she would be there for her brother as long as he needed her, for she loved him very much.

CHAPTER 39

New Jersey

"I'm glad so many of us could go to Sara's stepfather's funeral today," Mary Ruth said from her seat at the back of their driver's van. In addition to her and Willis, Michelle, Ivan, Yvonne, and Lenore accompanied them. Sara needed friends and family with her today.

"Since it's Saturday and I don't have to teach, it worked out so that I could come along," Lenore agreed.

Ivan had left his sons in charge of his business today, rather than having to close the store. When Willis talked to Brad last night, he'd said he also planned on coming to the funeral.

It would be nice to finally meet Sara's brother. Back when Sara's stepfather had called Sara and said he and Kenny planned to make a trip to Strasburg, Mary Ruth had been excited. She figured they would probably drive down sometime in the summer, after Kenny was out of school. But it was not meant to be.

It's unfortunate we won't get to meet Mr. Murray now, Mary Ruth thought. *I wish it were under better circumstances that Willis and I would be meeting our grandson for the first time.*

They'd crossed over the state line into New Jersey, so it wouldn't be long until they reached their destination.

Looking out the window, Mary Ruth thought about Rhoda. *Poor Sara. Less than a year after losing her mother, she's lost her stepfather too.*

Mary Ruth leaned to the right and loosened her seatbelt a little. She realized the importance of seatbelts for safety reasons, but was glad they weren't required to wear them while riding in their buggies. To her, at least, they felt too constricting. She leaned her head against the seatback and closed her eyes. Since everyone else in the van was quiet, including their driver, she thought it might be good to take a little nap. Today would be long and emotional, and since they'd gotten up earlier than usual, she wanted to arrive feeling somewhat refreshed.

Heavenly Father, Mary Ruth prayed,

please be with Sara and Kenny today. Let them feel Your presence, as if You are right there with them, holding their hands.

Newark

Brad entered the chapel where the funeral service was being held for Dean Murray and took a seat near the back of the room. Since he had arrived a few minutes late, all the other chairs had been taken.

A variety of flowers had been arranged up front, and a huge spray of white lilies draped over the closed casket. The fragrance from all the bouquets wafted through the chapel, and the sweet scent lingered everywhere. Next to the coffin was a small pedestal table adorned with a white doily. A framed picture sat on top. From where Brad sat, it looked like a family picture of Dean and three other people, who he guessed were Sara, her mother, and brother.

Craning his neck, Brad saw Sara sitting in the front row beside a blond-haired man, who he assumed was her brother. On the other side of her sat Sara's grandparents, her uncle Ivan, aunt Yvonne, and cousin Lenore. Michelle was there too, sitting to the left of Lenore.

Brad pulled his fingers around his too-tight collar, hoping to loosen it a bit. *Should have worn a different shirt,* he thought. *And I would have if there'd been a clean dress shirt in my closet.* Brad had been so busy at school the past week that he hadn't found time to do his laundry.

Brad caught sight of Stan sitting a few rows ahead. The Lapps must have hired him to bring them to the service today. If Strasburg hadn't been so far from Clarks Summit, Brad would have gone there to get them.

Sometimes Brad wished he had stayed at the Bible College in Lancaster to complete his studies, instead of going all the way up to the university he now attended. If things had worked out between him and Sara, he might have considered transferring back to Lancaster, or even moving there and taking some online classes. A long-distance relationship was not good, but since Sara was not a Christian, continuing to see her socially was no longer in the equation.

When the blond-haired man left his seat and stood behind the podium at the front of the room and to the right of the casket, Brad's thoughts refocused. Then as the young man began to sing, "Near to the Heart of God," Brad's wavering emotions threatened to overtake him. Not only were the words of the song appropriate, but the man's voice rang so true and clear, it seemed almost angelic. As though it had come straight down from heaven, an amber-colored light filtering through the stained glass windows shone down on the talented vocalist, illuminating his hair, and making it look like spun gold. To be able to sing that song without any musical instrument to accompany him made it even more amazing.

Brad glanced at the program an usher had given him when he'd entered the chapel. Kenny Murray had been listed as the vocalist. What Brad suspected had now been confirmed. The young man, who stood before them, looking upward as he sang the powerful words, was indeed Sara's half-brother. It had to be difficult for Kenny to sing at his father's funeral and not break down. Was the boy a Christian? How could he sing a spiritual song, and with such conviction, if he was not a believer? Had Sara been raised in a Christian home and strayed away from it? There were so many unanswered questions.

Brad's gaze went back to Sara. Her head was now bent forward. Her shoulders trembled, and when she turned her head to the left, Brad saw Sara dab her eyes with a tissue. Mary Ruth draped an arm around Sara, patting her shoulder. Brad wished he was sitting on the other side of Sara, to comfort and hold her hand. Yet another part of him was glad to be sitting in the back, not wanting to be emotionally tied.

Brad clasped the program he held. *I'd like to know either way where Sara stands on Christianity, and I'd like to hear it from her, not Michelle.*

Michelle was stunned to hear how well Sara's brother sang. He seemed nervous, choked up near the end of the song, but his vocal tone was on pitch, and Kenny had moved her to tears. Taking a quick glance around, she saw many others wiping their eyes.

Sara is lucky to have Kenny in her life, Michelle thought. She had met the young man before the service started, and he seemed like a nice person. Not like some teenagers she'd gone to school with, who had foul mouths and arrogant attitudes.

Once again, Michelle's thoughts went to her brothers. Had they grown up to be responsible citizens? Or did one or both of them end up like their parents — brash and rough around the edges? She hoped Jack and Ernie had made something of themselves and were living happy, fulfilling lives.

Michelle sighed. *Guess I'll never know the*

answer, so I need to keep my focus on the life I have in Pennsylvania and look forward to my future with Ezekiel.

When Kenny sat down and a man she assumed was a minister stood up and offered a prayer, Michelle reached up to make sure her head covering was properly in place. According to biblical teachings, the Amish believed a woman's head should always be covered whenever she prayed.

When the prayer was over and the preacher began to deliver his message, Michelle glanced over at Sara, sitting straight and tall.

I wonder if she will stay in New Jersey with her brother now that her stepfather is gone. Willis and Mary Ruth would surely miss Sara if she didn't to return to Pennsylvania. Michelle swallowed hard. *I'd miss her too.*

Sara couldn't remember when she'd felt more proud of her brother. Kenny had made it through the entire song without missing a note. And to be able to sing without accompaniment made it all the more astounding.

She reached across her chest and clasped her grandmother's hand, which was still around her shoulders. What a blessing and comfort it was to have Grandma and

Grandpa here today. Sara felt so grateful the Lord had led her to them after Mama died. She also appreciated the presence of Uncle Ivan, Aunt Yvonne, and Lenore. What a privilege it was to have such a special family.

And there was Michelle, who'd come to offer her condolences and support Sara. This young woman, whom Sara had once been so angry with, was now truly a friend. Sara could hardly wait to tell Michelle she had become a Christian and explain how it came about.

She listened attentively as the pastor spoke to those in attendance. He talked about life after death and stated that every believer had the promise of heaven.

Sara didn't know where her stepfather stood spiritually, but if he wasn't a Christian previously, she hoped he'd made a confession of faith before his death — perhaps during the song Kenny sang for him or maybe when the chaplain had visited. If the smile on Dean's face when he passed away was any proof, Sara had to believe it was true.

When the minister finished his sermon, he ended by telling everyone they were invited to go to the cemetery where Dean would be laid to rest. He also added that Sara and

Kenny wanted those who could to join them for lunch at the Adega Grill, one of Dean's favorite places to dine. After the announcement, he took his place at the foot of the open coffin and remained there while everyone filed by to pay their last respects to the deceased. Since Sara and Kenny went last, with the exception of the pastor and funeral attendants, the chapel was empty by the time she and Kenny walked out. In the hall, however, several people waited to speak to them and offer their sympathies. Sara's grandparents, her uncle, aunt, and cousin were there, along with Michelle. Toward the back of the group, Sara spotted Brad.

Sara's heart thumped in her chest as she made her way over to him. When she reached his side, he gave her a brief hug. "I'm sorry for your loss, Sara. I've been praying for you, as well as your brother."

"Thank you. I would have been disappointed if you hadn't come." Tears welled in her eyes. "If you plan on going to the cemetery, I hope afterward you can stay for lunch."

Brad shook his head. "Sorry, but I have to get back to Clarks Summit. It's a big study weekend for me."

"Oh, okay." Sara tried to hide her disappointment. "I'm glad you took the time to drive down for the service. It means a lot to me."

Brad nodded, then glanced down at the floor as though unable to meet Sara's gaze. "You're my friend, Sara. I wanted to offer my condolences in person."

Friend? Is that all I am to Brad? When he lifted his head, Sara noticed his subdued expression.

A wave of sadness washed over her, and it wasn't merely the mood of the melancholy service that had taken place moments ago. Sara felt something had changed between her and Brad. She suspected it might have to do with his friend Terri.

It doesn't matter, she told herself. *I have to stay in Newark until Kenny is able to be on his own, and I'll need to help sell the house and settle Dean's estate. It could be months before I'm able to return to Lancaster County. By then Brad could be engaged or even married.* Sara told herself it was better this way, because she had no time for love or romance. If she were being honest, she'd never been sure where her relationship with Brad was going. Her focus had to be on her brother right now.

CHAPTER 40

Throughout the months of April and May, Sara stayed at Dean's house with Kenny, and now here it was, the first week of June. They'd found a buyer for the house, and the couple who had rented the other side of the duplex when Sara moved to Strasburg had moved out. That meant the new owners could decide whether to rent out that half of the building or make use of the entire home for their family. Sara would oversee the estate sale that would take place two weeks before the new owners took possession.

Sara glanced at the calendar above the desk where she sat going over the bills that still needed to be paid. As executor of Dean's will, a lot of responsibility had fallen on her. She never dreamed so much paperwork would be involved in settling someone's estate, or that she would have to sort through all of Dean's personal items.

Sara remembered with fondness the day she'd gone through his bureau and found a box with her mother's wedding ring inside. She had never understood why he hadn't given the ring to her when Mama died, but at least it was in her possession now.

"I'm headin' out, Sara," Kenny hollered from the hallway outside the den where Sara sat.

"Okay. Try to be home in time for supper," she called in response.

"Sure thing."

Sara smiled when she heard the door click shut. Kenny's graduation had taken place last week, and even though he still missed his dad, he'd been in an upbeat mood. Sara knew it was because, thanks to the inheritance he'd received, Kenny would be attending the Curtis Institute of Music in Philadelphia. While the school offered free tuition, other expenses added up to thousands of dollars. But even more than being grateful he was able to afford such a great school, Kenny said he was glad he'd received his father's blessing to pursue his dream in music.

This was going to be a special summer for both Sara and her brother. Kenny looked forward to going with her to spend three months at their grandparents' place. It would give him a chance to really get to know them, plus he'd have the opportunity to work for Grandpa and earn some money as well.

Things were changing in Sara's life too. When she'd called Andy and Karen to inform them of her father's death, Sara had explained that she might not return to Pennsylvania for several months. She'd been about to suggest they find someone to replace her, when Andy said if they did hire another person, it would only be temporary, because he and his wife had decided to sell the floral shop sometime in June. At their age, the workload was getting to be too much, and it was time for them to retire. After Sara found out the reasonable price they wanted for the shop, she offered to buy the business. If not for the generous inheritance she'd received, it would not have been possible for Sara to even consider such a venture. This opportunity was a dream come true and most certainly an answer to prayer.

Sara missed being in Strasburg, but at the same time she felt thankful she could be in Newark to help finalize everything. Kenny admitted he could not have done all the work on his own and wouldn't have known where to begin when it came to going through all the household items.

Sitting back in her chair, Sara glanced out the open window, enjoying the warm breeze wafting in. The sounds of the birds singing made her yearn to be home. Home to her meant Strasburg, and it felt good knowing she'd soon be putting down roots in Lancaster County, where she would always be close to her grandparents.

I guess by now Grandma and Michelle have the garden all planted. Sara sighed. *I miss being there to assist.*

At least she and Kenny would be back on the farm to help with weeding and picking when the vegetables were ready. Grandma loved to can, and there'd be plenty of picking and processing to do for that.

Sara could almost picture Kenny helping Grandpa with the hogs and doing other chores around the farm. *My brother will get a real taste of country living with his grandparents.* She stretched her arms up and over her head, anxious to be surrounded by the sounds that could only be heard in the country. *If I was there now, I'd probably be strolling barefoot around in Grandma and Grandpa's yard.*

Sara wiggled her toes in the carpet, eager to feel the lush green grass under her feet. She was excited to get back home and help

Michelle with her wedding plans too.

The curtains floated out and back again. The fresh air sure smelled good. A dog barked in the distance, and Sara's thoughts continued to focus on Michelle. *Her puppy, Val, must have grown since I left.* Sara remembered watching an old movie when she was growing up about Irish setters. *They are such beautiful dogs.*

She recalled how Dean and Mama had taken her and Kenny to the drive-in theater when they were young to see their favorite movies. Sara closed her eyes, remembering those days, as more memories came to mind. On Labor Day weekend, the local drive-in had all-night theater, starting from dusk and ending at dawn. Sara had forgotten what fun she had during those times watching picture shows on the enormous screen from the comfort of their car. Each parking space had a small speaker, and Dean would attach it to their open car window. For the dusk-to-dawn movies, Kenny and Sara would go wearing their pajamas, and they'd take their sleeping bags along. At the time, they had a station wagon, and Mama and Dean would put the back seat down so they had a roomy area to crawl inside their sleeping bags in case they couldn't stay awake. Usually when the last movie was showing, she and her brother would fall asleep.

I'd forgotten what fun that was. Sara had recalled lots of good memories lately. For some reason, she had suppressed many of those. For too many years, she'd dwelled on negative things, which had done her no good at all.

Sara sat up straight when her phone buzzed. She had muted it before going to bed last night and forgotten to turn the volume on this morning, so until now, she didn't realize she had any messages.

The message was from Grandma, asking what day Sara and Kenny would arrive and wondering what they might like for supper that evening.

Sara smiled. *It's just like Grandma to be worried about what to feed us. She's always thinking of others.*

Sara listened to several older messages on her phone too. Some were from the Realtor about things pertaining to the sale of the house. Another was from Andy Roberts, and also an older message from Brad. She'd listened to it before but hadn't taken the time to respond since she had been so busy. Besides, Brad's message — telling her that he would soon be in the middle of finals but was still praying for her — was a statement, not a question he expected her to answer.

Sara still hadn't told him she'd become a Christian, but didn't see any point in telling him now. Brad's phone calls had gotten farther apart, and Sara figured he'd moved on with his life — a life that didn't include her. It was probably better that way — for both of them — since he would be going into the ministry after graduation. And soon, she would have a new business to run. Brad needed someone like Terri Conners, who'd been preparing for a certain phase of ministry. Sara hoped in time, with the busyness of her job, her memory of Brad would fade.

Clarks Summit

"Hey, Brad, wait up!"

Brad had started down the hall toward his next class when he heard a familiar voice. He turned and saw Terri coming toward him with a wide smile on her face.

"Hi, Terri. How's it going?" He hadn't talked to her in several days. "Are you feeling as edgy as everyone else due to finals this week?"

"No, not really. I'll just be glad to get them done so I can enjoy my summer." She smiled up at him.

"Will you be doing anything exciting during summer break or taking it easy till fall?"

"There won't be anything easy about what I'm going to do, but it should be fun and rewarding."

Brad tipped his head. "Oh? What might that be?"

"I've been asked to fill in for the youth pastor at a community church outside of Pittsburgh. He will be taking a three-month sabbatical, and since my uncle John knows someone on the church board, he put in a good word for me." Terri's eyes sparkled with exuberance. "Even though it won't be a permanent position, it'll be a great learning experience for me."

Brad placed his hand on her shoulder and gave it a tap. "Good for you, Terri. I bet your summer will be full of blessings."

"Thanks." She moved closer to Brad. "What are your summer plans?"

He turned his hands palms up. "Nothing nearly as exciting as yours. I'll go home first to see my folks in Harrisburg, and then I may head down to Lancaster County again and hopefully do some driving for the Amish, along with any work they might need to have done. The money I make will go toward next year's tuition of course."

"Makes sense to me." Terri gave Brad's

arm a squeeze. "Guess we'd better head for our next class. If I don't see you before we leave, we'll connect again in the fall. God's blessings to you, Brad."

He gave a nod. "Same to you, Terri."

As Brad moved down the hall, his thoughts went to Sara. He hadn't heard from her for quite a while, and figured she had continued to move forward with her life. But it was probably better that way. She was clearly not the girl for him.

Strasburg

Mary Ruth squinted at the words she'd written on her notepad. They looked a little blurry. "Think maybe it's past time for me to get an eye exam." As a young woman, Mary Ruth had enjoyed perfect vision. But as the years went by, she eventually needed glasses. At first it was for reading only, but then the doctor suggested she wear them all the time. Mary Ruth saw glasses as a nuisance — something she could easily misplace or lose altogether. Besides, her glasses would often slip off the bridge of her nose or the earpiece would dig into the back of her head behind one or both ears. So more often than not, she only wore her glasses for reading or close-up work.

"Whatcha doin'?" Michelle asked, stepping behind Mary Ruth.

"I'm making out a grocery list for when Sara and Kenny come, which will be soon." Smiling, she turned to look at Michelle. "Words can't express how excited I am about seeing them again. I'm especially looking forward to spending the whole summer with Kenny and getting to know him better."

Michelle took a seat next to Mary Ruth. "The last time I spoke to Sara on the phone she said Kenny would be going to college in the fall. Since it's in Philadelphia, I guess he'll only be able to stay here till then."

Mary Ruth nodded. "But Philadelphia isn't that far away, so Willis and I are hoping Kenny can come visit on some weekends and for extended holidays." Mary Ruth set her pen and paper aside. "And of course, we hope Sara will continue to live with us while she runs her new business."

"Everything's working out well for all of us." Michelle spoke in a bubbly tone. "I still can't believe I'm Amish now, or that I'll be getting married in five months."

"And that's another list we need to make." Mary Ruth pulled off the top paper she'd been writing on and handed the rest of the notepad to Michelle. "You've already started sewing your wedding dress, and we've

466

begun making plans for the food we want to serve your guests. Now you just need to make a list of everyone you want to invite to the wedding."

Michelle tapped the pen against the table as she tilted her head from side to side. "That's a good question. All of Ezekiel's family will be included, as well as the friends we've made here." She looked at Mary Ruth with an endearing smile. "That includes you, Willis, and Sara." Michelle's smile faded. "But of course, none of my family will be there. They don't even know where I am."

Mary Ruth reached over to gently pat Michelle's arm. "I know it hurts, but remember — we are your family now, and so are Ezekiel's parents and siblings."

"Danki." Michelle's eyes filled with tears. "I'm thankful for all of you."

When Michelle left the table to get a glass of water, Mary Ruth said a quick prayer. *Heavenly Father, on Michelle and Ezekiel's wedding day, when she and her groom stand before our bishop, please give her a sense of peace and comfort as only You can. And be with our granddaughters, Sara and Lenore, for You know who just the right men will be for them. Amen.*

CHAPTER 41

Newark

Sara's vision blurred as she closed the door of the home where she'd spent most of her childhood. The new owners would be moving in tomorrow, and it was time for her and Kenny to go forward with their lives. After today, this place would be filled with other people's possessions.

"There's one thing that will not disappear," Sara whispered as her hand moved to her chest. "That's the memories I'm keeping right here, close to me. I'm going to make sure I hold on to the good ones and, with God's help, try to forget those that once burdened me."

She glanced at Dean's SUV, which Kenny had inherited. It would be good transportation for him, going back and forth to Philadelphia. Sara had sold her old car, which wasn't reliable anymore. She would buy a newer one after they got to Lancaster

County.

"Hey, sis, are you comin'?" Kenny opened the window on the passenger's side and motioned to her. "We're burnin' daylight."

She nodded, looked one last time at the house, then climbed into the driver's seat. "Are you sure you don't want to drive, Kenny? After all, this is your vehicle."

"Maybe when we get closer, but for now I wanna enjoy the scenery." He clicked his seatbelt in place, and Sara did the same.

"Well okay then. Here we go." Despite the sorrow Sara felt over closing this chapter of her life, her brother's enthusiasm was contagious. A new door was about to open, and she couldn't wait to see what was on the other side.

Strasburg

Sara's first stop when they arrived in Strasburg was the flower shop. She'd made an appointment to meet Andy and Karen Roberts in order to pick up the keys and go over a few important things. As eager as she was to see her grandparents, it was necessary to make sure she had everything she needed in conjunction with her new business. The biggest hurdle would be finding someone to make up the bouquets and floral arrangements. But Andy had assured Sara the woman they'd hired to fill in for her while she was in Newark would be willing to keep working. The young man who made their deliveries had also agreed to stay on. If the business did well, Sara planned to hire one other employee to help at the store so she would be able to take some time off when needed.

After Sara parked the SUV, she looked over at Kenny and smiled. "Well, we made it." She looked at her watch. "It's almost lunch time."

"Yeah, my stomach has been tellin' me that for the last hour." He grinned. "I'm surprised you didn't hear it grumbling."

"Can you hold out awhile longer?" she asked. "After I'm finished talking to my former boss and his wife, I thought we could go to the restaurant in Ronks where my friend, Michelle, works. You met her at Dad's funeral."

"Oh yeah. Sure, I can wait a little longer." Kenny snickered when his stomach growled again. "Try telling that to my belly though."

"I shouldn't be too long. While I'm taking care of business, you can either check out some of the stores here in town or come inside with me."

"Think I'll walk around till you're done with business. This town looks pretty interesting, with all its old buildings."

"It is a fascinating place to visit," Sara agreed. "And with quite a history."

"How so?"

"For one thing, in the late sixteen hundreds, this area was visited by French fur traders. Then later it was settled by Swiss Mennonites and Huguenots from the Alsace region of France," Sara explained. "Some of the original log homes from the eighteenth century still remain."

Kenny whistled. "That's amazing."

"Of course, there's a lot more to tell about historic Strasburg, but I need to get into the flower shop now, so I'll have to share more of the town's history with you some other time." Sara was aware that her brother liked history and had done well in his high school history classes, so she was confident he wouldn't be bored walking around town.

"Okay, Sis. I'll meet you back here in an hour or so." Kenny opened the door, stepped out of the vehicle, then turned to face her. "One more thing . . . When we head for Grandma and Grandpa's place, would it be okay if I drive?"

Sara nodded. "See you soon."

Ronks

Michelle was glad she'd been given the

breakfast and lunch shifts today. With any luck, she'd be done working and back at the Lapps' before Sara and her brother arrived this afternoon. Although she was happy Sara could spend the summer with Kenny, a twinge of envy took over every time she thought about her own brothers and how she yearned to be with them.

As Michelle headed to the dining room to wait on her tables, the words of Philippians 4:11 popped into her head: *"Not that I speak in respect of want: for I have learned, in whatsoever state I am, therewith to be content."*

Annoyed with herself, Michelle's gaze flicked upward. *When am I going to quit fretting about this and learn to be content?* Lately with wedding plans being made, she had plenty of positives to think about. And as Mary Ruth had pointed out the other day, Michelle had a new family now, whom she loved and respected.

When she entered the dining room, Michelle was surprised to see Sara and Kenny sitting at one of the tables.

"Surprise!" Sara offered Michelle a sincere-looking smile. "We just left the flower shop in Strasburg and thought we'd stop here for lunch before heading to Grandma and Grandpa's. I was hoping you'd be working today."

"I asked if I could work the breakfast and lunch shifts today so I could be at Willis and Mary Ruth's place when you arrived. Your grandparents are eager to see you both. In fact, it's all Mary Ruth has been talking about for weeks." Michelle handed Sara and Kenny a menu.

"We're excited too. Aren't we, Kenny?" Sara bumped his arm lightly.

His head moved up and down. "I'll admit, I'm a little nervous though. I've never stayed in an Amish home before or lived on a farm. I'm not sure how I'll handle no TV or internet either."

Michelle chuckled. "You'll get used to it. And you never know. You might even enjoy the peace and quiet. I sure do."

"Same here." Sara looked at her brother. "As far as the internet goes, you can always come by the flower shop and log in on your laptop there."

His eyes brightened. "Seriously?"

"That's right. The shop has electricity and internet access." Sara bumped his arm again. "Can you imagine that?"

He snickered. "Okay. I'm no dummy. I figured it did."

The bantering going on between Sara and her brother caused Michelle to feel a pang of jealousy again. *Now stop it,* she berated herself. *Sara and Kenny deserve to be happy and enjoy their time together.*

Strasburg

Mary Ruth had a difficult time concentrating on the crossword puzzle she'd begun working on. The guest rooms were ready, the house had been cleaned from top to bottom, and supper was planned. All that remained was to wait for the arrival of her grandchildren.

"I wish they'd hurry up and get here," she mumbled from her rocking chair.

Willis gave a bemused smile. "Now don't start getting brutzich again. They'll get here in due time."

"I'm not fretful. Just wondering, is all."

He snickered and put his chair in the reclining position. "Think I'll take a little *leie.* Wake me when they get here." He leaned his head back and closed his eyes.

Mary Ruth wrinkled her nose and got the rocking chair moving. A nap was the last thing on her mind right now.

Her thoughts took her back over the year. She couldn't believe how much had changed. It was sad to think their daughter had died over a year ago. Although the pain had lessened, it still brought an ache to her heart thinking about all the years they were apart. But now so much happiness had entered their lives. They'd gained a granddaughter, a grandson, and also Michelle. Mary Ruth's life felt full, despite the longing she would always have for the daughter who left too soon. And because of the note Rhoda left in her Bible for Sara, three special people had come into Mary Ruth and Willis's lives.

Mary Ruth clasped her hands. *No matter how we end up finding it, God always has a plan for us.*

She was about to go out on the porch and wait for Sara and Kenny's arrival, when the grandfather clock struck two, and she heard a vehicle pull into the yard. Mary Ruth rose from her chair and went quickly to the window. "They're here, Willis," she announced when Sara and Kenny got out of the SUV.

Willis snorted, then put his chair up straight, instantly awake. "Okeydoke. Let's go outside and greet them."

Mary Ruth didn't waste any time getting out the door. Willis was right behind her. By the time they reached the vehicle, Kenny and Sara were out and getting their luggage from the back.

"It's so good to see you, Grandma." Sara

engulfed Mary Ruth in a hug, while Kenny hugged Willis. Then they traded. After all the hugging was done, Willis helped bring in the suitcases. Once inside, Mary Ruth suggested they all sit outside on the back porch, since the house was a bit stuffy and a cool breeze had finally come up. "I'll bring out some lemonade and homemade cookies I recently made."

"In a few hours Michelle will be home too," Willis added. "She's anxious to see you."

"We surprised Michelle a little bit ago." Kenny said. Then he explained how he and Sara had gone to eat lunch at the restaurant where Michelle worked.

"Well, that was nice." Mary Ruth smiled. "Now how about we do some of that porch-sitting? We have a lot of catching up to do."

"If you don't mind, before I sit and visit, I'd like to take a walk out to the barn and say hello to the horses. It's been awhile since I've seen Bashful and Peanuts." Sara looked at Mary Ruth and then Willis. "If it's okay, that is. It'll give you both a chance a visit with Kenny alone for a few minutes."

Mary Ruth blinked rapidly as she pushed her glasses back in place. Willis looked at her and shrugged his shoulders. *Our grand-daughter just got here and now she wants to run off to the barn? She never took an inter-est in the horses before. I wonder what that's all about.*

CHAPTER 42

It wasn't polite to head for the barn and leave her grandparents and Kenny sitting on the porch, but Sara felt compelled to go. She still had the slip of paper she'd found in her purse while in the hospital chapel and wanted to put it back in the prayer jar, where it belonged. She didn't know who had written the notes in either of the jars she and Michelle had found, but the person responsible must have had a reason, not only for the things they wrote, but for putting them inside the old jars.

Walking down the path to the barn, Sara was on the verge of skipping. Familiar sounds reached her ears as she swung her arms loosely at her sides. The burdens she'd shouldered when she was last here were long gone. The birds sang from the trees above, as if announcing her arrival. Cute little piglets that must have been born when she was away squealed in the paddock around their mother. Inhaling the scent of country air made Sara's heart swell. It was so good to be back with her grandparents again. This morning she'd left her childhood house, but here truly felt like she was home.

As the whiff of sweet-smelling hay and animals reached her nostrils, Sara entered the barn and found Sadie and Val curled up, sleeping close to each other. "Well, you little stinkers," she whispered. "No wonder you didn't come out to the yard to greet us when we arrived." Sara figured the dogs must be exceptionally tired not to have heard their vehicle when it entered the yard. Either that or they'd been out in the back pasture somewhere, chasing each other or some poor critter. Sara had seen Sadie go after squirrels in the past, but the dog had never attacked the animals. She supposed Sadie liked the sport of chasing.

Sara was tempted to wake the dogs and give them an official greeting, but that could wait. Right now, she had a mission to accomplish.

She pulled a ladder under the shelf where the old canning jars sat, then climbed up and took down the prayer jar, hidden behind the others. Holding it carefully, she seated herself on a wooden stool. Before putting in the piece of paper she'd brought with her, Sara read a few of the other notes inside the jar.

The first one said: *"We should always make allowance for other people's faults."*

Sara reflected on that a few moments. *Did the person who wrote this feel that someone had not made allowance for their faults?*

The next note Sara read included a thought, as well as a prayer: *"The reason we exist is to be in fellowship with God. Thank You, Lord, for being there when I need You."*

Sara put the notes back in the jar and added the one she'd found in her purse. Then, bowing her head, she said a short prayer of her own. *Lord, I have so much to thank You for — loving grandparents, a talented brother, my uncle, aunt, and cousins — and my special friend, Michelle. Please bless and protect each of them.*

When Brad pulled into the Lapps' yard, he noticed a beige SUV parked near the house. He figured Willis and Mary Ruth had company. Either that or the rig belonged to one of their drivers. *Maybe they won't need me anymore,* he thought. *Could be in my absence they've found someone else to work here on the farm. Even if that is the case, I'm sure there are plenty of Amish farms in the area who will need some extra help or a driver this summer.*

Since Brad would be staying with his friend Ned again, he wouldn't have to worry about a place to live while he was in Lancaster County. And with summer being a heavy tourist season, he felt sure he could secure a job, even if it wasn't driving or farming. He'd never had problems finding work before and assumed this summer would be no different.

Brad parked his van next to the other vehicle. He sat awhile, enjoying the pleasure of being back in Lancaster County. The last time he'd been here was during spring break in March when the weather was mild. Now the sultry air was heavily scented with the sweet smell of honeysuckle growing on fencerows along the road. During the trip down from Clarks Summit, Brad had noticed that the first cutting of hay had been completed.

He got out of the car and stretched his legs. Seeing no one in the yard, he stepped onto the front porch and knocked on the door. A few seconds later, Mary Ruth answered.

Her whole face seemed to light up when she looked up at Brad and joined him on the porch. "Well hello, stranger. It's been a while since we've seen you."

Brad nodded. "The last time we spoke was at the funeral of Sara's dad, but unfortunately we didn't get much time to talk."

"That's right," she agreed. "It was a busy day, and since you left before we did, neither Willis nor I had a chance to say more than few words to you."

"Who you talkin' to, Mary Ruth?"

She turned when Willis stepped up beside her. "Look . . . It's Brad."

Willis grinned and shook Brad's hand. "Sure is nice to see you again. Didn't know you were back in the area. Figured you were still at the university."

Brad shook his head. "I'm out for the summer and will be spending the next three months here in Lancaster County. I came to your place first, but I've only been here a few minutes."

"Ah, I see. Well, I was out on the back porch and didn't hear your vehicle pull in. When I stepped into the kitchen to get some more lemonade I heard my wife talkin' to someone." Willis gestured to Mary Ruth and looked back at Brad. "Will you be free to do some work for me while you're in the area?"

"Sure, and if you need a driver anytime,

I'll be available for that too." Brad rubbed the back of his warm neck. "Well, I don't want to interrupt since it looks like someone is here right now." He pointed to the SUV in the driveway. "I can come back another day to talk about what you might want to have done."

"You're not interrupting," Mary Ruth spoke up. "Sara and her brother just arrived. I'm sure our granddaughter would like to see you, and it would be nice for Kenny to get to know you better too. You barely got to meet him at the funeral."

"You're right. So . . . uh . . . how long are they here for?" Brad's voice sounded strained, even to his own ears. It wasn't normal for him to feel so jittery either. He glanced at the SUV again and squinted. *How dumb of me not to notice the New Jersey plates on that rig.*

"Kenny will be with us through August," Willis said. "Then he'll be heading to Philadelphia to a music college."

"But Sara is back here for good," Mary Ruth interjected. "Her stepfather's estate has been settled, and the house was sold, so she came back to Strasburg to live with us again."

"Guess that makes sense." Brad shuffled his feet. A part of him wanted to see Sara

483

right now and ask how she was doing. Another part said he should get in his van and make a hasty exit. But before he could make a sensible decision, Mary Ruth spoke again.

"The owners of the flower shop where Sara used to work are retiring, so she purchased their business." Mary Ruth's smile was so wide, it was almost contagious.

"That's great. I hope it works out well for her." Brad started to turn away. "I should really go and let you visit with your grandchildren. Give me a call if you need a ride somewhere."

Willis laid a hand on Brad's shoulder. "Wait a minute, Son. Don't you want to say hello to Sara before you go?"

Brad felt like a bug stuck to a strip of flypaper. He didn't want to appear rude, but seeing Sara again would only dredge up the feelings he'd managed to push aside with determination these last few months.

"Oh yes, you must say hello to Sara. She's out in the barn." Mary Ruth pointed in that direction.

Brad didn't feel as if he had much choice. "Okay, I'll go out there for a few minutes, but then I'll be on my way. Gotta head to my friend's place in Lancaster and get settled in."

"No need to rush off," Willis said. "You oughta get Sara and join us on the back porch for some cookies and lemonade."

"Maybe . . . We'll see." Brad stepped off the porch and headed for the barn.

As he approached the building, a cat ran past, chasing a fat little mouse. Brad shook his head. *I wonder which one of those critters will win out.*

Brad opened the barn door, but when he stepped inside, he heard Sara talking to someone. Was there another person in the barn — maybe Michelle?

Sadie and Val walked up to greet him. They weren't barking, but both dogs wagged their tails. He closed the barn door and stood off to one side. Instinctively, he put his finger to his lips. Somehow the dogs must have understood, for they remained silent.

Brad was never one to eavesdrop, but he didn't want to interrupt what he was hearing. Something compelled him to remain silent and listen as he hid in the shadows.

Sara set the antique jar on the floor and bowed her head. Speaking out loud, she offered another prayer. "Dear Lord, thank You for being so patient with me all these years. I am so happy and blessed to have given my heart to You. Thank You for showing me that I need to not only ask forgiveness for my own wrongdoings, but I've also forgiven others who have hurt me in the past. I pray that if I am given an opportunity to talk to Brad again, he will forgive me for deceiving him about being a Christian."

Sara heard what sounded like the scuffling of feet, and she opened her eyes. Seeing Brad standing a few feet away, with both dogs vying for his attention, she gasped. "Oh, you startled me! How long have you been there?"

"Just a few minutes."

"Were you listening to my prayer?" Sara's arms curled around her middle.

"Yes, I did hear you, but I wasn't eavesdropping, and I didn't know at first that you were praying." Brad moved closer. "I came in here to say hello, but I never expected to hear you saying a prayer. You told me before that you were a Christian. But later, I learned from Michelle that you weren't a believer. Then just now, you were telling God you were happy you had given your heart to Him." He crossed his arms. "So which is it, Sara? Are you a Christian or not?"

"I am now, but I wasn't back then." Sara explained how she had given her heart to the Lord when she visited the hospital chapel after Dean's accident. She lowered her gaze. "I'm sorry for lying to you, Brad. I didn't want you to think —"

Brad didn't let her finish. "I'll admit, our relationship was one I'd lost hope of ever continuing."

"I thought that too." Sara had to tell Brad now how she really felt about him, before she lost her nerve. "About our relationship —"

He stepped in front of her and put one finger against her lips. "You know what I think, Sara Murray?"

Tears sprang to her eyes, and she almost choked on the words. "Th–that I'm not to be trusted?"

"No, I don't think that anymore. What I do think though is that I'd like us to start over." He took her hand, holding it gently. "Would you be willing to do that, Sara?"

She gave a nod. "Yes. Yes, I would."

As Sadie and Val started barking and running around the couple's feet, the horses must have sensed their excitement and nickered in response. Sara glanced toward Peanuts and Bashful, both looking over their stall doors, nodding and shaking their heads. When she glanced back down at both dogs, they had settled and sat patiently at their feet. Sara giggled when Sadie whined and Val tilted her head — the whole time with their tails wagging in unison. When she looked back into Brad's eyes, her breath caught in her throat. At that moment, Sara could have melted in his arms, as he looked adoringly at her.

Brad leaned down and gave Sara's right cheek a gentle, feathery kiss. Then he kissed the other cheek, and moved to her lips.

Sara put her arms around Brad's neck, melting into his embrace. Both horses whinnied, and the dogs started barking again. Sara had no idea what the future held for them, but this time she would try not to do anything that could mess up their relationship.

As the sun began to make its descent in the west, Michelle and Sara sat on the swing, swaying slowly back and forth. Michelle had celebrated her twenty-fifth birthday a few days ago, but when Mary Ruth asked what she wanted for her birthday supper, Michelle suggested they wait until Sara and Kenny arrived, so they could be with them.

Michelle didn't want a big celebration; a cookout was fine with her. Willis had grilled some sausages and burgers that went well with the cucumber mixture and macaroni salad Mary Ruth had made. She'd also baked a three-layer lemon cake, iced with a white fluffy frosting. And the orange sherbet Willis bought at the store was a tasty frozen dessert.

"I'm sorry I didn't get you anything for your birthday." Sara's forehead wrinkled. "But I just found out about it after Brad left. When Grandma was upstairs helping me unpack, she let me know tonight we'd be celebrating your birthday."

Michelle brushed aside her words. "You being here is gift enough. I told Mary Ruth I didn't want to celebrate until you and Kenny came home."

"Well, even if it was a few days ago, I'm glad Kenny and I could be here to help celebrate your birthday this evening." Sara smiled. "He was so excited to come here. Probably as much as I was."

"I can hear him in there laughing." Michelle tilted her head toward the door.

"It's good he has this chance to get to know his grandparents. That's why I thought I'd sit out here with you for a while and give him some time alone with them."

Michelle looked at Sara closely. She sensed something different about her. She had noticed it earlier at the restaurant, and also during supper this evening. A sense of peace seemed to settle over Sara. She acted more carefree and talked a lot more instead of being within herself. "It's too bad Brad couldn't have stayed for the cookout."

"I'm sure he would have liked to, but he wanted to get to Ned's and get settled in. He had a mind-boggling week with finals and the drive down from Clarks Summit." Sara's smile grew wider. "I'm sure we'll be seeing a lot more of him this summer."

Michelle was happy for Sara when she explained how she'd admitted to Brad that she had deceived him about being a Christian but wanted him to know that she had since come to know the Lord.

"I know you offered to help me, Michelle, and I appreciate that," Sara said. "But when I felt God's presence in the hospital chapel, something very special came over me."

Michelle put her arm around Sara. "I'm so glad."

"It seems we both learned some valuable lessons this past year."

"We sure have. Now do you mind if I ask a question?"

"Go right ahead."

"Do you think yours and Brad's relationship will get serious?"

"I can't say for certain, but we both care about each other. I guess my only fear is if we were to get married someday, I might have to move away from the Lancaster area." Sara sighed. "I'm not sure how I would feel living far away from my grandparents if Brad decided to take a church somewhere else. I made a vow to myself some time ago that I'd never stray far from them. Then there's the flower shop. I could not believe it when the opportunity came up for me to purchase the business. It just sort of fell into my lap, and I grabbed the chance while I could."

"Sara, none of us knows what our future holds, but for now, just enjoy being back where you belong at this time." Michelle squeezed Sara's shoulder. "It's perfect, because you will also be here to help with my wedding plans."

Sara gave Michelle a hug. "I'm so happy for you, Michelle."

Michelle rubbed Sara's back. "Everything will fall into place for you too. Just wait. You'll see."

CHAPTER 43

The summer was going by much too quickly to suit Sara. Here it was the end of July already. Sara's business was booming, and word had spread about a new owner who'd taken over the flower shop. Some folks came in just to meet her or see if she'd done anything different to the store.

Basically, the shop itself had not changed, but Sara had shuffled a few things around inside. Instead of flower pots and vases being intermixed among the buckets of fresh flowers and potted plants, she'd designated one area just for those. Sara had even added a section with various sprinkling cans and some garden decorations. She'd also included a rack to sell the cards Lenore now supplied to the store, and had made a few beaded items to sell as well. Many of the patrons had made special requests for Lenore to personalize a card for a family member or friend.

But the real hit with the customers who came and went was the display window. Not long ago, in the back part of her grandparents' barn, Sara had found an old scooter. Grandma told her it had belonged to Ivan when he was a young boy. The scooter was quite old and had some rust in spots, but that's what made it unique. One Sunday, when Ivan and his wife stopped by, Sara asked if she could use it for something special. Ivan was more than glad to give it to her, especially when she told him her idea. Sara put the scooter in the shop's window, intermixed with a floral display. Many customers who came into the store commented on the old Amish scooter. She loved telling those who asked that the scooter in the window belonged to her uncle.

Sara had arrived at the store earlier than usual this morning, hoping to do some internet searching and make a few phone calls. In addition to taking care of some business matters, Sara had some personal things she needed answers for too, and social media in addition to some other places on the internet seemed like the best place to start.

Sara took a seat at her desk and turned on the computer. While she waited for it to boot up, she looked at her monthly schedule and also any orders that had come in the day before. She also did a walk-through to make sure everything in the store was in place.

Sara's social calendar was full, as she saw Brad every opportunity she could. With the exception of her uncertainty about the future, her life was going better than she'd ever expected. The more time Sara spent with Brad, the more attached she became. She dreaded the day he would return to Clarks Summit to continue his studies. But the ministry was Brad's calling, and she wouldn't stand in his way.

Sara's twenty-fifth birthday, on the first of July, had been special. Just like Michelle, Sara didn't want a big fuss made. She'd been happy with the small family gathering at her grandparents' home that evening. Instead of cooking on the grill, Grandma had made Sara's favorite chicken-and-rice casserole. Brad had stopped at a seafood restaurant and brought out a huge container of shrimp scampi to go with the meal.

Sara smiled to herself. *A little birdie must have told Brad I liked seafood.* Of course Michelle and Ezekiel were included in the meal. Sara liked it that way — nothing fancy — just the sweet fellowship with those she cared about. By now, Kenny was quite comfortable with everyone and had a good rapport with Brad and Ezekiel. After supper, they'd all gone out to the picnic table and enjoyed cheesecake for dessert.

Kenny was doing well and sported a farmer's tan from all the work he helped Grandpa with outdoors. He was eager to help in any way and had gotten used to living on the farm.

Sara wished she could help Grandma more, but between her new business and time spent with Brad, there weren't many hours left in the day. Grandma never complained or asked Sara to do anything. In fact, she'd said many times that she was happy Sara had acquired the flower shop and was home with them again.

Sara halted her musings and turned back to the computer. It was fully booted and ready to go, so she quickly went online. She had just begun her first search, when the bell above the shop door jingled. She looked up and smiled when Herschel Fisher entered the store. *I bet he's here to buy his wife more flowers. I hope she appreciates her husband's consideration.*

Sara saved the internet site she'd found and went to greet the Amish man. "Good morning, Mr. Fisher. What can I help you with today?"

"Roses. I need a dozen yellow roses."

Sara bit the inside of her cheek. "Sorry, but we are currently out of those. Would another color be all right?"

He shook his head firmly. "Nope. Has to be yellow."

Sara drew a quick breath. She hated to send Mr. Fisher to another flower shop, but what else could she do?

She was about to suggest the floral shop in the next town over, when Ezekiel entered the store. "I have some roses and other cut flowers from our greenhouse in the back of my market buggy," he announced.

Sara had forgotten he'd be making a delivery today. She hoped some of those roses were yellow.

"Please bring them in," she told Ezekiel. Then she turned to Herschel. "If some of the roses are yellow, I'll ask my assistant, Peggy, to make you a nice bouquet. If not, then feel free to take your business else-where today."

Herschel shook his head. "Nope. If I can't buy the flowers from you, I won't buy 'em at all." The laugh lines around his mouth deepened as he grinned at Sara. "You know, I've been comin' here for a few years now, and I was concerned when I heard the Roberts were planning to sell the store. But then when you bought the place, I felt better, 'cause you were always helpful when you worked here before."

Sara smiled. It was nice to be appreciated, especially by a customer she barely knew. After hearing Andy and Karen were retiring, other customers had also told Sara they were glad she'd become the new owner of the flower shop.

When Ezekiel returned with a box full of roses — some yellow and some red — Sara felt relieved. She gathered up a dozen yellow roses and headed for the back room. Peggy was an expert designer, and Sara felt sure she would create a beautiful bouquet for Herschel Fisher's wife.

I wish he'd bring her into the store someday, Sara thought. *I'd like to meet this special lady whose husband gives her flowers so often.*

Sara was preparing to close the store for the day when an elderly Amish woman came in. She walked with a limp and used a cane, but no evidence of pain showed on her face.

"May I help you?" Sara asked. She hoped the woman wouldn't want a special arrangement made up, because Peggy had gone home a few minutes ago. And while Sara had good customer skills, knew how to balance the books, and keep the shop tidy, she hadn't yet learned how to create any of the fresh-flower bouquets they sold in the shop.

The woman stepped up to the counter, peering at Sara through thick-lens glasses. "You need to stop selling my son flowers. It's a waste of money."

"What?" Sara was taken aback by the woman's harsh tone and pinched expression. "I–I'm not sure who you're referring to, ma'am."

"My name's not ma'am. It's Vera Fisher, and my son is Herschel. He comes here nearly every week and buys flowers for his wife, does he not?"

"Oh, you must mean Mr. Fisher."

The woman's head moved up and down.

Conflicted, Sara pressed her lips together in a slight grimace. "Is there a problem with your son buying flowers for his wife?" Sara wondered if Herschel's mother might be jealous or didn't approve of his choice for a wife.

Vera tapped the tip of her cane against the hardwood floor a few times. "There is most definitely something wrong."

Sara couldn't imagine what it might be, so she stood quietly, hoping the lady would explain.

"How long have you been living in Lancaster County?" Vera asked.

"I moved here to be with my grandparents back in October, and then I —"

"Just how much do you know about the Amish?"

"Well, my grandpa and grandma are Amish. Perhaps you know them. They live —"

The woman interrupted Sara again. "If you knew the Amish, you'd know that we don't put flowers on our loved one's graves."

Perplexed, Sara's eyebrows lowered. "I don't understand."

Vera pointed a bony finger at Sara. "Those flowers you've been selling my son end up on her grave marker, and that's just not done."

"Oh dear." Sara put her fingers against her lips. "I had no idea. I — I thought when Herschel first came into the store and said he wanted flowers for his wife that he would be giving them to her in person. I had no idea Mrs. Fisher was deceased."

"She died nearly two years ago, when a car hit her while trying to cross the street." Heaving a sigh, Vera placed her free hand against her breastbone. "My son's never gotten over his wife's death, and he began putting flowers on her grave soon after she was buried." She slowly shook her head.

"He knows it's not the Amish way, and he could get in trouble with our church leaders for doing it. So far, they've chosen to look the other way, thinking in time his grieving would subside and he'd stop what he was doing."

"I'm sorry for his loss, Mrs. Fisher. I had no idea."

"So you'll quit selling him flowers?"

Sara rolled her neck from side to side, trying to get the kinks out. She was really on the spot here. "The thing is . . . I really can't stop Herschel from buying flowers, but the next time he comes in, maybe I could mention that I'd heard about his wife."

Vera shook her head vigorously. "That won't do any good. You just need to tell him you're not going to sell him any more flowers." As if their conversation was settled, the woman turned and limped her way out the door.

Sara groaned. *Well, the day here in the shop may have started out on a good note, but it certainly didn't end that way.*

That evening, when Brad came over for supper, Sara waited until after she'd helped Grandma and Michelle do the dishes before she went to Brad and asked if she could speak to him privately.

"Sure can." He grinned at her. "In fact, I was planning to ask you the same question. I have something important I want to tell you."

"Sara, why don't you and Brad go out on the back porch, where it's cooler?" Grandma suggested when she entered the living room where Brad had been visiting with Grandpa.

"Good idea." He got up from his chair and led the way.

When they stepped out onto the porch, Sara took a seat on the porch swing, scooching over, so there'd be room for Brad. "What did you want to talk to me about?" she asked.

"No, it can wait. You go first."

"I had a little problem right before I closed the flower shop today." Sara went on to tell him about Herschel Fisher and how his mother barged in, asking Sara to stop selling her son flowers, and the reason.

"What do you think I should do, Brad? Knowing what I do now, I feel sorry for Mr. Fisher, but I wouldn't feel right about refusing to sell him flowers."

"Refusing to sell anyone what they come into your store to buy wouldn't be good business," Brad said. "Besides, if the man's church leaders haven't reprimanded him for putting flowers on his wife's grave, then you shouldn't either. I'm sure that eventually Herschel will come to grips with his wife's death, and then he will probably stop buying flowers for her grave." Brad shrugged his shoulders. "Who knows? He might eventually fall in love with another woman and remarry."

"True." Sara placed her hand on Brad's arm. "Thanks. You're certainly full of good advice. You'll make a great preacher."

"Speaking of which . . ." Brad took hold of her hand. "I've been praying about things, and I've recently made a decision."

"Oh? What sort of decision?"

"I'm not going back to the university in the fall."

Sara tipped her head. "How come?"

"I'm staying in Lancaster County and will do the rest of my studies through online courses."

"Really? That's a surprise."

He let go of Sara's hand and reached up to stroke the side of her face. "You must know why I want to stay in the area."

Sara moistened her lips with the tip of her tongue. "Well, I . . ."

"I love you, Sara, and I can't stand the thought of being away from you for the next two years while I finish my degree."

"You could come back here for visits."

Sara's heart pounded as Brad gazed into her eyes. She wanted to make sure he would not regret his decision to leave the school in Clarks Summit.

"I could, but it wouldn't be enough for me. I want to see you as often as possible. I want to give our relationship a chance to really deepen."

"I–I want that also, because I have recently realized that I love you too."

Brad wrapped his arms around Sara and pulled her close. "And I hope you'll be prepared with an answer, because someday I plan to ask you to be my wife." Before she could offer a response, his lips touched hers in a gentle, yet firm kiss.

As Sara enjoyed being held in Brad's arms, her concerns about the future evaporated. All she could think about was how happy she was to have found such a wonderful Christian man. Sara felt thankful for God's love and forgiveness. She would have never experienced any of this if it hadn't been for a prayer jar that led her to the truth.

CHAPTER 44

Four months later

Sara sat on a backless wooden bench inside the Kings' barn, watching and listening as Michelle and Ezekiel said their vows in front of the bishop. The oversized building had been cleaned from top to bottom, leaving no sign that it ever housed any animals. The horses had been put in the pasture, and the Kings' dogs were secured inside a temporary enclosure. In addition to Ezekiel's father and brothers, Uncle Ivan and his sons had come over a few days ago to pressure wash and clean every nook and cranny inside the barn. Bales of hay and straw had been put in the loft above, and if it hadn't been for the shape of the structure, no one would have known they were sitting inside a barn.

Sara heard some sniffles and glanced at her grandmother. Sure enough, tears had splashed onto Grandma's cheeks, and she was none too discreetly blotting at them with her delicate white handkerchief.

Sara struggled not to cry as well, for the look of joy radiating on the bride's and groom's faces made her feel like tearing up. She clasped her hands together in her lap. *A year ago, who would have believed I'd have a friendship with the young woman who had impersonated me for over four months, let alone be one of the guests at Michelle's wedding.*

So much had changed in Sara's life that she sometimes felt as though she'd imagined it all. She glanced at the men's side of the room and caught Brad looking at her. She couldn't help but smile. His love for her was obvious, and she felt the same way about him. Sara wondered if some day she and Brad might be saying their vows, with a whole new life starting for them. So far, however, he'd made no reference to them getting married since their conversation four months ago. *Brad knows how much I like living near my grandparents. Maybe he hasn't asked because he's afraid I'll say no.*

Smiling, Sara looked at two young English men who sat on the bench behind Brad. When the wedding was over, she would introduce them to Michelle.

Michelle took her groom's hand, and as the

bishop pronounced them husband and wife, she struggled to keep her emotions in check. Today was the most special day of her life. Even the weather cooperated, giving them sunny skies and mild temperatures for the month of November.

The other day, Michelle had called her foster parents to let them know how much her life had changed and to invite them to her and Ezekiel's wedding. Al and Sandy Newman were the only link she had to her childhood after she was taken from her parents. Al had been delighted to hear Michelle's voice when he picked up the phone and immediately yelled for Sandy to get on their other extension. The three of them talked for nearly an hour, and the Newmans said they wished they could come to the wedding but unfortunately had made other plans for that day.

Michelle thought about the letter she'd previously sent to her parents. Unfortunately, it had come back with no forwarding address, so she had no way of getting in touch with them. *They probably wouldn't have come to my wedding anyhow,* she thought. *And maybe it's for the best. I'm sure they would have had unkind things to say to me, Ezekiel, and even the Lapps.*

For a moment, Michelle leaned her head

back and looked up. *The only thing that would have made today any better would be to have Ernie and Jack in attendance.* But it was an impossible dream, and she needed to keep her focus on Ezekiel, for he was all she could ever want in a husband. Michelle looked forward to having a family someday and teaching their children about God. If only she'd had a personal relationship with Him when she was a child, it would have been easier to deal with all the trials she and her brothers had faced.

Better late than never, Michelle thought as she gave her groom's fingers a tender squeeze before they returned to their seats.

When the wedding concluded and people milled around outside the tent where the first meal of the day would be held, Sara searched for Michelle. She found her talking to Ezekiel's sister Sylvia.

"I don't mean to interrupt" — she said, stepping up to them — "but I'd like to give Michelle the wedding present I got for her."

Sylvia blinked a couple of times. "Can't that wait until later, when the bride and groom open all their gifts?"

"No, this gift can't wait." Sara took her friend's hand. "Will you come with me?"

Michelle glanced around as though she

507

might be looking for Ezekiel, but then she nodded.

Leading the way, Sara hurried in the direction of the greenhouse. That's where she'd asked Brad to wait with her surprise wedding present for Michelle. He had told Ezekiel to meet them there too.

As they approached the greenhouse, Michelle stopped walking. "What are we doing here? Is this where you put my wedding gift?"

"Yes, it is, and you'll see when we go inside." Sara pulled her along.

When they entered the building, Brad stood beside Ezekiel and the two young men who had been sitting behind him during the wedding.

Michelle looked at them with a curious expression, and then she turned to face Sara. "I am confused. Who are these men, and where is the gift you promised me?"

Sara could hardly keep a straight face. "These men are your wedding present." She pointed to them. "Michelle, I would like to introduce you to Ernie and Jack Taylor."

Michelle's eyes widened as she clutched Sara's hand. "M–my brothers?"

Sara managed only a nod because the lump in her throat made it impossible to speak.

The young men moved forward, and Michelle ran toward them. Exclamations of joy and tearful sobs could be heard, as two auburn-haired brothers were reunited with their now-Amish sister. Ezekiel stood by with a loving expression as he witnessed the scene. Sara also noticed a few tears escaping his eyes.

"But how?" Michelle asked, turning to face Sara.

"It took some doing, but thanks to a lot of internet searching and a good many phone calls, I was able to locate them."

Michelle looked in awe at her brothers. "I — I still can't believe it." She hugged them both again.

Brad stepped up to Sara and pulled her to his side. "You did a wonderful thing, Sara, and your good friend is one happy bride."

She flashed him a smile, struggling to keep from breaking down. "Yes, I can see that. I couldn't think of a better gift to give my good friend."

"Let's go outside and allow them to visit for a bit," Brad whispered in Sara's ear. "There is something I want to ask you."

"Okay." She followed Brad out the door.

As they stepped into the sunlight streaming down from the sky, Brad suggested they move off to the side, away from the building. Then, catching Sara completely by surprise, he got down on one knee.

"I can't promise you a life with no complications, but I can promise to always be there for you, in good times and bad."

Sara held her breath as he continued. "The life of a minister will have its challenges, but with God's help, and you at my side, I am up for the challenge." He paused and took a small jewelry box from his jacket pocket, opened the lid, and held it out to her. "Sara Murray, will you marry me?"

With tears of joy streaming down her cheeks, Sara nodded. "Yes, Brad, I will marry you." She held out her left hand, and Brad slipped the ring on her finger. It fit perfectly, as if it had been made just for her. Her worries about Terri were completely gone. Becoming a pastor's wife wouldn't be easy, and it might mean moving to some other town or state. But Sara loved Brad enough to make that commitment and felt certain God would bless them and direct their lives. As much as she wanted to continue running her business and living closer to her grandparents, Sara wanted to share in Brad's ministry that would involve touching people's lives and ministering to them when they were hurting. Just as Sara's life had been touched by the notes she'd read in the forgiving jar, she wanted to be by Brad's side as they shared the Good News with others.

SARA'S PUMPKIN BREAD

Ingredients:

4 eggs
3 cups sugar
1 teaspoon cinnamon
1/2 teaspoon salt
1 teaspoon nutmeg
1 cup pumpkin puree
2/3 cup water
2 teaspoons baking soda
1 cup olive oil
3 1/2 cups flour
1 cup chopped nuts

In large bowl, beat eggs. Add remaining ingredients and mix well. Pour into three well-greased loaf pans. Bake at 300 degrees for 1 hour or until done in center.

MARY RUTH'S TURKEY VEGETABLE SOUP

Ingredients:
1 cup diced carrots
1/2 cup diced celery
1/3 cup chopped onion
2 tablespoons butter
2 cups diced cooked turkey
2 cups water
1 1/2 cups peeled, diced potatoes
2 teaspoons chicken bouillon granules
1/2 teaspoon salt
1/2 teaspoon pepper
2 1/2 cups milk
3 tablespoons flour

In large saucepan, sauté carrots, celery, and onion in butter until tender. Add turkey, water, potatoes, bouillon, salt, and pepper. Bring to boil. Reduce heat, cover, and simmer for 10 to 12 minutes or until vegetables are tender. Stir in 2 cups milk. In separate bowl, combine flour with remaining 1/2 cup milk. Blend until smooth. Stir into soup. Bring to a boil. Cook and stir for 2 minutes or until thickened.

DISCUSSION QUESTIONS

1. Could you be as brave as Michelle when, after Ezekiel's urging, she returned to the Lapps' to confess in person what she did and to apologize?

2. Sara didn't like the idea that Michelle got to know her grandparents before she did. Can you understand why Sara felt the way she did about Michelle? Was there a better way for Sara to cope without allowing resentment to take over?

3. Willis and Mary Ruth each had a talk with Sara and Michelle but let the girls work it out themselves. Do you think they should have intervened more?

4. Were you ever in a situation where you longed to have someone love you the way Sara saw how Michelle and Ezekiel cared

for each other? Were you envious of the couple or happy for them?

5. Could you have been as patient as Ezekiel, giving Michelle time to decide for herself if she wanted to learn the ways of the Amish and join the church?

6. Were you happy to find out Michelle made a commitment to join the Amish church? Did you feel she found her faith through the prayer jar notes and was not just persuaded by her love for Ezekiel and wanting to have a life with him?

7. Do you think Sara was right in not questioning her grandma about the prayer jar and forgiving jar messages?

8. What did you think about the way Ezekiel's mother and sister acted toward Michelle? Do you understand why they were concerned about him being interested in a woman who wasn't Amish?

9. Has someone close to you passed away and afterward you discovered that they had deceived you, the way Sara learned that her mother kept her heritage a secret?

Since you could not confront the person, how did you handle your feelings?

10. Have any of your children ever upset you by going to someone else's house for a meal on Christmas, when traditionally your family has always been together on this special day? Would you have reacted the way Belinda did when her son Ezekiel went to the Lapps' for Christmas dinner instead of staying at home with the family?

11. Do you think Michelle handled herself well when she waited on her ex-boyfriend Jerry and his new girlfriend at the restaurant where she worked as a waitress? Could you have confronted your ex as bravely as Michelle did Jerry?

12. Was it wrong for Sara to deceive Brad by telling him she was a Christian when she wasn't? After feeling guilty for lying to Brad, should she have confessed right away and told him the truth?

13. Even though Brad told Sara that Terri Conners was only a friend, she still had doubts. Do you think she should have

shared her doubts with Brad instead of remaining quiet and just observing?

14. In this story, did you learn anything new about the Amish and the way they handle certain situations?

15. What scripture verses in this book were your favorites and why?

ABOUT THE AUTHOR

New York Times bestselling and award-winning author **Wanda E. Brunstetter** is one of the founders of the Amish fiction genre. She has written close to 90 books translated into four languages. With over 10 million copies sold, Wanda's stories consistently earn spots on the nation's most prestigious bestseller lists and have received numerous awards.

Wanda's ancestors were part of the Anabaptist faith, and her novels are based on personal research intended to accurately portray the Amish way of life. Her books are well read and trusted by many Amish, who credit her for giving readers a deeper understanding of the people and their customs.

When Wanda visits her Amish friends, she finds herself drawn to their peaceful lifestyle, sincerity, and close family ties. Wanda enjoys photography, ventriloquism, gardening, bird-watching, beachcombing, and spending time with her family. She and her husband, Richard, have been blessed with two grown children, six grand-children, and two great-grandchildren.

To learn more about Wanda, visit her website at www.wandabrunstetter.com.